The I

Ashley Hough

First published in 2023 by Blossom Spring Publishing
The Maze Copyright © 2023 Ashley Hough
ISBN 978-1-7392955-1-6
E: admin@blossomspringpublishing.com
W: www.blossomspringpublishing.com

Prologue

Most architects dream of skyscrapers or concert halls. Diego Flint was different, though. His dream was to change the world. To change the way people thought about the Correctional System. Five years ago, he had his vision of a new prison, and now the masterpiece was complete. Well, for now, anyway. It had taken less than five years. He couldn't believe his eyes as he took it all in.

Diego Flint was the only person in the world who knew in full the design of the largest and most expensive maze in existence. But this wasn't a maze that families would visit for a fun, if not frustrating, day out. No. This was, in fact, to become the new solution to the correctional programme. A maze that would hold hundreds or even thousands of prisoners, their every move watched, waiting to see if they would change in their ways.

The Maze currently had forty-seven kilometres of pathways, criss-crossing underground in the American wilderness. The paths were covered with tiny, hidden cameras that would be watched by operators twenty-four seven, tracking the progress of the inmates. A single construction company only ever covered five kilometres of the Maze, meaning Flint kept his status as the only one with a full understanding of his creation.

Unfortunately, this came with its drawbacks. As of the day of opening, Flint would be placed under maximum security, even greater than that of the President of the United States. After all, the Maze would host some dangerous criminals, and there would always be those who wanted to 'help' from the outside.

As well as the one thousand, six hundred and twenty-four operators newly hired to keep a close eye on the thousands of cameras, there would also be a large team of highly trained 'Janitors' who would maintain the Maze's facilities and lighting, which was essential to the project. These Janitors would use the top of the ten-foot concrete walls that forged pathways in the underground system.

Flint stood at the end of one of the long, stretching alleys and breathed in its glory. It was a proud moment. He looked up at the ceiling, some thirty-feet above, and truly realised what a marvel this place was. In truth, he couldn't actually see anything above him, but that was the point. The fact that the ceiling was so high was an architectural miracle.

Ahead of him, Flint could see the regular glow of the golden lanterns lighting up the corridor for as far as he could make out. These were something he had campaigned relentlessly for. One thousand, nine hundred and twenty vintage lanterns, secured with cages to protect them from harm, though Flint expected it wouldn't be long anyway before they started falling victim to careless damage. They were partly in place to light the areas covered with cameras, of course, but Flint liked the eerie effect they brought to the place.

It was strange. Flint found this place quite calming; the darkness and silence could well be endless, with equal opportunity. Of course, Diego Flint knew he could leave at any time. He imagined it would be very different for those entering tomorrow, not knowing if, or when, they would ever get out.

Chapter 1

McKenzie woke, sweaty and feverish. Today was the day. He still hadn't taken in that it was time. How could anyone be expected to take in something this huge, as if it were just another stumbling block? There was one thing that was troubling him more than anything, though: why him? He wasn't a dangerous criminal, so why was he sentenced to the Maze?

Like everyone else in his position right now, he had no idea what to expect. During his court de-briefing, he had been told he was to be part of the first forty-seven people to be released into the Maze. The weird thing was, he hadn't seen any other prisoners at all. In this disconcerting, modern, and clean new complex, there must be forty-six other people like him somewhere.

The whole place was a little confusing. When McKenzie thought of prisons or correctional facilities, he thought of two stereotypes. One was the typical place you saw on telly, somewhere in southern America with crazy drug lords that are head-to-toe in gang tattoos, walking around a dusty, sand-coloured courtyard. The other was a plain, dingy, dark, and grubby cell block that had no life within it. This place was definitely neither of those. All around, there was natural light filtering through large panes of glass. The whole place was clean and in order. It was more like staying in a fancy hotel or spa retreat. Even the bed was unexpected; it was soft and comfortable, making it much easier to sleep despite everything that was rushing through his head.

Noon would mark the last moments of his life before the Maze. This morning, he had been allotted time for his loved ones to visit. However, McKenzie had found, like a lot of people in his position, that he wasn't expecting flocks of loved ones to appear. He hadn't spoken to his family for weeks, and the likelihood of him ever seeing Jessie again was very slim.

He wandered over to his window, gazing into the glorious wilderness beyond. He had been locked in a secure prisoner transport vehicle on the way to this place, so he wasn't sure where this place was at all. All he knew was that his window provided a glorious lookout over a beautiful plane full of grasses and shrubbery. It was almost taunting him, showing him this wonder when he was trapped like an animal at the zoo, unable to go beyond the glass that separated him from the open air. His eyes seemed a little wider than before the trial. When you know you might not see the light of day again, everything seems more beautiful, as if the world is mocking you, trying to prove a point. The morning sun seems that little bit more golden, and every blade of grass a perfect shade of green.

The glass door opened smoothly, the brushes underneath the frame rubbing on the tiled floor in a gentle whisper. It allowed one of the well-dressed facility workers to enter. McKenzie didn't bother to look. A deer had wandered into view from his window, and he stared longingly, wishing he could be free to run the lands as this doe was. If he was to ever escape the hellhole he would soon move into, he couldn't imagine ever sitting still for more than ten minutes again. There was so much he hadn't seen. The facility worker cleared his throat.

'I'm sorry to have to tell you,' he began softly, but paused, sighing deeply. 'But... erm... unfortunately nobody has come to see you.'

McKenzie let out a small snort. He had known this would be the case for some time.

'That's okay. It's certainly not your fault, so there's no need to apologise.' McKenzie's voice was a little croaky.

This was the first time he had spoken today, or for a while, when he thought about it. The verdict had stunned him into a kind of stupor.

'Well,' the young man continued sympathetically, 'you have the morning free, and we would like to offer you a choice of activities before…'

McKenzie chuckled again. Everything seemed futile. The man walked over and brandished a leaflet in McKenzie's face. McKenzie snatched it from him and began flicking through the pages with disdain. Then, he stopped, suddenly. He had turned to a page featuring an image of someone holding a bow and arrow. His first thought was how amazed he was that they allowed convicted prisoners to be in control of potentially dangerous weapons, then he was quickly taken back to the first time he'd held a bow. His dad had taught him. They had taken a camping trip out to the lakes, and his dad wanted him to learn to catch his own food; he'd always supported him and wanted him to be as practical as possible. They had spent hours wandering around looking for animals, and every time they found one, McKenzie fired too hurriedly and his arrow fell well short. Yet, his dad had not lost his temper or shown any frustration at all. They had been completely unsuccessful, but despite this it was one of McKenzie's most treasured memories.

'Oh! I almost forgot!' the young man exclaimed suddenly, bringing McKenzie back into the room. He realised he had been standing in silence for some time. The man was now rummaging in his pockets and soon pulled out an assortment of objects and placed them unceremoniously on the polished wooden table. There didn't seem to be a clear pattern to the objects at all. The first item he had withdrawn was a deck of pristine playing cards complete with a luxury travel case, which was quickly followed by a nifty penknife with several attachments. Then followed a small pen, like one from an old catalogue shop, and finally, a bungee cord and a soap bar.

'What's all this?' McKenzie asked, a little bemused.

'Well, Flint decided he wanted to allow all entrants to the Maze three items. Despite many meetings and constant beratement from his superiors, he was insistent that these could be absolutely anything, regardless of any potential injury they could cause. Normally, these are provided by your visitors, but, uh,' he tailed off and smiled politely. McKenzie turned back to his window. 'Anyway, these are the basic choices provided by us here at the Maze.' He paused once more, apparently expecting McKenzie to hit him with a flurry of thanks, or at least show some sign that he had registered any of this. 'Erm, if you did want to do an activity this morning, come and find me at the reception.' He stood there for a moment, watching McKenzie with an inquisitive look, then turned and slowly left the room. McKenzie knew he had left when he heard the gentle noise of the door smoothly opening and closing once more.

McKenzie was not necessarily someone you would expect to see in a correctional facility. He looked smart and well-kept despite his shoulder-length hair; even that was neat and under control, matching a fashionable stubble on his handsome face. You could tell he liked to be outdoors by his sun-worn skin. He looked slightly older than his age because of the crow's feet and blemishes on his face. Dressed casually and comfortably, he wore a relaxed fit: stonewashed jeans paired with a loosely fitted, chequered, yellow and black shirt.

He sat down on the small bench that stood adjacent to the window, trying to focus his mind and decide on whether to take up the offer of a morning of archery, but for some reason it was completely blank. It was as if so much was happening in his head that nothing new could be done. Instead, he watched the deer vacantly, content to imagine a simpler life of freedom. Eventually, the deer ambled away out of view, further emphasizing the difference between it and McKenzie. How he would love to just wander out of sight right now.

With little more to distract him other than an array of small birds, he got back to his feet, returning to the random selection of items laid out on his table. The man had said he was allowed to take three with him. He was immediately drawn to the gleaming penknife. It featured a small blade alongside numerous other metal attachments; a nail file, an Allen key, a mini screwdriver, and two other arms McKenzie couldn't work out. Thinking heavily, he tried to picture why he might need any of these tools in the Maze, but again, his mind came up blank.

Nevertheless, he pocketed the knife and started perusing the other items. He couldn't really see a need for any of them in the Maze, not that he really knew what he was going into, anyway. He hadn't even seen a picture from inside the Maze. Nobody had. Over the last six months, more and more information about the Maze had been released. McKenzie had seen an interview on the news with the creator, Diego Flint. He remembered being surprised at how normal he seemed. McKenzie had expected some twisted old man who had designed this place to torture others. Instead, he had spoken very well, explaining his vision for the Maze eloquently and passionately.

At that time, McKenzie had been watching Flint as anyone else did, intrigued by his ideas, fascinated to see the man behind them. It wasn't long after that he was watching news articles about the Maze with a whole new level of interest. He had begun researching everything he could find out about the Maze, but he had never once found any pictures. He couldn't see why any architect, even if he had just designed a new prison, wouldn't want his design up in lights.

Snapping back to reality, he quickly picked up the deck of cards and the soap bar, stuffing them into his pockets along with the penknife. He strode out of the room and headed to the reception. Within fifteen minutes, he was standing in the open air, breathing in the crisp breeze cutting across the archery lawn. It was so odd, to be standing there, about to be locked away for years, and yet holding a dangerous weapon. The bow was so similar to the one he'd used as a kid that it made McKenzie feel a little disturbed. He had already been wary that he was given the option to do archery, something connected to a very personal memory to him, but this bow was so similar in every way. The unusual nature of this place had put him on edge; now he was almost certain that something unnatural was going on.

For an hour, he disappeared into his own world, pushing his worries to the back of his mind and instead focusing on a happier time full of the freedom of nature. He took shot after shot, then collected his arrows, trudging along methodically. At last, another of the staff approached, with caution, McKenzie noticed. He was half tempted to pretend to raise the bow at her but figured that might be taken the wrong way in this situation. She already seemed jittery as it were. The nervous girl told McKenzie it was time to head inside, and everything came crashing down. The bubble he had disappeared into during the morning's archery was quickly burst. He numbly started plodding back towards the main building in the compound.

The doors opened smoothly as he strolled his way back in, unaware of everything around him. He hadn't even realised he was still holding the bow. One of the staff standing at reception quickly came and took it from his numb hands. One thing he did notice was that there seemed very little sign of anyone who would stop him from trying to run. It's like they knew. Deep down, he was desperate to find out what the Maze was like. He ambled along casually down the hall, following the nervous young girl who occasionally glanced back in his direction before quickly turning away with a little jump.

McKenzie found it very amusing. The girl seemed to be terrified of him. For one, the idea that he was scary to someone was a fairly new sensation; he wasn't used to it. Also, he felt this girl was unlikely to last long in this field if a minor criminal like himself was enough to terrify her. After a short while walking, turning another corner in an ironic maze of corridors, the pathway began to slope downwards, and McKenzie knew it meant only one thing.

Chapter 2

At exactly the same moment, twenty-five kilometres away in an adjacent correctional facility, Penny was stood waiting, surrounded by four concrete walls. This room was far more like any prison she had expected. It was dark and dingy with no natural light and gloomy grey walls. It was a complete contrast to the rest of the place — that she had seen, anyway. The only slightly unusual thing was that there was a door on either side on the two longer walls. She knew what the second door was for, of course. It stood, intimidating and tall, bearing down on her.

Only one of the workers had accompanied her to the room, and even though she was not armed, Penny didn't feel the desire to run. Somehow, she knew she wouldn't get far, despite the apparently lackadaisical security. She had spent the morning painting freely in a completely empty studio. It was like a dream come true. Everything she had ever wanted or needed to paint was there. It was so peaceful and so quiet she could have stayed there forever, creating to her heart's content. The only thing that had made it hard to focus was the knowledge that she couldn't stay there forever. In fact, she knew it would be merely hours before somebody turned up with a solemn face and graver news. Sure enough, little more than an hour after she had sat down on the wooden stool, she was summoned away.

She couldn't be angry for long, though. The stern-looking lady led her swiftly back to her room where her mom, brother and boyfriend waited. There was a mix of emotions on their faces; the same emotions she had been feeling towards herself over the last week. Pity and sadness that almost stretched to mourning, but also, smiles. Penny tried to focus on the positives. It had been some time since she had seen any of them properly. The last time she had seen their faces was in the courthouse, and the shame she had felt that day meant she couldn't look any of them in the eye. Even now it was hard, but she was so happy to see each one of them that she forced herself to seem brave and untroubled.

'H- hi,' she began nervously. She felt like a child being scorned, despite the fact that none of the three people in front of her looked in any way angry. Her mom sighed and walked forwards, her arms outstretched. It was nothing like in the movies. There were no heartless guards stepping forward to stop the joyous embrace. The blissful moment seemed to last forever, but eventually her mother pulled away, still smiling, though Penny noticed a tear fall down her left cheek before it was quickly wiped away.

'How is it here? It seems... weird,' Toby, her boyfriend, asked hesitantly.

'Yeah, it is a bit,' Penny giggled. 'But I think that's because I didn't expect anything like this. I think it's actually how these places should be.'

Toby was scanning the room with intrigue. It seemed like he didn't agree, based on his expression.

'We brought you your things,' her brother, Leo, said in a matter-of-fact way. He was always very down to earth and resourceful.

'What things? You mean, like, my suitcase?' Penny chuckled.

'No, as in the three things you can take with you, remember?' Leo replied, exasperated.

In truth, Penny hadn't remembered. She vaguely recalled something about it being mentioned during a long spiel she was given straight after the court verdict, but she was so zoned out at that moment that she'd heard almost none of the information that was given to her. For all she knew,

... that the table ... Leo was leaning
had a bag on it. Rushing over, she grabbed the bag
enthusiastically to see what they had brought, a sudden
positive energy causing her heart to race. In a way, she was
glad she had forgotten about her allowance of three items.
It was exactly the boost she needed this morning. She
rustled hastily through the bag and pulled out the first item.
Inspecting it closely, she noticed it was a roll of film filled
with images. She held the film tightly between her hands
and held it up to the light. She saw herself and Toby
smiling back, enjoying a sunny day in the park. She
remembered it well.

Shifting the film between her fingers, she now saw a
scene at the beach in which her and Leo, much younger,
were arm in arm with their father. She quickly rolled the
film roll back up neatly and stuffed it into her pocket. The
bag was still heavy, which intrigued Penny. She pulled the
other two items out together. One was an ornately designed
chisel with a patterned wooden handle. Its sleek silver blade
shimmered beautifully in the midday light that glared
through the numerous windows. Alongside the chisel was a
matching hammer which was shaped with stunning
precision. All three of her guests were watching her
intently, as if she were opening presents on Christmas
morning.

'We thought... well, we thought, seeing as you won't
have anywhere to paint in there, maybe you could use these
to create some art on the walls,' her mom said cautiously.
Something on Penny's face seemed to have conveyed
displeasure, as they all looked a little nervous. She quickly
tried to refigure her features and face them, keen to correct
their worries. She loved the thought they had put into each

item.

'I love them. I think it will really help me pass the time in there.' She hugged her mom again, and then Leo and Toby, too. She pulled away from Toby and turned to her mom and brother.

'Would it be okay if we have a minute alone?' she asked warily. She didn't want to offend them or seem ungrateful for them coming all this way.

'Yes, of course,' her mom said casually. She left the room, closely followed by Leo. Toby took her hands and moved closer.

'Um- look. I don't really understand what happened,' Toby said, stumbling over his words. Penny rolled her eyes and turned away.

'You know what happened, you were in the courtroom. You heard it all.'

'So, that's the truth?' Toby asked sharply. Penny nodded slowly, her back still turned away from Toby. She couldn't bring herself to face him.

'But- why?'

It was an inevitable question. Penny had known it was coming. She couldn't help it, but she quietly welled up.

'Honestly,' she said after a long pause, 'I just don't know. I guess I just got a bit desperate.'

In the reflection of her small window, Penny caught Toby hang his head.

'I didn't know you felt like that. I thought we were happy. I thought we still were, until just now.' Toby sounded defeated.

'I am happy.' Penny turned desperately to face Toby. 'I love you, you know I do. I didn't do it because of us,' she gesticulated wildly. 'I did it because I wanted a better life for both of us.'

'How'd that do for you?' Toby cut in harshly.

Penny gave a short snort of laughter.

'Oh, pretty well, actually. This is exactly how I had intended to be living my twenties,' Penny replied, full of sarcasm.

Toby sighed heavily. It seemed he was deep in thought.

'Look, I didn't want to do this. Especially not today. I can't imagine how hard this is for you, especially given all the uncertainty-'

'What are you saying?' Penny interrupted quickly.

'I can't do this anymore. You're not the person I thought you were. I'm sorry.' Without another word, Toby turned and strode purposefully past Penny's mom and brother, who watched him go in shock. Penny's mom rushed into the room and squeezed Penny tightly in a hug. Tears were now pouring down her face. She couldn't believe she had allowed herself to be so positive this morning. At this current moment, she couldn't see herself being happy again for a long time. All she could see was a darkness ahead of her. Leo was stroking her back reassuringly.

'I'm sorry,' her mom said softly. 'It was probably for the best, though.'

'You think?' Penny implored.

'Absolutely,' her mom said confidently. 'This is a fresh start. A chance to rediscover and reinvent yourself without anyone or anything holding you back.'

The rest of their short time together was spent with Leo und her mom reassuring Penny. After what seemed like an incredibly short time, the stern lady reappeared in the doorway. Her voice surprised Penny. It was oddly calm and soothing, not at all in keeping with her strict-looking face. She informed Penny's mom and Leo that it was time for them to leave, standing aside to allow them out of the door. She then turned to Penny, signalling her to follow. On her way out, Penny got one last glimpse of her family at the end of the corridor, but didn't get a chance to say anything. The woman was soon rushing through the hallways, Penny following reluctantly.

Chapter 3

The door opened and Yazmin breathed deeply in anticipation. A bundle of emotions hit her like a freight train; nervousness, excitement, dread, fear, and despair, all mixed together to cause a wave of butterflies in her stomach. The giant door swung forwards to reveal little more than darkness. It seemed a massive anti-climax. Yazmin looked at the man standing in the room with her in concern. He simply nodded once, his face emotionless, and stood waiting.

'What, so that's it?' Yazmin snapped angrily. 'I'm expected to just walk through this door into... nothing?' She waved forcefully at the empty frame.

'You are expected to oblige. It is the law,' the man stated plainly.

Yazmin stood resolute. She had always been stubborn. Now it seemed she had reached her last. How was she supposed to fight the verdict from this immeasurably miserable place?

Time passed as she just stared into the void in front of her. The man to whom she shared company made no sign of calling for support or backup, he merely watched on with intrigue. Eventually, one of them had to break.

'The only way is forward,' the man mumbled.

'What?' Yazmin yelled. 'What does that mean?'

'You cannot go back. There is no way back. The only way is forward,' he repeated. This time, he waved towards the doorway Yazmin had entered through, except it wasn't there anymore.

'Huh,' Yazmin said with surprise. 'Pretty literal.' She sounded impressed, a begrudging respect showing on her face. She paused, thinking hard. It seemed her legs made the decision for her. As she began to edge her way forwards, the darkness soon began to consume her. Walking along the pitch-black corridor, the only light came from the room she had just left. Slowly, the corridor grew darker and darker, until every step could lead to a three-hundred-foot drop, with very little chance to react. Yazmin could still sense the walls close on either side, and a ceiling a couple of feet above her head. Her eyes had not adjusted to this darkness as well as her other senses; at this moment, she couldn't see a thing.

Her hands stretched out before her, fumbling for the walls on either side and for any unseen obstructions ahead. It was just as well that they were. After several minutes of groping thin air, her hands hit something very solid; a wall. It seemed there was no way forward. Turning back, she could no longer see her entrance and guessed that it had been closed, just like the one back in that strange room. Panic beginning to settle in rapidly, she swivelled all around on the spot. Her heart began to race wildly, beating out of her chest, when she noticed the smallest of lights to her left. A golden, flickering light. The temptation was insurmountable.

Her heart slowing with each step, Yazmin made her way along this new path at a very gradual speed, the light growing ever stronger. An opening appeared ahead, and her mind began to clear. The feeling of dread she had fallen into so willingly within these tiny, dark corridors appeared to be lessening. At least, in part. At last, she reached the end of the cramped, narrow passage. It opened into a glorious chasm that stretched on for miles. Although she could make out very little of the space above her, she could sense an immense cavernous arena.

To her right, left, and ahead were new opportunities, new pathways lit by vintage lanterns shining golden light for brief circles of relief. Above her, she could see nothing but darkness. The ceiling must have been twenty feet high at least; she felt a sure sense of open air above her. Strangely, there was a slight breeze, too, though it was not apparent where this could be coming from. It certainly didn't seem like there were any windows nearby.

She stepped forward and ran her hand across the smooth, cold wall. It felt like granite, but Yazmin thought it was probably impossible to get that much granite to cover the entire Maze. She wondered if there were even that much to be found in the world. After all, the wall must have been three feet in width. It was more likely to be a compound of some sort.

Every single wall was a constant gunmetal grey. The lanterns brought a sense of great character to a place that was otherwise incredibly dreary; the whole place felt magical. The sheer feat of design and engineering left Yazmin in awe. Edging forward inch by inch, her focus was drawn to the nearest lantern; something about it radiated curiosity. Looking around at her surroundings, it struck her that it was the only reminder of the twenty-first Century. Just about, anyway. It was definitely electric, at least, but Yazmin thought it was a bit twisted to use a design that seemed to fit the eighteenth Century much better. Yazmin couldn't imagine that oil lanterns would even work down here, and it wasn't what she would call cosy. In fact, as she thought that, she noticed her breath rising in front of her eyes in the form of smoke.

She stared at the beautifully simple lantern for some time before realising her eyes were beginning to burn. Blinking constantly as she fought against the strain, her mind quickly moved towards the Maze. She had three options at this moment: left, right, or forward. She tried to imagine the thought process of that man, Diego Flint, as he designed this place. This was the first fork, the first junction, the first decision. Most people would go straight on, he would have expected that. The next thing she figured would be obvious was to go right. It was well known that a massively disproportionate percentage of the population favoured their right side. No, she had to go left. One thing she had decided days ago was to stick with her decisions. If she started doubting herself, it was a downhill slope.

She set off, this time moving at a quicker speed. Her mind was set. She passed the first light, then quickly a second and a third. The passage was long, straight. Yazmin passed countless more lights, working up towards a pace that was basically jogging. Still, she could see no end in sight.

Yazmin stopped suddenly, breaking her now ferocious stride. She cursed herself loudly. She was being naive, trying to complete the Maze in a day. That wasn't going to happen. She wasn't about to break the system. Taking a deep breath, she closed her eyes to clear her mind and then set off once more at a far gentler pace. She tried to imagine she was on an afternoon stroll on a summer's day.

After just the one very brief mental breakdown, she finally reached the end of her first passage. At this moment, she decided it was necessary to use the first of her three items: a compass. Of course, a compass is at its most useful when you actually know where you're going. Yazmin didn't, but she figured that keeping track of her direction would be smart. The last she had heard, this place measured over thirty kilometres. Getting lost was not a good idea.

The compass showed that she was currently facing east. A little confusing already, as she was moving left from where she had started. Although now that she thought about it, there was that other left turn back in the dark passage. She must have started by walking to the west.

Already a little disorientated, she had to compose herself once more. This was going to be harder than she had imagined. The pathway split into two right-angles: left or right, north or south.

It had taken her just two junctions, but she suddenly realised there was no logic. This place was so big, there was no point attempting to follow a pattern or thought process. A great feeling of hopelessness fell over her like an icy shower. She didn't know where she was trying to get to, let alone how to get there. As if caught in an avalanche, everything came tumbling down. The hardened version of herself that she had tried to create for this place was dwindling away to leave her in her most vulnerable state.

She slumped to the floor and sobbed openly. She wept more then she had for years, more than she could ever remember. She felt completely and utterly useless. How was she supposed to get out of here? How could anything anyone has ever done in their life prepare them for a place like this? A dark, silent dungeon, with nothing but your own thoughts.

Yazmin had always been someone who allowed her emotions to take control very quickly, and right now her feeling of helpless dread was quickly overtaking her entire headspace. She closed her eyes and tried to empty her mind, but before she knew what was happening, she was drifting off into an uneasy sleep. She hadn't had a minute's sleep over the last few days, feeling too uncomfortable in that mental hospital-looking place. She guessed that it reminded her too much of that summer when she was younger. These days, Yazmin did everything she could to forget about that part of her history.

Chapter 4

It had taken some time to get used to, and Aaron knew he still wasn't fully accustomed, but after several hours of walking purposefully he was content to stop for the night, or whatever passed for night in here. There was no concept of night and day at all, no light or dark. Just the Maze, the walls, and the lanterns.

Aaron loved to work methodically. It had already helped him in the Maze. Everything was a process. It was about a steady trudge, passing the lights one by one. Something else that came in handy was a photographic memory. He had been able to memorise whole pages of books since he was young. When he was reading *Mr. Men* books this wasn't particularly useful, but being able to know the encyclopaedia front to back certainly was. In the Maze, it could be quite easy to lose your bearings, especially as everything looked the same. As in, exactly the same. At least he had the advantage of knowing for sure he hasn't gone in a circle yet.

He had decided to stop near a T-junction, right at the end of a long corridor. That way when he inevitably moved around in his sleep, he wouldn't be left confused when he woke up. Aaron had no idea how long or how far he had been walking today, but it was definitely enough to make him tired – and hungry, for that matter. The woman who had met him after his verdict had informed him there would be restroom and refreshment facilities, but he hadn't found any yet. Running through this in his head he was a little concerned. He must have been walking for what he had worked out as around eight hours. At an average walking pace of an adult, he knew this would mean around four miles per hour, therefore he must have covered at least twenty-five miles, about forty kilometres.

The last he'd seen the Maze had only just passed forty kilometres of pathways in total. This had only been around two weeks ago. He must have nearly walked the entire Maze and found no sign of another person, any facilities, or any sign of life at all. He lay there, leaning against the cool wall, thinking about this issue. His eyes were unfocused, gazing distantly off to the dark ceiling in the distance. Then the strangest thing happened.

A light appeared a little above him. It looked like a window or something; it seemed very square and definitely man-made. Then, after a few moments, it disappeared again. What on earth could that have been? Maybe it was a lookout spot for Flint and his cronies, keeping an eye on their inmates.

He had begun to feel drowsy, eyes gradually drooping. Now, he was suddenly wide awake, his mind racing. What if that was the way out? He quickly ferreted through his pockets and pulled out the three items his sister had brought him earlier that day, trying to think how they could help him. In his hands he held a switchblade, a pen, and a copy of the first book he ever memorised; *Ulysses* by James Joyce.

It said a lot about him, and his sister, that he was holding the blade backwards and would have cut his wrist open if he had pressed the small button on the handle. He understood why she had brought it, but he wished she hadn't. He really hoped it wouldn't ever be needed. Now he had a moment to sit and think, the book was really pointless. Sure, it had sentimental value, but other than that it held little purpose. He didn't want to say it to his sister at the time, but the whole reason it carried any sentiment is because he had memorised it. As in, he knew every word. He didn't even need to open the cover to know that the book opened with: "Stately, plump Buck Milligan…" As for the pen, it was nice, but it was pretty useless without anything to write on, and he wasn't about to defile the classic *Ulysses*.

Once again, it seemed he would have to rely on his own wit and intelligence. He pushed himself back onto his feet, ignoring his already aching joints and muscles. Forcing himself to focus once more, Aaron set off chasing the mystery light. Immediately he faced a tough choice. His direct path to the light was blocked and he would have to go either right or left. Making a swift decision, he set off to the left. Before he charged off down the corridor, though, he crossed to the wall facing the junction and pulled out his switchblade. Pressing hard against the stone, he carved out a large "L" and then set out on his new mission.

All the time, he tried to keep an eye on that spot above the Maze in the distance. A ray of salvation, perhaps. One thing he really regretted now he was here was his choice in clothing. He was never much into fashion anyway, but he had been torn on what the most practical outfit would be. He had decided on comfort. Loose fitting and simple. He chose an oversized t-shirt and baggy joggers. Unfortunately, he hadn't accounted for the weather. He had been told it was indoors so didn't expect it to be this cold. In hindsight, that was incredibly naive. As if they would just place him in a nice cosy maze. There was certainly no heating down here, or sun for that matter. Now, he shivered as he made his way along the newest path.

Reaching the end in a surprisingly short time, he had hoped there would be a right turn, and he was in luck. To his enormous surprise, however, when he turned the corner, he was greeted with a glorious sight: a doorway was lighting up the pathway in heavenly white light. Inside the doorway was a simple restroom, a basic yet spectacular restroom. Never had Aaron been so excited to see a sink.

Looking around for any fellow prisoners, he stepped in and immediately felt like his cornea's were permanently damaged. It felt like what he imagined a rapture to be.

Closing the heavy door behind him, he locked it with a loud clunk and quickly started relaxing. This place was safe. The Maze had left him on edge. The lack of any sign of security was certainly worrying. If he was to bump into someone who wanted to start a fight, there wasn't much to stop them. Sure, Aaron had his switchblade, but he really didn't want to use it. The only reason he hadn't ditched it straight away was because he didn't want anyone else to find it.

In the corner of the room furthest from the door sat a plant pot holding a perfectly kept house plant. Thanks to *One Thousand and One Plants For Your Home* Aaron recognised the plant as a Boston Fern. The fact that it was so well-kept made Aaron think these lights were probably of the UV kind. It was a common plant that could be found in a lot of homes, but for some reason, at that moment, it was the most beautiful plant Aaron had ever seen. He walked over, once again pulling out his blade, which was seeing far more action than he had expected. Leaning over the plant, he carefully held one of the branches between his fingers and neatly cut it off at the stem. This was much more useful and pertinent than any of the three items his sister had left him. It would serve as a great reminder of the outside world. A world full of life.

Life was certainly easy to forget here. He hadn't seen anyone, heard anything, or, until this moment, had any sign of life, human or otherwise. Looking around at the strange sleep far better here than he could out there. The light could wait until the morning, or whenever he woke up. If anything was going to ruin his internal clock, it was sleep.

Chapter 5

'Alex, what's the report from 1200 hours?' Diego Flint called, striding into the control room. A woman in her mid-twenties stepped forward from a desk at the front of several rows of computers.

'No incidents, Diego. Nobody has crossed paths, as of yet. We have seven currently on the move, three criers,' she answered confidently.

'Good, good. Any technical glitches?'

'Nope. All of the lanterns are in order, as are the cameras.'

'Awesome!' Diego smiled contentedly. He wasn't like a normal boss. After all, he was still only twenty-one. He sat down, putting his feet up on the white desk, showing his brown boat shoes and bare ankles. His long, wiry chestnut-brown hair brushed against the leather of his chair as he leaned back.

'Mr Flint,' another well-dressed man pronounced as he bounded jubilantly down the steps to the front row. 'Great news, section seventeen is ready.'

'Excellent, what a day!' Flint called out to the whole room. Alex could tell he was ecstatic. He had been so stressed during the past months of preparation — now it seemed everything was coming together. 'Is there anyone near the entrance, Scottie?'

'No, sir,' Scott replied.

Flint nearly fell off his chair — he had been precariously rocking on two legs. He swivelled around, taking his feet off the table. 'Please don't call me sir, man! I'm younger than you!'

Scott chuckled nervously. 'Sorry.'

Flint rolled his eyes. That was exactly the point he was trying to make. He didn't want people treating him like a big boss. He was an ideas man, not a leader.

'All clear for section seventeen?' Flint called to the room. In front of him was an enormous screen with forty-seven red dots spaced across a giant live map of the Maze. Each dot was tagged with a name, and underneath that, a notice of the crime they were sentenced for. Scanning it, he could see a clearing around the wall connected to section seventeen which was currently shaded in grey, rather than white like the rest of the map.

'All clear,' came the response from multiple different operators.

'Let's do it, then.' Flint clapped excitedly. Instantaneously, section seventeen faded from grey to white after a couple of flashes, and the map zoomed in on the camera nearest to the doorway. He just about saw the last of the previously solid wall slide into its new place as part of the newly created long corridor.

'Everything has gone according to plan,' Alex said, intently watching the tablet strapped around her shoulder. 'The Maze now stands at fifty-one point two kilometres in distance.' This was echoed by the bottom right of the screen, which showed a breakdown of the activity within the Maze, and was now updated to the same figure.

The big screen zoomed back out, showing the Maze in full. Flint followed a red dot tagged with "McKenzie Symms". It was one of the only dots still moving, and, interestingly enough, was heading straight towards section seventeen. Flint sat back down and grabbed the sharing bag of crisps that was on the desk in front of him.

'Can we get a camera on Symms, please?' he asked Alex.

'Yeah, sure. Camera on Mazer Zero-Zero-One, please,' she called over to her operating team. Flint winced a little but made no comment.

'Come and sit down,' Flint said kindly to Alex, patting

the chair next to him. She did so, a little nervously.

'This is the whole point of all of this,' Flint began, chucking a crisp into his mouth and crunching loudly. 'Learning about a person, their traits and behaviourisms. The first day of any Mazers time here is one of their most important. We get to see where they are coming from. The start of their journey, if you will. It's like watching an epic movie, just over the space of months or years.' He grinned broadly.

Alex smiled. It was hard not to appreciate the passion Diego showed for his work. It wasn't just a job for him. It was his life's dream and ambition. He truly believed this was the answer, that this could solve people's lives from going down a darker and darker path. Together, they sat in silence as McKenzie continued steadily along the empty corridors. Occasionally the camera flicked to the next one along to keep him in focus. Alex looked at Flint's child-like face as he watched on in intense fascination.

'Tell me about this guy,' Diego instructed inquisitively. 'What has he been up to today?'

Alex nodded to one of the junior operators loitering behind them and within moments Flint was handed a tablet with a full fact file on McKenzie Symms. The file included a tab labelled "Highlights", along with data on *distance covered*, *rest time*, *sleep time*, and *average pace*, amongst others.

Flint noticed that Symms was ranked number one for *distance covered*. In contrast, he was number forty-seven — last — in *rest time* and *sleep time*. He clicked on the *distance covered* rankings and scrolled down to the bottom. To his amazement, number forty-seven had covered just two-hundred and seven metres. Intrigued, he clicked on the name to find out more. The woman's name was Yazmin Tracey. She had been sitting in the same spot now for eight hours, but had not slept for more than thirty minutes. Alex, watching over Diego the whole time, noticed a line of concern spread across his face.

He quickly clicked on the "Highlights'" button and was presented with a number of videos, all relating to Yazmin at various points of her first day in the Maze. She can't have been much older than Flint himself. He watched as Yazmin walked casually up to one of the hundreds of T-junctions within the Maze and paused for a moment, looking resolute but troubled. Then, within an instant, she slumped to the floor, shrinking as small as she possibly could.

'Have you been watching Yazmin Tracey at all, Alex?'

'Yes, Mazer Zero-Three-Two. Definitely one we are keeping a close eye on. I took a special interest in her, it seems she might be one of the most interesting cases within the initial batch.' Flint winced once again, but this time he decided to speak his mind.

'Please don't call her that, call her Yazmin.' For the first time Flint had sounded forceful and a little angry. Alex was taken aback, being so used to a gentle Flint.

'I- I'm sorry. It just helps us operate. It's okay right now, but when we have hundreds-'

'It's okay, I understand that. I just don't want any of you to forget that these are people, though, not just numbers.'

'Of course,' Alex said solemnly. Flint brushed it aside as if it hadn't even happened.

'Could you keep a close eye on Yazmin, please? I would like a report compiled for the next twenty-four hours.'

Alex replied with the same answer. She knew Diego cared about these people. She was also aware that he was under a lot of pressure to succeed in his great experiment. His superiors and the families of those within the Maze were a constant threat, should anything go wrong. A negative case in the first forty-eight hours of the Maze opening would not help this pressure.

'Speaking of the next twenty-four hours,' Diego said, changing the subject quickly, 'what's the plan for tomorrow?'

'Ah,' Alex smiled. She was back in her element. 'Lot's more to do tomorrow. There are six new Mazers to be introduced.'

'Excellent!' Flint exclaimed. 'It's really beginning to take shape, isn't it?' he asked rhetorically, checking his watch. 'You know, I feel like heading for a drink. Would you be up for it? Lots to celebrate.'

Alex thought as quickly as she could. She didn't want this to be awkward, but it didn't seem appropriate.

'Scottie, Luka, Michelle, wanna head for a drink in a bit?' Flint called to the quiet room before Alex had a chance to answer. She felt a wave of relief spread over her. There was a general murmur of agreement from the others in the room. Alex actually thought blowing off a little steam wasn't a bad idea. It *had* been a stressful few weeks, — months, even.

∗

The next morning at a quarter to eleven Diego was awoken by a gentle buzzing. It was his phone on his bedside table. He leant over and grabbed it hastily, prepared for the worst possible news. It was Alex.

'Hello,' he croaked, coughing quickly to awaken his vocal chords.

'Hi, Diego, have you heard the news yet?' Alex seemed much more awake than he was. Diego's worst fears seemed to be being realised.

'No, what's happened?'

'There's been an incident with one of the new Mazers,' Alex spoke quickly. 'I'm heading in now. I suggest you probably should, too.' Diego sighed heavily, heaving himself out of bed as he put the phone on speaker.

'Okay, I'll be there in about ten minutes,' Diego stated to the room.

'See you soon,' Alex said shortly. Diego could tell she was driving already. He waited a moment for the call to end before turning on the spot.

'Anthony!' he called, seemingly talking to the door. Oddly it spoke back to him. Or at least someone behind it did.

'Yes, sir,' came a deep voice.

'Can you get the team ready ASAP, please?'

'Of course, sir.'

Diego heard Anthony quickly muttering on the radio as he dashed into the bathroom. His mind was racing with the possibilities of what Alex had meant by an "incident". He quickly brushed his teeth and had an even swifter face wash in the basin. Grabbing a can of spray, he raced back out of the en-suite and went to get dressed.

Within three minutes he was stood outside with Anthony, the head of his personal security, still panicking. They made their way down the hotel corridor towards the elevator where another member of the security team waited for them. The elevator doors pinged open and revealed yet another burly man waiting in the elevator, alone. Diego and the two guards entered and within five minutes of Alex's call, Flint had made it to the hotel lobby.

The main base of Maze control was situated on the ground floor of this hotel. In fact, the entire hotel was built as a cover for the base. Another member of the security team had joined the party, and the four of them walked Diego purposefully through the hallways in a formation like a five on a dice, with Diego in the middle, until they reached a coded doorway. The most recent member of the team to join them, Anna, stepped forward and entered the code, which was changed daily, along with a thumbprint.

Anna led them through the metal doors, revealing a much contrasting décor to the front provided by the hotel. Just as the doors began closing behind them, they heard a frantic scuffling coming from the hotel side. Anthony stepped in front of Diego and put his hand on his holster. Alex came running in as quickly as she could manage in her pencil skirt and heels. Anthony reached for his gun, but, just in time, Diego grabbed his arm.

'There'll be no need for that, Anthony,' Diego stated, eyeing the gun warily. 'This is Alex, one of my Deputy Head of Operations.'

Alex looked startled, her eyes wide. Slowly, the tension broke, and Diego quickly remembered the reason for his hurry.

'So, what's this incident about?' Diego said calmly, beckoning Alex to walk beside him. Alex already had her trusty tablet out in front of her — Diego was beginning to think it was attached at the hip. He was glad he had been able to convince her to have some fun last night for once. It seemed she had been deep in dialogue with Benji, her fellow deputy, all morning.

'One of the six new Mazers today was a high-security case. The protocol was followed throughout, but he decided to take his opportunity when he was in the transition room. As normal, there was only one of our team with him. Rather than following his path, the Mazer chose to attack. We have been locked in a hostage situation ever since.' All the time Alex had been briefing him they had been walking at a brisk pace through the corridors and now they entered the Control Room. It was almost unrecognisable from the calm of last night.

Operators were dashing chaotically here and there; phones were ringing, and paper was being exchanged rapidly. The screen was now split into two, one half still showing the Maze in full, the other a live feed of transition room twelve, in which two men were struggling with each other in one corner, surrounded by three heavily armoured members of an advanced security squad and one man dressed in a three-piece suit. Flint couldn't help but chuckle to himself. He admired Benji for heading straight to the front lines and dealing with the problem himself, but he could have at least taken off the waistcoat.

'What's this guy's name?' Diego enquired, his eyes fixed on the scene developing on the screen before him.

'Toni Jeremiah Bogle, otherwise known as TJ. He is here after he was stopped at a bank robbery in which he shot three civilians whilst attempting to get away with eighteen million dollars.'

Flint nodded knowingly; he remembered this story. He admitted it was perhaps their most ambitious coup so far to take TJ into the Maze. The failed bank robbery was just the final in a long catalogue of previous connections to illicit activities.

'So, what's happened since?' Diego asked calmly. He wanted to make sure he conveyed confidence with everyone around him panicking.

'As you can see, Benji is currently keeping TJ occupied-' Alex began.

Diego couldn't help but smirk.

'What are you laughing at? This is serious, Diego!' Alex retorted.

'Sorry, it's just Benji. I don't think I've ever seen a negotiator in a waistcoat before.'

'Laugh if you will. At least he's in there. I'm not sure I could have handled this so well,' Alex said sternly.

'You're right, I'm sorry.'

'Anyway,' Alex said, getting back to the point, 'there hasn't been much progress, yet. It seems TJ hasn't really thought through his great plan. Benji thinks it's a matter of time until he gives in. They just have to be careful. He *is* armed.' She gave Diego a meaningful look. It was his idea to allow prisoners to bring any items they wanted to take with them. If he hadn't insisted on that, this might not be such as issue.

'Has anything broken to the media yet?' he asked, a little nervously.

'No, of course not. There is no reason it has to, either.'

'Okay, good,' Diego said thoughtfully. 'I've got to go.'

'Where?'

'Down there, of course.' He nodded to the screen, and without another word turned and walked out, accompanied by his private security team.

Chapter 6

TJ had regretted his decision almost immediately. When the door had opened, he just panicked. He hadn't been given an exact sentence in court, which worried him. A man like him would more often than not spend the rest of his life in a normal prison. Now he was heading into the depths of hell, and he couldn't pass the gates without a fight. But he was never going to win. There was nowhere to go. Even if by some miracle he managed to escape this god-forbidden place and found freedom, it wouldn't be true freedom. He would be running for cover the rest of his life — how different could that be from what awaited him through the impenetrable darkness of the doorway?

Everyone in the room knew it, too. There were three men pointing guns at him, but not one of them showed signs of firing. TJ knew a man who had the capability of killing — and these men were not killers. Not in the conventional use of the word. They were the type of killers who were content to condemn a man to a life of misery and go home without a heavy conscience. He would always be seen as the bad guy in this world, and maybe he was. But there were plenty more out there who weren't recognised for what they were.

Then there was this other man, Benji he said his name was. It was fair to say he seemed out of touch with the real world. TJ actually laughed in his face when he walked in, up on his high horse, wearing that ridiculous two-toned blue suit. How can anyone be expected to be taken seriously in a situation like this when they are dressed like that? He kept trying to remind TJ about what is right and wrong. TJ had to grind his teeth to stop himself jumping at this Benji.

The room had been silent for some time — Benji had stepped back outside to make some calls. TJ thought it was worth keeping this up just to spite him. Just as he thought this, the door swung open again, letting in a brief glimpse of natural light and a much-needed wave of fresh air. It also brought with it someone new. TJ recognised him at once but couldn't put his face to a name. This man was a stark contrast to Benji. He was smartly dressed, but had not overdone it. His shirt sleeves were rolled up fashionably and he clearly hadn't had time to sort his hair out this morning. TJ got the impression he had woken this man up. Something about this idea made him relax around the new man. His whole demeanour was refreshing, having dealt with the annoyingly middle-class Benji for an hour.

'Hello, TJ,' the man began calmly, his voice cracking a little. 'My name is Diego Fl-'

'Aw, yeah, that's it. I knew I knew you!' TJ blurted out. 'You're the guy who came up with this twisted dungeon thing. Man, I didn't recognise you at first. I thought you'd be all done up like that bud before you.'

Amazingly, Flint actually laughed at this. Not a nervous laugh, but an actual show of amusement.

'Yeah, I just made a comment about that myself. He didn't mean to belittle you, you know. He just didn't think he had time to change.'

'Yeah, whatever. Who wears a waistcoat to work, anyway?'

'I guess there's nothing wrong with looking smart,' Flint chuckled. 'It's more than you're managing right now.'

'Hey!' TJ yelled, tightening his grip on the trembling man he still had a hold of who let out a terrified squeak. 'What kind of negotiating is that, man? Don't you know the first rule is not to antagonise me?'

'Is that right? Well, I guess I don't really play by the book, as this place goes to show,' Flint said a little smugly.

'Why are you here, anyway? Don't you have enough

bodies working under you for someone else to come down here?'

'Of course, but this whole place is of my creation. Its problems are my problems.'

TJ contemplated this for a minute. This guy was literally like the God of this new world he was about to enter. Yet, he really wasn't what TJ had expected. He was even younger than he remembered seeing him on TV, and he was confident, but not over-confident. If anything, he was a little humble given his position. This all threw TJ off a little.

'So, aren't you going to give your little speech?' TJ asked, trying to get back on track.

'What would be the point of that? We both know you *will* go into the Maze. I was just going to ask if you could give us poor Ben back.' He nodded at the man that TJ had one arm around, who looked like he might pee himself at any moment. TJ took a deep breath.

'Fine,' he conceded, 'but only cos I don't wanna be smelling of urine when I go in that *Maze*'. He loosened his grip on Ben and pushed him forwards. The three armoured guards stepped forward to retrieve him.

'Thank you. So, you admit that you *will* be going into the Maze, then?'

'What other choice do I have?'

Flint shrugged. 'Fair point.'

'Can I ask you something first, though?' TJ's voice suddenly changed.

'Sure.'

'Have you got any tips?' TJ asked cheekily.

Flint smirked.

'I'm afraid I can't be doing that, now. That wouldn't be fair.'

TJ's shoulders dropped a little, but he nodded his understanding. 'Worth a try,' he mumbled, turning to face

He turned quickly.

'I have one bit of advice for you,' Flint said. 'Don't ever assume to know the Maze completely. You never know when it might surprise you.' He smiled again. He seemed quite proud of that one. TJ thought for a moment, then nodded his appreciation to Flint and turned into the darkness.

Chapter 7

Yazmin had never been so nervous. The jury were currently off in their private room, deciding her fate. It was one of the weirdest feelings ever, knowing that she was innocent yet staring down the barrel of a prison sentence. If only she had proof of some sort.

She was facing charges of assault and grievous bodily harm after a young woman was found unconscious, bruised, and bloody. Security cameras in the area had shown Yazmin walking along the same road that the girl was found on at around the right time. She had just left David's, crying, and freezing cold in the dead of night in mid-December. Not only that, but they had seen nobody else on this road at the approximate time of the attack. On top of this, when she was called in for initial questioning, she had been foolish enough to tell the police that she had seen no-one else at that time.

She had thought she was simply there to help the police. She believed she was being treated as a potential witness. Never had it occurred to her that she could be a possible suspect. She sat there on the metal bench in the hallway of the courtrooms, surrounded by her family as she cried once again. Everything that had happened in the last three weeks since that initial call from the police seemed to flash through her mind every five seconds.

She did have a few things on her side. Firstly, she had no motive. She had no connection to the young woman and, as far as she knew, they had never met. Secondly, there was no evidence which linked her to the attack. The forensics team had found none of her DNA on the girl's clothes or body. Unfortunately, they had found no DNA belonging to anyone else, either.

The other mystery is how the young woman got there. It

was a quiet road on the very outskirts of the city, and at that time there weren't many people around, yet no security camera had picked her up. The only one on the street was situated towards the end that Yazmin had come from, but the woman had never made it that far. Yet, cameras on the two streets she could possibly have entered from did not pick her up on route. Typically, the girl was still in a coma and unable to give evidence, for or against Yazmin.

Yazmin was forced to hope that the lack of damning evidence was enough to help her out of this mess. After all, any number of things could have happened to the woman. She could have come from one of the many houses on the road, or perhaps from a car. She had tried to suggest these to the police to investigate but was told, in no uncertain terms, to allow the police to do their jobs and focus on her own defence. This didn't fill her with confidence.

After fifteen minutes or so there was a sudden flurry of activity. Yazmin looked up to see the judge marching past on his way back to his chair. Shortly after, a man in the navy and black uniform of the court security approached and summoned her and her family to return also. Yazmin's knees nearly gave way as she stood to make her way back, forcing her to grab the bench tightly. Her whole body was shaking as she gave her mom and dad a quick kiss.

There was a kind of sick murmur of excitement as Yazmin re-entered the courtroom. This case had provided a surprisingly large media following, possibly because of the unusual circumstances that encircled the whole case in mystery. She quickly found her seat next to her attorney, unable to stand for much longer, such was the violent nature of her shivering.

The judge entered and everyone automatically stood, as usual, before being seated promptly. She wasn't the best judge of character, but the judge seemed a little less grave than usual. His worry lines certainly seemed less apparent.

'I have just this minute received a phone call from the hospital,' he began in his deep, sultry tone. Yazmin knew this was going one of two ways. Either the woman had died, and she sat in even greater lumber, or- 'I am pleased to inform you that Miss MacDonald has become responsive.'

Yazmin's heart skipped a beat.

'In light of this information, I have made the decision to postpone the hearing for the time being, with the hope that over the coming days and weeks we will be able to get a clearer picture, thanks to any evidence the young lady is able to provide. Thank you, you are dismissed.'

A feeling of elation filled Yazmin with ecstasy. Surely this was it? The girl would be able to clear her name and she could begin to put this all behind her.

She tried not to look too happy as she stood, feeling returning back to her legs, and turned to see her family smiling back at her. It was important she didn't start counting her chickens too early. Nothing was decided yet. Her parents didn't seem to feel the same way. They had never had a doubt in their minds that their little Yaz was innocent. She found herself forced into a celebratory meal at her favourite Italian restaurant, gulping down overly extravagant wine. For a while she began to fall into the folly of belief that she could live a regular life.

Two weeks later, after enjoying a walk on a crisp winter's morning with her family, this came to bite her in the backside. As they turned their way onto their street, Yazmin spotted the police car waiting outside number forty-seven — their own house. They came to a halt, her dad throwing the car into the driveway with a little additional aggression than was necessary. Yazmin could tell he was furious, the little of his face that she could see was a deep shade of scarlet. He was the first out of the car, slamming the driver's door so violently the whole car shook.

Yazmin was torn. She wanted to race after him and find out what the hell was happening, but then again, she felt like shrivelling up into the backseat and never leaving the car again. It was pretty clear that it wasn't good news, the police showing up unannounced at her door. They don't tend to bring around "congratulations, you're innocent!" balloons to their old adversaries.

After an interminably long time sat in silence with her mom giving her furtive looks from the front seat, she finally gave in to the temptations of the muffled voices talking by the police car on the roadside. Her trembles returned as quickly as they had disappeared in the courtroom.

As she opened the door, she heard her dad yelling in full flow: '-Shame on the family! You could have called, but nooo! Instead, you march on over here to make a scene for the neighbours.' The policeman wasn't getting a chance to give his side of the story. '-Enough funny looks from them when we leave the house as it is! I don't even know what you want! What is it you want?'

The officer tried to seize his chance as he spotted Yazmin walking over to them.

'Miss MacDonald has given her first statement, Mr. Tracey. Based on her evidence we would like another chat with your daughter, Yazmin.' He nodded in Yazmin's direction. His voice was steady and soothing, providing the whole scene with a state of calm previously missing. It seemed he was well experienced in calming relatives, victims, or even criminals.

Yazmin's dad had a look of mingled confusion and anger on his face. He turned incredulously towards his daughter, sure that she would have some explanation for this latest intrusion into their personal lives. Unfortunately, Yazmin had no answers. She was surer than anyone that she was innocent, and after the girl, Missy, had woken, she was sure there would be no further problems. She didn't understand. The look on her father's face didn't help either, a look that Yazmin had never seen before. It seemed like he was slowly understanding. Understanding something that wasn't true.

The police officer opened the door gently, a soft smile on his face that reflected a little pity. Yazmin's dad was clearly in two minds. He wanted desperately to save his daughter from another horrible ordeal, but it was plainly obvious that more than a little doubt was seeping into his mind. Yazmin didn't put up a fight, she didn't say a word. It may have been naïve, especially given what happened last time, but she still knew deep down she was innocent. That fact had not changed.

Chapter 8

'I have to say, that was pretty incredible,' Alex stated casually. Flint had returned from transition room twelve in Facility B. He smiled cheekily.

'Thanks,' he said smugly. 'I would take it as a compliment but for the fact you sound so surprised.'

'And well done to you as well, Benji. You did so well to keep TJ under control.'

'Thanks,' Benji muttered. He had been sulking all the way back from the transition room and still had a sour face. It didn't quite fit his three-piece suit much. Flint knew he had to be careful not to upset him further.

'She's right, Benji. You kept everything under control. I couldn't have asked for more. I think you can go home early now, get some rest. Alex has got it from here, right?'

'Yeah, I'm here anyway. No point me going home now,' Alex agreed.

'Excellent. Before you go, though, could I have your night report please, Benji? I hope you remembered I wanted a full report on Miss Tracey?'

'Yeah, of course,' Benji said, already unbuttoning his waistcoat. He moved over to the Deputies' desk and picked up his own tablet.

'It was a very quiet night, Diego, much like we had expected. Most of the Mazers still have a rough sleeping pattern and were unmoving throughout the night, so no incidents. We have all but one on the move again now, though. Miss Tracey.' He paused for breath, looking grave. 'She hasn't moved since twenty-five past twelve yesterday afternoon.'

'What has she been doing?' Flint asked with interest.

'Mostly crying,' Benji said, getting straight to the point. 'I guess the good news is she can't have too many tears left, though.' He added dryly, though there was no hint of laughter on his face.

'Very well,' Flint said, disappointed. He turned to face the map, his brain working in overtime. 'I'm guessing we avoided room nine for confrontational purposes?'

'Yes, of course, as is protocol.' Benji was always one to play by the books. Flint was clearly brewing up a plan. 'Will that be all then, Diego?'

'Yes, yes. Thank you, Benji. I'll see you tomorrow,' Flint said distractedly.

Alex waited in silence for Benji to leave. She pretended to be intently studying the map in front of her as he collected his things from the Deputies' desk. She waved goodbye as he left the control room, waiting a few moments for him to be out of earshot, then quickly hurried back over to Flint who had taken up a random seat to watch on from.

'Sooo…'

'Yes?'

'What's your great idea then?'

'I might not have one,' Flint tried to say innocently. He was given away by his face breaking into a boyish grin. 'Oh fine,' he said, spotting Alex's sceptical face. 'The way I see it, there is no reason for Miss Tracey to move. She seems quite content to wallow in her own self-pity. The only way this will change is if we make it change. We have the means to do exactly that.'

Alex nodded her understanding. 'So, you want to put someone in from room nine?'

Diego thought about this for a moment.

'What's happened to our friend TJ?' Diego asked.

'What?'

'Mr Bogle. What's he up to now he's finally made his way into the Maze?'

Alex grabbed her tablet and began looking through.

'Looks like he's pretty much the same as everyone else,' she stated, looking through Mr. Bogle's information. 'He's moving pretty slowly at the moment, but he hasn't stopped yet.'

'Okay. I think it's time to put *Operation Roadblock* into action for the first time,' Diego said, a little giddily. He seemed like a kid in a playground, desperate to get his new toys out.

'What, you mean to get those two together? That seems like a disaster waiting to happen.'

'Maybe. There's only one way to find out.'

Chapter 9

McKenzie wasn't sure anymore, but he estimated that about a week had passed in the Maze. The loneliness of this place was beginning to grate on him. He had come across two people so far and, on each occasion, they had simply nodded to each other. He had been desperate to say something to both people, to scream out for a bit of company, but had fought the urge with his own social anxiety issues. This place certainly didn't help any anxieties. When you don't talk to anyone for an entire week, all insecurities begin to grow stronger.

On top of the loneliness, the darkness seemed to be growing heavier and heavier on his shoulders. He was sure the place had become bleaker since his first day in the Maze. He thought his eyes would become more accustomed to the poor light, but it seemed to be going the opposite way. Boredom, too, was an issue. There was nothing to do to pass a few hours. McKenzie remembered when he used to get bored as a kid. His mom would always tell him to read a book or watch a film. That wasn't really an option here. At least, he hadn't found a cinema complex or a library just yet.

Something that had amazed him was his own ability to remember the pathways. Or, lack of ability. At times he felt sure he had already been down a pathway, and then suddenly a new turning would appear that hadn't been there the last time. This created a horrible sense of unknowing for McKenzie, a feeling that only added to the anxieties of this place. He was becoming unsure of his surroundings, unsure of himself. Maybe that was the point.

This extra time on his hands meant he had more time to think about his life. Of all the mistakes in his past. Occasionally, a random memory would flash up in his mind as he was walking along, and it was never one of the positive ones. It was always something embarrassing or something that would make him hate himself further. More often than not, it involved Jessie. He had been thinking a lot about her. In a way he wished he could stop. It was just too painful.

The Maze was beginning to show signs of life after a week of the weirdest civilization ever. It had its own little quirks of character. Every now and then, McKenzie would come across small scratchings of graffiti on the walls. Sometimes these would be small things like directional advice at a junction. McKenzie had to laugh when he came across one that had been scratched "left", then crossed out and underneath it said "right". The funniest thing was this had been crossed out again, only for "left" to be written again.

Once, he had come across something much more extravagant than a simple "left" or "right". One of the other prisoners had created an entire piece of art. It was pretty simple, but impressive nonetheless. McKenzie imagined the person's tools for the job were pretty limited. They had crafted a tree, complete with branches and roots. At first McKenzie had *thought* it was simplistic, but the more he studied the tree the better and more complex it became. There were different depths of grooves in the trunk that showed the aging of the tree and more lines than he could count. He became captivated with its beauty, carefully feeling the grooves with his fingers.

By this point, he was on the verge of exhaustion. He couldn't remember feeling this tired, if ever. There wasn't much room for comforts like sleep in the Maze. No beds, no soft pillows, not even a private room, unless you were fortunate enough to bump into one of the rare bathrooms. Even then, it was not an easy task. Trying to sleep in glaring light was not something most people were accustomed to.

Today, he had set his task to find the most easterly point of the Maze. Or, seeing as he didn't have a compass, the most "righterly" point to where he stood right now. He would head in that direction until he could go no further, searching for new paths along the edge of the Maze. He had done the same yesterday, but he had a strong hunch that today he would find something different. He had begun to understand the Maze now, and today he was hoping to confirm his suspicions.

After walking for over an hour, he was forced to retrace his steps for the third time, trying to find a new route to the right. It was frustrating work, but he was confident of finding an answer that would make it all worthwhile. Having a purpose to each waking day had made his life here more bearable. He turned left twice, well aware that he was now heading in the wrong direction, before he was rewarded with a glorious sight. Another left turn. He followed the path for no more than fifty yards before he hit a dead end. He let out a derisive, slightly evil laugh. He was sure the people behind the Maze were playing a game with him.

Another two hours later, he had finally found what he believed to be the edge of the Maze, the most easterly point. More importantly, more than ever he was convinced he was correct. He was almost certain that the Maze was not a constant, but an ever-changing stroke of genius. Subconsciously, he was very aware that the Maze had changed him, made him think darker thoughts and presume the very worst, but on this occasion it wasn't a bad thought. He was impressed. The rumour was that this Maze was only around forty kilometres in pathways, at least that was what McKenzie had last heard. In truth this Maze could cover hundreds of kilometres, if

McKenzie was correct, at least.

Chapter 10

Aaron had never found the source of the mysterious light from his first night in the Maze. Part of him wished he hadn't stopped in that restroom to sleep, but most of him knew that wouldn't have made the slightest difference. This place seemed to have a mind of its own, and it was affecting his mind, too. Normally he was so sure of his senses, particularly his sight, but it felt like at every corner he turned that his eyes were playing a trick on him.

No matter which combination of turns he made, he couldn't seem to make any progress towards that place the light had appeared. He had been using the pen he had been given by his sister to try and keep track of his movements, pointing it towards the light and then turning it in his outstretched hand whenever he turned a corner. Sporadically he would come across a stretch of path he believed he recognised, only to be proven wrong by a turning that he was sure had not been there before.

Most people would pass this off as a trick of the mind; an error, on their part. Even Aaron had tried to convince himself that was the truth. Unfortunately, being able to memorise things perfectly like Aaron could came with its drawbacks. When he recognised a pathway, it meant he had been there before — and his mind did not make mistakes.

So far in his time in the Maze, Aaron had read *Ulysses* three times, once backwards. It made for an interesting read. It seemed to provide a new meaning to the writing, making Aaron wonder if there was something behind that, if it had actually been intended to be read backwards. Of course, some of it made no sense at all because of the sentence structuring, but the overall message was interesting. This had led Aaron to spend some of his new-found time attempting to recite other books backwards. It had started to drive him a little bit insane, making the same mistake in the same sentence four times in a row as he attempted to find a hidden message in the *Harry Potter* series.

Not only was it incredibly infuriating, but it was also a little bit addictive, and with each book he tried he began to think more and more that it was all connected by some "big plan". With every passing day he was beginning to believe more and more in the possibility of an illuminati. This didn't exactly help keep nasty, intrusive thoughts away. It only increased his feeling of being on his own in a place in which he hadn't spoken a word for an entire week.

He hadn't heard anyone else speak either. He had once spotted someone's foot as they turned a corner, and he decided to hang back. He wasn't about to risk a confrontation when he didn't need to — after all, everyone was in here for a reason. He was, too, but he doubted many others here had committed such tame crimes. In truth, he didn't really understand why he *was* here. Everything about this place was set up for far more high-profile prisoners than he.

Before his new life in the Maze, Aaron had been an investment banker. He was a good one, too. His intelligence and ability to understand patterns made it almost easy for him. But naturally, like so many of his type, he became too greedy and eventually made one too many dodgy deals. He had made millions of dollars in non-taxable accounts, but it was all worth nothing now.

His trial had not been a long one. He had confessed immediately, well aware that the evidence would tell true soon enough. It was a known thing amongst bankers like him that if they were arrested they were all but doomed. The police didn't come around arresting people without solid evidence, and a bank trace is about as blatant as it gets.

Following his confession, he was hoping — almost expecting — to receive a lighter sentence. Upon the judge's final verdict he collapsed into his seat, stunned. He was expecting a relatively short sentence, after all it was a somewhat petty crime with nobody hurt. Now he had no idea how long he would spend in here.

That weird yellow light that had popped up a week ago still haunted Aaron's thoughts. Every time he stopped for a break in his parading of the corridors, or before he slept, he would closely watch the dark ceiling in the distance, as if he was praying for the sun to suddenly rise. That would be something. As he prepared to sleep one night, or what he thought was night, he thought that perhaps the light he had seen wasn't the only one. When he thought about it, it was quite unlikely that it was in fact the only light. If his belief that the light was a lookout spot was correct, it would be impossible to watch the entire Maze from one spot, so there must be more somewhere.

Of course, he hadn't ruled out the possibility that the light was actually something else. He liked to theorise what the light could be. With little more to entertain himself with, it became one of his regular daily activities. So far, he had come up with the idea that it was a signal to the prisoners, perhaps designed to tempt those within the Maze to follow its intrigue. This idea was not helped by his growing concerns of conspiracy. Everything had a deep-seated explanation, and most of it had unpleasant and heinous themes. This very thought made him start to doubt whether the light was even worth troubling over. It was just as likely to be a misleading ruse created by the designers of the Maze, to distract him from other routes and other importance's that lay within.

Then again, on other occasions when the dark thoughts

strayed away, he thought perhaps the strange light had been a doorway or window of some kind. It was plainly evident that there was no heating within the Maze. Maybe it was just a way of creating a suitable environment. On his brightest day of his week so far, he even began to hope that it was *actually* the exit. Conceivably it was a door to a stairwell, or yet merely a signal to let others know when a fellow prisoner had escaped.

On his seventh night, Aaron sat slumped, twiddling his pen between his fingers absent-mindedly. This had become much of a habit over the past nights as he watched the horizon. As had become his norm, he found a corner to cosy into, able to see from both directions should anyone come across his path in his sleep. He was just gazing off to his right when he heard the unmistakable sound of rubber on concrete. He scrambled to his feet and quickly hid around the corner, peering around his shoulder like a spy in a movie. Only, he didn't have a gun.

After a minute or so a woman, who must have been in her late twenties to early thirties, stepped cautiously around the corner. She appeared to be limping. Immediately, Aaron's whole body relaxed from the tense state he had found himself in. The woman looked harmless, verging on helpless. Aaron watched on, careful to stay completely still as the woman paused, deciding which way to move. It was like looking in a mirror — something Aaron hadn't done for a while now. The woman looked as bedraggled and debilitated as he had felt for the last few days. The lack of regular food, drink and general opportunities for self-care meant that it was almost impossible for anyone to keep up the appearance of a healthy person.

The woman's clothes already hung loose on her body, her face a sickly pale shade with a hint of green. Aaron was glad, at this moment, that he did not have longer hair. He suspected this woman had considerably shortened her hair ahead of the Maze, yet her now shoulder-length locks were already matted and dirty. It was clear it had originally been a much brighter colour than it was at current. Her breath seemed short and shallow, full of a panic which matched her wide eyes, the only part of her appearance that made her seem awake.

A few moments passed and Aaron suddenly made a decision. If she were to walk in his direction, he didn't want to startle her as she turned the corner. It made more sense in this situation to make a steady approach. Slowly he stepped around the corner, watching the woman all the time. He was very conscious not to intimidate her, and he made sure to show his hands away from his pockets.

For a moment he waited in awkward silence, arms out to his sides as he gradually approached the woman. However, she seemed too deep in thought to even notice him. She was staring at the wall ahead of her, unblinking. After a while he gave up on the idea of ever being noticed by the woman, though he wondered if she was deliberately ignoring him. He coughed gently to announce his presence and his belief was quickly answered. The woman clearly had not known he was there; she jumped backwards making a high-pitched squeal. She turned to face him with a look of shock on her face, the little colour that had remained in her cheeks gone completely. Aaron noticed she quickly reached towards her pocket, trying to grab something to protect herself with. It took a few seconds but after a while she began to breath easily once again.

'How long have you been stood there?' she asked slowly.

'Only a few seconds, I swear. I heard you coming so I hid around the corner.' Aaron gestured to his hiding spot.

'Were you watching me?'

'Well, yeah. But only because I thought you might be

dangerous,' Aaron said defensively.

'I might still be dangerous. How can you be so sure I'm not?' the woman asked, mocking.

'That's true, but I generally trust my judgement,' he replied, smiling in a friendly way. It felt odd. The muscles in his face were not used to smiling at the moment. 'I'm Aaron, by the way.'

'Penny,' the woman replied, still a little wary of the sudden appearance of another person. 'So, what are you doing here?' she asked politely.

'The same as you, I guess, unless you are very lost,' Aaron stated, as if it were incredibly obvious.

'I meant right here. Have you been following me?'

'Oh! Oh, no. I was just about to head to sleep in the corner there.' He pointed to the shady corner he had been resting in a few minutes earlier. Penny eyed him suspiciously.

'Why would you sleep in a corner, surely that's really uncomfortable?'

'Isn't everywhere? It means I can see people from both directions if they sneak up on me.'

Penny seemed impressed by this idea, she clearly hadn't thought of it herself.

'You sleep with your eyes open, then, do you?' she laughed. Aaron laughed, too, for a moment forgetting the depressive nature of his surroundings in a moment of genuine happiness. For a moment there was a silence as they both considered their next move.

'Have you met anyone else yet?' Penny enquired. She seemed quite willing to keep talking.

'I met one person, but I didn't stop to talk to them. He didn't seem the friendliest. What about you?'

'Yeah, same here. You're the first person I've spoken to since I got here.' They both pondered what else there was to say. They couldn't exactly talk about the weather.

'Look, I know this will sound a bit weird,' Aaron began, tentatively, 'but I know I could do with someone to talk to, for a bit. Other than the back of my hand, that is.'

Penny chuckled again.

'You know what, that sounds great. But first, I want to see what's in your pockets, if that's okay?'

'What's in my pockets?' Aaron asked, surprised by this request.

'Yeah, as in the things you brought with you.'

'Oh, right. Yeah, that's fine.' He took a step forward as he ruffled through his trouser pockets and pulled out the three items he was carrying: the book, the pen, and the switchblade. Penny's eyes widened a little when he showed her the knife, but she didn't overreact. He dropped it on the floor, and she soon seemed quite okay with the idea. Especially when he explained it was his sister's idea and he had wanted to ditch the knife as soon as he had got in the Maze.

'Okay, that's cool,' Penny said, having examined Aaron's items. 'And in the interest of fairness…' She pulled out her three objects, and Aaron wondered what she had been worried about. Her items were fair more dangerous than his. She had a magnificent little chisel with a matching hammer, and also a roll of film, though she didn't allow Aaron to see this up close. Something suddenly clicked in Aaron's head.

'You're the one who made the tree!' he exclaimed, excited. Penny nodded humbly.

Chapter 11

A week ago, Penny could never have imagined befriending a complete stranger when she was this vulnerable. That just summed up what the Maze had done to her. Judging by her brief introduction to Aaron, he seemed to be facing similar affects. She imagined it was hard for anyone not to struggle facing weeks and months alone with no social interaction.

She didn't want to get her hopes up just yet, but Penny was delighted for some company. For some reason she didn't feel threatened by Aaron. He wasn't a particularly well-built man, though he was still comfortably taller than Penny. She was surprised at how much his appearance contrasted his personality. He was clearly an intelligent man. If Penny was to make a quick judgement, she would guess he was used to spending much of his life in a suit. Down in the Maze, however, he seemed at a level playing field. After just one week in this place, his clothes were worn and grubby. Probably not helped by the fact he slept in the dingy corners.

One thing that Penny had quickly learnt in here was that you couldn't judge anyone based on how they looked. Aaron's hair was greasy and unkempt, matching his grubby and oily skin. The thing that troubled her the most was knowing she probably looked just as bad at first sight, if not worse, with her hair being considerably longer than his.

After a brief exchange, Aaron had suggested they follow the path he had been intending to take after he slept. They had now been walking in silence for a while, as if they were walking along a riverbank on a Sunday afternoon. Even in silence, it was nice to have someone around. The load she had been carrying on her mind seemed to half just by being in Aaron's presence. If she wanted to talk about something now, she could. They walked on for some time, both content just to keep the company. Eventually they reached their first junction, and it seemed the silence must now be broken.

'What do you think? Have you been following a particular route?' Penny asked, looking left and right.

'Sort of, but it seems pretty impossible to find one, to be honest.'

'What do you mean?' Penny questioned, a little confused.

'Well, haven't you noticed?' Aaron prompted, though he quickly noticed by the look on Penny's face that she clearly hadn't. 'The paths change, don't they?' he said, as if it were the most obvious thing in the world.

'What? How can you be sure, have you seen them?'

'No, obviously they do it when no-one is around. But I have a photographic memory and I can memorise almost anything I see. I've walked down paths that I have been *sure* I've been down, only they aren't quite the same as before.'

This statement came with a heavy silence. Penny eyed Aaron with confusion and disbelief. She didn't quite believe what he was saying, but also, she didn't *want* to believe it. This small detail seemed to make this task an even greater mountain to climb. If the Maze really did change, it could be ten times bigger than she had thought. Penny also felt a little ashamed. She had been walking around aimlessly since she had entered the Maze without even noticing that at all. A question she had been dying to ask quickly came to the tip of her tongue.

'Did you come into the Maze on the first day?' she asked casually.

'Yeah, I'm guessing you did, too, based by the way you worded that?'

'Yeah, I did. And how long do you think we've been here, now?' This had been what she had really wanted to know. She had lost all concept of time since she had entered the Maze. With no clocks or watches to keep track of time, this wasn't really surprising.

Aaron was thinking hard about his answer.

'I think we've been here seven days, now, but I couldn't even guess what time it is.'

Penny nodded as she considered this. She would have said about the same, too, which gave her a little a comfort. She continued to stare along the gloomy path to their right when another thought came to her.

'Weren't you about to go to sleep, back there?' she blurted out, remembering their earlier conversation.

'Yeah, but it's not like I'm exhausted. It's just something to do.'

Amazingly, Penny understood this perfectly. She had not long woken up when she had come across Aaron. She hadn't been tired, but she figured it was best to try and sleep regularly, otherwise any concept of time would be lost completely.

'Well, if you still wanted to sleep, I'm happy to keep watch for a bit,' she suggested.

Aaron thought about this for a minute or so. She could understand his concerns. If this was the other way around and Aaron had suggested he would keep watch, she doubted she would have trusted him enough to agree.

'I'm not sure. No offence but we really don't know each other,' Aaron said hesitantly.

Penny noticed his eyes dart to her pocket where her chisel and hammer were kept.

'Okay,' Penny thought quickly, 'what if we both put our things over here?' she suggested, walking twenty metres back down the path and placing her items on the floor. This seemed to ease Aaron's mind. He quickly followed her over to the spot under one of the many lanterns and placed his things in clear view. Together, they walked back to the end of the path and sat against the wall, facing back down the T-junction. They sat in silence for a moment, Penny content to allow Aaron to rest. However, after a minute or two with no sounds other than gentle breathing, Aaron said something that had clearly been on his mind.

'You know, on my first night, I was sat just like this, about to sleep, and I saw something I still haven't worked out.' He spoke softly, as if they were looking up at a sky full of stars on a knitted blanket. This thought seemed to relax Penny enormously.

'What was it?' she said, low. The smoothness of her own voice surprised her. She was so used to it being croaky and hoarse now.

'A little square light, miles away, somewhere above the Maze.' He pointed to a spot just above the outlines of the walls, squinting with one eye. 'It was only there for a moment, but it was definitely there.'

'What do you think it was?' Penny asked, a little more alert.

'I don't know,' he admitted, seemingly a little defeated by this. 'But ever since then it's all I've thought about. I've been trying to spot it, trying to reach it ever since.'

Something about his story was devastatingly sad. This could well be an answer to their problems; it could be the way out, or it could be nothing. Yet, because of this place, an incredibly intelligent man like Aaron had been driven to the point of obsession verging on madness as he chased his pursuit with desperation. Even he had not been able to the find an answer to this mystery. The Maze had befuddled him, just as it had her. Neither of them said anything more after this and it wasn't long until Penny heard Aaron's breath become slower and more pronounced.

Chapter 12

Flint couldn't believe it had been just four days since the Maze had welcomed its first inhabitants. He couldn't help but be drawn in, fascinated by the social study of the inhabitants. Once again, he found himself glued to the giant screen at the front of the control room. In the bottom right, the stats had been updated to now show fifty-nine Mazers, and fifty-four point seven kilometres of pathways, with section eighteen of the Maze being completed on day four of the Maze's opening.

It was amazing to see how quickly the Mazers showed new traits and behaviourisms. On the first day, almost all the Mazers were running on similar timings. Almost all of them slept at similar times and followed a clear routine. It didn't take long for this to change, though. Even by day two, some slept longer than others, some moved faster and farther than others. The most common thing among all the Mazers, however, was a loss of time.

It was fascinating for Flint to see that it took just one day for almost the entire batch of Mazers to lose all concept of time. It had always been said that time was a social construct. If this Maze proved anything, it was that that was true. Flint could have gone down there and told them it was any time at all and they would have believed him.

For the first few days the Mazers were incredibly tentative, tip-toeing their way around the passageways, all carefully avoiding any unnecessary confrontation. Occasionally they would meet one another by chance and quickly continue on their separate ways. Flint had watched as loneliness began to affect them. Their actions became more irrational, more desperate, as they realised the gravity of their situation. Many of the Mazers had resorted to racing through the corridors, determined to discover the "exit" as quickly as possible.

There was the odd exception, of course. Those with a little more intelligence and wits than others had soon realised there was more to the Maze than a simple exit. In fact, Flint had been shocked to see how quickly some of them had discovered the primary secrets.

Despite their struggles, Flint had been more disappointed by the lack of social interaction within the group. The Maze had been designed to provide a new environment to help stimulate a change in the inmates' mindsets. Most of this was based on their place within society and subsequent interactions with fellow human beings. Unfortunately, for the first few days there was no interactions at all. Meaning no proof that anyone's personalities had been changed. It had taken until day four for any meaningful communication between any two Mazers, and even that had been forced by Flint.

*

After four days without moving, Flint had been forced to find a solution to the Yazmin Tracey issue. Since her first day in the Maze, she had still moved just two hundred and seven metres before breaking down into tears. Flint had been correct; her tears had eventually stopped, but she still showed no sign of moving. She hadn't eaten or drank at all and Flint knew she needed some help, otherwise it was he who would face the music.

It went against everything he had wanted, but he knew he had to intervene. He had wanted complete freedom for the Mazers to decide their own fate, but this was too far. If one of the Mazers starved themselves to death within a week of opening, the whole place would be shut down in minutes and his work would all be over. This was the only chance he was going to get at his great idea.

yet. He was still going to give the Mazers the chance to sort out their own problems. He had made a quick decision to put *Operation Roadblock* into place, designed to deliberately direct someone down an exact route. On this occasion, he had chosen TJ Bogle, despite Alex's protests. Alex had tried to argue that TJ's record of violence and disruption showed him to be incompetent in the situation, but this convinced Diego even further. He had remonstrated with Alex that this was the whole point of the operation. They had created this entire place to offer opportunities of redemption in social situations. He knew full well that this was a risk, but it was the kind of risk he had to take for it to succeed.

On day four of being in the Maze, TJ had "accidentally" come across Yazmin, as planned by Flint and his team. It was a tense moment in the control room. The whole unit watched with bated breath, like a re-enaction of the moon landings, as they watched TJ approach the diminished Yazmin. He was surprisingly cautious in his approach, slowly moving towards the young woman, but it soon became clear by his actions that this was out of concern.

Yazmin's eyes were closed, and Flint could see TJ's worries. She was remarkably thin, her face sallow and gaunt, her hair frizzy and fluffed up on one side. Despite a clear lack of care to her appearance, there was still a beauty evident in her pale face. TJ was clearly fearing the worst, though. Looking up and down the pathway as he approached, his face became extremely solemn. He bent forward to shake her shoulder gently and leapt backwards when she had stirred gradually.

'Who are you?' she whispered, barely audible despite the silence all around.

'My name is TJ,' he said calmly, in a tone Flint had not

believed possible of TJ. 'I was just passing by. Are- are you okay?' he asked, a little afraid to find out the answer.

'Yeah...' Yazmin said airily, without any real conviction. TJ looked Yazmin up and down once more, concern etched onto his face. Flint could tell he was debating whether to help her or not. He sat forward on his chair, his fingertips pressed together on his lips. Everyone in the room knew how important this moment could be. TJ was a priority case. In an ordinary prison, someone such as him would usually face further trouble and more than likely a relapse after release. This was an opportunity to prove that the Maze was a better way.

Yazmin had closed her eyes again, apparently unable to stay conscious for more than a short period of a time. Seeing her like this, in more focus, reminded Flint of the urgency of the issue. It also seemed to make up TJ's mind. He put both arms around Yazmin and, as easily as if she were a fluffy pillow, picked her up. TJ was a solid and formidable man, but it was a statement of Yazmin's condition that he was able to pick her up so easily.

Flint breathed a minor sigh of relief. The first part of his plan had worked perfectly but he didn't intend to leave it there. This was going to be a long night. The camera changed to a new angle around the corner, in which TJ came into sight, walking purposefully. He turned in a full circle, apparently trying to find something. It swiftly occurred to Flint that he must be looking for a refreshment room. He sharply rose to his feet, moving into action.

'Benji, where's the nearest food hall?' he called across the room. He wanted a fast answer and didn't care who gave it. An old man sat in the row in front of him quickly came forwards, holding a tablet. He brought up a map which showed the two dots that represented TJ and Yazmin, and locations for all six of the refreshment rooms.

There was one within a two kilometre walk from the unlikely duo.

'Thank you,' he muttered to the man, who must have been at least in his fifties. 'Can we *Roadblock* it please, and make sure it's clear for them.'

The man nodded respectfully. Flint wondered if he would ever get used to that. The man was at least thirty years his senior, yet, with the way he looked at Diego nobody would have known. Several of the junior operators began rushing around the rows of computers, talking in rapid tongues as they tried to organise a clear route to the refreshment room. The old man was directing several of his colleagues to tasks which they duly rushed into without a word. It was evident that the whole team was desperate for this to succeed. It was like an epic military mission to spare a hero. Everyone seemed to have forgotten that Yazmin was there for a reason.

Little more than five minutes later, the entire path was set up to direct TJ and Yazmin towards some salvation. TJ's progress was steady as he struggled along the paths, his strength wavering under the weight of Yazmin. Yazmin's feet dragged against the grey stone walls and after ten minutes of constant straining, TJ was forced to gently put her back down for a rest. Flint could tell by the expression on TJ's face that he was still considering if this was the best thing to do, or if he was even going the right way. He sat down next to Yazmin's limp form, his heavy, steaming breath billowing out of his mouth.

As Flint watched on with the rest of his team in hope and fascination, he heard the door behind him swing open. Taking his eyes away from the screen for a moment, he was amazed to see Alex walking over to him, dressed down in what he could only presume was her loungewear.

'What are you doing here?' he said, unable to disguise his

surprise.

'I came to see how it was going,' she stated, as if it were obvious. Flint looked at her in a way that said she really needed to get a life. 'What? You'd do the same. Besides, I couldn't sleep thinking about it, so I thought I might as well find out for myself.'

'Fair enough.' Flint turned back to the big projection of the two Mazers. 'As you can see, we got TJ to Yazmin. She's in a bad way. Malnourished. We've been directing them towards the nearest refreshment room.'

'It's going to plan, then,' Alex said, a clear note of surprise in her voice. Flint looked at her in mock hurt.

'I know you were sceptical, but I promise I know what I'm doing,' Flint asserted. Alex nodded her acceptance. 'Now we just have to keep watching,' he added.

'Coffee?' Alex suggested. Flint didn't really like coffee. He thought it to be a classic case of twenty-first Century following-the-herd mentality. He was sure that there couldn't be that many people in the world that enjoyed the taste of something that bitter. Then again, now seemed like the right time, so he agreed.

By the time they were back in the control room, TJ was back on his feet with Yazmin in his arms. If it were possible in that short an amount of time, she seemed to have gotten thinner and looked even limper than before. It was quite a heroic look for TJ, struggling along with the young damsel in his arms. As he walked along the diverted corridors, Alex busied herself by studying one of the junior operator's tablets. She had not brought her own for once, and Flint thought it was the first time he had seen her without it in around two weeks. At least he knew it actually *wasn't* attached to her.

'What's happening with these two then?' Alex asked.

'What two?' Flint queried back. Alex exhaled a laugh and

rolled her eyes.

'You haven't been watching the rest of the map, have you?'

'No, I've been a little pre-occupied,' Flint said defensively. 'Why?'

'We have another pairing,' she stated excitedly.

Flint almost choked on his coffee and began spluttering. He quickly recovered himself and leaned over Alex's shoulder. Sure enough, he saw two dots right on top of each other, labelled Penny Bishop and Aaron Jones.

Flint was staggered at his own lack of attention. How had he not noticed this? More surprisingly, how had nobody in the entire room packed full of operators not spotted this new development, either? What an exciting night.

'Benji! Benji! Get a camera up on Penny Bishop and split the screen!' he called to the well-dressed man at the front of the room. Benji came striding over immediately.

'What's up, Diego?'

'We've got a new interaction,' Diego said with clear delight in his voice.

'What? Where?' Benji cried in shock. Alex rolled her eyes once again, muttering something along the lines of, 'Men.' Benji too leant over the tiny screen in Alex's hand, bumping into Diego in the process.

'Just a thought,' Alex said dryly, 'but do you think maybe we would all be able to see the two people in question if we used the big screen?'

Benji clearly thought this was probably the best thing to do, too. He scampered off to the front, giving instructions to several of the operators who were all busy at work with pieces of paper and tablets in their hands. Within a few moments, the giant screen at the front of the room had changed and now showed the struggling TJ on one side and two new people, Penny and Aaron, on the other. It appeared Aaron was fast asleep, and Penny was sat silently by his side, looking out on the three passages that converged on their position.

'Can we find out how this happened, please?' Diego enquired towards Benji.

'Yeah, of course,' Benji replied before he turned back to the operators and called a one-hour rewind on Aaron Jones. Once again, within moments the screen changed. Penny had magically disappeared, and Flint could just about make out Aaron's form in the shadows of a dark corner. For several minutes he was almost completely still, and Diego wondered if he was asleep — it was hard to make out in the dark. Then, just as Diego was sure he was sleeping, his head turned. It appeared he had merely been watching something intently. Diego tried to think what that could be.

Aaron again went very still, watching something in the other direction, something far off. His behaviour was completely baffling Flint.

'What do you think he's looking at?' he muttered to Alex.

'I don't know,' she said, also looking on with intrigue. 'He seems pretty intent on whatever it is, though.'

After several more minutes, something suddenly brought Aaron to attention. His vision quickly flicked to a nearby corridor. Something, or someone, must have made a sound that had alerted him. He jumped to his feet in an instant and moved across the passageway, hiding from view of the corridor. A few moments later Penny appeared around the corner, pausing as she looked up and down the path. Aaron remained hidden for a while, unsure whether to show himself. Eventually, after a minute or so of neither person making any positive movements, Aaron finally stepped out from around the corner, though Penny was so deep in thought she didn't notice him.

'Can we make sure we have sound for this, please?' Benji called urgently. Just in time, the sound from the corridor was echoing around the control room. They heard Aaron clear his throat, and then the two Mazers began a brief exchange. After a few minutes of conversation in which very little of any importance was said, the two decided to walk together. Diego's heart skipped a beat through excitement. This is what he wanted to see. Sure, there had been no life-defining epiphanies within their brief exchange, but this could be the start of something huge.

They fast-forwarded ahead as the two strangers made their way along the stretching alley. There didn't seem to be much conversation at this point. All the while, TJ trudged ever closer to the food hall, seemingly untroubled by the lack of turnings available. After a short while, Penny and Aaron reached a turning, and Diego's attention was drawn back to the pair. The volume was turned to maximum as they listened in to the conversation. It really was fascinating to listen to the pair discover more about the Maze through each other's eyes. Despite barely knowing each other, they seemed comfortable and relaxed; they could have easily been mistaken for a husband and wife as they sat down together, discussing the Maze.

Then, Aaron suddenly started talking about a light. He had spotted something that had been on his mind ever since seeing it, making him obsessed with finding an answer. Maybe he needed the obsession to get by, but it was a harsh reality for Diego to see what these people were being put through. For a brief moment, a seed of doubt opened in his brain. He knew, of course, what Aaron was referring to and felt sorry for him that he believed it could be a solution. The truth was that this light would offer no escape to him or anyone else.

After a little period of silence, Diego came to the conclusion that Aaron had fallen into the sleep they had initially found him in. He quietly waved for the left portion of the big screen to be cleared. He wasn't quite feeling the thrill he had expected to feel from the conversation. In fact, he felt a little deflated, but worked hard to make sure this didn't show on his face.

The left portion was cleared, and the entirety of the giant screen was filled once more with the image of TJ and Yazmin. Through a small map in the corner, Flint saw that he was now just one corner away from the refreshment room. Once again, everybody was focussed on this moment of history for the project. It deserved some dramatic music to fit TJ's heroic effort.

Finally, after an age willing TJ on, there was a collective cheer of enormous magnitude as he crossed the threshold into the refreshment room. The room comprised of a very basic set-up. The left and far walls were lined with tables, full of a range of food and drink, all designed to help keep the Mazers healthy and replenished. TJ looked around in awe as he took in the trays of food, and quickly moved to place Yazmin down gently on a wooden chair provided in the middle of the room, next to a matching table.

The furniture looked like it belonged in a canteen of some sort, but it was more than a welcome sight to somebody who had been struggling under the weight of two people for the previous hour. TJ looked as though he could easily have gorged himself on the platters of food, but his first action impressed Diego massively. He dashed over to the water cooler that stood in the far-right corner and hurriedly filled a plastic cup with the cool fluid. He didn't think of himself, but scanned around the room frantically, and soon spotted something that he had been looking for.

Dashing across the room, he grabbed hold of a sachet of sugar and shook it into the cup. He stirred the cup with his finger, unable to find any other tools to use, and moved back to Yazmin. He held her head back and forced the liquid into her mouth until the entire cup was empty. He seemed to breath more easily after that and turned back to the tables full of food. It was his turn to replenish himself. As he forcefully grabbed a handful of crisps, Yazmin stirred in her chair, her eyes flicking open. This was greeted by another immense cheer in the control room. Diego noticed several people wiping tears away and had to admit he felt a certain amount of emotion watching the scene.

Chapter 13

Not a single eye was drawn away from the slow recovery of Yazmin that afternoon; it was definitely a success story for the Maze and Flint's belief in redemption over punishment. However, Flint himself was surprisingly quiet and seemed less buoyed than even he had expected by this set of events.

He was in silence, thinking deeply, as he sat in the back row of computers, hidden away from view. Within the next hour, he had his first weekly report meeting with the committee board. He knew he should be happy about this timing, but he knew he would have to explain the manner in which Yazmin had become in such a bad state. On top of this, something about the conversation between Aaron and Penny was nagging at the back of his mind.

Alex had left again, feeling more comfortable knowing that Yazmin was beginning her recovery. She didn't seem to believe TJ to be capable of that level of care. That, if anything, showed Flint that he was correct about the possibilities available within his new correctional facility. Before she had gone, Alex had given Flint a very surprised look. She clearly wasn't used to him doing busy work. He currently had several sheets of paper in front of him and was frantically taking notes as he flicked through the different Mazers' highlights on multiple tablet screens, his brow furrowed.

The meeting would only report the first week of the Maze, so Flint wasn't overly concerned. The board couldn't expect results already — unless they were completely irrational. Albeit he was glad to be able to report some interaction. It wouldn't look great if he had nothing to report at all. Flint knew a lot of people had gambled a lot of money and their own positions to back this new venture and he didn't want to let them down. Most of all, though, he didn't want to let himself down. This was his project, at the end of the day. The buck stopped with him.

After another half hour of note-taking and over-analysis of statistics that were more or less futile, he packed all of his papers together and hastily stuffed them into his satchel bag. At the same time, he took out his tie and comb and exited towards the bathroom, his jaw clenched and hands shaking a little. As he left the control room, three armed and suited members of his security team turned on their heels and followed him out. Together, they headed towards the meeting room hidden on the second-from-the-top floor of the hotel, making a quick detour to the nearest bathroom so that he could smarten himself up. All the while, he ran and re-ran through his report.

After what seemed like an eternity in the elevator, the doors opened to reveal a corridor full of blues and greys. Flint imagined the colours could be quite intimidating, but to him they came off as oddly calming. Perhaps he was too used to seeing the grey of the Maze. The corridor was lit with very similar lanterns to those within the Maze, though they were slightly more modern. All around, there were small hints and tributes to the giant labyrinth some hundred feet below them.

At the end of the corridor there was a solitary glass door with a single frosted panel so that Flint could make out mere shapes of what was going on in the meeting room. The room seemed full of activity; several bodies moved past the door as Flint watched on. Flint took a deep breath and marched purposefully down the corridor. Unsurprisingly, another security officer stood guard and Flint gave the man, who towered over him, a quick nod as he made his way past.

A moment of panic abruptly hit him as he approached the door. Should he knock? He didn't want to seem disrespectful, yet he also didn't want to seem timid and afraid. He gave a surreptitious look towards Anthony, his head of security, who had accompanied him along the corridor. Clearly his concern had successfully been portrayed on his face. Anthony gave a swift nod as he casually waved his hand forward, signalling that he should walk straight in. Flint smiled appreciatively.

He opened the door with confidence, and the two security men who had accompanied him (one had doubled back to the elevator) held their position outside of the room. As Flint had thought, the meeting room was a hub of activity. The six board members all sat around the white marble table in the centre of the room, one dauntingly empty chair left empty. Around them several secretaries and personal assistants were busy compiling files and passing them amongst each other. As the door closed behind Flint, they all stopped to look up and the room went deadly silent. It was as if he had wandered into an unknown saloon during the goldrush era. This thought made Diego let out a nervous chuckle which made the board members raise their eyebrows.

The board itself seemed a bit of a mismatch. Only one of the members really met the image Flint had in his mind. This was the first meeting they had ever had, this board having been set up solely to watch over the progress of the Maze. Prior to today Flint had only met with general correctional system and justice system boards. He was pleasantly surprised to find a diverse range of people. Maybe they had been selected for that very reason, Flint thought. After all, the Maze was supposed to bring the correctional system a new revelation into the Twenty-First Century.

After a few moments of awkward silence, a black man gestured gently for him to take the empty chair. Flint swiftly took his satchel bag from his shoulder and took up the invitation. The man who had gestured appeared to be the head of the board. Even though he was sitting, Flint could tell that he was tall and commanded respect just by the way he sat so formally. He must have been twice Flint's age, but he could tell, even at first glance, that the man was in very good shape. He had a stern face, raised eyebrows, and nostrils that flared slightly as he took in Diego. He made no sign of speaking, but smiled in a comforting manner as Diego caught his eye, before adjusting his square-rimmed glasses and returning to his notes.

To his right sat the kind of board member Flint had expected to find. He didn't want to jump to conclusions, but the man seemed very typical of the position. He must have been at least in his sixties, with wrinkled and blotchy pale skin and receding white hair that was combed over and wispy. He was pushed further away from the table due to his protruding stomach, which was making his shirt buttons work hard.

Furthest on the right sat a stern-faced woman who wore a look of scorn as she looked over Diego. From first impressions, she seemed like a strong-willed woman, the no-nonsense sort, someone with whom he would have to work hard to get her on his side. Her glossy dark hair was tied up neatly in a colourful hairpiece, which indicated some sentimentality, much like the dainty silver necklace she wore. Opposite her sat another man who showed clear pride to his heritage. The man wore striking earrings of brightly coloured feathers. He appeared to be

most surprising in the way. Neither of the men could have been much older than Diego himself, though they were contrasts of one another. One was suave and sophisticated. It looked to Diego as if he had been born in a boardroom; it occurred to Diego that he probably had been, though, not literally. He had to stifle another laugh at this thought. This man looked like he belonged, his royal blue suit was bespoke, clearly tailor-made with a matching tie and pocket square in an artic blue. In contrast, the other young man sat next to him seemed a long way from his comfort zone. Instead of piles of paper, he had a large laptop screen which had been detached from its keyboard. He seemed more nervous than Diego was, and his eyes kept darting between the other board members as if they were suddenly going to realise that he shouldn't be there.

'Mr. Flint, how are you?' the man who had gestured him into his seat asked as a way of beginning the meeting formally.

'Very well, thank you, Mr...?' Flint suddenly realised he knew none of these people's names. *Not a great way to make a good first impression*, he thought to himself.

'Ah, yes, Jenkins. Paul Jenkins,' the man said, relieving Flint of a little embarrassment.

Jenkins nodded to the older man to his right.

'Andrew Downes,' the wispy-haired man said quickly.

'Amelia Tompkins,' the woman on his right followed.

'Tarlo,' the man opposite said shortly.

'Gavin Robertson,' said the suave man. Even his voice was cool and collected.

'James Smith,' the final board member squeaked timidly.

'Now that we have made our introductions, shall we begin,' Jenkins stated rather than asked. 'We have received a little information, but would like a report of the Maze from your viewpoint, Diego.'

'Of course,' Diego stammered, unsure whether he

should stand for this. In the end, he opted to lean forward slightly. He hadn't expected the board to have been keeping track on their own accord and it threw him off a little.

'I'm not quite sure how much you are up to date on, but I will try to give a good overview of the events so far,' Diego began. He thought this at least covered his own back a little. He paused to make it seem like he hadn't rehearsed this over and over in his head fifteen times. 'As we expected, the first couple of days were very quiet as the new inhabitants of the Maze grew accustomed to their surroundings gradually. In fact, for the first three days there were no interactions between any of the Mazers.'

'Sorry, Mazers?' Downes interrupted.

'Ah, yes, sorry. That is just a term we have begun using to describe the inhabitants. It stops us referring to them as criminals, inmates, or prisoners. We feel it helps separate the Maze from a regular prison.'

Andrew Downes didn't seem to agree with this statement, but he nodded to Diego to allow him to continue.

'As I was saying, it took until day four before it began to get a little more-' Diego caught himself mid-sentence. He had almost said 'interesting' and figured the board might not appreciate this terminology. Not everyone shared his views that studying the behaviour of the Mazers was interesting. In fact, some believed it to be unethical. He quickly corrected himself: '-social. In the last few hours alone, we have had two pairs of strangers interacting. One of them has shown little to report yet, but seems amicable. The other is a little more complex.' He paused for breath, taking in the nonplussed expressions of the board members. He didn't seem to have won them over just yet.

'We had a minor issue with one of the Mazers, Miss Yazmin Tracey.' At these words all the board members became rapt with attention. 'Yes, by your expressions it seems you have heard of the issue,' he prompted. Again, he paused, unsure how to word this next part. He had to explain that it was his plan that had helped Yazmin, but he was sure the board wouldn't like what they heard. 'We decided to intervene with the issue indirectly. We had an issue with another Mazer, TJ Bogle, at the start of the week, and decided it would be a good opportunity for the troubled young man to prove he was capable of a good deed.' He felt he had worded the situation diplomatically, but was pleased to the see that the board were at least not too horrified by what they were hearing.

'I am pleased to report that this afternoon Mr. Bogle found Miss Tracey, and with a little help from our operations team, was able to get Miss Tracey to one of the refreshment rooms, where she is currently recovering well.' At this, the board certainly seemed more positive, and Mr Jenkins even smiled at Diego.

'That's excellent news, Flint,' he said pleasantly. 'It seems the Maze has certainly had its-' he searched for the correct word, '-hitches. But I for one am pleased to see that these can be ironed out and are being dealt with swiftly.'

'Thank you very much, sir.'

'What about the other fifty-five *Mazers*?' Mrs Tompkins asked harshly, with extra emphasis on the final word. 'So far we have heard about only four that have made any contact with a fellow human.'

Diego thought for a moment.

'Yes, like I said, the majority of the Mazers seem content at this moment to keep to themselves; many seem nervous to make contact. All the Mazers have come into contact with one of their fellows, but, as of yet, only twice has this led to any kind of interaction.'

Most of the board nodded with satisfaction. Mrs.

Tompkins and Mr. Downes did not.

'Good, good!' Mr Jenkins said positively. 'We appreciate there isn't too much to report at this time, so I think it's best if we keep this meeting short for today,' he asserted. Again, Mr. Downes and Mrs. Tompkins didn't seem best pleased about this. They certainly seemed tough to win over. The other three, on the other hand, seemed quite content to keep quiet. In fact, James Smith looked delighted at the thought of getting out early.

Chapter 14

Yazmin didn't think she'd ever felt this drained in all her life. Her eyelids drooped heavily, though this was not helped by the strong light glaring down on her. It wasn't easy to get used to after four days in the gloom of the Maze. Her body felt bruised and battered as she drew in raspy, shallow breaths. She knew she needed to eat and was beginning to realise how stupid she had been, but forcing herself to eat when she felt completely incapable wasn't easy.

TJ was still strolling around the room, helping himself to the platters of laid out food. For a moment, she pondered why anyone would leave this place. Sure, eventually the food would run out, but if you rationed it well then everything in here could last you at least a couple of weeks, if not a month. She thought about this for a moment, then her eyes drifted over the still open door. That was certainly an issue. Anyone who occupied this place certainly offered themselves as a target to the other inhabitants of this place. What was outside the door was the biggest lure, though. You could keep yourself sustained by staying in this room, but it didn't give you a chance of escaping and returning to the real world, where food was always readily available.

She briefly studied TJ as he stuffed a bread roll into his mouth. He spotted her looking and she pretended to be scanning the room. On first appearance he certainly didn't look like the hero type, but he had already got her this far and she was grateful to him for that. Her eyes flicked back to him and again their eyes met awkwardly. They hadn't spoken since reaching this room and remained very much strangers despite the circumstances that had led them here. TJ seemed to take this as a sign that it was time to talk.

'How are you feeling?' he asked, ambling over to the

odd canteen-style table she sat at.

'Much better, thank you.' Her voice was still husky, her throat dry. TJ looked at her, frowning.

'What happened to you? Did someone attack you?'

'What?' Yazmin was surprised at first, then glanced up and down herself and figured that was a reasonable assumption. 'No, nothing like that.' She didn't feel ready to tell him why she was in this state, though she knew he was going to keep pushing.

'I don't understand,' TJ said, his arms crossed.

Of course you don't understand, she thought to herself as she looked up at him. He was strong and powerful, which didn't necessarily mean *mentally* strong, but in a place like this, it didn't hurt. She sighed heavily; even that hurt her weak lungs and ribs.

'Look. I lost it. I shouldn't be here, and I know what you're thinking: no-one should be here, this place isn't fit for humans. But, I mean, I didn't do anything to get here. I was wrongly accused of... something. As soon as I got here, I just broke down. I hadn't moved from that spot you found me since I got here.'

TJ's eyebrows raised.

'Were you part of the group on the first day?' he asked curiously.

'Yeah, why?'

'It's been like... five days or something. I'm not too sure to be honest, but I came on day two, I *know* that much.' He added a lot of emphasis, undoubtedly expecting Yazmin to be shocked by this news.

'Huh,' she said plainly. 'I guess time flies when you're... in a ball on the floor crying your eyes out.' She sniggered feebly. The fact that she had made it this far without dying was something. It seemed to add a bit of resolve to her mentality. TJ was still taking her in with interest. His appearance had definitely made a difference. Inside of her, she felt her own belief in fellow people growing once again. She was careful to catch herself, though. She didn't know much about TJ. Then, it suddenly struck her that he must be in here for some reason.

'What about you?' she asked, trying to sound casual.

'What do you mean?'

'Why are you here? Wrongly accused, too?' she crossed her fingers behind her back.

TJ looked away for a moment.

'Err, no. Unfortunately not. Bank robbery that went wrong,' he stated.

Yazmin took this in for a moment. It could be worse, she thought, at least it wasn't a violent crime. She forced herself to try and forget about TJ in the outside world. After all, he had saved her; he must be a reasonably good person, at least.

'Do you want some food?' he asked, obviously keen to change the subject.

'Yeah, I guess I should, really,' Yazmin replied. She stretched her arms and legs weakly and turned in her chair, looking at her options. 'I'll need something easy to start with. Nothing too solid,' she stated.

'How about some fruit? Maybe a slice of melon,' TJ suggested, pointing to one of the more colourful platters.

'Yeah, that sounds good.'

TJ went scurrying across to the fruit and brought back two pre-cut slices of melon. Yazmin took him in for a moment before she accepted the fruit. She couldn't have asked for much more, really.

A minute later, she sat nibbling away at the melon, juice dripping down her chin as she giggled away. It felt joyous, as if this melon had magical qualities. She had her eyes shut tight as she took in the gloriously exotic flavours and felt the sugary juices spitting onto her cheeks and fingertips. She was suddenly transported to a place far away from the troubles of the Maze, where she felt like a child once more. When she opened her eyes, wiping the juice from her chin with her hoodie sleeve, TJ was looking at her like she was a madwoman. She grinned broadly, and he snorted with laughter.

*

They spent several hours taking in their fill of food. TJ didn't eat too much more, but occasionally helped himself to some meat or a bit of fruit. Yazmin had to take her time. Her stomach felt bloated, so she couldn't manage much more than a handful of something every half an hour. Before they left, however, they both crammed their pockets with an assortment of dried foods, making sure to take as much as they could manage. Yazmin even suggested they put stuff in her hood, before TJ reminded her she wasn't a cargo mule. They both laughed extensively at this, causing much of the food to come tumbling out of the multiple pockets they each had. If anything, this caused them to laugh even harder. Yazmin felt high, such was her feeling of ecstasy. She knew only a few hours ago she was in danger of dying from malnutrition, but that seemed a million years ago right now, the way she felt. Eventually, they made their way to the murky light of the doorway and looked in both directions. There wasn't much to help really, not that Yazmin had expected a signpost saying: "Maze Exit — this way". That wasn't really the point of any Maze, let alone this one.

'I came from that way,' TJ said, pointing to the right. They therefore agreed that in the spirit of progress they should go left. They hadn't even discussed whether they would travel together. All that Yazmin knew was that she trusted TJ, she felt safe with him around, and having some company made this miserable place seem slightly less impossible to handle. TJ didn't seem to need company. He had been managing perfectly fine on his own since he had entered the Maze. Yazmin was impressed. Sure, it had only been four days or something, but she didn't see how anyone could cope with this place on their own.

They walked in silence until they reached another turning that forked left and right. Yazmin had a horrible recollection, of the last time she'd been faced with a choice in here, and she had to catch her breath as she pretended to look to the left, trying to hide her panic-stricken face from TJ. After a moment, she gathered herself and looked back to her accomplice. They both shrugged aimlessly at each other. Yazmin let out a brief snort. Already the moment of ecstasy she had felt in the food room seemed a long way away. After a moment's thought, TJ suggested they go left and together they set off once more.

'I met the guy who designed this place, you know,' TJ said thoughtfully.

'No way! What's he like?' Yazmin blurted out.

'He's not what I expected,' said TJ. He paused for a moment then began to tell Yazmin his story of meeting Diego Flint. Yazmin tried to keep her face neutral but was slightly concerned by TJ's actions. She wondered if he was prone to sudden moments of aggression.

'-And just before I came in, he said...' TJ paused for a moment, screwing up his face as he tried to remember. *'Don't ever assume to know the Maze completely. You never know when it might surprise you.'* He looked to Yazmin, as if she was going to give him an answer to this cryptic message. She just looked back, dumbfounded, and shrugged again.

They reverted to silence once more. They reached another turning, and, more decisively, TJ decided they should turn right this time. Yazmin didn't say anything, but already the hopeless nature of the Maze was wearing her thin. TJ didn't seem bothered — he seemed happy to trudge along, corridor after corridor, hoping he would come across the exit.

'Shall we play a game?' TJ asked abruptly.

'Er… Okay, but I think hide and seek could go very wrong in here,' Yazmin replied sarcastically.

TJ sniggered appreciatively. 'How about twenty questions?'

'Ooh, how do you play?' Yazmin's sarcastic streak was suddenly very evident. TJ didn't look so appreciative this time. 'Sorry,' she muttered.

'I'll go first, you ask the questions,' TJ carried on, deciding to ignore Yazmin.

'Fine,' she replied.

After half an hour, Yazmin had to admit this was a good idea. She had been drawn into the game and now it allowed her to think of the world above, distracting her from thinking too much about the troubles of the here and now. She had great fun teasing TJ as he tried to work out her go of "spoon". They whiled away an immeasurable amount of time before Yazmin began to become tired. It had certainly been a long day for her — but a good day, too.

Chapter 15

McKenzie was really feeling the burden of the Maze. He estimated it had been ten days since he had entered, and he was still yet to have a conversation with a fellow prisoner. The loneliness was something he was really not used to. He was the middle of five children, so there hadn't been many dull moments growing up. McKenzie wasn't used to being left to his own thoughts for ten minutes, let alone ten days. As it turned out, he didn't like his thoughts much.

That may have something to with this place. It was hard to think of anything positive or optimistic in the eternal gloom. He was sure he had started seeing things, too. On several occasions he passed a turning and caught a glimpse of a bright light at the opposite end. Each time, for a fleeting moment, he felt his heart fly out of his chest, believing he had truly found the exit, only to find nothing but darkness when he retraced his steps and looked again along the corridor.

During the first few days, McKenzie was able to rely on his sleep to help him escape the misery. He allowed himself to drift off, content that he would soon be seeing the outside world. He was able to revisit some of his favourite places: the park, the beach, the Yankee stadium. On top of this, he could see his favourite people, as he remembered them from before his arrest. He saw Jessie's gorgeous smile looking at him, and his family sat around the Thanksgiving table, celebrating another year. However, over the last few nights, all of that seemed far away. It became harder and harder to separate his dreams from reality. All he saw at night were empty corridors lit with familiar lights. He had one particularly rough night where every corner he turned led to a bottomless pit, until he eventually turned to face a mirror and saw himself looking back, only he wasn't normal. His skin had turned red, and his eyes were completely black. He had woken sharply, his hands clammy and his head in agony; he had slipped down the wall and banged it against the solid floor.

He had attempted to come up with daily plans to discover more of the Maze and keep himself moving. He had awoken with a crooked neck as usual; sleeping on a hard concrete floor wasn't something many chiropractors would recommend. Once he had stretched for a while and loosened his neck thoroughly, he thought about what he could try and achieve for the day. Then, he heard a scurrying of footsteps nearby. He listened intently, trying to figure out the source of the intruding sound. He was stood at a T-junction and could clearly make out a clear stretch of pathway in each direction.

The only possible place it could have come from was a turning just along the path in front of him. He edged along the corridor, grabbing hold of his penknife as he neared the corner. He leapt around it, expecting to find someone cowering beneath his raised weapon, but there was no-one in sight. Before, with the weird lights at the end of the corridors, he had been able to accept that it was simply his mind playing tricks. This time it had seemed very different, though. He was *sure* he had heard something, but clearly, he was wrong.

Shaking his head indignantly, he looked all around one final time. There was definitely nobody there. He went back to working out his plan for the day, trying hard not to think about what had just happened. So far, he had gone as far as he could in every direction and followed each wall methodically, assuming there would be an exit somewhere on the outside, but to no avail. He figured his first action should be to try and find some food. So far, he had only once found a food room. He wasn't sure if it was the only one, but despite his efforts to retrace his steps he had been unable to find it again. He hadn't eaten now for over two sleeps.

He went into his pocket once more and clumsily pulled out the deck of cards, which were all loose. He had attempted to come up with a code to make it easier to remember his previous steps. Using the face cards and aces, he tried to put the pack into an order that would help him find his way back to the food room when he was desperate. He had been trying all day yesterday to do so but, despite following his own code exactly, he had not had any luck. He looked at the coded cards once more, desperately trying to remember if he had missed a turning or misread the cards somehow, but no explanation came to him. He shoved them angrily back into his pocket. It had been a stupid idea anyway. For several days now he'd had suspicions that the Maze was changing around him. Any one of the corners could have moved, and that would have ruined his entire plan. He needed to rely on guesswork instead. He knew roughly which direction the food room was in; he would just have to keep moving around until he found it.

He hastily moved to set off when he heard voices. Actual voices, of actual people. He was sure he was not imagining it. They were moving closer, too, until he could make out a man and a woman. The voices were coming from the stretch of path he had slept on. He hid around the corner of the nearby turning, leaning around it as the voices grew louder.

'Are you… an elastic band?' said the woman's voice.

'Yeah,' the man's voice said, disappointed. Both voices stopped. McKenzie was frozen in his silence.

'What do you reckon?' the woman's voice said.

'Straight on, I think.'

McKenzie saw the two figures come into view: a well-built man supporting a woman who looked diminished, to say the least. They walked straight past the pathway McKenzie was hiding down and he stood there, paralyzed, wishing he could scream out for company. What had happened to him? Was he incapable of talking to another person now?

'How rubbish are you?' he heard the woman's voice say, slowly edging further away. 'You could have chosen anything in the whole world, and you go for an elastic band!'

Then he heard something amazing: human laughter. It was magical, maybe the best thing he'd ever heard. Then it was gone again. He slumped to the floor and stared at the wall opposite, hands running through his hair. He felt like crying, but it seemed he was too dehydrated for that.

Dehydrated. That thought quickly reminded him. He needed to find the food room. No matter how glum he felt right now, he would feel much better with some sustenance. A thought came to him. Those people seemed remarkably happy. Too happy for this place. That could only mean they had recently eaten. He jumped back to his feet and ran to the end of pathway. He checked the two unknown figures were well gone and quickly headed in the direction they had come from.

He must have looked like a cartoon character, walking around sniffing violently, trying to get even the merest scent of food. He stumbled around the confused corridors, gradually becoming more and more desperate in his pursuit. He hurried along, skidding to a halt when he reached a junction and leaning awkwardly, trying to spot the out-of-place light that would signal the end of his search. After a frantic spell of searching, in which he probably went around the same square of pathways several times, he finally found some relief. At the far end of the corridor he had just turned onto, he could make out a light very different to that emitted by the lanterns. He raced his way down the corridor, almost skipping with glee until he finally crossed the threshold to refreshment.

He turned the corner and was left stunned by what he saw. The entire room was splattered with chaotic mess. The water cooler that had once sat neatly in one corner now lay in the middle of the floor, with much of its contents spilled around it. The platters of food had been slammed against the walls, leaving splattered marks of red and yellow over the entire room, including the ceilings. He took in the scene with an air of desperation. He had been relying on a little relief. This food was about all he had to look forward to, and not only was this food mostly left in ruins, but it had left the idea of food rooms tainted. It must have been those two he had seen together. Nobody else could have been in here between them and him.

He suppressed his rage, knowing he would have a hard job finding them again, anyway. Instead, he made his way into the room. He would just have to fix it himself. He picked up the water cooler first, careful not to spill any more. He could still use that. He carefully tried to reattach it to its stand, which was exceedingly hard as the seal had already been broken. After a fair amount of struggle, he managed to click it into place and duly poured himself a cup of the slightly less cool water, taking in the rest of the room. There wasn't much he could do for the walls and ceiling. He hoped whoever came and topped up the food would be able to sort that out.

He restored the scattered chairs and the flipped table and tried to straighten up the food trays that had not been completely destroyed, helping himself to the few scraps he could find. He didn't even care what it was at this point. Taking another look at the room, he felt proud to have done something positive and productive. It wasn't much, but it was more than he had managed so far in the Maze.

Chapter 16

Aaron had not slept for long. Penny had asked him if he had slept as much as he normally had whilst inside here, to which she got the answer she expected. This made her think a lot about the concept of time within the Maze. They could invent a whole new way of living if they wanted to. She explained to Aaron her theory that they had probably been in the Maze much less time than they had thought previously, based on Aaron's short sleep cycle.

The problem with falling asleep in this place was that once you did there was no way of keeping track of the time unless you had an incredible internal clock. It helped that they had each other, now, to tell them roughly how long they had slept for. Once Aaron had properly awoken, they had swiftly began making their way through the corridors once again. Aaron had tried to insist that Penny get some sleep, too, but she pointed out that if she did that they would end up in a cycle where they didn't move because one or the other of them would always be asleep. Besides, she wasn't tired anyway. She very rarely was in here. Sleep seemed far more of a chore, a necessity, now they were trapped here.

They meandered along together, both seemingly aware that they barely knew each other yet but more than happy for the company. They both began asking questions about their lives outside of the Maze, trying to learn more about the person they were travelling with, though it was clear neither of them wanted to ask the other why they were here. Penny wasn't afraid of Aaron; she didn't believe him to be capable of an act of violence. Though a thought occurred to her, a saying: *it's always the quiet ones.* This nagged at the back of her mind, but more than this she didn't want the question to be flipped on her. She was sure

Aaron wouldn't want her as a companion if she told him her darkest secret.

Instead, they talked about their families, their old jobs, places they had visited, and anything in-between as they attempted to distract themselves from the reality of the situation. Aaron was still in awe of the tree Penny had created and quickly led her on a tangent about its meaning and purpose. In truth, Penny hadn't created the tree as a symbol of anything at all, though Aaron was sure that subconsciously she probably had. She just wanted to practice with her new tools, and figured a tree was a pretty basic design to start with. They both decided it would be good to try and find it again, so they set themselves that task for the day. Aaron told her it was pretty far to the right, based on where they were right now. She was staggered that he was able to know this.

Aaron's story about the mysterious light still played in Penny's thoughts. They hadn't really discussed it in detail before he had fallen asleep, and Penny was curious to find out his thoughts on it.

'I honestly don't know,' he said ponderously after she had prompted him.

'You must have a few ideas.'

'Well, yeah. Like I said, I thought at first it must be some sign of an exit, but I don't think it could be, anymore. My best guess is it's some kind of lookout room for that Diego Flint to keep an eye on us. There's probably loads of them around us.'

Penny thought about this. She wasn't overly fond of the idea that they were being watched all the time, but if it were true, she supposed it had its uses. It would certainly be useful for security purposes. Penny doubted even someone as twisted as Flint must be to create this place would let someone be killed under his watch.

*

They continued to plod along in silence for some time. It wasn't easy to come up with anything to talk about, really. Neither of them had any interesting stories about people or things they had found in the Maze. In fact, the most interesting thing about the Maze was that there seemed to be no landmarks, other than perhaps the lanterns, but it was hard to tell them apart anyway. Penny didn't know what she had expected, but she did think maybe the Maze would offer more than just these plain grey walls and floors for forty kilometres.

'I've got something to help us pass the time,' Aaron announced abruptly.

'Okay,' Penny said, unsure where this was going.

'It's a bit of a thinking game, really. Something to take our minds off of-' he gestured to the Maze in general.

'Okay,' Penny repeated, more enthusiastic.

'Top five films of all time,' Aaron stated. 'Have a think.'

Penny laughed a little; it was a bit stupid and not something she would normally have thought was worth thinking about, but she decided to humour him. After a few minutes thinking, not only had she come up with a list she was fairly happy with, but she had quickly changed her mind about the game. It was a good idea, she had to give Aaron credit.

'You ready?' Aaron smiled.

'Yeah, I guess. Why don't you say yours first?' she said nervously. Penny felt they were quite different people, and she didn't want to be judged by Aaron. Her choices weren't exactly cultured.

'Fine,' Aaron smiled. 'But I warn you, you might not like them.'

They spent a long time debating and arguing their lists of films. To Penny's surprise, Aaron chose films that were clearly his favourite comfort films such as *Back to the Future* and *Jurassic Park*, whereas Penny tried to think of so-called classics she liked, such as *Psycho* and *Forrest Gump*. She was fairly pleased with this as it made her seem a little more cultured in comparison, but Aaron insisted on repicking his choices. After a further raucous debate in which Aaron reeled off a list of films, Penny realised she had not thought about her current predicament for some time.

But she didn't want to stop there. She didn't want the distraction to end. Swiftly, she moved the topic onto music, and soon they were arguing over that instead. This was much harder, though. Music was something that was independent to each person, so it was hard to argue with another person's choices, no matter how different they were. After a long day of hard distraction work, Penny was becoming a little drowsy. She wasn't overly fond of the idea of sleeping yet, despite getting to know Aaron better over the course of the day, but she had to accept she would need to sleep at some point.

They had still not found the tree she had made before her second sleep in the Maze, so she decided she would rest when they found it. As ever when someone was dreading something, however, it came around far too quickly. No sooner had she thought that very thought, at the next corner they turned it was right in front of her. She looked at it in a humorous disbelief. Turning to Aaron, she announced her plan to sleep here. He, meanwhile, was looking from the tree to Penny and back in sheer awe.

'Why haven't you done any more yet?' he asked curiously.

'How do you know I haven't?' she replied defensively.

'Probably because I've been round this Maze twice over and not seen any,' Aaron laughed. Penny accepted this as a fair point.

'I thought about it, but I just couldn't think what to make.' She paused, looking down at her feet. 'It's not the best atmosphere for creativity,' she stated despondently.

They sat down either side of the tree. Penny's tangled hair flowed to its trunk as she glanced sideways towards her piece of art, craning her neck a little. She noticed lots of fingerprints along the wall face. She was staggered to see that people were clearly stopping to take it in. It annoyed her slightly that they couldn't just look with their eyes, but it meant a lot to her that she could make even the slightest of difference. It opened her eyes a little to a communal struggle everyone was facing together. At that moment, she knew they needed to do more.

Chapter 17

Over the days following TJ helping his fellow Mazer Yazmin, the mood in the control room was evidently more upbeat. It was idealistic for Flint to have that kind of incident to support his case for the continuation of the Maze. Everyone who had seen the footage of TJ carrying the limp body of Yazmin down the corridors had been inspired, their belief in the Maze's potential changing, hopefully, for the good.

A moment that positive could have easily been forgotten, though, had a few negative moments contradicted it over the next day or so. Again, Flint was fortunate that this wasn't the case. It was an emotion-sparking moment to watch Yazmin smiling and laughing giddily as she ate a piece of melon — certainly the poster moment of the Maze's opening week — but soon after eyes were fixed on the development of two new friendships: TJ and Yazmin, and Penny and Aaron.

The best thing about these friendships, Diego thought, was that they were clearly people who never would have been friends outside of the Maze. This proved that the Maze forced people to change in their ways, even if it was just a small change, such as who they interacted with.

It certainly hadn't all been positive. There had been moments in which McKenzie Symms appeared to be struggling. On more than one occasion he had thought the screen had frozen whilst he watched the troubled man, only to realise he had become completely still. However, Flint's plan to help McKenzie find his feet by getting the Maze officers to trash the food room seemed to work brilliantly. Although McKenzie had only managed to find a little sustenance in the food room, he emerged looking a different man.

Familiar patterns were beginning to emerge within the other Mazers, too. So far, they still only had the two pairs that were staying together, but elsewhere more Mazers were beginning to strike up conversations when they crossed paths. Those that were struggling to reach out to others were the ones who were struggling most of all. Every day they went without speaking, the worse it seemed to become, and the harder it got for them to start conversations.

Flint too was beginning to feel the burden of the Maze. There wasn't much of a future in sight for him at this moment in time. Any way he looked at it, he would be here watching over the Maze for the rest of his life, unless it failed miserably. He couldn't leave because he was the one who knew all its secrets. He wasn't even allowed to leave the safety of the hotel complex above him. This made small things such as fresh air feel like a luxury other people didn't appreciate. He had to look at the positives, though; at least he had any number of people to talk to. If he didn't want to speak to Alex for some reason one day, he could easily go and chat with Benji instead, who seemed to have recovered from his minor sulk.

Today would mark an entire week of the Maze playing host to its first detainees. It was 10a.m. now as he watched the dots move infrequently, some of them not moving at all thanks to their detached sleep patterns. In two hours, the Maze would officially be a week old. It felt like a year.

Something Flint had always been very keen on was creating a set of "favourites", much like in a TV show. He figured it would help create a deeper understanding of the pressures of the Maze if he were to follow a select group of individuals more closely. Even after just a week he was fairly sure he could pick out five that would be included within that list. Right now, both of his star pairings were on the move, heading to opposite corners of the map, whilst McKenzie wandered alone, quite separate from the other dots scattered amongst the ever-growing Maze. Flint was perhaps most concerned for him of all the Mazers.

Flint called to Benji, asking him to focus the screen on McKenzie for a while. Benji was in charge again this morning, with Alex due in shortly to take over from the night shift. Meanwhile, Flint had taken up his favourite spot in the far left of the room, hidden away from the action. Not that there was much action right now. The Maze had been quiet since last night and that reflected in the lack of excitement within the control room.

The screen showed McKenzie. He was stood still, not walking anywhere at that precise moment, but seemed jumpy and agitated. He kept rapidly turning his head to look down the corridor and then back the other way. Flint's brow furrowed as he tried to figure out what was going through his head. Benji had wandered over, looking thoroughly bored. Diego couldn't really blame him, but he knew what he had signed up for. It wasn't a bad thing that there wasn't constant excitement.

Flint had been quite enthralled by the heated debates brought about by Penny and Aaron. Their discussion on films had been watched by many in the control room and it had caused an uproar of noise for the next few hours as the operators argued energetically with each other. Now, though, it was back to relative silence.

'Mind if I sit?' Benji asked, gesturing to the chair next to Diego.

'Of course not,' Diego said nonchalantly. As usual, his mind was elsewhere. For a moment there was silence between them as Benji clearly tried to come up with a topic of discussion.

Flint started to follow McKenzie's actions with his own

head, darting to one side then the other, trying to imagine what he was thinking about.

'Err… are you okay?' Benji asked, looking from him to the giant monitor with a confused expression.

'Yes, yes. I'm fine. I- I'm just trying to work out what he's thinking about,' Flint muttered, still moving his head from side to side. Benji frowned for a moment then half joined in. If anyone looked over at them at that precise moment it might have looked like they were trying out a very odd new dance craze.

'It seems pretty hard to reason with,' Benji said casually, like it was no big deal. It was a big deal to Diego, though. He wanted to understand the inner workings of the people in the Maze more than anything. If he was to be doing this job for the foreseeable future, it was best to have a strong understanding of every aspect.

After a minute or so, McKenzie finally stopped this weird motion, and just like that set off along the corridor once more. The two men who had sat copying his movements were forced to give up on their pursuit and return to normal conversation.

'What have you made of the first week then, Benji?' Diego asked, trying to take his eyes away from the Maze for a minute. He spent far too much time looking at the screen as it was.

'It's definitely a start,' Benji said, trying to sound meaningful. Flint didn't really think Benji was much of a thinker. 'The Maze has shown its promise, that's for sure,' he added. It was a very one-dimensional answer.

'Okay. What would you say you have learnt from the Mazers?' Flint tried to prompt him to think a little deeper.

'Not to commit a crime, I guess.' He chuckled. Flint's face remained stony still and Benji soon stopped, and actually considered his answer a little further. He coughed a little, trying to cover up the awkwardness. 'I guess… to take advantage of the luxuries we have up here.'

Flint smiled broadly at this, and Benji breathed a big sigh, clearly relieved.

'Exactly!' Flint exclaimed. 'That's not the point of the Maze, really. It isn't designed so that they appreciate what they have, but it can be a lesson for anyone and everyone. For example, what are you going to do today when you leave this place?' Flint asked, full of energy. Benji looked a little startled.

'Probably go to sleep,' he said honestly.

'Sleep!' Flint yelled even louder. 'Don't get me wrong, I know we have to sleep and rest for our own health, but there is so much you could be doing out there! You never know when it could stop,' he added meaningfully, nodding towards the screen at the front.

Benji suddenly seemed like he wished he hadn't sat down. He clearly wasn't expecting a lecture on life. He looked over to the nearest computer screen, looking for an escape, before muttering that he had to take care of something and sheepishly dashing away. As Flint watched him go, he spotted Alex making her way in, a fruit smoothie and a gloriously bulging sandwich in hand. She was watching Benji rush off, too.

'What did you say this time?' she asked, setting down the drink and sandwich in front of Diego carefully.

'Nothing he didn't need to hear,' Diego murmured, taking his feet off the desk to grab the smoothie. Alex sat down again. She carried on to drink her coffee.

something moment, she passed a sip of her coffee.

'Nothing much,' Diego sighed. 'Is there anything happening today?'

'Yes, we've got a busy day today. Well, busier than the night has been by the looks of it.' She looked around the room at all the bored faces.

'Thank God. What's happening then?'

'Well, we've got a new Mazer joining today,' she stated, knowing this would get Diego excited. 'She is our first foreign Mazer, too. She was charged with causing political unrest in Russia. Apparently she is part of one of the women's rights' groups. Could be a handful,' she finished, raising her eyebrows towards Diego.

Diego nodded thoughtfully. She certainly sounded strong-minded, but maybe that was what the Maze needed right now. Nobody within the current group of Mazers seemed willing to take a risk or do something bold to change their destiny.

Another hour of passed with exceedingly little of interest to occur, and Benji bid them goodnight, even though it was half past eleven in the morning. Flint suspected very little of their conversation would sink in, and Benji was, in fact, going home to sleep. He couldn't exactly blame him today. It wasn't the kind of watching that would fill you with energy; even Flint was a little bored, and he was usually able to find interest in the smallest of details. He sat there in silence for some time, staring blankly at the dots on the screen as Alex attempted to busy herself and the operators with work that didn't really exist.

Finally, at a quarter to twelve, Alex instructed for the screen to be split in half so they could watch the entrance of the new Mazer. Diego was half anticipating being called upon in the transition room again. He leaned forward with intrigue as the Russian woman was escorted into the room. An excited buzz filled the control room, full of anticipation. It was a little bit sick how much everyone reacted to the difficulties of these people as if it were just another TV soap. Scottie was stood at the end of Diego's row, watching on with interest like everyone else.

'Scottie, what's this woman's name?' Flint asked. It felt weird saying woman. She looked like she was definitely younger than Diego, and that was saying something.

'Err…' Scottie fumbled for his tablet, hastily. 'It's Natasha. Natasha Oleksandr.'

'Thank you, Scottie.' Diego returned his gaze to the young woman. When he had been watching others enter the Maze previously, he had noticed that their pockets had been heavy with their personal belongings, but this didn't seem the case with Natasha. He wondered if she had been given any belongings. Of course, he knew they were offered the standard options if they were not brought belongings by family, such was the case with Mr. Symms, but Natasha might have chosen not to bring any of those. The pockets of her baggy grey joggers didn't exactly seem to be overflowing.

'Hey, Scottie?' he said again.

'Yes, s- Diego?' Flint's eyes flickered dangerously. Scott had almost called him "sir", despite several remonstrations against such terms. He ignored it and continued.

'Do we know what Miss Oleksandr is taking with her into the Maze?'

'I'm afraid not. We don't keep a record of that until they use them,' Scott said confidently.

'Really? That seems… dangerous,' Diego said, surprised. Scott frowned at him as if to say: *surely you should know this?* He must have agreed to it, but with so much administration work in the weeks leading up to the grand opening, sometimes he signed papers that he hadn't necessarily read fully. He quickly went silent, trying to pretend this hadn't happened. Fortunately, he was pretty sure Scott was so scared of him he would never mention this to anyone.

The door to the Maze had now opened and Natasha looked at the woman who had escorted her into the room. It seemed every single Mazer did the same. It didn't matter who you were, nobody would just walk into a dark void without some form of confirmation of some sort. The staff member, who Diego didn't know by name, nodded casually. Without a second for thought, Natasha strode purposefully into the dark. She didn't look back once. Diego was slightly stunned by this. Everyone else he had watched go through the transition room would usually edge their way forward slowly. Natasha didn't seem to want to mess about. Diego worried for a moment that she was going to be another who tried to find the exit in a day. He had seen this happen too many times already and once they had learnt it wasn't going to be that easy, they had spiralled dangerously.

They saw nothing for the next minute or so as Natasha found her way through the passage of darkness that separated the Maze from the transition room, then soon she rushed out into the dim light of the cavernous Maze, watched closely by the camera fixed on the entrance point. As ever, she took a few moments to acclimatise to her new surroundings. She looked around at the corridors stretching before her, took in the lanterns, and inevitably looked up towards the ceiling thirty feet above her. Nobody would ever be able to make out the ceiling above them, but it didn't stop them all looking. Perhaps it was a reflex of acceptance. Being unable to see the sky seemed to reaffirm to the Mazers that their situation was real.

Natasha seemed to take much less time to acclimatise than most. After a brief glance at her new surroundings, she quickly set off, heading straight along the path directly in front of her. Again, this was unusual. Nearly all the Mazers at this point had been trying to work out some kind of mind game. In truth, it was far simpler than that; Flint knew only too well. He was pleasantly surprised to see someone just go straight forward. If the first two minutes of Natasha's time in the Maze had told Flint anything, it was that he had been correct. She was definitely strong-minded. He hoped this would last.

Chapter 18

Natasha felt at a great advantage to her fellow prisoners. Some of them had already been in for a week and hadn't had a clue what to expect when they had first walked in. Sure, Natasha still hadn't seen anything from inside the Maze, but at least she had a bit more information than those first people had.

Naturally, the Maze had received global interest. It was an incredibly bold experiment and across the world people were launching into arguments about the ethics behind it. In the last week Natasha had listened intently to any news reports she had been able to hear, but more than this she had heard snippets of conversation between the workers in the weird spa resort she had been held in for the last four days. This had given her a plan of action for the Maze. She had contacted her sister and asked her to bring a very specific set of items that she could use to help her and everyone else in the Maze.

Her mind was extremely set. This dystopian freakshow of a prison wasn't about to throw her off course. She power-walked purposefully along this impossibly long corridor, which had already taken up five minutes of her time, as she looked for the next turning. All she could think about was finding a good spot to complete her plan. In her mind she had envisioned a perfect opening where several paths came together. Already she was under the impression that this probably didn't exist, but her plan could still work.

Another five minutes of intense walking later, she finally reached a junction. She didn't pause to think but immediately turned right. She didn't really care where she was going at this point, she just wanted to get a good distance away from the entrance before she stopped. She was so preoccupied with this thought that she wasn't paying attention to where she was going. She stumbled over something as she turned the corner blindly. Or more accurately, someone.

'Sorry, sorry,' she said quickly. Not wanting to get drawn into a conversation, she quickly turned away and made to continue walking.

'You're not from 'round here, are you?' a man's voice said quietly.

She looked up at the darkness above her, then turned back. As much as she wanted to get moving, she didn't want to be rude. The man was fairly young, though not as young as she was, and it seemed he had seen better days. He was a little thin, his facial hair growing in patches, covering his greasy face. His messy hair was a sand colour which actually suited him quite well. She guessed he had opted to wear baggy clothing like her, but she was troubled that they seemed extra loose.

'Do you mean the Maze, or America?' she asked calmly.

'Well, both, apparently.' He too had been taking her in. Her clothing was still fresh and her shoes un-scuffed, and her deep purple hair still glistened healthily. It was fairly obvious she hadn't been here long. 'How long have you been in here for?' he asked weakly.

'About fifteen minutes,' she replied bluntly. The man's eyes lit up.

'No way!' he exclaimed. 'And- and how long have I been here?' he asked, embarrassed.

She tried to smile supportively. She had no idea how hard it must have been for him and the others who had already been here for a week.

'Were you one of the people who came in on the first day?' she asked, looking to confirm her suspicions.

'Yeah. How long ago was that?' he asked a little desperately. She almost didn't want to tell him.

'Err… one week, exactly.'

'A week! Only a week?' he yelled, making Natasha jump. He then went silent thinking this through. At first, he had seemed devastated by this, but then his face began to change. 'I have so much time,' he muttered to himself.

'Look, I don't mean to seem rude, but I have a plan to help everyone and I kind of want to get on with it.' The man looked up at her hopefully.

'A plan? What are you going to do?' he spluttered hurriedly.

'Want to come and see?' She smiled knowingly. She figured it wouldn't be the worst thing to have someone with her to share the moment with. It might help spread the word faster. The man jumped to his feet excitedly. He looked different already to the man she had first seen sitting against the wall dejectedly.

'My name's McKenzie, by the way.' He held out his hand. Natasha looked at it for a moment.

How very American, she thought.

'Natasha,' she stated blandly, taking his hand, nevertheless.

Chapter 19

McKenzie couldn't believe his luck. Part of him had begun to think that this was fate. He had been unable to speak to anyone for days, and then someone goes and trips over him, practically forcing him to speak. Then that person goes and changes everything about the Maze, and tells him she has a plan to help him and everyone else. McKenzie couldn't help but notice that Natasha also happened to be very attractive. This was probably exacerbated by not seeing another woman for an entire week, but it did make him feel incredibly conscious of the current state of his own appearance.

She led him swiftly along corridor after corridor, seemingly full of energy. McKenzie thought that he had probably also walked at that pace on this first day. A combination of limited sleep and a growing defeatist approach had slowly worn down his willingness to keep up the endless tirade.

McKenzie still had no idea what Natasha's big plan was. She didn't even seem to have a clear destination in mind, other than apparently as far away from where they were coming from. She looked over at McKenzie after a while of silence and apparently noticed his heavy breathing. His lack of proper nutrition over the previous week had severely damaged his breathing capacity and now he was wheezing as he tried to keep up. Natasha abruptly stopped with a look of concern on her face.

'Sorry, I didn't realise you were struggling,' she said awkwardly. 'Let's take a breather.'

McKenzie wanted to say something but was struggling to gather his breath. Besides, he wasn't really sure what to say.

'Tell me about this place,' Natasha requested, and she

actually seemed interested as she looked around them, taking in every inch of the constant, grey walls. McKenzie rolled his eyes behind her back. Couldn't she tell he could barely speak right now?

'There isn't much to tell, to be honest,' he said after a moment. 'That's probably the most interesting thing about this place. That there isn't anything interesting.'

Natasha smiled softly.

'What about food? There's no way you could have lasted a week without something.'

'Yeah, there's these weird refreshment rooms,' McKenzie replied, 'but they're really hard to find. Everything is. There is more to this Maze than you think,' he said darkly. Natasha clearly didn't understand what he meant as she looked at him, perplexed.

'I don't know exactly how, but it's almost impossible to retrace your steps. I have a feeling the walls move,' McKenzie continued, thoughtfully. He had been doing a good job of pretending this wasn't true, that he had imagined it for that brief spell, but it was no good; all the evidence suggested it was true. Either that, or he was going completely mad — he would much rather believe the walls were moving.

He hadn't wanted to break this to Natasha on her first day, but it was probably better to know now than in a week or a month's time. She was looking around again, but this time with a much different expression. It seemed much less innocent, much more resolute.

'Is there any landmarks at all here?' she asked, a little snappily this time.

'One, I guess. It's just about the only flaw in the entirety of the Maze's walls. It's a tree. Not a real tree,' he added hastily, noticing her look of surprise. 'Somebody carved this tree in the wall. It's really good.'

'Are we far from this tree, by your guess?' she asked quickly.

'Err... No, I don't think so actually. I can take you if you want. Or try to, at least.'

Natasha nodded vigorously.

'But you have to promise you won't get too angry if we get a little lost,' he said cautiously. 'If the Maze has taught me anything, it's to have a little patience.'

'Fine.' She rolled her eyes, but smiled at him, too.

'Oh, and we're going at my pace this time,' McKenzie added. Natasha let out a little giggle that was far more becoming of her age than anything she'd done previously.

They set off once more, this time at much more of a steady plod. McKenzie felt like a clan elder, teaching a young one the ways of the Maze. The only thing was, he was really hoping she could make a difference. Something about the Maze had to change. He couldn't see himself lasting more than a month if it continued like this.

'Tell me about the outside world,' he said casually. 'What's it like up there?'

'Basically exactly the same as when you left it,' Natasha answered, incredibly dry.

'Yeah, fair point. I guess it seems like a long time, but it hasn't been, really.'

'The president of the United States got shot yesterday,' Natasha said, as if this was an everyday occurrence.

'WHAT?' McKenzie exclaimed. Natasha's face broke into a grin.

'Wow, that was far too easy,' she said disappointedly.

After that they didn't speak for some time. McKenzie led them onwards at a meandering pace. He could tell Natasha was getting frustrated, but she kept to her word and didn't say anything. McKenzie had been desperate for someone to talk to for the past seven days and he was glad he had someone to pass the time with, but it was weird. All McKenzie could think about was the Maze. All he wanted to do was discuss it with someone, yet Natasha was not the person to have this conversation with. She had only just arrived and had no idea about what it was truly like to be alone in here with nothing but your own thoughts. Plus, she was a little short with him. He could understand why. His brain wasn't exactly functioning at full speed, making him seem a little dopy. She must also have felt a little intimidated. She didn't know him, didn't know why he was here, and she was all alone with him. McKenzie figured telling her why he was in here wouldn't exactly help the situation, anyway.

They walked on for some time and after a while McKenzie began to get that dreaded feeling he occasionally felt down here; that he wasn't sure where they were. He tried to keep his face neutral, determined not to show the panic that was setting in. Natasha was already becoming impatient to see this tree and he didn't want to seem lost. He continued on, making the occasional turn until at last Natasha could wait no longer. She put out her heavily tattooed arm to stop him as he made to turn left.

'This doesn't make sense,' she snapped.

'W- what?' McKenzie stammered.

'Why are you turning left again? We're just going around in circles!'

'Well, I know it's over there, somewhere.' He pointed to his left, waving his hand vaguely.

'Oh, that's reassuring,' she said sarcastically. This time there was no sign of a smile. 'Look, we can't just keep walking along the same paths and hoping we'll come across the tree. Why don't we try going a different way?'

She was right, of course. McKenzie felt a little foolish being told how to navigate the Maze by someone who had literally just entered. He reluctantly nodded his agreement and Natasha started storming through the paths again, apparently giving up on the pretence of allowing McKenzie to lead.

Within mere minutes they had made a breakthrough, finding a new path McKenzie could have sworn wasn't there a minute ago. It's like the Maze Gods were *trying* to make him look stupid. They raced down the new pathway at an alarming speed, and when they reached the following junction, McKenzie spotted the tree a little way along the path to their left.

Natasha dashed over to the carving, running her fingers over it just as McKenzie had the first time he had found it. Something about its very nature seemed to make people do this. As McKenzie approached, he noticed lot's more shining fingerprints littered across the wall. Natasha stepped away from the tree for a second and McKenzie stepped forward to touch it himself, as if it were some religious ritual you had to do whenever you passed this weird monument. When McKenzie thought about that a little more, he realised that was truer than he'd first thought. This was the sole landmark of the Maze, meaning the reluctant cult that had been thrown together within the Maze were almost forced to show some sign of respect to it when they came across it.

He also wondered if the artist planned to do any more. It seemed weird to make something this powerful and meaningful, something this beautiful, and then just stop at that. McKenzie looked around at Natasha and noticed she was busying herself, reaching for something in her pocket. To his amazement she pulled out a watch and told him to hold on to it. She then returned to her pocket and found a packet of Blu Tack and a small pad of paper, which she began rifling through. She must have found the page she was looking for as she quickly stopped and then tore out the page she was on.

Within a few minutes, Natasha had completed her mission, with a little help from McKenzie. As he stood back and took in the slightly bizarre moment, McKenzie soon realised what she had meant earlier. Natasha was clearly very intelligent, and had come in with a much clearer idea of the Maze than McKenzie when he had arrived. She had used the Blu Tack to attach the watch to the wall, accompanied by the small note which read:

Dear fellow people of the Maze,
As of twelve o'clock on this watch it has been seven days exactly since the first of you entered the Maze. This watch will become the first item of a new monument and will help all of us keep track of time within the Maze. If any of you have anything on you that you do not need/want, please use the spare Blu Tack to add to the watch.

McKenzie felt emotions bubbling as he stared at the watch. It was so simple, yet it would change the Maze forever onwards. McKenzie didn't think he'd ever met anyone with such a sense of purpose as Natasha; he looked at her, full of admiration. She spotted him looking and something in his face must have given away his feelings. She scowled at him in a way he had quickly learnt was normal of her. Natasha wasn't like him. She didn't seem to get overly emotional, or if she did, she was very good at hiding it. She took a deep breath and turned to face McKenzie, who smiled back full of naivety.

'Thank you for helping,' she stated, devoid of any feeling, 'but this is only half the job. We need to work together to spread the word to others.' McKenzie felt a sudden jolt of excitement. She was talking about them working together. 'The best way we can do this is to split up, especially as you know the Maze so well.'

McKenzie's stomach dropped a little. He had gotten excited too early and now had to work hard to keep his expression steady. The last thing he wanted to do was come across as needy. Besides, they were trapped together in a fairly small space; he was confident he would be seeing Natasha again soon.

'You're right,' he said after taking a moment to gather himself. 'But, before we go, I have to tell you how much this will mean to everyone in the Maze. Sincerely.' It was a stupid thing to say, and he didn't know why he had bothered; she already knew this. That's why she'd done it.

'Thank you, again,' Natasha replied, smiling brightly. 'Well, I guess you go that way,' she pointed down the corridor beyond McKenzie, 'and I'll go this way,' she pointed the opposite way. McKenzie nodded firmly. He didn't feel like saying anything more. In fact, neither of them said another word. Natasha turned with a final glance to McKenzie and began walking rapidly down the corridor. She was out of sight before McKenzie had reached his turning just a short distance away.

Chapter 20

This was more than Flint could have dreamt of. He and Alex had watched on in amazement as Natasha stormed her way through the Maze, dragging the previously shy and lost McKenzie along with her. Then she had created this shrine to the Maze. A "monument" that would provide the Mazers with a stronger link to the outside world than they had ever previously had: time.

The whole control room had a stunned silence about it. Nobody quite knew what to think. It had been such a simple act, yet so brilliant Flint couldn't help but stand back and applaud, though he didn't literally. That would probably be deemed quite inappropriate. As they had taken in this new development, Alex had wandered over to Flint.

'Do you think we should do something about this?' she asked nervously.

'Like what?' Diego thought aloud.

'Like, take the watch away,' Alex suggested. Diego looked at her in surprise, a little disappointed.

'Why would we do that?'

'Because it's going to cause problems. Because that's not the point of the Maze.'

Diego didn't appreciate this comment.

'And you know what the point of the Maze is better than me?' he asked accusingly.

'No, that's not what I'm saying. It's just... it's just sometimes you can get lost in the people.'

Diego was a little blown away by this. He was the first to admit he had a greater interest in the Mazers themselves than many of his colleagues; he was fascinated by their behaviours. That being said, he still understood the needs of the Maze better than anyone. It wasn't a bad thing that the Mazers weren't going to go completely mad and lose track of time and society. The whole point of the Maze was to help these people re-enter society as decent as possible. He could only imagine how that would go down if they didn't have basic human necessities such as the ability to tell what time it was. He explained this to Alex as well as he possibly could, and she left the topic alone —though, she did not seem overly convinced. Diego knew this would come back up soon enough.

*

As the afternoon wore on, Diego watched as the dot marked Natasha made its way around the Maze at remarkable pace. Every now and again she would find another Mazer and quickly tell them about the new "monument" and about the time-keeping device. Most of them just nodded along, seeming quite bored as they listened to her. Diego suspected that they thought Natasha was a little crazy. It seemed they had all had their fair share of breakdowns within the Maze, and they probably figured this was just an extreme version of one.

It wasn't until a full two hours after she had created this new monument that the first Mazer stumbled upon it. Diego had lost track of whether Marcus Morgan had been one of the Mazers that had been told about it by Natasha or McKenzie, or whether he had just found it of his own volition. He kind of wished he had made notes to help him keep track. Diego was nervous as he watched the broad-shouldered man approach the delicate watch. There was no-one else nearby and as he thought about it, that watch had almost instantly become the most valuable item within the Maze. Marcus could so easily have stolen it and become the master of time in there. If anything were to scupper Natasha's plan, it was this.

Marcus moved closer to the watch, reading the small note that Natasha had added. Diego was annoyed that he wasn't able to read the note. They just couldn't find a camera angle that made it clear enough for him. He imagined it just explained the watch, but he wished he could know for sure. Perhaps he would send a Maze officer to take a photo of it. This would be no easy task, though; he imagined there would be people converging to check the time quite consistently from now on.

Marcus stood motionless for a minute as he read and re-read the note, taking in the watch as he did so. His stillness was reflected by the operators in the control room who were acting like making sudden movements might scare him off. They were all thinking the same as Flint, it seemed. Speculating as to whether Marcus would take the watch for himself.

Several more minutes of nervous tension passed as Marcus took in the watch and then looked at the tree as if he'd never seen it before. Flint noticed on the map that several of the dots appeared to be heading towards the watch now, and he hoped that one of them would reach it before Marcus could make any decision. Just as he thought that, Marcus reached for his trouser pocket. To Diego's amazement, he didn't make to take the watch, but instead pulled something out of his pocket. It was a roll of Sellotape.

The first thing Flint thought was why anybody would give him a roll of tape to take in the Maze. He wondered if Mr. Morgan had been another who didn't have any relatives visit. Nevertheless, he quickly used his teeth to cut two strips of tape and placed them over the watch's straps to fasten it more securely on the wall. This was just about the last thing Flint would have expected Marcus to do. He then bent down and placed the rest of the roll next to the Blu Tack on the floor. There were a few raised eyebrows and gasps of surprise around the control room. Flint just smiled, as if this had all been part of his great plan.

After another moment of taking in the time, Marcus turned away and quickly scampered off along the corridor. The giant screen did not change to follow him as it normally would have, but instead remained fixed on the watch. Diego quickly decided he had seen enough for the time being. He could sit there all day and watch people filter in, but he had already been in the control room for eight hours and needed to take a break. He stood and stretched widely, keen to leave before anything else could distract him.

'I'm heading to the pool. Let me know if anything important happens,' he retorted coldly to Alex. He was still seething about her comments, though he knew she was just trying to look at all the information. She looked a little crestfallen as he left, and Diego regretted his tone a little. This was the first time they had argued about anything. He had relied on Alex as his number two throughout the entirety of the Maze's existence and it felt odd to be distant.

Chapter 21

'Maybe you should go walk for a bit, leave me to it,' Penny had snapped at Aaron. She hadn't meant it, but she didn't like him loitering around behind her whilst she worked. He had given her a hurtful look but didn't argue. He'd appeared fidgety for a while as he'd watched Penny begin her precise work on a new piece of art. 'Don't go far, though,' she'd added kindly, before he had skulked away silently. She felt so ridiculously dependant on Aaron already, which was crazy considering they'd only met about two days ago.

They were far away from the tree carving that she'd made such a long time ago. At least, it felt like a long time ago. In truth it probably really wasn't that long at all. Penny had decided to be a little more ambitious with her next design, but she wanted it to be a surprise for everyone, including Aaron. That was partly why she had sent him away. She didn't want him stood behind her trying to guess what it was before she had even finished. Aaron didn't seem to understand quite how long it took for her to make a simple tree, let along something more complex.

He had been gone for a while now. Penny pondered if he had taken her a little too literally. He had to understand that artists really don't like to be disturbed. She tried to forget about him, to forget about the Maze, and zone out into her own creative world, only focusing on the intricacies of her hammer and chisel as they scraped away at the solid wall. It was cold being sat there for so long and it had become quite hard work to stop her hands from shaking as she held her chisel steady. Once or twice she slipped a little, giving her desired image a little more motion that she had been aiming for.

She thought back to that empty studio back in the weird

pre-Maze place that she had briefly inhabited. Despite her grave situation, it had somehow become her happy place. A place she was able to focus on completely and forget about the Maze. Perhaps because it was so contrasting to the Maze's gloom with its white walls that glowed with rays of natural light. Penny missed natural light. She missed the paints and the chalks in that room. She had known at the time that her stint there would be bittersweet, but it seemed ten-fold once she'd ended up here.

She was so in her head, so in the moment with her work, that she had no idea how much time had passed; not that she ever did anyway in here. All that she knew was that her new carving was nearly finished, and yet Aaron had still not returned. She didn't like the feeling of neediness she felt right now — it wasn't something she was used to. Her relationship with Toby had been a good one, but a relationship in which both of them were content to be casual. Her and Aaron were not a relationship, but it was already far more co-dependent.

Persisting on with her work, trying to take a positive twist on the moment, she thought she might be able to finish before he returned. Sure enough, after another half hour she was just adding some final touches, standing back to take in the work in full and to check she hadn't missed anything. She squinted with one eye, as artists often did. She'd never actually seen anything differently by doing this, but she didn't feel like a proper artist without doing it. She moved forwards once more, making a final adjustment, when she heard the sound of approaching footsteps.

'Aaron?' she called nervously to the darkness.

'Yeah, it's me,' Aaron's voice said, and he soon appeared around the corner. He noticed Penny lowering her chisel and hammer that she had briefly raised in readiness for self-defence.

'Is that thing even sharp anymore?' he joked, eyeing the chisel.

'Barely,' she chuckled. 'But I could still hit you pretty hard with it.' She paused for a moment. 'Where have you been?' she demanded.

'Long story. We've got to go,' Aaron replied urgently. He seemed distracted, but excited.

'But, hang on. You haven't even looked at my work,' Penny said, a little disheartened.

Aaron sighed. Clearly something had happened to him whilst he had been away. He looked around at Penny's finished piece of work and nodded, impressed.

'It's awesome,' he said, trying to sound convincing. Penny rolled her eyes; she wasn't buying it.

'What's the rush then?' she said, getting to the point. Apparently there was no way of getting around it.

'We've got time,' Aaron said, excited. Penny was suddenly confused.

'That's what I've been saying! What's going on?'

'Like I said it's a long story, but I can explain it on the way.'

'The way where? The exit?' she said hopefully.

'No, no. Back to the tree.'

Penny didn't say anything more for a while. They had quickly set off after Penny had stored her tools away once more, full of worry. She hoped it was nothing bad, but she almost didn't want to ask Aaron. She didn't even know how he found out about whatever it was. There was no way he could have walked all the way to the tree. The silence became too painful, and after a few minutes Penny had to ask what was going on.

'Is it bad?' she asked weakly. She almost shut her eyes. She really didn't want to know if it *was* bad.

'No, No. It's definitely good,' Aaron replied cryptically.

Penny stared at him, disgruntled, and he quickly got the message. 'I met this guy whilst I was walking.' He paused, looking at Penny poignantly. 'He told me about a new girl who's just joined the Maze. She had an idea before she came in that could help us, and now she's done it. She's put up a watch right by your tree!' he said breathlessly as he sped along, Penny struggling to keep up.

'You're joking!' Penny breathed heavily. By the expression on Aaron's face, she knew he wasn't. His face was full of a feverous giddiness that Penny couldn't help catching. The fact that they had chosen a spot right next to her tree meant so much to Penny. It reaffirmed Aaron's suggestion that it had great importance to those in the Maze, as clearly somebody else had thought so, too. At that moment she wanted to create a whole forest of carvings. Penny figured she would need to sharpen her chisel first, though. Fortunately, there was quite a lot of spare stone around to do so.

They dashed through the corridors, both excited to reach the tree. Penny cursed her luck that they happened to be just about as far away as possible from the tree within the confines of the Maze. As she strode as fast as she physically could, she felt an excited buzz within the Maze, almost coming from the very walls as if they knew something important was happening. She wasn't sure if she was just imagining it.

They had been walking for at least an hour when they came across a rare opportunity. On their left, as they came towards the end of one of the many stretching corridors, there stood an open door with luminous white light flowing out into the dim hallway beyond. Penny shielded her eyes which were really not used to this sort of lighting — they had grown accustomed to the general gloom of the Maze.

Penny and Aaron looked at each other. They had both

been awake for an unusually prolonged time, with Aaron walking around in exile as Penny worked on her newest artwork. Penny knew full well there were several hours of walking between them and the tree. She was sure Aaron would have realised this too, what with his photographic brain. She expected he had a full map of the Maze in his head at all times. Though, this wouldn't necessarily help, with the Maze always changing.

The moment was a little awkward. Penny had learnt to trust Aaron with confidence by now and they had both slept in the open with the other sat nearby. It was an entirely different scenario if they were both to sleep in the locked bathroom together. Aaron didn't seem to want to make the decision for her, which she appreciated, but it didn't make it any easier for her to make. It felt to Penny as if they stood there in a palpable silence for hours, but eventually she had to make the decision.

She stepped forward into the bright light, feeling a slight warmth spread over her skin that made her arm hair stand on end. Aaron followed slowly. Penny noticed he was working hard to not make anything awkward in a potentially uncomfortable moment, and she appreciated him trying, but if anything it made the situation a little more awkward. If he'd pretended as if nothing was wrong then there would have been far less trouble. Penny quickly busied herself at the simple basin, determined to avoid eye contact wherever possible. Soon enough they had both had a thorough wash, and they settled in opposite sides of the room without a word spoken. It was the first time Penny had felt uncomfortable around Aaron since they'd first met. Aaron was too busy looking at the small plant in the corner, at that moment, to notice her looking at him.

'On my first day, I cut a piece of that tree off and I've carried it ever since,' Aaron said quietly, breaking the silence. It was something so simple, but it reminded Penny of Aaron's quirks and she soon began to relax once more, eventually drifting off to sleep

*

The next morning, or rather after they had both woken up, they set off in a hurry. For a while, Penny had been forced to forget about their target of reaching the tree to see this watch. Her focus had been on more immediate matters, but now it was all she could think about. It took surprisingly little time for them to reach their destination; Penny's mind had been preoccupied with other things, and she and Aaron passed a lot of the time quibbling over another of his brainteasers. Penny wasn't a massive fan of some of Aaron's discussions, but there was little else to do to pass the time.

When they turned the corner to the tree, knowing this time exactly where they were, Penny was shocked to see several people stood around the corridor. These people were all staring at the wall and acting very oddly. It was as if they were statues; they were stood so still. As Penny and Aaron approached, only one of the five people looked around in recognition of new arrivals.

Penny quickly followed their eyeline and her own eyes fell upon the watch that was causing such a stir. She had barely seen this many people in the entire time she'd been in the Maze, and suddenly these five people were all stood together in a single corridor. With Penny and Aaron, that now made seven people.

The watch was fairly basic as watches go. It wasn't flashy with gleaming gold straps, but still held a simplistic splendour. The centre was white, with no numbers, only markings showing the hours. The rim of the watch gleamed a shiny silver, reflecting a distorted version of the seven people opposite. The straps matched the hands; bold and

124

black; and were apparently made of leather, though Penny suspected it was faux leather.

Penny looked across at the five people to her left and noticed they were all acting peculiarly, and all doing the same thing, as if they had been hypnotised by the watch. For a moment Penny was a little troubled by this notion, until she worked out what the people were doing. Each of them would occasionally look at the watch for a few seconds, then shut their eyes for around ten seconds. The woman furthest away from Penny, who appeared to be the oldest, had had her eyes shut for a full minute before she reopened them. Penny quickly realised they were trying to learn to memorise time. It was a little ambitious, Penny thought, trying to learn how to count in exact minutes. What if you wanted to think about something else for a while? Penny noticed, when she glanced back at the watch, that there was a small note next to it. She cleared her throat, stepping forward slowly.

'Err, do you mind if I…?' she asked cautiously, pointing delicately to the note. Nobody replied. She took that as a yes and leaned forward to read it. It told her that at twelve it had been seven days since she had entered the Maze. The only problem with that was she didn't know how many twelves ago that was.

'Does anyone know how long ago that note was put up?' she asked hastily to the crowd — if you could call five people a crowd. Down here in the Maze it definitely was, at least. Nobody replied again. She walked huffily back to Aaron who was still busy taking in the scene and told him to read the note. He did so, and soon returned.

'It's been a day, I think. There's some scratching underneath the note which I think says days, and then a single line.' Penny didn't want to think what that person had used to scratch that into the stone. Aaron appeared to think the same thing as he all of a sudden reached for his pocket. He pulled out his tiny pen and his copy of *Ulysses*, and looked meaningfully at them for a moment, then moved to turn back to the watch.

'Are you sure, Aaron?' Penny asked quickly. She knew exactly what he intended to do. 'Those are the only things you have from your sister. You might not see them again.'

'I can see them whenever I want,' he said, pointing to his head and smiling gently.

After a few minutes, three of the gathered group had meandered off alone. Penny wondered why they weren't talking, why they didn't want to reach out to others while they could; this seemed like the perfect opportunity. *Maybe they're foreign, and can't speak English,* she thought. Eventually the other two drifted off, too, leaving Penny and Aaron alone with the watch.

Penny had taken everything in by now, but she still wanted more time to just look, kind of like when she used to go to the zoo. You could stare at a penguin all day and never get bored, even though you've seen everything it could do. Penny guessed that was because they were out of the ordinary, just like this watch, it was something different. If she had seen a penguin every day of her life she probably wouldn't be as interested in them.

The truth was that this watch *had* changed a lot, but at the end of the day it was *just* a watch. Penny marvelled at the idea. Just over a week ago she probably wouldn't have

Two days had passed since McKenzie had met Natasha, and he hadn't seen her since. He had returned to the watch three times in the hope that he might meet her there, but each time he'd had no luck. There was almost always somebody there now, though. Sometimes there was a whole group of people. From what he guessed, just about every person in the Maze must have seen it at least once.

He never spoke to anyone when he had visited. He would try to wait around the corner for them to leave but the last time he had done so, he had waited so long he became fed up and just walked over silently. Just like everyone else he had tried to get used to keeping track of time in his own head, but this had its drawbacks. For one, he wasn't very good at it. He had started with ten second intervals, but no matter how hard he tried he kept opening his eyes on nine seconds. He tried to correct this by just waiting for well over ten seconds but ended up looking at twenty-two seconds; a little *too* overcorrected.

The other downside was that as soon as he left the watch and his mind began to wander off, he had no idea what the time was again. It was impossible to keep track of time constantly. His thoughts kept drifting to Natasha instead, theorising about how she was handling the Maze on her own, then questioning if she would even be on her own. He remembered his first few days in the Maze, alone for days on end, slowly losing sense of himself. In fact, other than that brief but brilliant time with Natasha, he had been entirely alone. He began to doubt if Natasha had even really been a prisoner like him. Maybe it was all a plan by that Diego Flint because he'd begun to feel sorry for them.

McKenzie felt nothing but contempt for Flint. No matter how much he thought it would help them become "better people", there must be a better, less cruel way of going about it. Maybe just stick someone's head under the water until they see the light. That seemed far less tortuous.

After another two days of solitude, McKenzie had begun to feel dark thoughts creeping their way into the back of his mind. The brief moment of hope and excitement had intensified them, if anything. He began to think everything was a twisted joke being played on him. He cursed himself for not saying anything to Natasha and just agreeing to go their separate ways. Everything had seemed so bright and brilliant at that moment when he naively thought he would be seeing Natasha again in an hour or two. He'd forgotten how this place could be.

From the brief amount of time he'd gotten to know Natasha, McKenzie guessed she was probably exploring every nook and cranny trying to find an exit, trying to discover every little secret this place had. He almost resented her resilient attitude. He wished he was someone who could just get up and go when the going got tough. But he was too busy feeling sorry for himself.

This was never helped when he was hungry, and he was certainly hungry now. The last time he had eaten was the scraps he had collected not long before meeting Natasha. He wished he'd come across those two people again, those that he was certain must have trashed the food room. He wasn't sure what they looked like, as he had only seen a little of them, but he was sure he would recognise their voices. They had been playing in McKenzie's head ever since. He just didn't understand why anyone would do that. It didn't much help the limited spirit of community within the Maze.

That had become his main focus. He had given up on Natasha for the time being and tried to focus on finding another food room, hoping this one wouldn't be trashed.

He was beginning to get that feeling when he was so hungry that he didn't even feel hungry anymore, but he knew he needed to eat. He felt weak and his vision was a little blurred as he stumbled his way along. It was like being drunk, but less pleasant.

He turned a corner on his way and nearly stumbled backwards, he was so shocked. Stood before him was none other than his old fiancée, Jessie. But it couldn't be. *How could it be?* She was a good person, there was no way she would end up in here. Then again, she had probably thought the same thing about him. He looked her up and down in silence, still a little stunned.

'W- what… h- how?' McKenzie stammered.

'Hey, Mac,' Jessie said with a straight face. She appeared to have a faint glow, though McKenzie wasn't sure if this was just his hungry brain imagining it. He had thought about Jessie so much over the last week that he'd built up a flawless image of her in his mind. McKenzie didn't know what to say. He had so much he wanted to say, but he just didn't know where to start. Sorry seemed like a good place.

'What did you do?' he asked in shock.

'I didn't do anything, you idiot. This isn't me,' Jessie said affectionately. McKenzie was now thoroughly confused.

'What do you mean?'

'I'm not really here!' Jessie spelled out plainly, and finally the penny dropped. Of course Jessie wasn't really here. He had been correct; she was a far better person than he was.

'Why are you here?' he asked after another minute's silence.

'Oh, I don't know that. Come on, you've seen enough films. I'm in *your* imagination; if you don't know, I won't know either. The only guess I would make is that maybe there's something you want to say.'

McKenzie nodded solemnly. He knew this, but it was so

hard. Probably the hardest thing he had ever done. He had never had an opportunity to say anything to the real Jessie. Pretty soon after his arrest he was in court and then within a fortnight he was here in the Maze. It had all happened so quickly, and he had been so self-involved, he had never thought about the fallout from Jessie's side.

Chapter 23

Yazmin's life in the Maze had been an extreme rollercoaster of emotions. The first few days had been a bottomless pit of misery — and then she had met TJ. For some time, she had felt almost happy, though she wasn't quite sure what happiness felt like anymore. The moments they had spent in the food room together had definitely been her highest so far, closely followed by the time they had found the watch.

Each of these moments had brought her closer to the outside world, where Yazmin knew she belonged. That was the hardest thing for her in the Maze. She was most likely the only person in here who knew for sure that she shouldn't be. Ever since the food room, Yazmin's mood had slowly deteriorated. She was incredibly grateful for TJ and everything he had done for her, but they were very different people. He tried to occupy her troubled mind with distracting games and conversations, but nothing seemed to help her. She had begun to rely on moments like finding the watch to keep her going, but these were rare at best. In fact, she couldn't see what else could come their way to help her now.

Neither Yazmin nor TJ had any ideas left. Their conversations had become a little stale as both began to wear a little thin. Each of them relied on the other for new ideas on coping with the Maze, on new conversations, and on new ideas to help them find an exit. Unfortunately, neither of them had a clue. There was nothing to help them down here. This highlighted the difference between TJ and Yazmin's personalities: TJ fought hard against difficulties. He was clearly a competitive person and when he faced troubles like this it made him strive harder to beat them. Yazmin was at the other end of the spectrum. Her personality was content to let the waves crash over her limply.

This came to fruition after ten days of the Maze, six days since they had met. They hadn't been able to find any food or a bathroom for an entire day — the only thing they had to look forward to — and they were both on edge. Every little thing TJ did started to wind her up. The way he swung his arms like a gorilla as he walked, constantly bashing against her, his random loud sighs that interrupted lengthy silences, along with his stomping footsteps. Deep down she knew none of this was his fault, in fact quite the opposite. He had done everything for her. Without him, Yazmin probably wouldn't have even made it this far. But these rational thoughts had been overtaken by her distraught brain, taking all logic out of the question.

They had reached the end of a corridor and they both stood still, as they often did. They had no idea where to go or what they were even aiming for by this point. They must have circled the entire Maze three times together, yet there didn't seem to be any sign of an exit anywhere, no silent and wispy breeze of fresh air. As usual, they looked at each other for answers, but soon realised the other person had little more idea than they did.

'What do you think?' TJ asked, trying to sound calm.

'I don't know,' Yazmin replied desperately.

'Well, I reckon that the food hall is…' but Yazmin never heard where TJ reckoned the food hall was. She wasn't listening. She couldn't listen to another long speech in which he thought out loud about the possible whereabouts of food, when in actual fact neither of them had a clue. '…What do you think?' TJ asked at last.

'Like I said: I don't know,' Yazmin snapped. TJ looked hurt by this; he was just trying to help. 'Why don't we just rest for a bit?' she added weakly, slumping to the floor and leaning against the icy wall.

'We've only just got going again!' TJ said, exasperated.

'Yes, but neither of us has a clue anyway, do we? At least if we stay still we can't be getting any further away from the food.' Even as Yazmin said this, she knew there was absolutely no logic to it, but she didn't really care. Sure, they weren't getting any further away, but they weren't getting any closer either.

'That doesn't even make sense!' TJ yelled.

'Whatever. Look, if you want to carry on, just go,' Yazmin said harshly. There was a long silence after a moment. TJ looked shocked that she would even suggest this, but after a minute he recomposed himself.

'I can't keep carrying you,' he said softly.

'I'm not asking you to carry me,' Yazmin replied bluntly. She knew he had meant metaphorically. She just wanted some time alone; she actually *wanted* him to leave now. A further silence came as TJ just stared in disbelief at Yazmin. She couldn't bring herself to look back, so resolved to stare directly at the floor between her feet.

'Fine,' TJ said, defeated. He turned his back on Yazmin, still slouched against the wall, and made to head to the right of the junction. Yazmin didn't break her gaze from the floor, as if it were the most interesting piece of flooring she had ever seen, but she could tell TJ had paused to look back. After a moment or two in which he waited, expecting her to say something, he stomped away and out of sight. Yazmin allowed herself to let out a deep breath she had been holding on to and with it flowed more tears. It felt like a dam had been built in her tear ducts over the past few days and it had finally been broken.

Chapter 24

Jessie sat in the old, worn armchair, vaguely watching a repeat of a nineties sitcom on the TV, waiting for McKenzie to get home. She was curled up in a ball under a knitted blanket that her mother had made her when she was little. It barely even covered her legs, but she didn't care. Somehow the warmth of memories carried through it, making it warmer than any other blanket she'd ever owned.

Laughter rained from the TV screen, which glared out around the room it was too big to fit into, after a particularly funny quip from one of the characters. Jessie let out a snort of laughter despite the fact that she had seen the show at least twenty times before. She was a little worried about McKenzie, and the comfort of something she knew so well seemed to relax her nerves better than any herbal teas or other remedies recommended to her. He had been working hard for weeks now in the build up to Christmas and it was beginning to take its toll.

He'd been snappy on the rare occasions they'd actually been able to spend some time together, and she was worried he was overexerting himself. He was a long-distance haul driver, and tiredness and the road were never a good combination. Jessie had expected him home by now; he'd messaged to say he should be home by seven but it was now half past eight and there was still no sign. Naturally, she checked her phone every minute or so to check she hadn't missed a notification, not that she ever did. It was quite hard to miss her notification sound; it was the voice of Shaggy from *Scooby Doo* shouting "Zoinks", which often made her chuckle.

She checked again and still nothing. Instead, she contented herself to scroll through her social media feeds for the fifteenth time in the past hour, reading people's updates that she really didn't care about. One thing that seemed definite, she must have been the only person from her school year that didn't have a child yet. That didn't bother Jessie really, she wasn't the kind of person who had to compare herself to others, she just wished they could not post pictures every five minutes.

She quickly locked her phone again, feeling the strains of a long-running headache that had begun at work earlier that day. Jessie was a "Play Supervisor" at a nursery in the town centre and the children had been particularly raucous that day. She didn't think they were old enough to go crazy about Christmas, but apparently she was wrong. Ever since, she had held a dull ache in her temple that reappeared whenever she strained her eyes. It probably wasn't helping that she was checking her phone every minute.

After another half an hour, the pain was becoming too severe and the show had finished, leaving nothing else worth watching. It was quite impressive to cover four hundred channels with pure drivel, just orange people shouting at each other and the like. She switched the TV off and climbed out of the chair slowly, her head throbbing a little as she stood. Hoping she could close her eyes for a while to ease the pain, she headed straight upstairs to bed, quickly changing and brushing her teeth before cosying up under a thick duvet. It was much needed on a cold night like this. It didn't take long for her to drift off. She didn't even have to read like usual, after all the kids had been running her ragged all day.

She woke three hours later, looking to her right to see if McKenzie had returned and was shocked to see he wasn't beside her. She hoped she had just been woken by his return, but she could hear nothing from downstairs but for the gentle humming of the fridge in the kitchen directly below her. She got up hastily, pushing the warm duvet off and making her way to the closed bedroom door.

She silently made her way down the steps, carefully avoiding the squeaky spots as she was so used to, feeling McKenzie might have decided to sleep downstairs to avoid disturbing her. She was partly correct. McKenzie was indeed asleep in the very armchair she had vacated earlier in the night. However, judging by the reek of alcohol emanating from his direction, he hadn't decided to sleep there out of curtesy. It looked like he had passed out pretty quickly; he hadn't bothered to turn the heating on or even cover himself, and now his hands were pink in the cold.

Jessie understood that he needed to unwind, but she didn't know why he hadn't just messaged to tell her he was going for a drink. Maybe he thought she would object. She swiftly walked over and pulled his own blanket over him. She also thought it would be nice to put on their little electric fire, so he was nice and cosy when he woke up. McKenzie didn't stir as she moved around him, sound asleep with only the streetlight outside breaking the darkness of their living room, until the fire sparked into life. Before she went back upstairs, Jessie placed a small glass of water next to McKenzie on the small table next to him, then returned to bed as quietly as possible, intending to read for a while. Typically, she didn't really feel tired now she had woken up.

She read for almost an hour before her eyes began drooping once more as she lay on her side in the gentle light of the bedside lamp. She finished the chapter she was reading and almost instantly she dozed off into an uneasy sleep. She was expecting McKenzie to emerge at any moment and was wary he'd be in one of his moods again. They seemed to have become far more regular as of late.

Indeed, soon enough she was woken by the heavy footsteps of McKenzie downstairs. She switched the bedside lamp back on, blinding herself in the process, and rushed to the door, swinging it open quickly as she heard McKenzie heading up the stairs. She tried to force herself into a welcoming smile.

'Hey Mac,' she said softly as he came onto the landing.

'Don't play dumb with me,' McKenzie replied aggressively. Jessie's smile quickly faded into a look of worry.

'W- what do you mean?' she stammered, gripping the door tightly with her left hand.

'Where were you? Out with those stupid friends again, I suppose?'

'What? No, I went to bed early, I-'

'I don't want to hear your made-up excuses. I'm sick and tired of working all day and then you're not even here when I get in!' McKenzie yelled, spitting in his anger.

'I'm sorry. As I was going to say, I had a long day-'

'Long day! Really? Those kids a bit too much for you?' he said in mock concern.

Jessie looked at him in incredulity. He had never once insulted her job before.

'What's going on with you?' she asked firmly, giving up on defending herself. She was fed up with being treated like this lately. This wasn't the McKenzie she had first met.

'Oh, I'll tell you what's going on,' McKenzie started. 'I've been working my ass off for months now, whilst you go off enjoying yourself with our money. I come home and there's no food, no heating *and* no you.' His voice was alarmingly loud, and Jessie began to get a little worried that the neighbours would hear. The walls in their terraced house weren't exactly the thickest.

'Look,' she said quietly, trying to ease the situation, 'why don't we get a coffee or something and then we can talk. I'm here now, aren't I?'

This didn't seem to work. McKenzie stepped forward intimidatingly, bearing down on Jessie who was considerably shorter than he was.

'Why are you talking to me as if I'm a mental patient?' he said through gritted teeth.

Jessie didn't know what to say to this. She didn't know what to do. She felt strangely scared of someone she trusted more than anyone. There was a moment of fractious silence as McKenzie loomed over her threatening and finally, she decided she needed to leave, quickly making to move past.

But McKenzie didn't allow her to get past. He pushed her firmly backwards and she crashed painfully into the bedroom door, letting out a small squeak, more from shock than pain. She quickly tried to back away from McKenzie as he advanced, but he was quickly upon her again. He shoved her forcefully once more. Her head hit the wall as she fell backwards.

She crumpled to the floor, whimpering with tears of desperation. This person in front of her wasn't McKenzie, it was somebody else. Something else. She wanted the old McKenzie back, who would surprise her with a souvenir from his travels every day, the one who had proposed in the park at sunset. As his shadow from the landing light loomed over Jessie's quivering form once more, there was suddenly another noise. McKenzie didn't seem to have noticed. He picked Jessie up, grabbing a handful of her lavender-coloured nightshirt, ripping it slightly at the seams. Just as it appeared there was no escape, Jessie heard footsteps below them. McKenzie still didn't notice. He slammed her against the wall, her shirt still clenched tightly in his fist. A moment later their neighbour, Dan, came bounding into the room, followed closely by his wife, Hannah.

For an instant the four of them stood motionless, Dan and Hannah taking in the scene in shock as McKenzie relinquished his grip on Jessie's shirt. She breathed heavily. It seemed like McKenzie had suddenly realised what he had been doing, like he had been possessed. He walked away from Jessie with his hands on his head. Jessie quickly scampered over to Dan and Hannah, and Hannah embraced her kindly as violent sobs erupted from her. Dan was staring at McKenzie heatedly. The next thing Jessie saw was the flashing of blue and red lights from outside.

Chapter 25

The Maze had certainly settled down considerably after the first week. After a flurry of activity following the arrival of Natasha and the watch, the Mazers had quickly become quiet. The only exception was Yazmin and TJ, who had been involved in an epic fallout. It was plainly evident this needed to happen for both their sakes, but Flint now worried for Yazmin. She had immediately reverted to first day Yazmin and had been the in the same state now for three days. He didn't want to repeat the cycle; that wouldn't exactly show progress.

Flint was facing his own personal battles, too. He was fighting a losing battle to control his patience, always tempted to throw in curveballs to speed up the process of the Maze. He kept reminding himself that only two weeks had passed. In a normal prison, the prisoners would barely have settled in by this point.

The previous day, Diego had returned to the daunting board room for his weekly update, which had been relatively uneventful yet painful, nonetheless. He had expected much of the same as the previous week, but it appeared that had been a one-off. The board covered every detail in great scrutiny, with particular focus on the watch. Flint explained eloquently his feelings on the topic but judging by the unconvinced faces, most of the board members were very much in agreement with Alex. Flint got a little frustrated that nobody seemed to understand the concept of the Maze; it wasn't to make the Mazers miserable wretches incapable of feeling normal human emotions. They needed basic human necessities to facilitate their recoveries.

He and Alex had settled their brief quarrel. Alex had insisted on joining Diego for a drink in the hotel bar. She had far greater empathy for his situation than anyone else and Diego figured it was because she actually saw him as another human being, not just the creator of the Maze, or as their boss — he appreciated this more than he'd been able to let on. Diego had relaxed whilst they sat at the bar together; it was the first time he'd been able to since they had opened. It didn't last long. He was soon being called back to the control room through his beeper, a little worse for wear than he should have been after a few more drinks than he'd planned on having. He thanked Alex for being a good friend and apologised profusely once more before steadily making his way back to the control room, determined not to waver in his line. He didn't want anyone, not even his security team, to think he was drunk.

Naturally, he didn't pull this off. Scott had been left in charge for the night whilst both Alex and Benji were away, under the pretence that Diego could help in an emergency. Diego walked into the room as calmly as possible, trying hard not to get too close to anyone for fear of them catching his breath; that would be a big giveaway. Immediately Scott came bounding over like an excitable puppy and started talking to Diego far too quickly for him to comprehend. After a moment's pause, Diego asked him to calm down and say it again, as if he had been talking too fast for *anyone* to understand. It said something about Scott that he thought this was perfectly plausible.

It turned out Scott had been trying to tell Diego about an issue with McKenzie, but from what he could discern there was no immediate danger, so he frustratedly told Scott that he was only to be called in an absolute emergency, continuing his act that Scott was being completely irrational. Somehow it seemed to work, or at least he thought it had. Scott had said, 'OK,' and marched back off to the front of the room, and Diego quickly turned away, looking to escape before any more questions came his way.

Only the next morning when he saw Scott again did he realise he hadn't been so subtle.

Scott brightly asked him, 'Are you feeling better this morning?' and Diego soon realised Scott was well aware of his level of intoxication. He ignored the question and quickly hurried over to his usual spot, where a fruit smoothie was already sat waiting for him, along with Alex. Her eyebrows were raised humorously as she watched him sit down beside her.

'Thought you might need that this morning,' she said as Diego picked up the smoothie.

'Yeah, thanks.'

'Maybe one too many last night, for someone on call?'

'No-one died, did they?' he said defensively. 'Scottie had it under control. Besides, you can hardly talk. How are you so… normal this morning?'

'It's called coffee,' she joked, waving her empty cup.

'Yeah, I might need some of that today.'

After a few minutes of sitting in silence Diego got to work on catching up on the night's action, starting with McKenzie. Watching back his night's movements, something was certainly troubling him. Over the past two weeks Flint had seen several incidents which had led him to believe McKenzie was struggling mentally, possibly even hallucinating. When he stopped fast forwarding his brief recap, he was sure something was wrong. He could see McKenzie's lips moving. He had no audio, but he could only presume he was talking to someone, someone who wasn't actually there. He waved Scott over, still watching McKenzie's odd actions intently.

'How can I help, Diego?' Scott asked. He'd finally gotten used to not saying sir.

'Did you get any audio on McKenzie?' Flint questioned him hastily.

'Ah, yes.' Scott paused for a moment, fidgeting his feet a little. 'It appears he thinks he's talking to Jessie,' Scott said uncomfortably.

'Jessie?'

'His ex-partner,' Scott prompted.

'You mean, the one he-'

'Yeah…'

'Oh, wow,' Diego said meaningfully, looking at Alex. They had discussed McKenzie's backstory just the other day. He didn't seem that type, but then again is there a set type of person? He must have been carrying an immense sense of guilt around with him. Diego felt goosebumps appear under his crisp suit as he watched a teary-eyed McKenzie converse with the imaginary Jessie.

'Do we know if Diane is in yet?' Diego asked Scott and Alex. Diane was head of a three-strong Psychologist team based within the compound that Flint had hired to help give evaluations of the Mazers and assess odd behaviours. This certainly seemed like her area of expertise.

'Yeah, I think I saw her light on as I came in,' Alex said.

'Good. I think we should get her opinion on Mr. Symms, here,' Diego asserted. 'Malcolm. Could you go and fetch Mrs. Cooper please?' he called to an older member of the operating team that happened to be walking past. Diego knew the name of just about every member of the operating team by now. They probably thought he was trying to be a good boss by getting personal, but in truth it would have been awkward if he didn't know their names. He sometimes spent up to ten hours at a time in the same room as them.

Ten minutes later Malcolm walked back in with Diane in tow. Diego had been beginning to wish he had asked one of the spritelier young operators to go in Malcom's place. He'd moved away from his usual spot, thinking it would be more professional to sit at one of the circular meeting tables at the very back of the room as opposed to the small desk filled with papers and computer screens. Diane took a seat opposite. Her face was difficult to read, but Diego felt a certain coldness coming from her. It made him a little nervous, as if he were back in the board room. After all, Diane was easily ten years his senior.

'Hi Diane, thanks for coming so quickly. I wanted to get your professional opinion on a couple of the Mazers, if that's okay?' he asked politely.

'That's what I'm here for,' she replied bluntly.

'Right, okay. So, the first is Mr. McKenzie Symms,' Diego persevered, pushing the tablet showing McKenzie's file across the table.

'Ah, yes. I thought it would be,' Diane said coolly, not looking down at the tablet. 'What did you want to know?'

'Well, we believe he is talking to Jessie. Is that right?'

'Yes, it appears so.'

'Obviously this isn't normal behaviour, but should we be concerned?' Diego asked tentatively.

'I don't think so,' Diane said calmly. She seemed to defrost a little, losing some of her coldness, more comfortable talking about what she knew best. 'Often in cases like this there is a large amount of guilt, particularly towards one person. It is not uncommon, therefore, for the person in question to become apparent in the offender's mind, and in some cases think they can see them. Either way, this usually only lasts for a short time. Just long enough for them to say what they need to say.'

Diego nodded thoughtfully, running a hand through his stubble. From what Diane was saying, it seemed McKenzie just felt he needed to get an apology to Jessie in whatever form was possible. Diego thought about whether McKenzie had managed to do this yet, but he doubted it, as it appeared McKenzie was still talking to someone. Diane had suggested Jessie would dematerialise in McKenzie's mind only once he had made peace with her.

'Okay, what about Miss Yazmin Tracey?' he asked, trying to sound as formal as possible. He got the feeling Diane assumed this was all a big experiment to him, that he didn't care about the people at all. He was keen to prove her wrong.

'Another interesting case,' Diane stated. 'It is much harder to get an understanding of her thinking process without speaking to her...' She broke off, almost suggesting that she be allowed to speak to Yazmin.

'I'm afraid I can't allow that,' Diego said softly. He quickly noticed the look of disappointment on Diane's face and sought to explain himself. 'If Yazmin were to get an experience of the outside world, even a conversation with you, it might damage her position within the Maze. She may circle to even greater depths,' he finished. This sentiment seemed to please Diane considerably. 'What can you infer from her behaviours? What possible explanations can you come up with?' Flint asked, looking to seize on the opportunity.

'Well, the most obvious deduction is that she appears depressed. Usually with depression there is some kind of trauma involved. This could simply be the trauma of being within the Maze, but it *does* seem more than that.'

'Yes?' Flint raised his eyebrows hopefully. Diane sighed heavily, as if she were unwilling to say what she was thinking.

'It... it would suggest she feels she does not belong in the Maze. As in, she does not believe she was guilty,' Diane emphasised. 'If I were to give an honest opinion, I would suggest that her case should be re-investigated. I have taken a brief look, and something doesn't quite add up,' she finished dramatically. Diego frowned, looking straight at Diane.

'Okay, thank you,' Diego said. Diane made to stand.

'Erm, before you go, just one last thing.' Slowly, Diane returned to her seat. 'You have been watching the behaviours of the Mazers closely. Is there anyone else you feel we need to keep a closer eye on?'

'Natasha Oleksandr,' she said, smiling knowingly. 'She does not appear to possess any danger to herself or others, but she is the only person who seems completely unaffected by the Maze. She has a purpose.'

'Thank you,' Diego said again. This time it was clear that was the end of their conversation. Diane stood, straightened her blazer, and left with a nod to Diego. When he was certain she was gone, Diego stood, too, returning to his messy work corner.

'Julie, get me all files on Miss Tracey's court case, please, and hurry. Take Lisa with you,' he instructed the middle-aged operator who happened to be passing him.

'Yes, Diego,' Julie squeaked before hurrying off to grab Lisa.

Diego was pleased to see her scurrying her way over to him with a wad of papers just a few minutes later.

'Thank you very much,' he said, impressed. She smiled and half-curtsied before straightening her glasses and scurrying away once more. Diego rolled his eyes again. Sometimes he liked the power of his position, but he would never get used to the reverence that came with it. He immediately got to work burying himself in the intriguing case, trying to figure out exactly what Diane had meant.

Chapter 26

Penny and Aaron hadn't spoken for almost an entire day now. Penny found it was just about comforting enough to have someone by your side to justify the stiff silence, but it was becoming harder to ignore all the time. Neither of them had said anything when they had woken up, without much to be said. That was the problem. They had run through a whole range of topics to talk about, and they had just about run dry of anything in common. Down here, there was never anything new to talk about. For a while they had discussed the watch and some of the new objects that appeared alongside it. Soon after they first found the watch, a lonely pen appeared followed quickly by a sharp knife and an empty flask. The items had stopped appearing so frequently, and those that remained had become tiresome far too quickly, just like every other topic. The biggest issue they faced was a lack of any common ground. They had been thrown together into the Maze, and if it weren't for that they would never have spoken, let alone spent every minute together for an entire week.

Occasionally they met another person, but the fact that there was two of them seemed to scare them off pretty quickly. They all seemed scared they would be overpowered, two-to-one. They had brief conversations, that never satisfied Penny's need to talk to someone other than Aaron for a change, and then quickly moved on. It seemed incredibly difficult to come up with small talk in this place, and more often than not these brief encounters were punctuated with awkward silences, none of them able to entertain a decent discussion.

As they ambled along another long corridor, they came across something different for once. They walked past lantern after lantern, split in their regular intervals of twenty-nine paces — for Penny, twenty-seven for Aaron — when, suddenly, they reached a spot of darkness. One of the lanterns had gone out, leaving forty paces of pitch-black darkness between the two lanterns on either side, still glowing gold. It was so unusual to come across something different in the Maze that both Penny and Aaron looked at each blankly; these lanterns had always been a guaranteed constant. It appeared they might finally need to break their stubborn silence.

'Do you think we should go through?' Aaron asked uncertainly.

'Yeah, it should be fine,' Penny replied nonchalantly, taking a step forward. Aaron grabbed her arm to stop her.

'What if someone broke it on purpose?' he asked, full of suspicion.

'We'd still be able to see their silhouette if they were hiding, wouldn't we?' Penny indicated. They both squinted into the darkness. They could see all the way through to the next patch of light, and there certainly didn't seem to be anyone hiding, unless they were lying flat on the ground. Aaron got on his hands and knees to check and finally seemed convinced there was no issue. They set off once more, but Penny had to stop to investigate the light. It wasn't smashed or damaged, it had just gone out.

'I don't know why, but I never really thought about the lights going out,' Penny thought out loud. 'I assumed they would last forever, but I guess they are just the same as any other bulb.'

'Mmm,' Aaron sounded in agreement. He seemed skittish and kept looking around sharply. Penny sighed heavily and continued through the dark in a mood. They couldn't even hold a conversation for two minutes anymore, thanks to Aaron's neurotic ways.

They continued on, returning to the silence only broken

by their echoing footsteps as they trudged onwards. Penny began to think about Toby again, like she had been a lot recently. She knew it was stupid; he'd let her down at the worst possible time. She wondered what he was up to at the moment and, as most people did, she wondered if he thought about her. She wished he knew what she was going through and hoped he felt bad about what he'd done.

Thinking about her history made her consider what Aaron was thinking about during their lengthy silences. She didn't even know if he had a girlfriend outside of here, or if he had been rejected just like her as soon as things got tough. Now that she thought about it, she didn't know where he was from or in fact anything about his life before the Maze. They'd been too busy talking about completely superficial things such as their favourite films and their choices for desert island discs.

She had just opened her mouth to voice this when they reached a turning and were shocked to see a young woman looking worse for wear, crumpled on the floor. Once again, they looked to each other as they both took in the young woman. It was a bit callous, but one of the first things Penny could think was hoping that *she* didn't look that bad. She hadn't seen herself since entering the Maze, and she hoped her hair wasn't so matted and her skin not so pale as this girl's.

Penny bent over to check on her, considerably concerned, given her appearance at first sight. At least she was still breathing, but her breaths were weak and shallow. Even compared to the slightly deprived people Penny had met in the Maze so far, this girl was *thin*. As she tried to get the girl to sit up, she could feel every bone in her spine. She hoped there was nothing more sinister involved than a simple lack of nutrition. Penny would struggle to ever sleep again if she knew this girl had suffered any sort of assault in here. So far, Penny had done a pretty good job of pretending that wasn't an issue in here, and at least she had Aaron around for now.

The young woman didn't seem capable of waking or of acknowledging their presence at all. Penny shook her a little to test her reactions but got no response.

'What do you think we should do?' Penny asked Aaron, her voice shaking a little. Their idea that someone was watching over them here in the Maze was unravelling in front of Penny's eyes. Surely someone watching this wouldn't just allow this girl to get into this state Aaron was watching on with concern, too, but he also seemed a little reluctant to help.

'I'm not sure we can do anything,' Aaron said, still stood several feet away.

'What?' Penny said, indignation strong in her voice.

'Look at her,' Aaron said, a slight hint of disgust on his face. 'She obviously wants to be left like this.'

'What are you talking about? How can you possibly know that?' Penny snapped angrily.

'I can't, for sure. It's just… it's just I've never believed in helping people who don't want to help themselves,' Aaron said hesitantly, trying to avoid a confrontation.

'We don't know that she hasn't been trying to help herself. We don't know anything down here. Maybe she got lost. Maybe she got attacked. WE DON'T KNOW!' she yelled.

Aaron sighed.

'I don't think we should help her,' he said stubbornly. Penny really didn't understand what was going on in his head at that moment.

'Well, I can't leave her like this,' Penny stated in a dangerously quiet tone. She was just daring Aaron to disagree with her. His silence said enough. 'Leave, then!'

she roared, waving her hand dismissively. Aaron didn't need telling twice. He turned heel and disappeared the way they had come.

Penny looked down at this young, helpless woman. At that moment, she felt at the same level. She had committed to helping someone struggling, someone in the same boat she was in, but she didn't even know where to start. She was pretty sure she wouldn't be able to carry her, even at her strongest, let alone at this present time. She was undernourished, at best, and weaker for it. All she could think was that she needed to get this girl some sustenance. She needed to get her to food, even if that meant dragging her.

Chapter 27

McKenzie had spent an entire day avoiding the inevitable. Well, partly that, but also selfishly he wanted to spend more time with Jessie. The real Jessie, and the real him. They'd laughed as he'd given her a grand tour of the Maze's "sights". It had been the best day of his existence within this messed up place, only disturbed by the constant nagging in his head telling him none of it was real. That it had to end.

McKenzie had taken Jessie to see the watch, though she hadn't seemed as awestruck as everyone else in the Maze. It had also been a little awkward, as there were two others stood nearby, giving him odd glances whenever he whispered something to Jessie. It was testament to how much the Maze toyed with a person's brain that they didn't say anything and took it as a given. Who hadn't started talking to themselves in this place?

He never mentioned Natasha. It didn't feel right to say anything to Jessie. He had been the one who had thrown everything away and didn't deserve anything better than a lonesome existence. Whilst walking around on his own, he'd realised that he'd subconsciously been isolating himself on purpose. He knew he didn't deserve anything more.

*

After several hours of avoiding what was to come ... reached a juncture that ...

... things, two of ... ere right next to one another. Now, it seemed there ... nothing else to do. He turned to Jessie meaningfully and stared into her olive green eyes, words momentarily failing him. He had to look away. It was the only way he could get through this. He sighed morosely as he looked down at his tattered shoes.

'Err... look. I- I know this is too late. I know it will never change anything, partly because I'm not saying this to the real you, but I really let you down. I will never have an excuse for the way I treated you and I will never try to find one, but I want you to know I will never forget my mistakes. I promise I will learn from them. I know that's not much good to you, but it's the best I can do for now. Anyway, I'm truly sorry and... and goodbye.'

The entire time he spoke he didn't raise his eyes from his scuffed-up, grey trainers. As he said his final words, he finally worked up the courage to look up and see Jessie for the last time, but she was gone. In truth, he had seen the last of Jessie some time ago in the courtroom. She had been crying then and never once met his eyes. McKenzie sniffed heavily and turned away, keen to put distance between himself and this spot. As he turned, somebody stepped out from a turning just up ahead.

'Who were you talking to?' Natasha asked curiously. McKenzie couldn't believe it. Of course she just had to turn up now.

'No-one,' he lied, blatantly. Natasha put her hands on her hips as she gave him a sceptical look. 'Fine,' McKenzie added, figuring now he was on a roll he might as well keep it up. He walked past Natasha and began talking at speed. It felt surprisingly freeing to be honest with someone. He told her exactly why he was here. He told her that he had been talking to Jessie and just about everything in between as she walked beside him; she made a good audience. The most amazing thing about it was that when he finished, she didn't seem to judge him differently. She simply nodded her understanding.

'You know, I've been looking for you for days,' she said once he'd finally stopped talking. The pit of sorrow

McKenzie had felt in his stomach did a quick somersault and he tried to control himself.

'Why?' he asked, a little bemused.

'Because despite your mistakes, you seemed like a decent person,' she stated sympathetically. 'I didn't know why you were here, and I didn't necessarily want to know. I was just happy to know this version of you. You know you're the only person who's actually spoken to me properly down here?'

'Yeah, it's weird, isn't it? You'd think people would be desperate to talk to one another, but it seems like the opposite,' McKenzie said. Then he thought about his own issues trying to talk to people in his first week here. It was likely many of his fellow prisoners faced similar feelings of guilt. Maybe some were just scared. Everyone was here for some reason or another, though McKenzie had yet to come across anyone who he thought looked particularly dangerous.

McKenzie suddenly walked with a weight lifted from his shoulders. Somebody knew his greatest secret and they were willing to give him a chance to redeem himself. More than that, he had begun to make peace with himself. Maybe he would survive this place after all.

Chapter 28

Penny was exhausted. For the first time within the Maze she had worked up a genuine sweat trying to heave the limp girl along corridor after corridor, desperately trying to find a food room. After hours of struggle, she had set the girl against the wall and slumped down next to her. 'You know, I could really do with a little cooperation,' she muttered satirically to the girl, unsurprisingly to no response.

She sat there trying to catch her breath, her lungs exhaling heavily, trying to think what to do next. It was like trying to save someone who was drowning. She could either jump in and risk drowning herself, or leave this girl to fight off the current on her own. Looking at her greying face, Penny figured the girl wouldn't last much longer if she did leave her. Penny's brain seemed to be whirring faster than it ever had in the gloom of these corridors. Then it suddenly struck her, and she wanted to slap herself in the face. She would have to leave the girl here for a while and try and find the food room on her own. Otherwise, she could be carrying her in circles for hours.

'Stay here,' she chuckled hoarsely as she pushed herself to her feet, exerting more of her waning energy. 'The things I'll do for a damsel in distress,' she laughed, looking down at the girl. She set off once more, this time moving much more freely and much faster without the extra weight. As soon as she turned the first corner, she heard a dark voice in the back of her mind telling her she didn't need to go back. She was free of the girl now, so why not just forget about her? But she couldn't do that. She had resolved within herself to be a better person following the mistakes that had led her here. If she was to ever escape this place, she wanted to have learnt from her lessons.

It didn't take long to find the food room in the end, but

that hadn't been possible for her to know. When she found the light-flooded room she told it too to stay where it was, which funnily enough was probably less likely than the girl being where Penny had left her. Penny quickly scampered off, retracing her steps back to the girl and checking every few yards that the door hadn't suddenly disappeared. She checked one last time before swinging around a turning to the right, running as fast as she could. Unsurprisingly again, the girl had not moved. Perhaps what was more surprising was that the door hadn't either when she finally got back to it.

She didn't think about the girl at first, but instead took a long drink from the water cooler. Penny felt she had at least earnt that. Once she had quenched her significant thirst she then got to work on the young girl. She brought cup after cup of water over, forcing it gradually into the girl's open mouth, then collecting one last cup and pouring it straight over the girl's head. Still there was no sign of consciousness in her willow-coloured eyes as Penny rolled her eyelids open. Her concern grew and she rushed over to the food, thinking fast. She tried to remember anything she had learnt in science class, or just absolutely anything that might be useful.

Finally, she figured sugar, if nothing else, would give the girl some energy. Frantically scanning the wide selection of foods, she picked out an orange and peeled it quickly with her grubby hands. She forced a slice into the girl's mouth and pressed her jaw shut, allowing the juices to release, then sat back and hoped for the best. After a nail-biting — not that she had much nail left to bite after all this anxiety — few minutes, the girl's eyelids finally began to flutter with signs of life. Penny watched on as she slowly chewed on some questionable bread.

Chapter 29

It was the worst case of déjà vu Yazmin had ever experienced. There she sat, once again being salvaged back to some version of health in this oddly blinding food court by a complete stranger and all she could taste was fruit. She had almost choked as she came to, making to take a deep breath, completely unaware that there was a piece of orange in her mouth. The woman she was with gave her a moderate slap on the back and she soon spat the orange out, though now her back hurt. Yazmin got the impression this woman wasn't as good at this as TJ had been.

She looked into the woman's kind eyes and that was where the déjà vu ended. TJ's eyes had never shown much kindness. They held more of a steely resolve about them; at times a little sympathy, too.

'What's your name?' Yazmin croaked.

'Penny,' the woman smiled kindly.

'Well, thank you, Penny,' Yazmin said. It was getting a little embarrassing that she kept being in a position that she had to thank someone for saving her. That, more than anything, was a wake-up call to her. She couldn't keep getting into this mess. She had to stand up and be counted.

'You're welcome, I guess-'

'-Yazmin.'

'Anyway, I couldn't exactly just leave you there, could I?' Penny said, trying to deflect the thanks.

'You'd be surprised,' Yazmin said darkly, cradling her knees as she sat in the plastic chair. Penny's forehead crinkled and something suddenly struck Yazmin. A memory that didn't really exist. 'Hey, weren't you with someone?'

'Err... yeah. I guess I found out all I needed to know about him, though,' Penny said, though she clearly felt she needed to explain herself. 'We weren't together or anything,' she said a little defensively. 'We just met in the first week, and I kind of thought it would be good to have someone around. It got a bit tiresome, to be honest.'

'Yeah, I feel that,' Yazmin said dryly, but then she realised she'd have to explain TJ. She couldn't face the embarrassment of being saved twice, she would just have to lie. 'I met this guy, too. We were travelling for a while, but we weren't very similar,' Yazmin said vaguely. It wasn't a total lie, she'd just avoided the whole truth. However, this seemed to create concern in Penny's face.

'He- he didn't do… anything to you, did he?' Penny asked uncomfortably, eyeing Yazmin warily.

'Oh, no, we just fell out. I just got kind of tired and fed up of this place. I think he just got tired of me. I can't say I blame him.'

Yazmin hoped TJ was doing okay. She had been telling the truth; they were just too different to be travelling around this place together, or anywhere for that matter, but she couldn't forget what he had done for her. When she had come around, she had half expected to find TJ looking down at her, it was quite a surprise to find this woman, who must have been a few inches shorter than Yazmin, stood there watching. Yazmin thought for a moment about how she'd managed it. She noticed a pain in the small of her back and after looking at her arms she quickly realised that the woman must have dragged her; they were covered in grazes and friction burns. Yazmin was filled with admiration. This woman really cared. Yazmin could be a mass murderer for all this Penny knew, yet she was willing to help Yazmin no matter what.

Penny brought over a tray with a variety of foods piled upon it and Yazmin looked down upon its contents, completely unperturbed. If she hadn't needed to eat to survive, she wouldn't have bothered — none of it looked overly mouth-watering. In fact, food in general just seemed like a necessity now, a fuel to keep her going. In the outside world Yazmin had loved all different kinds of foods, but a little perspective within the Maze had made her realise this was just gluttony.

Despite their brief introductions to one another, there was still a great deal of awkward silences between the two women. Yazmin wasn't overly appreciative of the troubled looks Penny kept giving her, but also after more than two weeks in the Maze, there was very little to say to one another. There had been no exciting news or developments to share, they couldn't talk about the regular conversation starters of their previous lives like what TV they had watched last night. Penny instead made her way through copious amounts of food. Yazmin figured she had probably worked up a fair appetite getting her here.

For some time, neither of them spoke as they both ate, Yazmin picking slowly at bits and pieces of the platter in front of her. Penny looked like she wanted to say something, but didn't voice whatever was bothering her. Eventually, Penny stopped eating and came to sit opposite Yazmin at the canteen-style table, dragging an uncomfortable chair out loudly.

'Sorry, but I kind of have to ask…' Penny muttered, 'but if this guy didn't do anything to you, what exactly *did* happen?'

Yazmin considered this for a moment. How was she supposed to answer that in a way that didn't make her seem completely weak and vulnerable? There didn't seem to be a way around it.

'Nothing happened, as such,' she began, looking away with shame. 'It's just this place, isn't it? It's draining me. I can't cope, seeing the same stupid grey walls day after day.'

To Yazmin's surprise, Penny actually laughed. Not a mocking, cruel laugh, but rather a derisive, understanding laugh.

'Yeah, I'm beginning to feel like I'm going colour-blind,' Penny joked, continuing to chuckle. Yazmin smiled. TJ had always been so wrapped up in his own toxic masculinity that she'd never been able to voice these concerns. It was nice to talk to someone who seemed to recognise the same struggles she was going through.

They sat and talked openly for a while. Yazmin explained her situation, that she never committed the crime she was in here for and talked about the feeling of crushing hopelessness that had been sat heavily in her chest since the first day. She didn't ask how Penny ended up in here. Penny didn't exactly seem keen to give away that information, anyway. It was just about the only thing a person could be judged for in here, which was ridiculous as they had all made mistakes to earn their place here. Of course, some were always going to be worse than others. Yazmin's only mistake had been walking down that road at the wrong time.

Soon enough they got onto the topic of the exit to the Maze. They both agreed that they didn't believe there was one. At least, that they believed there wasn't just a doorway that they could walk through and be free to live a normal life again. Yazmin wondered if she could ever go back to a normal life after the trauma she'd been through over the last few weeks. She didn't even know if she would ever get out of this place at all. If there really was no exit, how were they supposed to leave?

She was sinking quickly in her own head, revolving around the same questions over and over again. Questions that, no matter how hard she tried, she couldn't come up with answers for. Having Penny around might be useful, though. She may not know any more than Yazmin, but at least she felt comfortable talking things through more thoroughly than she had with TJ. Around two hours had passed whilst Yazmin picked at her food, and they discussed all things to do with this tortuous place. Yazmin quickly began to feel comfortable, before Penny turned sharply towards the doorway, jumping a little. They both froze, watching the empty doorway. Nobody appeared, yet Yazmin still felt incredibly jumpy. She suggested they moved on, away from the open. Penny agreed, so between them they swiftly packed up as much food as they could carry and headed on their way.

Chapter 30

Today was a big day for the Maze, possibly the biggest it had faced so far, and maybe even the biggest it ever would. There would be four new sections opened to the Mazers and within these sections, the very first exit. Flint had known that there'd been no point enabling the possibility of an exit within the first month as it would take more than a month for any of the Mazers to prove their qualities enough to justify their freedom.

*

The last two weeks had passed with little event to note, besides Yazmin being saved again. Flint had perhaps been even more relieved on this occasion, though. He had quickly passed on Yazmin's case to his best team to further research. Diane had been right; there was definitely something off about the entire case, and Yazmin's actions throughout. She didn't act like a guilty person, and she hadn't ever since Flint had been watching her in the Maze. Despite two weeks of work, the team had not yet found Yazmin's innocence, so for now all Diego could do was watch on and pray she was able to get through this rough patch.

The introduction of Penny had been a surprise to Diego, but a very welcome one. The two women had similar personalities and at last they were able to open up about their personal struggles. Diego was hopeful that Penny would be able to drag Yazmin through at least a few more weeks of the Maze, if that was what it took.

The openings of sections nineteen to twenty-two brought with it Diego's favourite part of his entire masterplan: a giant brick tunnel, full of moss and the smell of sea air. The first possible exit. The genius of it came in the detail. The door to this new cavern of possibility would not be opened unless those in the control room deemed any passer-by to be worthy, and even once they took this new pathway, it wasn't necessarily the end of their journey within the Maze.

So far only two had come even a little closer to gaining their freedom: Penny and TJ. Both had shown compassion and basic human sentiment in their efforts to help a fellow Mazer, Yazmin, who was in dire need. Whilst this was certainly a heroic act, Diego had decided long ago that it would take more than one good deed to prove somebody had changed. Flint had, in fact, created a points system to be used by the operators as they watched the Mazers' progress. Positive moments such as these would be rewarded with a gain in their points, whilst negative incidents would take away points. Flint was pleased to say that, as of yet, none of the Mazers were in negative points, though fifty-one out of the sixty people wandering the corridors were still marked at zero — a long way from their targets.

Of course, with each of the Mazers coming in through different routes and different crimes, the points targets were varied depending on the severity of the crime. For instance, Aaron had a much lower target than TJ, though at this moment in time TJ stood ahead of Aaron on points. Aaron's total had taken a significant hit when he had refused to help Yazmin. Diego still didn't understand his actions in that instant. He didn't get why he was so opposed to helping such a desperate young lady. He had been more than willing to befriend Penny, after all.

Each Mazer's personal points total now shone in green or white, — depending on if their score was positive or zero, respectively — besides their name on the giant screen. On most days, none of the scores would change at all and it would always give Diego a little flutter of excitement whenever he saw one move.

Excitingly, on top of the four new sections being added today, there would also be an addition of eleven new Mazers. These would be the first to enter since Natasha had joined over three weeks ago and would take the total number up to seventy-one. Whilst Diego felt a small margin of excitement about this, he also felt jabs of anxiety. These new eleven were far beyond the level of criminals the Maze currently held. At the moment, TJ was considered a high-profile case, but his actions in the Maze had proven he was not a major threat to anyone else. The new eleven would be a different story. This would be a true test of the Maze and the people within it. Diego was sure that soon enough some of these Mazers would face difficult decisions that would greatly affect their future.

'Are we ready then, Diego?' Alex asked. He had been caught staring at the screen blankly.

'For what?' he answered dimly.

'The new sections…'

'Yes, yes. Sorry, miles away. I presume you've checked for the all clear with the entrances?'

'Yes, some of us are with it,' Alex said, exasperated.

'Very well, then, get on with it.' Diego waved his hand authoritatively. In one swift animation, the four new sections showed up on the Maze, adding a great swathe of new spaces to explore. In the very top left corner, the tunnel to freedom was currently blocked off and shaded, hidden from the Mazers' grasp.

Within another hour, the new Mazers would join, too. Diego had been thinking about that when Alex had interrupted and was glad to be able to return to his thoughts promptly. He had formed an attachment with many of the current Mazers and only now was he beginning to grow concerns for them. He was responsible for their lives, and he couldn't take that lightly. In all honesty, he didn't really want to send the new Mazers in, but deep down he knew the Maze would never be a true success if he held back. What benefit would it hold if it were only capable of housing petty criminals such as Aaron?

Maybe the new Mazers would create some more interest; Diego hoped so, anyway. After all, based on the current pattern, none of the Mazers would be leaving the Maze any time soon. There wasn't enough happening for them to prove themselves. Most were keeping to themselves, following consistent patterns in their continued search for freedom. Penny and Yazmin were still sticking together as, interestingly, were McKenzie and Natasha.

Natasha's watch had caused quite a stir and slowly items had appeared alongside it, like some out-of-the-box library. Books seemed to be the most common donations. Flint was staggered by how many of the Mazers had been given books to head in with. He guessed by now they would have read and re-read the book from cover to cover and were well and truly finished with it. Indeed, from what Diego could make out in the dim light, most of these books looked tattered and bent. McKenzie himself had added a pack of cards he had taken with him, whilst others, such as Marcus, had left small items including tape, pencils, pens, and even a torch. It appeared somebody's family thought it would be darker in the Maze than it actually was.

When McKenzie and Natasha had returned to the watch, Natasha has spent a moment collecting some of her own Blu Tack from the wall before they had set off once more. Diego was sure she had further plans to make changes within the Maze. He couldn't help but smile at her tenacity.

After the slowest hour of Diego's life, the digital clock finally flashed twelve o'clock and he watched as eleven new dots appeared simultaneously. He had almost expected trouble from the off — he didn't know why. He'd pictured a wave of chaos as a rampaging group of new Mazers charged their way through the corridors. Though, they were just people after all; perhaps they would be much the same as the current crop. Interestingly, not one of the eleven put up a struggle before entering the Maze like TJ had. Diego had been sure one of them would have done something drastic.

Slowly, the eleven new dots dispersed into the main Maze structure, appearing from their darkened transition tunnels into the gigantic cavern. Meanwhile, on the other side of the Maze, section nineteen had its first visitor. Diego speculated, wondering if they sensed that this was a newly revealed area. Perhaps the fresh, smooth walls might be a giveaway. Diego had noticed a growing number of scratches and markings on the walls in sections one through eighteen. Some were mere doodles, others attempted to give directional instructions, either to their future selves or to those following in their footsteps.

The design of the four new sections meant that the Mazers would have to move through sections nineteen to twenty-one before they could reach section twenty-two. Diego was giddy with excitement at the prospect of someone coming across section twenty-two. He was sure they would be able to taste the sea air, possibly even hear the distant crashing of waves echoing along the stony corridor. It would be interesting to see how the Mazers dealt with this. It could be torture, knowing there was something so close that they couldn't reach, though their brains were so frazzled right now many of them might simply think they were imagining it.

Diego had been in his own bubble all morning, deep in his own concerns and thoughts. He was always going to be under pressure in this role, though, at the moment, that was mainly his own doing. His interactions with the board had not come to anything substantial, as of yet. The Maze was only a month down and fortunately the board members seemed to recognise this. They weren't demanding to see instant results. Just as Diego was thinking back to his most recent meeting in the icy board room, he was disturbed by a flurry of activity behind him. He wasn't in his usual spot today, but instead he was stood almost directly in the middle of the room, in the aisle between the rows of computers looking directly up at his great project. He swiftly turned when he heard someone calling his name.

'Mr. Flint! Mr. Flint! We need to talk!' It was Anderson, the lead in Miss Tracey's case. Diego suddenly felt a rush of excitement.

'Go on,' he prompted.

'We have been to see Miss Macdonald, the victim in the case. You were right, she wasn't telling the truth,' Anderson said breathlessly. Diego was stunned, he had sent Anderson off on a hunch, he hadn't really expected it to be right.

'Okay. So, what happened?'

'Well, it seems Miss Macdonald was visiting her boyfriend that night, not her family as she first told the investigators.'

'Okay, what does that change, though?'

'Oh, it changes everything!' Anderson said excitingly. 'We were able to track down photos of Miss Macdonald's boyfriend's car that night. She was in it.' He brandished a slightly blurred photo in front of Diego, who snatched it up.

'Okay, but that still doesn't prove-'

'Oh, but that's not it. Here is another picture, which is slightly clearer. Notice Miss Macdonald's face.'

Diego took the new picture and looked closely. It was

much clearer to see; Missie clearly had a large bruise under her eye, and another on her temple. She had already been hurt. Diego's mouth opened in understanding.

Anderson continued, 'We managed to get an image of the car heading towards the road Miss Macdonald was found on, and we believe the boyfriend threw her out on the roadside. It certainly appears Miss Tracey was completely innocent.'

'How can we prove this?'

'We have just this minute arrested Mr. Thompson, the boyfriend.'

'I want to question him myself,' Diego said firmly.

'Erm… are you actually allowed to do that, Mr. Flint? You know, you're not actually an officer of the law…' Anderson trailed off under the fierce glare Diego gave him.

This was an incredibly rare treat for Diego. For the first time in a month, he left the confines of the hotel complex. It was strange seeing the outside world again. It felt so distant that he'd begun to think everything would have changed. That was, of course, not true. The streets were still lined with the same fast-food restaurants and coffee shops. If Diego hadn't been in such a rush, he would have been tempted to stop off for some fried chicken. He wasn't even allowed to order it to the hotel anymore, so his mouth watered hungrily as he passed his favourite restaurant.

They had a long drive ahead, across two states, to reach the station in which Mr. Thompson was being held, but the journey seemed to pass by in an instant — Diego was so thrilled to be out of his own trap. He watched out the window in awe of everything, like he was a child again. Just as the sun was setting, they reached their final destination. Diego felt like just driving on forever and leaving the Maze behind, but he owed this to Yazmin, at the very least. A tight cramping of guilt circled his insides thinking of how she had suffered at his hands, once again adding doubt into his previously assertive mind.

Mr. Thompson was waiting in a questioning room when they arrived. Immediately, Diego got the impression that the chief inspector of the case felt the same way as Anderson and didn't think he should be going to question the young man, though he held limited resistance at the same time. Diego walked into the questioning room authoritatively. He'd had a long drive to come up with the right words; he was sure of himself in this situation and knew what he wanted to say immediately.

'Hello, Mr. Thompson,' Diego said calmly. 'My name is Diego Flint. I am the designer of the Maze. I assume you are familiar?' he asked, judging by the confused look on Mr. Thompson's face.

'Err... yeah. What are you doing here?'

'Well, it's funny you should say that. I have a young girl in the Maze currently, her name is Yazmin Tracey. Know it?' Mr. Thompson shook his head, nonplussed. Diego continued, pacing up and down. He was enjoying this a little too much. 'And what about Missie Macdonald? I'm sure you know that name,' Diego said. This time Mr. Thompson nodded reluctantly.

'So, if you wouldn't mind, could you tell me why you dumped the aforementioned Miss Macdonald at the side of the road, considerably battered and bruised, and fighting for her life?'

Mr. Thompson looked stunned. He didn't say anything.

'Very well.' Diego persevered. 'I can tell you're not a decent person. You're not about to fess up just like that. Each to their own,' Diego added poignantly. He paused for breath, knowing what he was about to say would work.

'As we've established, you aren't an overly nice person. But I tell you who might be: Miss Yazmin Tracey. Did you know, she is so distraught, so upset by the events, that she has nearly died *twice* within my Maze?' he asked, knowing Mr. Thompson couldn't possibly know that.

Again, Mr. Thompson did not respond.

'No? Fair enough. Now, if I had even the tiniest shred of decency in my little finger, I would consider a complete stranger dying because of my actions quite awful, would you agree?'

'Yeah, I guess,' Mr. Thompson muttered. 'Why don't you just let her go, then?' he asked through gritted teeth. Diego knew he had got through to him.

'Oh, that would certainly seem the easiest solution for everyone, wouldn't it? Unfortunately, the law-' he glanced at the two-way glass, '-doesn't really work like that. They can't just let someone go without proof they are innocent. The only way, it seems, that Miss Tracey can be relieved of her misery is to get a confession from somebody else.' Diego looked Mr. Thompson square in the eye. 'So, what's it to be? Confess here and now, or have another young girl's blood on your hands?' Diego spat, tossing a pen towards Mr. Thompson. He knew he wouldn't be able to catch it as his hands were tied up, so Mr. Thompson could only watch as it hit him in the face and dropped onto the table. Mr. Thompson stared solemnly at the pen, and Diego turned and walked out, clapping his hands.

'That must be some kind of record,' the chief inspector said, dashing to catch up with Diego. 'I've never seen anything like it.'

'Thank you. I would love to stay and chat, but I do have an innocent prisoner to release, I hope you understand,' Diego said implicitly.

'Yes, of course. Good luck.'

'Thank you,' Diego said again, turning and striding out of the electronic doors and jumping into the car waiting

170

directly outside. He immediately went to his phone and dialled Alex's number. The quicker they could get to Yazmin, the better.

Chapter 31

TJ had never been one to fret over the future, or the past for that matter. He didn't understand the point of troubling yourself with things you cannot affect at that exact moment. Unfortunately, the Maze had an uncanny way of bringing out these thoughts in even the most stubborn of minds. TJ had found himself wandering the at-times deserted corridors looking back on his biggest mistakes and worrying over his bleak future within the Maze.

"What if" always seemed to be the question in his head these days. He looked back at the bank robbery and thought of everything that could possibly have gone differently to avoid his current predicament. It was amazing to consider how many different moments could have had a pivotal effect on his life. TJ had always been a strong-minded person, but now he began to realise that he was always trying to remain strong for those around him. Having Yazmin around had been perfect because she'd needed him to be strong, more than perhaps anyone he had ever met previously. She had been in such a dark place, ready to give up, that he needed to be the complete opposite. Now she was gone, he had a lot more time to himself. And it wasn't an enjoyable experience.

He spent too much time in his head now, having long in-depth debates with his own conscience. Most of this was focused on his past. He kept re-watching mistakes and embarrassing moments from his childhood, like when he fell off his bike and broke his arm. The scar on his left forearm didn't help him forget about that. Then there was the time he fell down the stairs at school, ripping his trousers in the process. He had replayed that particular moment on multiple occasions; sometimes he found it hilarious, on others it was merely painful.

Over the first two weeks he had endeavoured to be as active as possible, to keep moving at all times. After a month, he found himself demotivated. On some days he barely moved, he might walk for an hour or so and then settle down once again. It was hard to convince himself to keep moving when it seemed incredibly unlikely that there was an active exit. He was ninety-nine percent sure that he had covered the entire Maze by this point, and he had found no sign of any exit. That was the most difficult thing to comprehend; if there truly was no exit, it didn't exactly help anyone in here to stay positive.

One of the other main issues was the monotonous nature of everything around him. Nothing ever changed. There were only two genuine imperfections in the gunmetal grey walls, the two carvings that had been made. One was a tree, which at first had seemed beautiful in its simplicity, but after the first few sightings it had become as monotonous as anything else is this grey wasteland. The other carving depicted the Statue of Liberty. This struck TJ as incredibly ironic. The carving itself was brilliantly put together, yet he didn't understand what possessed the creator to recreate a statue that was created to symbolise freedom. It didn't really suit a dystopian prison-maze.

Other than those two carvings and the countless scratchings in the walls made by knives or pens, the Maze offered nothing of interest. It was a joyful moment to stumble across a bathroom or a refreshment room, more because it offered something different from the norm than for its actual purpose.

TJ felt himself becoming weaker and weaker as the weeks had passed. He had always been in very good shape before the Maze, but without any motivation or space to keep himself strong, he felt his previous strength waning. The malnourishment of only eating once every three or four days didn't exactly help. He wasn't sure what he missed more; his physical strength or his mental strength.

Chapter 32

Diego had encouraged his driver to break a few rules on his way back to the Maze, promising tongue in cheek to be generous if he ended up in Diego's control. As such, their journey back was considerably shorter, though with Diego's new nerves it did not feel so.

He dashed back into the control room and quickly found Alex, who was clearly comfortably in control of the situation. The room was a hubbub of excitement; today would be the first of many exits from the Maze. Of course, it wasn't quite what Flint had been hoping for and expecting — it wasn't the glorious redemption story. Nevertheless, Yazmin would be the first Mazer to re-enter society. It was an important moment and handled poorly it could cause serious problems.

Diego strode over to Alex's side, quickly barraging her with questions. It became clear that she had developed a very clear plan. Yazmin and Penny were currently still together and appeared to be working on some new art for the Maze. Alex explained that she planned to evacuate Yazmin when they next visited a bathroom, which she estimated would be soon, based on their pattern of activity. The two women had developed a regular routine which seemed to be benefiting both heavily. The only dilemma Diego and Alex faced was Penny. Unfortunately, she was not in a position to leave the Maze yet, and she couldn't be a witness to Yazmin's exit as it would change her perception of the Maze, so they had to find a way to make sure the two women were separate. The only time this ever happened was when they stopped at a bathroom.

Alex had already been in contact with the Maze officers, and two were on route to the nearest bathroom to Penny and Yazmin, running up high along the numerous Maze walls, instructed on any necessary diversions by a team of operators. In the top right-hand corner of the giant screen there was a camera focused on one of the brave officers. The second officer was wearing the camera around his head and Diego watched as the film bounced up and down sloppily in time with the man's strides. The officer at the front was dressed all in black and looked incredibly reminiscent of a classic burglar, his head covered in an old-school balaclava and the rest of his body in skin-tight, black material. It was even darker up above the Maze. It had to be to keep the officers unnoticed by those below. Diego squinted to be able to keep track of the two black-clad officers moving in sync.

The officers quickly came to a halt as one of the Mazers passed by below, completely unaware of the activity above him. The camera followed the man turn left and away from the two frozen officers. Diego recognised him as Marcus Morgan. He was one of the people who'd had very little interaction with any fellow Mazers. Even now he was a good distance away from anyone else.

Diego's mind was flowing with thoughts and ideas, as if he'd had about four espresso shots. It suddenly struck him that they could speed the process up by putting one of his favourite operations into motion: *roadblock*. As soon as Yazmin and Penny got back on the move, they could be gently directed in the right direction, leaving no possible room for error.

Chapter 33

Penny was enjoying her best days in the Maze so far, talking the days away with Yazmin. It was a completely different feeling to being with Aaron. Being with Aaron had been okay, a convenience during a tough time in the first two weeks of the Maze. This was different; Penny and Yazmin actually got on really well. They were able to reference the same TV shows as they walked around. Yazmin, like Aaron, had been fascinated by Penny's wall designs. Unlike Aaron, however, she seemed keener to try it out for herself. She was interested in the techniques and thought process behind Penny's work, not just the aesthetics.

Shortly after they had gorged themselves on food, they found a wall with limited amounts of graffiti already on it. Penny began showing Yazmin how she worked and talked about how she came up with the designs without being able to sketch them first. It was incredibly refreshing for Penny to be able to talk passionately about something she truly cared about. It brought her closer than ever to the outside world and the wonderous artwork within it.

Yazmin certainly had some natural talent with a chisel in her hand. Penny had reluctantly handed over her prized possession, entrusting Yazmin to do no damage to it. She hoped she realised what an honour this was. Between them they whiled away the hours creating their separate designs. Yazmin always watched on with an awe-struck expression as Penny did her work. Penny, too, was impressed by Yazmin's creation. She had created a very respectable bird soaring through the air with its wings stretched to their fullest. It was a great metaphor for the feelings Penny felt inside and could only assume that's what Yazmin felt, too. The will to be free to fly. To be free, full stop.

Penny herself had created a wolf, her favourite animal.

Again, it reflected her will to be running free in the wild, but also her desire to be in the company of others. Of course, it was a common expression to say a "lone wolf", but that was because it was an exception from the norm. Wolves were almost always part of close-knit packs, something Penny could only dream of right now. As they sat back and marvelled in their work, Penny went about sharpening her chisel, scraping it forcefully against the corner of the wall.

Eventually they stood, in silence, both worn out by their day's work, and headed away in search of a bathroom. The pathway they followed was like nothing Penny had seen before. She began to feel that something unnatural was happening. They walked for ages without passing a single turning. When they came across a turning that would often have had two options previously, they could now only turn right. Then the next, only a left. They walked and walked for another hour without a single opportunity to choose their direction, until they reached the bathroom.

They were both considerably concerned by this development, though there appeared nothing sincere in the immediate future. Both Penny and Yazmin had been constantly scanning their surroundings as they became more and more aware of something happening around them with every false turning. Now they stood outside the

looked at each other

Penny felt obligated to go into the bathroom first. She told Yazmin to wait close to the door and confidently stepped forward, pushing the door open to its fullest as she took a deep breath. Penny had no idea what she had expected to find, but she was left a little surprised and disappointed. By now Penny had been dying to find something out of the ordinary to brighten her life in the Maze, but as she opened the bathroom door, nothing unusual came screaming towards her. The small plant still sat placidly in the corner whilst the white walls and matching basin and toilet remained as unchanged as any other time she'd visited this or any other bathroom in the Maze. She should have been relieved that nothing had attacked her, but in truth she kind of wished something had. At least it would be a story.

After an incredibly uneventful time cleaning herself as best as possible in the polished basin and using the facilities as she had so desperately needed, Penny exited the bathroom, shrugging in a bemused fashion to Yazmin as they passed in the doorway. Perhaps the changing walls had simply come up with an exceptionally unusual pattern of pathways that, in fact, had no meaning.

Penny sat against the wall opposite, waiting patiently for Yazmin. It wasn't like they were in a rush to get anywhere. Now she was alone she thought about the circumstances of their friendship. It had been almost forced, yet Penny couldn't have wished for a better companion to be stuck in here with. Yazmin had really opened up over the last two weeks and had shared her feelings freely with Penny, which had been a huge relief for Penny to hear. The idea that anyone was going through a similar struggle to you was always comforting. It really was true; misery loved company.

The door to the bathroom was so thick that Penny couldn't hear anything from the other side, so she had no idea what Yazmin was up to. She seemed to be taking an unusually long amount of time and Penny hoped she was merely having a very thorough wash. As thorough as it could be with no soap or shampoo to help, that is. After even more time passed, Penny got a little worried that

Yazmin had maybe fallen asleep, or worse. She got up and knocked on the door. There was no reply. She knocked again, harder this time. Still, there was no reply, yet there was nothing more she could do. She sat back down, befuddled, and hoped Yazmin had simply drifted off to sleep. Penny was tired, too, so she began to relax, assuming she would sleep outside the bathroom.

Just as her head began drooping to the left, lolloping onto her shoulder, she heard the bathroom door's lock click open. She stood up hastily, rubbing the sleepiness from her dozy eyes.

'What've you been doing?' she asked before the door had even opened. But the door didn't open. She began to wonder if she had just imagined the door unlocking. Stepping forward, she gently pushed the door to see if it would open. It did. She pushed it all the way so that the whole bathroom was in view and felt her jaw fall in shock. Yazmin wasn't there. She frantically hurried around the room, trying to find some secret doorway that would explain this most mysterious turn of events. She pressed on the walls, turned the taps, and tried to press them down, too, and even tried moving the plant pot, but nothing worked. There seemed to be only one way in or out of the room.

At first Penny was simply confused, unable to connect this mystery to any emotions. She was sure there must be a simple explanation. Then, slowly, as the gravity of the scene became clearer in her mind, it hit Penny and she began to cry. She had finally found a friend that she truly needed at this time, and she had been taken away in an instant, without the opportunity to even say goodbye. Penny was angry, too. Why hadn't Yazmin said something? Why was she the one who had disappeared and not Penny? Where had she even gone? Was she free from the Maze?

Penny pounded the wall with her fists, letting out her emotions in a barrage of anger, frustration, and hurt. She just couldn't comprehend what had just happened. She locked the door, fell to the ground, and melted into her own self-pity, heaving with intense sobs as she lay face down on the cold bathroom floor.

Chapter 34

Aaron had been surrounded by walls for over a month now, but none of them seemed to trap him in quite as much as the walls he had created for himself. Since he had parted ways with Penny, he had fallen into a deep rut of despair, darkening every day. He hadn't spoken to anyone since, and constantly considered the consequences of his actions.

He didn't really know why he hadn't helped the girl they had found, but he hoped Penny had managed to help her. He felt a growing feeling of animosity towards himself for his actions. Over the last few days, he had been frantically trying to find Penny, hoping the girl would still be with her, but he'd had no luck. Aaron was pretty sure the Maze had grown over the last couple of days. He wandered around areas he didn't recognise at all, and it seemed to take him longer to find either of Penny's designs than he was used to.

This was the first place he had ever been in in his life that he had not felt fully in control of his own senses. Usually, he would be so extremely confident of his surroundings that he could almost close his eyes and know where he was going. The Maze didn't allow for that. Even after an entire month, he was yet to find any pattern to the changing of the pathways. The only area that he was confident about was around Penny's tree and the watch. Aaron had concluded that Flint and his team had stopped the pathways moving around that area as it was now such an important part in the lore of the Maze. Aaron often spotted fellow prisoners coming from or going to the watch when he went near. He was careful to avoid them now, even more than he had when with Penny. His level of paranoia and terror had risen considerably recently.

It had become a lot harder to put one foot in front of the other over the last week. He had searched every inch of this place, down to the minute details on the golden lanterns and the tiny scratchings on every wall. There was no answer coming to him. No brilliant solution helping him on the way to freedom.

Aaron was now walking along a pathway he was sure belonged to a new area of the Maze. The walls were certainly cleaner, with much less in the way of random scratchings from those who had visited in the past.

He turned a corner and something incredibly unexpected hit him. A wave of fresh, salty air. It caused him to freeze completely. He took another deep breath and was carried away to a cold Christmas day walk on the beach, the crisp sea wind battering his much younger face. By his side, his mom and dad trudged through the wet sand. He actually heard the waves crashing in, but then his daydream came to a stop as quickly as it had begun.

He stood, back in the dim, grey corridor, and he actually felt a gentle breeze against his oily forehead, ruffling his wispy fringe. Feverishly he began scanning his surroundings, looking up towards the ceiling for a sign of where this blissful scent was coming from. There was nothing obvious. In all directions the ceiling was as dark and distant as ever. On both sides of him and behind were thick, heavy walls. But he was sure he wasn't imagining it. If it had been a brief second, he would have probably conceded it was his brain concocting another mental image of the outside world, but he could feel the salt lingering on the tip of his tongue.

He must have stood in that exact spot for at least half an hour, spinning around in search of an answer. This was something new. A taste, literally, of the outside world. The most connected he had felt with it for at least three weeks.

He decided to sit down in the corner he had just passed, and he allowed himself to relax, filled up with the tingling sensation of a fresh ocean breeze flowing through his nostrils. Quickly, he fell into the deepest sleep he had managed in the Maze, drifting to a comfortable place somewhere far away from his troubles.

Aaron had no idea how long he had slept for, but the next thing he knew he was woken abruptly. Someone had kicked him aggressively, his leg now throbbing with numbness. He looked up, dazed, to see who had bothered him and quickly scuttled back against the wall as far as he could go. The man towering above him let off an aura of danger. He was tall and well-built, and Aaron could tell he mustn't have been in the Maze for long. He still seemed to be at full strength, for one, but there were other signs, too. His clothes seemed clean and fresh, and his hair remained neat. He was looking down at Aaron with a look of malcontent. Aaron knew he was in trouble.

'H- hi, who- who are you?' Aaron asked timidly. He felt like a child being bullied in the playground.

'M' name's Antonio,' the man said gruffly, still staring down at Aaron.

'I'm A- Aaron,' Aaron stuttered.

'I don't care,' Antonio growled harshly. 'I want your stuff.'

'My stuff?' Aaron asked, his voice unusually high pitched.

'Yeah, y'know, the stuff your family gave you to come in here. Unless you didn't have anyone to bring you stuff?' Antonio let out a harsh laugh.

Aaron was thinking quickly. He only had his switchblade left, and he really didn't want to lose that. He would have nothing left from his sister, then. Antonio certainly had the stronger hand right now, though. He was a much bigger man and Aaron was currently cowering at his feet. It was either stand and fight or bow down like a coward and lose the only defence he had, the only thing he had left from the outside world. He glanced back up at the steely eyes of Antonio and knew he wouldn't stand a chance in a fight. Slowly, he reached into his pocket and pulled out the switchblade, holding it out towards Antonio and looking down at the ground.

Antonio snatched up the blade and examined it quickly, seeming unimpressed. He then looked down at Aaron again.

'And the rest,' Antonio said.

'I haven't got anything else,' Aaron muttered, down beaten. He could still smell the salty air and was amazed to remember how recently that feeling of elation had hit him.

'Why not?' Antonio asked sharply.

'I left…' Aaron stopped himself. He was about to tell Antonio about the tree, and about the items there, but based on this encounter he was sure Antonio would go straight to it and take everything for his own. He couldn't let that happen. 'I gave it away,' he said quietly, thinking quickly. Antonio eyed him suspiciously.

'Guess someone else caught your weak ass snoozing, huh?' Antonio chuckled to himself. 'This will have to do, then,' he added, waving the blade. 'See ya around.'

'I hope not,' Aaron muttered to himself as Antonio lumbered away.

Chapter 35

Diego had rushed down to the officer's entrance to meet Yazmin. As she came stumbling over the threshold Diego could see clearer than ever how weak and thin she was. He had intended to speak to her immediately, but upon first sight he knew she needed to rest first, to gain some actual rehabilitation above the level provided within a basic food room in the Maze.

He greeted the slightly confused yet relieved Yazmin and guided her swiftly away from the Maze exit, straight towards his own personal suite in the hotel. There, he allowed her to rest thoroughly, and he called for a wide assortment of foods. Rest she certainly did. Diego waited and waited, and then waited some more, until seventeen hours later Yazmin finally awoke.

Diego was down in the control room when Anthony called to let him know she had woken at last. He headed straight up, glad for the excuse to leave the library-esque room which had last night been such a buzz of activity. Yazmin had showered and eaten a little by the time Diego made it up to his room in the penthouse of the hotel. He sat down at the end of his bed as Yazmin continued to nibble on various foods, sat on his previously untouched desk chair.

'I'm sorry you had to go through such an ordeal,' Diego said quietly. It was stupid, he knew, but he couldn't think how else to start this conversation. He couldn't help but think of his own role in this story. He hoped that Yazmin could forgive him. Yazmin didn't answer at first but continued to munch her way through the melon slice she was holding. It seemed to have become a personal favourite. Diego held his breath as he waited for her response. He also had to hold in a chuckle as he looked at

Yazmin wearing some aviators. It appeared her eyes were extremely sensitive to light after a long stretch without any.

'It wasn't all your fault,' Yazmin said, at last. Diego couldn't help but let out a sigh of relief in his own self-indulgence.

'Thank you for saying that, but I can't help thinking you needn't have suffered as you did.'

'You couldn't have known,' Yazmin said weakly.

'Maybe. You know I could use your help, if you wanted to?' Diego asked. He had intended to ask this since he had learnt of Yazmin's innocence.

'What do you mean?' Yazmin asked curiously.

'You know more than anyone about the struggles of life in the Maze. That could come in very handy.'

'You want me to work for you? To help you torture people like you tortured me? I nearly died!' Yazmin retorted.

'My intention has never been to torture anyone. You suffered more than anyone else in the Maze because you were aware of your own innocence. It prevented you from being able to open your mind to your own failings, because you had none.' Diego paused, noticing the expression of anger and disgust on Yazmin's face; maybe this wasn't the right approach. He needed to prove himself. 'Did you know, TJ would never have found you if it weren't for me, for us, in the control room?'

This seemed to get Yazmin's attention.

'How? Did you mind trick him or something?' Yazmin speculated. Diego chuckled.

'No, no. Nothing like that, we merely rearranged the Maze in such a way that it was impossible for him to miss you. We redirected him.'

'So, it's true, then,' Yazmin stated. 'The walls move?'

'Of course. Otherwise, you lot would have gone mad

after a week!' Diego exclaimed.

'Oh, yeah, and this way was much better,' Yazmin uttered sarcastically. Diego didn't know what else to say. Fortunately, the empty silence was broken by a knock on the door. Diego called for the knocker to enter, and Anthony emerged.

'They're here, Diego,' Anthony stated.

'Thank you, send them in,' Diego replied, then turned to Yazmin. 'I'll give you a minute alone,' he muttered softly, standing and walking towards the door, but before he reached for the handle he turned and said, 'Please think about it. God knows I could use your personal insight.'

On his way out, Diego passed two people that he knew must be Yazmin's parents. Her father looked angry. He was red in the face and his expression was hardened. Diego thought he was probably someone he didn't want to cross. Unfortunately, in a way he already had. Diego stood waiting outside with Anthony and they chatted away the time talking about the Dodgers, whom they were both fans of. However, their chat was soon cut short as Yazmin's father came storming out from Diego's room looking furious. He made a beeline straight for Diego, and Anthony was quick to step between them. Diego grabbed Anthony on the arm to allow him to step forward.

'You! You evil sod!' Mr. Tracey yelled, pointing a chubby, wrinkled finger at Diego.

'Maybe you would do well to remind yourself who helped your daughter prove her innocence. Then maybe you might stop pointing your finger at him,' Diego said coolly. Mr. Tracey immediately lower his outstretched arm.

'You? You saved our little Yaz?' he asked, thoroughly confused.

'Well, I didn't personally go down into the Maze, and it wasn't I who personally traced down the ex-boyfriend of

Miss McDonald and discovered the truth, but I was certainly the one who restarted the case. I was the one constantly looking out for her welfare, yes. I was the one who went all the way across two states to make said ex-boyfriend confess to his crime, thus allowing your daughter her freedom.'

Mr. Tracey didn't seem to know what to do now. He looked like he wanted to hug Diego, a vast contrast to the man who had come storming out.

'Erm… I don't wish to tell you how to live your life,' Diego began hesitantly, 'but maybe you should make the most of the extra time with your daughter.'

'Yes, yes, you're right,' Mr. Tracey said, a little embarrassed by his actions. He turned and scurried away back into Diego's room.

'I'll tell you something,' Anthony said once Mr. Tracey had disappeared once more, 'you have some way with words.'

'Thank you,' Diego mocked sincerity, laughing.

*

Over an hour later, Yazmin, her mother and her father re-emerged from Diego's room. Her father seemed much calmer, whilst her mother had evidently been crying for most of the hour. Diego accompanied them down the elevator and asked to borrow Yazmin for a while on the pretence of debriefing her for the outside world. They sat down in the hotel bar area whilst Yazmin's parents waited in the car outside.

'So, have you thought about it?' Diego opened the conversation.

'Yes, but I'm still not sure. I just don't think I can help you run this twisted prison.'

'You see, that's what I don't get. I don't see why you describe it as twisted. I understand that it is unconventional, but why twisted?' Diego asked, a little agitated.

'The whole place is just weird. The darkness, the loneliness, the constant battle with your own mental fragilities.'

'It's not supposed to be like that, you know,' Diego said quietly. 'I realise that so far it's been pretty lonesome for everyone, but don't you think that over time, with more people joining, that there'll be more of a sense of community?' he asked hopefully. Yazmin thought for a moment.

'Honestly, the Maze felt so detached from the outside world that talking to other people felt weird.'

'Okay, so what do you think we can do to change that?' Diego smiled; his plan seemed to be working.

'Well, you could start by…' Yazmin trailed off and smiled too, noticing what Diego was doing.

'I tell you what,' Diego said suddenly, tapping both hands on the table. 'Let me show you something quickly.'

'What?' Yazmin asked, glancing quickly out to the car park where her parents were waiting.

'The control room. Don't worry, it won't take long,' Diego replied, noticing Yazmin looking out of the window.

'Fine,' Yazmin agreed. Together they stood and Diego led them away.

Chapter 36

Natasha had allowed herself to become closer to McKenzie than she had to anyone else for a long time. They traded long stories about their lives. McKenzie seemed fascinated by her life in Russia and her campaign for women's rights. It was fair to say his own life was considerably different. There was quite often a lengthy silence in which both of them worked hard to think of a new topic, but after a while they got back into conversations about anything and everything.

Natasha was happy to walk in silence. The weeks that passed whilst she was on her own had been some of the hardest of her life. She had always prided herself on being mentally strong and her willingness to overcome stereotypes and systematic oppression, yet being alone and unsure of anything down in the Maze had left her feeling more vulnerable than ever before. Now just having someone to walk alongside seemed to soothe her worries. She had learnt quickly that it was no good bottling up insecurities, so having someone around whenever she felt a shadow of doubt in her mind was comforting. It was even more comforting to know that McKenzie was going through exactly the same struggles.

He told Natasha about his low moments and how she had helped him when she stumbled over him on the first day they'd met. McKenzie said he had felt close to giving up before that moment. It wasn't hard for Natasha to feel empathic towards him; she understood that feeling perfectly.

The only thing that had disturbed Natasha was the moment she had found McKenzie for the second time. He had been talking to an invisible person, which had turned out to be his ex-fiancée. That was certainly disturbing behaviour. More disturbing was the story that McKenzie had subsequently told her, but Natasha had resolved in herself a long time ago to give people second chances. McKenzie didn't seem to be that person from his story and, most of all, he seemed to truly regret everything that had happened.

Despite his face lighting up when Natasha had appeared, McKenzie still appeared distant. He was always careful to remain in neutral, safe conversation that offered no danger of becoming more intimate. Their conversation had almost always resembled small talk about movies, music, and their jobs. Only occasionally had Natasha managed to break through McKenzie's high walls of defence. She was trying hard to get him to open up, but she also didn't want to scare him away.

Each day they walked for several hours, aimlessly turning corners in the hope that something new would appear. Nothing ever had so far, but they had to believe. After two weeks together, Natasha felt comfortable enough around McKenzie to stop herself freaking out. If he hadn't been by her side this place would have crushed her spirit some time ago. Instead, she tried to focus on the peace and quiet; the opportunity to reflect.

That night they had slept next to the Statue of Liberty carving. Amazingly, despite them both travelling the entirety of the Maze spreading news of the watch, neither of them had ever come across the maker of these designs. Not that anyone had owned up to, anyway. Before he had dozed off, McKenzie had been mumbling a children's story that he remembered his mom telling him. Having been brought up in Russia, Natasha had never heard the story and she was fascinated by the moral hidden within. She didn't even think McKenzie knew why he had suddenly remembered the story, but somehow he had put the link together in his mind. It was funny to Natasha that someone could be so intelligent yet so dim all in the same moment.

Once they both had woken, drowsy and cold, they began ambling along the dimly lit corridors again. Natasha knew it was good to have a routine which they could follow every day, but right now they were dangerously close to falling into a rut. They had no purpose here, no-one did. There was nothing they could do to help themselves or anyone else down here, and so every day was just about getting by and not going insane, finding even the smallest victory to help them get through, one day at a time.

After only a few hours, they stumbled across a bathroom. It hadn't been too long since they'd last visited one, but it was always best to use the facilities when they came about. There was no way of knowing when they would next find one again. McKenzie allowed Natasha to go first, and she took her time cleaning herself up. Her glossy purple hair was beginning to grow out and lose its colour; it was incredibly hard to keep hair maintained in the Maze. McKenzie had been kind enough to share the small amount of soap he had remaining, but this didn't do much to help her split ends.

It didn't help her temperament to know that she couldn't look after her own appearance. Fortunately, there were no mirrors in the bathroom so she couldn't get too hung up on it. Maybe they were worried someone would break it and use the shards as a weapon. That wasn't overly in tune with the idea that they were allowed to bring whatever weapons they wanted with them into the Maze, however.

Nevertheless, the ice-cold tap water had a remarkably refreshing effect on her face. She even washed her clothes to the best of her ability, rinsing them in the basin using the mildly warmer water that came from the hot tap. The only issue that came with this was the beyond damp clothing she had to put back on straight away.

Finally, she exited the bathroom and allowed McKenzie to take over. They had non-verbally agreed that they would be best entering the bathroom separately to keep at least a little privacy in their relationship. Besides, it was nice to have some time to herself sometimes. She'd never had a single moment of hostility with McKenzie, but everyone needs at least a small moment with their own thoughts. She didn't like to show her emotions in front of anyone, let alone someone she had only relatively recently met, so she used the time to release any emotions she had stuffed away, usually resulting in a river of tears.

Natasha was stood outside for quite a long time waiting for McKenzie. When he appeared his clothes were also wet and his out-of-control hair was slicked back over his ear. The biggest issue with the wet clothes was that the Maze was cold at the best of times. With wet clothes sticking to your body, this was increased ten-fold. Just looking at the slightly bashful McKenzie standing there unassuming, Natasha suddenly had the urge to do something. She stepped forward swiftly and kissed McKenzie. At first, he returned the kiss, a little unprepared, but then he quickly backed away.

'No, no. I can't,' McKenzie said, holding his hands up. Natasha didn't know what to say.

'I'm sorry,' she found herself saying, though she wasn't sure what for. Where she was from, kissing somebody didn't usually lead to an apology.

'No, it's just- I can't. I- I've got to go,' McKenzie stuttered, avoiding Natasha's eyes. He turned rapidly and sprinted away down the corridor. Natasha watched him run out of sight, completely stunned. She had not expected that to backfire quite so heavily, but she figured she should be flattered. She knew what McKenzie was afraid of and what he was doing.

Chapter 37

Aaron was absolutely exhausted. After his encounter with Antonio, he'd sprinted as fast as possible in the opposite direction. He knew he had to make it to the tree before that selfish psycho. He'd run for hours, his head spinning wildly as he twisted around one corner after another. He had paused for a minute, trying to catch his wheezing breath. He was trying to focus on the forked pathway ahead of him so he could make a rational decision, but he was seeing double.

It took him several minutes to gather himself — he was still shaken by what had happened. He couldn't believe it. Well, he could, actually. This was the kind of behaviour Aaron had expected when he'd entered the Maze, only he'd fallen into a sense of security after a month of safety. That had been rapidly shattered by Antonio. He wondered if there were any other new entrants into the Maze that he should be worried about.

He tried to shake that thought out of his head, focusing on the main issue in front of him. His eyes finally focused, and he concluded that he needed to turn left. He broke into a frantic run once again, the physical effort helping to calm his nerves slightly. Even now his heart was racing at an alarming rate.

He turned another corner, grabbing the steely wall to help carry his momentum, then within an instant came across a doorway. Something about the doorway drew him in and he came grinding to a halt. The door was almost completely closed, which was odd in itself. Whenever he'd come across either a food room or a bathroom, the door had either been wide open or locked. Over the heavy beating of his heart, thudding rhythmically in his ears, he could make out a muffled noise coming from the other side.

Gradually he reached forward and gently pushed the door inwards. The first thing he saw was a pair of feet, which he dearly hoped belonged to a body. He also recognised the shoes and pushed the door more forcefully to reveal Penny lying there. She was heaving with dry sobs, making a horrible rasping noise that came deep from within. Looking around at the state of the bathroom, Aaron could tell almost immediately that Penny had been here for a while. There were patches of water on the floor where the sink had overflown, and the plant in the corner was lying on its side, much of the soil that had been in the pot scattered around its base.

Aaron suddenly remembered that Penny had been with the young girl the last time he had seen her; he wondered where she'd disappeared to. Maybe that was the reason he now found Penny in such a state. He rushed forward and turned Penny onto her side, though she seemed reluctant to acknowledge anything in the world. She rolled back over so that her face was pressed against the cool tiled floor, her eyes still tight shut. This happened twice more as Penny refused to be helped.

'Leave me alone!' she yelled, taking enough of a pause in her frenetic wheeping to vent her anger.

'No,' Aaron said simply. He wasn't about to make the same mistake again. Besides, he cared about Penny. She had been as close to a friend as he had known in the last month, and he wasn't going to stand back and let her suffer. Something in Aaron's response seemed to hit Penny, maybe she recognised his voice, but her breathing became lighter and less pronounced, less desperate. After a minute or so in which she remained still, lying flat on the floor, she finally began to stir. She lifted her head and looked up at Aaron.

'What are you doing here?' she whispered, her voice raspy and dry.

'Well, actually, I was just passing. But…' Aaron looked away at the plain wall, tailing off.

'Go on then, pass. I know you don't like to help those in need,' Penny said bitterly.

There was an uncomfortable pause.

'I'm sorry,' Aaron said at last. It didn't seem like much, but he knew better than anyone that those words rarely came from his mouth. 'I wish I had an excuse. The truth is, I don't know why I didn't help.'

'Yeah, well, it was probably for the best,' Penny muttered. She was still lying on the ground, now despairingly curled in the foetal position.

'Umm… so, where's the girl?' Aaron asked casually, looking around as if he suddenly expected to find her sat in the corner of the room.

'Gone,' Penny stated.

'Gone where?' Aaron asked, confused.

'Well, if I knew that I probably wouldn't be lying here,' Penny replied dryly. Aaron still didn't understand what she meant, though he got the feeling he shouldn't blunder on with further questions. He waited, instead, for Penny to expand on her statement of her own accord. At last, Penny sat up, dragging herself along the floor to lean against the wall.

'She came in here to use the bathroom,' Penny began slowly, as if recounting a horrible memory. 'I waited outside, but she was taking ages. I figured she'd fallen asleep or something, so I began to doze off. Then I heard the door unlock. I got up expecting to see her coming out, but the door didn't open. I pushed the door open but there was no-one in here. It was like some kind of sick magic trick, only with a bathroom instead of a cabinet or something.'

Aaron listened intently, but he didn't understand. How could that be possible? He looked around the room, trying to come up with an explanation. There must be another exit somewhere.

'There isn't any other way out,' Penny stated, watching Aaron and reading his mind. 'I looked. A lot.'

'Where did she go, then?' Aaron asked desperately. People didn't just disappear from bathrooms.

'I reckon she got out.'

'What, you think the exit is in here?' Aaron blurted, suddenly excited.

'No... well, not for us, anyway. Yazmin kept telling me that she didn't commit any crime to end up in here. I think they came and took her away.' Penny sounded defeated.

'Okay...' Aaron thought for a moment. 'Then why were you in here crying?'

Penny looked directly at Aaron for the first time. She stared at him as if she couldn't believe he just asked that question.

'Maybe because I just lost a friend. Or maybe because this place is simply impossible, and I just wanted to dive into my own pit of self-pity and give up.'

There was a prolonged silence after this heavy statement. Aaron couldn't think of anything to say. What were you supposed to say to someone who had just told you that wanted to give up? He let an awkward silence to envelope him, until an idea popped into the back of his mind. He remembered that he had his task. This was perfect; he could give Penny a purpose once more, if nothing else.

'I need your help,' he stated quickly. Penny looked at him with a puzzled expression.

'What with? I'm kind of busy here,' she replied. Aaron

had noticed a sense of depressed cynicism within Penny that hadn't existed before. The Maze was certainly getting the better of her. Aaron fully understood that. It was the worst place he'd ever been, and he'd been to Times Square on multiple occasions. He explained about his run-in with Antonio, how he had lost his last memento from the outside world, and his need to reach the tree before Antonio did. Only now did he realise how stupid this plan had been before he'd met Penny.

He hadn't stood a chance against Antonio on the previous occasion and now he was even more defenceless. Antonio had taken his only weapon and he wasn't about to take him on in a fist fight. He needed Penny, at least, and maybe more.

'Why do you need to stop him, though? What difference does it make? Why don't you just let him take it, it's only a stupid watch,' Penny argued. Aaron hadn't expected he would need to justify his case.

'It's a principle, isn't it? The watch made everything more bearable down here. We can't just let him take whatever he wants,' Aaron said, a little desperately. Penny certainly didn't seem convinced.

She looked quizzically into Aaron's face, trying to work him out, then she looked down at her grubby hands and the grimy clothes that hung from her body. It was amazing to witness. It was as if something clicked in the back of her mind in that instant, and she looked up with a completely different expression.

'You're right,' she said stubbornly. 'The only way this place is going to feel like the real world is if we do it ourselves.' Aaron smiled at her. He had missed Penny immensely in the last two weeks.

Chapter 38

Yazmin's eyes had been opened by the vast control room. For some reason she had never once considered that there were people watching her in the Maze. She suddenly became very self-conscious, aware of her pitiful actions and how these people must have judged her.

Flint showed her around the room and talked her through the giant screen. Yazmin watched as the red dots that signalled each member of the Maze gradually floated around. Her eyes were drawn first to the dot that was marked "TJ Bogle". He was still alone. That didn't really surprise Yazmin. He wasn't the type that wanted or needed anyone else around; the only reason he and Yazmin had spent so much time together was because he'd been looking after her.

Yazmin's eyes scanned the screen, searching for Penny. Eventually she spotted her, apparently still in the same spot that Yazmin had left her. This concerned Yazmin, though as she watched another dot approached her position. This one was labelled "Aaron Johnston" and Yazmin felt a jolt of relief. If Penny was suffering, hopefully Aaron could help her. Though, from her own experiences, he wasn't someone who seemed overly helpful in this kind of situation.

Flint watched her all the while as she remained glued to the screen, watching the shaded walls move from time to time when nobody was near. It was fascinating. Then something occurred to Yazmin, and she turned back to Flint. He was sat in a distant corner, silently observing the activity in the room. Yazmin had expected him to be right at the forefront, barking orders. Everything about Flint was different to her expectations. He was quiet and philosophical, a far cry from what she had anticipated.

'What *exactly* do you want me to do here?' Yazmin asked tentatively. 'It seems like you've got everything pretty well covered.'

'You'd think,' Flint replied dryly. 'I need someone who truly understands what it's like to live down there. We can watch from here all we like, but we don't truly know what's going on in the Mazers' heads. That's where you'd come in. You can be a... Maze Psychological Advisor.' He plucked the title from the air with a cheeky grin. Yazmin couldn't help but let out a chuckle. She was beginning to like this Flint, which she had certainly not expected before meeting him. He let off an air of casual comfort that was infectious.

Another twenty minutes later, Yazmin left the hotel's front doors, a wave of fresh air hitting her like ecstasy. She squinted her eyes against the blazing sunlight that filtered through her sunglasses. Now her head was spinning with all new thoughts, mainly around the process of explaining her decision to her parents, particularly her father. She knew he wouldn't be pleased in the slightest. He hated the way she'd been treated, and Yazmin appreciated him for that, but even he had to admit there was another side to the Maze. After all, if it hadn't been for Flint, she wouldn't be breathing fresh spring air into her lungs right now.

The conversation with her dad had been as predictable as it could have possibly been. She had decided to get it out of the way as soon as she got into the back of his burgundy estate car.

'The cheek of it!' he remarked. 'After all they put you through, I can't believe that Flint even asked!'

'This is a good chance for me to get back on my feet,' Yazmin protested softly.

'So's a brothel, but don't expect me to endorse that either!'

'Roger!' her mom exclaimed in shock. 'There's no need

for that,' she added sternly.

'Sorry, Debs, but you can't tell me that you think this is a good idea?' Yazmin's mum stared at the car in front awkwardly, fidgeting with her seatbelt.

'Actually, I think this is perfect. She'll certainly know what she's talking about. And... and she might actually be able to make a difference — y'know, stop the next Yazmin coming out looking quite so dishevelled.'

'Oh, thanks, Mom,' Yazmin retorted.

'Well come on now, honey, you can't say you're looking your best right now.'

Yazmin shrugged her agreement.

'Look, can we leave it for now and just get going, please?' Yazmin requested. Nothing more was said, but Yazmin was beginning to regret her words; it was going to be a long drive based on the fractious silence filling the stuffy car. Fortunately, Yazmin was soon distracted by the world she had so dearly missed. The store fronts they passed seemed brighter than ever, despite the sunglasses tinting her vision. They were crammed full of an assortment of fascinating objects that Yazmin was only now realising she had missed in the last month. In truth, they weren't very interesting at all, but as Yazmin had seen nothing but grey walls, golden lanterns, and the odd stone carving her eyes couldn't move quick enough to keep up.

*

Four hours later, as they pulled into the driveway of their suburban home, a thought struck Yazmin. This would be a very long commute on a daily basis. She thought she would save that conversation with her dad for another day.

Chapter 39

A week had passed and still there was no sign of Antonio at the watch. Penny and Aaron had set up camp on either side of the collection of real-world artefacts, waiting for the inevitable. But the inevitable seemed to be a little slower than Aaron had expected. Even now, with the two of them working together, Aaron wasn't overly confident. They were both severely diminished from their outside selves and neither of them stood within a foot of Antonio.

Aaron had watched on cautiously as the occasional visitor would come by to check out the collection of goods or check their timings. He'd tried to explain why he and Penny were there to a few of them to gain some extra support, but no-one seemed very willing, though they were all more than happy to keep stopping by to check on the time and take their pick of the surprisingly large selection of books that had turned up.

Penny and Aaron hadn't spoken much in the last week. She still seemed distant and distracted, and Aaron didn't feel comfortable trying to get her to open up. He felt a lot of blame for the condition he'd found her in and couldn't bring himself to discuss it. After two days, Aaron had suggested Penny go and find some food. They knew there was a food room not too far from the tree and she hadn't eaten for days. Aaron could see a noticeable difference in her pallid appearance.

She'd returned from the food room several hours later with her pockets overflowing with an assortment of food for Aaron. This had made Aaron feel a lot better, as clearly she wasn't too mad at him. She had even remembered that his favourite sandwich was egg and cress. After a short and awkward conversation, they'd returned to silence, sitting a few feet apart as Aaron made his way through the food

Penny had provided.

Now, after several uneventful days, the pair continued to wait patiently. Aaron still had no idea what he planned to do when Antonio turned up. The very thought of meeting him again was terrifying. He couldn't imagine standing up to anyone, let alone a man so clearly stronger than himself. As he pondered that very issue, he heard someone approaching from the adjoining corridor, walking slowly with heavy, deliberate footsteps.

He looked around at Penny with a look of panic on his face and quickly jumped to his feet, chucking the copy of *Harry Potter* he'd been reading to the side. Penny scrambled to her feet, too, steely-eyed but shaking a little. They both stood rooted to the spot as the footsteps grew louder, but when the owner finally showed himself, it wasn't Antonio but another similarly built man. Aaron relaxed immediately, though Penny didn't. Aaron suddenly realised she didn't even know what Antonio looked like. The man looked bemusedly at the two of them, Penny with her fists raised comically.

'Who are you?' the man asked, raising his eyebrows at Penny. She quickly lowered her fists, catching on that this man was not, in fact, Antonio.

'Erm. I'm Aaron, this is Penny,' Aaron said hesitantly.

'Right... and what are you doing? Acting as guards or something?' the man chuckled.

'Well, kinda, yeah,' Aaron replied awkwardly.

'From what?'

Aaron went into a long explanation of his meeting with Antonio. He knew having someone of this man's stature on their side would be a great help, and he was more than keen to go into detail about how terrible Antonio was. The man nodded patiently as Aaron told his story, and at the end he let out a deep sigh.

'I know this Antonio,' the man said. 'I didn't know his name, but I met him a couple of days back. He tried the same thing on with me, but I wasn't having any of it.' Aaron noticed a bruise underneath the man's gristly beard. He figured there was a little more to that story, but he wasn't prepared to ask.

'Great, so will you help us?'

'When you say "help us"…' The man looked the two of them up and down. 'I feel like I'd be doing most of the work.'

'Yeah… I guess so.'

'You know what? I will help, though,' the man said, thinking.

The man, who had introduced himself as Marcus, told Aaron and Penny a surprisingly emotional story of his first encounter with the watch. He marvelled at Penny's pieces of artwork — as everyone who learnt she was the artist did — and talked them through a plan of attack, or rather defence, that made their initial plan of just sitting and waiting seem remarkably juvenile. Eventually the three of them set up at the opposite end of the corridor to the tree, crouching low in the wall's shadows to avoid being seen. Aaron already felt much more confident with Marcus around; it was as if he had defended a wall-mounted watch before.

Finally, five hours of unbearable silence later, the man they were waiting for finally lumbered around the corner. Immediately his eyes widened as he took in the watch for the first time. The three of them waited in silence as Antonio approached the watch, looking up and down the corridor — they were far enough away that he wouldn't spot them lurking in the dark. Antonio stepped right up to the watch and stared at it intensely for several seconds. Marcus had insisted they give him a chance to prove himself, but Aaron was fidgety just watching him. Antonio could reach out and grab the watch for his own at any second, along with everything else that lay congregated on the floor below it.

For several minutes the three of them watched on in silence. Aaron was certain that Antonio would take the watch, but he was left in shock as Antonio slowly turned away and began walking straight towards them.

'Come on, let's move,' Marcus whispered. Aaron didn't need telling twice. He turned, grabbed Penny's hand, and bolted down the corridor. He felt a little ashamed that he had judged Antonio so quickly, but, then again, he did steal his only possession so maybe he wasn't that rash.

Chapter 40

McKenzie really regretted running away from Natasha, but he knew he had to. He'd proven himself unworthy of relationships and he actually felt scared. But it wasn't normal fear. He felt scared of himself, terrified of what he might do if he got too close to another human. He'd never considered himself capable of any such act before meeting Jessie, but for some reason that relationship had brought out the very worst of him and he would wear the scars forever.

As soon as he was out of sight of Natasha, McKenzie had fallen to the floor, curled up in shock. He was so incredibly torn. He did like Natasha, maybe even more than he ever liked Jessie, but that just made it harder. He couldn't risk hurting another person he cared about. He really hoped she wouldn't come looking for him; he couldn't deal with explaining his feelings and the subsequent arguments that were bound to follow.

After a few hours of wallowing in his own ball of shame, he recomposed himself and decided he needed to put some distance between himself and Natasha in the hope that they wouldn't run into each other any time soon. Over the days following he didn't sleep at all. Everything seemed futile. For about a week he continued onwards, alone. He deliberately avoided the watch as he figured he stood a stronger chance of bumping into Natasha there, or anyone for that matter. He wanted to be alone now; he'd realised it was the best thing for him. If he knew Natasha at all, he was sure she would be lurking around the watch, expecting him to appear. He was determined not to, despite how hard this made his own life.

McKenzie was back in a space with no knowledge of time. Having the watch in the Maze had definitely helped his time-keeping abilities, but not being sure made everything harder. He didn't know if he'd been ambling along for three days, five, or even seven. Something felt different about this loneliness though; he felt stubbornly controlled in his exile from anyone and everyone. Before, when he had first entered the Maze, McKenzie had always felt a sense of hopelessness verging on insanity as he struggled to cope with the constant companionship of only himself. Now, however, he felt at ease with his position because it was of his own accord — it was freeing to feel so independent.

Then again, McKenzie knew it was a slippery slope once you became comfortable with your own solitude. The people McKenzie did meet were becoming more and more sallow, a sickly shade of grey that seemed to be emanating from the walls themselves. It wasn't healthy to be out of the sunlight for this long. In the days that followed McKenzie didn't meet a single person whom he would consider healthy. The haunted faces he passed were gaunt and depressed, as if from an apocalyptic film. He knew he must look the same way, malnourished and sleep deprived as he was. The only sense of his appearance he had any more was his touch. His greasy beard was thicker than it had ever been, covering a lean jawline that had never existed before the Maze.

Under his eyes he felt bulging bags which carried his fatigue for all to see. On the top of his head, scruffy, oily hair was ruffled messily in all directions. McKenzie had no desire to try and fix this issue. He knew nobody would be judging him down here. There was no one *to* judge him anymore.

He felt more focused on the barrier that stood before him than ever before in the last month. He began to think a little outside the box. Certain there was no physical way out of the Maze, he began to consider what he must do to get out of this hell. It was clearer than ever to him that the Maze could not just be a dead end. There would be riots if it came to light that all of them had effectively been trapped away to die slow and painful deaths, locked in their own heads. If Flint had been that twisted, McKenzie doubted he would have given them such luxuries as food or bathrooms.

With these irrational worries behind him, what was ahead became much easier to think about. Some way or another, his previously addled brain had come back to life and everything seemed obvious now. Perhaps he had finally recovered from the initial shock and anguish which he had allowed himself to be swallowed by. He realised that there was almost certainly some way in which Flint's team was watching them all, which comforted him but also embarrassed him at the same time. He also realised this must mean they were watching his behaviours, assessing his progress. He considered this very thought for some time. It was an issue he couldn't avoid. If they were looking for some sign of reconciliation, a moment in which he would prove he had learnt his lesson, surely he would need to be around fellow people. Only actions could prove this, unless they were in some way reading his mind.

As he played with this thought in his head, separated from the reality of the many grey walls in front of him, something snapped him back into focus. A smell. An actual real-life smell that wasn't the same as every other waking minute; not the mixture of his own odours, the weak smell of urine, and the ever-present stony smell. It was the smell of the sea, McKenzie was sure of that. But it couldn't be, could it?

His mind raced. He was so disorientated that McKenzie had no idea if he could actually be by the sea. He didn't even know where he'd entered the Maze in the first place.

McKenzie supposed it was more than possible he was near the sea, though he hadn't expected to be able to actually smell the salty air or feel the fresh breeze it brought with it.

Ironically, the salty scent seemed to come and go in waves. No sooner had he smelt it, it had disappeared without a trace, leaving him sniffing the air like a blood hound and questioning his sanity. Fortunately, it soon reappeared, and he began searching for some sign as to where it was originating from. There was no sign that he was near the edge of the Maze. The ceiling was as distant as ever in all directions, an apparent infinite expanse beyond the nearest wall. It didn't make any sense, but McKenzie was determined not to obsess over the mystery. It was a magnificent moment because it was finally something different, but it wasn't going to help him, so he braved on, marching away down the corridor, the scent slowly diminishing.

Chapter 41

It was now eight weeks since the Maze had begun operating. Diego watched on nervously as the Maze officers attempted to pull off the most ambitious operation yet. On Yazmin's orders, they were placing a large number of speakers on top of the Maze walls. It had already taken two days so far, with a large portion of the Maze still to be completed. Each speaker needed to be connected to the electronic circuit which had also been created during the project, as it was impossible to get to the only electrics in the Maze without causing a large disturbance.

Yazmin's idea was simple, yet she believed it would really help the Mazers feel more connected to the outside world, giving them hope and motivation. She told Diego of the despair she had felt at being so distant from what was going on in the world and pitched to him the idea of reading out a daily piece that would be heard across the Maze. In this, the Mazers would be able to hear a brief update of the world's news, as well as weather and any other necessary announcements.

Diego was proud to see Yazmin stepping into her role so whole-heartedly. She'd been tentative to say her piece at first, but it was remarkable to see how quickly she'd grown in confidence. This entire, expensive operation was her personal doing, and Yazmin didn't doubt herself in the slightest. Diego supposed that was the kind of confidence that came with experience; she knew exactly what she was talking about.

She was still remarkably thin, and Diego often sat with her for hours at a time without seeing her eat. He figured she was just used to a sporadic eating pattern. That was a little concerning, as it put a dent in his ambitions to see these people enter society seamlessly. That already seemed almost impossible to achieve. Yazmin still had to occasionally wear her sunglasses indoors to protect her fragile eyes, and she was so thin and grey that Diego wouldn't be surprised if someone mistook her for a zombie.

Still, she seemed happy enough. Diego had been delighted to see her smile on her second day in the control room. Thinking back, he couldn't ever remember seeing her smile other than that brief moment in the food room when she had first met TJ. That was another matter Yazmin had been keen to discuss. She had eventually agreed to Diego's incessant petitioning for her to be the one to deliver the daily news, as it was her idea, but on one condition. Diego had been forced to agree that she would be allowed to personally thank TJ and Penny. He wasn't overly keen on the idea, as he felt this offered them a little too much insight into the world beyond the Maze. He wanted to keep them as secluded as possible in their own little bubble.

Nevertheless, he had been forced to agree to Yazmin's proposal, trusting that she had their best interests at heart. Tomorrow morning Yazmin would deliver her first speech to the Maze. Diego could tell she was nervous — she had been wide-eyed and on edge all day, frantically making notes so quickly she wrinkled the paper. Her hands were constantly shaking and, if possible, her skin had become even paler. Diego had caught her practising in the corridor outside the control room the previous afternoon. Her voice was still hoarse and dry even almost a month on, as if she'd suffered some horrible chest infection.

Yazmin knew more than anyone how much this would mean to the Mazers, and she wanted to get it exactly right. Diego admired that commitment and passion. Meanwhile, he was still busy attending board meetings that he'd deemed completely pointless. He now approached the meetings with a new kind of dread. For the first couple they'd seemed terrifying, but by now it was simply the dread of sitting in a dull, colourless board room for an immeasurably long time bored out of his wits. The board didn't seem very interested at all in the finer points of the Maze. In fact, Diego began to wonder if they would even bat an eyelid if he told them the entire Maze had burnt down — not that that was really possible due to the limited amount of flammable materials in the Maze.

In fact, the entire process of the Maze had become far more of a nine-to-five, dreary affair than Diego could ever have anticipated. Everyone within the control room had fallen into a similarly boring routine to those on the screen in front of them, eagerly awaiting something exciting. Unfortunately, these exciting moments had become more and more sparse as the weeks went by. At one point, it was an entire week before any of the Mazers' point totals were changed.

Unfortunately, the Maze now featured multiple negative scorers. The most recent wave of entrants had briefly ensued on a tirade of violent and nasty acts upon their fellow Mazers which involved thievery and, in more than one case, physical assault. Despite the chaos, Diego's meeting with the board that week had been his shortest to date. He'd been particularly dreading the backlash he would be facing, but nothing. The board were remarkably dismissive.

That week of chaos was certainly a setback, more in Diego's head than anything. Ever since the Maze had opened, Diego's unerring confidence had been wavering. More and more regularly he would have moments of doubt that grew like an infestation in his brain. It was unsettling at best.

Fortunately, the new Mazers had slowly begun to settle into their new home. The violence became less frequent until it eventually ebbed away completely. It seemed the new Mazers found the Maze similarly despairing, though in this case with a slightly less detrimental effect. The biggest issue Diego was facing was the serious lack of interactions between the Mazers. He had noticed that some of the longer serving members were beginning to seek out others more frequently, going out of their way to reach out to their fellows. He could only hope this would become more apparent over the coming weeks. The Maze was designed to help people reconcile themselves in a much faster way than in any other prison. At the moment, that was looking like a pipe dream.

Diego forced himself to focus on the positives in his moments of doubt. The Maze had been open for two months without any major incidents. There were currently seventy people in there, unsupervised by any guards, that had successfully avoided any catastrophes. There had been minor physical attacks, but if Diego was honest, this was as good as he could have hoped for. The likelihood of locking seventy people up together, many of whom were armed, and not needing to intervene once was rather unlikely. The only thing stopping him celebrating this achievement was the voice in the back of his head telling him it had to end at some point.

The following day, Diego woke at the crack of dawn, full of excitement. Today would be momentous in the history of the Maze; the first contact from the outside world. Thinking about it like that it felt more like the first contact with an alien race. Diego supposed that the outside world was so distant to the Mazers that it might as well be a message from some Martians.

He wondered how Yazmin was feeling this morning. It

didn't take him too long to find out. Diego got dressed and ready for the big day and went down to the hotel lobby, accompanied by his usual security patrol. Every morning he ate breakfast in the small restaurant, almost always the only person in the entire room. However, to his surprise when he walked in to the oddly burgundy-set room, his feet sinking into the thick carpet, he found Yazmin already sat at his table.

She looked as reminiscent as she did the day she had been withdrawn from the Maze. The bags under her eyes were a sure sign that she had managed little, if any, sleep. She grunted an acknowledgement of Diego's arrival as he sat down, playing with her scrambled egg listlessly.

'Long night?' Diego asked well-meaningly.

'Yeah. Except time seems to be going much faster than normal,' Yazmin bemoaned.

'It does have a tendency of doing that when you really don't want it to,' Diego smiled.

'What a great comfort,' Yazmin stated sarcastically.

'So, how are you feeling? Ready?'

'Yeah, I guess so. I must have rehearsed about a thousand times, so I'd like to think so.'

'You know, these people haven't heard anything from the outside world in months. They will appreciate this no matter how many times you stumble over your words.'

'Oh, that helps.' Yazmin rolled her eyes. 'That's what's making me nervous! This is going to be *so* important to them.'

Diego shrugged. He didn't want to linger on the subject, knowing how much Yazmin had already been obsessing over it.

'Are you settling in now?' he asked, trying to change the topic. Yazmin had moved into the hotel on the floor below Diego's. She'd struggled to get settled into her new home at first, this being the first time she had moved away from her childhood home and her parents.

'Yeah, I guess so. I think it would have been easier if my first adult home hadn't felt so much like a prison.'

'Do the prisons in your head have swimming pools, then?' Diego sniggered without thinking.

'No, the prisons in my head have ten-foot-high walls and no exits,' Yazmin retorted, making Diego feel terrible.

*

Three hours later, Yazmin's trembling hands held a microphone, a palpable silence spreading around the control room as everyone watched on eagerly. Her face was set in a stony expression, a combination of nerves and a steely resolve to make this occasion a great success. Diego sat in the front row, keen to be at the forefront of activity for once. He watched anxiously as Alex gave Yazmin a thumbs up, signalling her to begin. Yazmin took a deep breath and gently cleared her throat.

'Testing. One, two. One, two. Ah, man I always hated the dads that did that,' Yazmin joked. 'Are we good?' she added, looking to Alex. Alex nodded.

'Hello to everyone in the Maze. My name is Yazmin, and this is a very special, first daily announcement from the outside world…'

Diego watched as Yazmin's shy demeanour slowly disappeared. She was a natural. His attention was quickly drawn to the giant screen she was addressing. Several different images filled the screen, each with a different Mazer within the frame. Every single one of them had frozen, stiff as a board, looking up to the ceiling above them in amazement.

'…I will be discussing news from the outside world every morning for the foreseeable future. Today might be a bit longer than usual as there is quite a bit to catch you upon,' she giggled heartily.

'So, let's begin. Today is March the first, as I know first-hand how hard it is to keep up in there. It is eleven o'clock. Today, it's pretty sunny out, spring is definitely on its way. Anyway, on to catching you up.'

Diego listened intently in unison with every single Mazer. All seventy dots had stopped moving completely, their owners too busy focusing on every word out of Yazmin's mouth. Yazmin discussed all the major events that had taken place in the world over the last two months, from the winners of the Super Bowl to the outbreak of a civil war in Venezuela. For the entire twenty minutes, nobody in the entire Maze moved a muscle. Nor did anybody so much as twitch in the control room as they hung on to Yazmin's words. Diego felt goosebumps spreading along his arms and neck as he listened in awe. Finally, Yazmin made it to her final juncture. The one she had been most excited yet anxious for.

'Finally, I wanted to take a moment personally to thank those that helped me. Most of you won't know, but I was, myself, in the Maze for over a month. During that time, I had more than my fair share of struggles and two people particularly helped me get to where I am today, and I would like to take a moment to thank them. So, to Penny and TJ… it's hard to put into words how grateful I am for your help when I was at my lowest. Please know that I won't forget what you did, and I will be willing you on throughout your time in the Maze. Thank you all for listening.'

Something inside of TJ did a loop-the-loop the moment he heard that amplified voice echoing through the corridors. It was Yazmin. He had been certain from the second he heard her voice. It filled him with a sense of jubilation to know that she was safe, but it was conflicted substantially with the spiteful feeling of jealousy burning him up. He hated himself for that. TJ had always thought Yazmin was a better person than him, but it was hard to know it really was true.

Still, her message had been an incredible lift. Just to know that the outside world hadn't gone up in a mushroom cloud brought some relief to an otherwise dreary life in the Maze. It was amazing to hear her talk normally, almost confidently. TJ learnt something new, too; it was March. Who knew? Despite the count by the watch that was updated daily, TJ had lost track of an association with days of the week or months. Every day was the same, so it didn't matter if it was a Saturday or a Wednesday.

It wasn't like he could look forward to the days getting longer or the weather getting warmer either. If anything, a longer day at this moment in time struck TJ as his worst nightmare; simply more time to spend wondering these endlessly tedious hallways. It was like walking a never-ending maths corridor knowing there was no way to reach the lunch hall.

It was tough to even picture what the outside world must be like at this moment. For some reason it felt so long since TJ had seen it that he imagined flying cars filling the sky like a scene from *Metropolis*. Spring had always been TJ's favourite time of year, so full of a youthful hope in great expectation of the times coming in the following months. Right now, he couldn't imagine a crisp wind blowing through the Chicago streets or the sight of a glorious morning sun framed by pearly white clouds. He felt no attachment to that world anymore. This was his home now.

But it couldn't stay that way. His life before had been horrible, a real-life disaster movie with very little comic relief. Yet, for some inexplicable reason, he was desperate to return to it. To go back to that messed up reality that everybody just accepted as the given way of living. Perhaps people were just too comfortable to try and make any major changes in their lives.

Chapter 43

'Do you think he saw us?' Penny asked hastily.

'Oh, that's easy! *Jurassic Park*!' Aaron replied. They were playing another of Aaron's brainteaser games. However, for some reason, it felt less forced and much more enjoyable than before. They were naming lines from famous movies that the other person had to guess.

'Okay, if it's that easy, you go then!' Penny stated resolutely.

'Hmmm. Let me think,' Aaron said, smiling. He had clearly been saving one but wanted to make it seem off the hook. 'Oh, I know! Don't cross the streams.'

There was silence for a minute as Penny thought, but it wasn't an awkward silence. There was a new lease of life in their relationship that had brought an energy that was otherwise non-existent before. Penny desperately tried to rack her brains for the answer. She knew she'd heard that before, but she couldn't quite place it.

'Do you want a clue?' Aaron interjected tauntingly.

'No, no. I'll get it in a minute,' Penny replied stubbornly.

They continued to walk on absent-mindedly, with no intent or purpose. Aaron had been keen to put as much distance between themselves and Antonio despite his apparent revelation in front of the watch. It was weird to see how terrified of Antonio Aaron was. He certainly didn't seem overly intimidating, though Penny had only seen him from a distance. Something about their meeting had changed Aaron, though — he was jumpy and alert now, insistent that one of them should always be awake, which meant they had much less time for travel. Not that there was anywhere new to go.

'I've got it!' Penny suddenly blurted out; it had suddenly hit her mid-thought. '*Ghostbusters*! I knew I'd heard it.'

Aaron nodded in concession; he was clearly a little disappointed it had taken her that long, though. He didn't understand that Penny didn't have the same memory as him. Hers was closer to a goldfish's than to Aaron's.

'Well done,' he said. 'Your go again.'

'Okay, let me try and come up with a harder one this time,' Penny said excitedly as they strolled on.

As they returned to silence Penny's thoughts fell back to Yazmin's message. She'd been thinking about it a lot. Yazmin had always insisted she had been innocent, and clearly she'd actually been telling the truth. Penny was glad she'd found the safety and comfort she clearly deserved, and it'd certainly eased some of the bitterness she felt towards the whole ordeal; she just wished Yazmin could have said something before vanishing. Anything.

The news she'd delivered was most welcome. It was fantastic to hear from the outside world after all this time. It seemed to give the entire Maze a new lease of life, which was direly needed. There was suddenly something else to talk about other than how grey a particular wall looked at any certain moment. Penny was glad she had Aaron back to talk about what Yazmin had shared with them — they'd discussed at length the developments in climate change. Knowing Aaron had been a Wall Street banker, Penny was surprised to hear his liberal views on the matter. Maybe they weren't all as bad as she had imagined. They did get a bad rep in films and TV, which probably hadn't helped Penny's assumptions.

In fact, Aaron was far from what Penny expected from a banker. Rather than being ruthless and cocky, he was actually shy and nerdy. It appeared his only real flaw was a lapse in his morality which had led him to make a selfish decision, one that Penny could tell he regretted. Unfortunately, his regret felt more like a selfish one. He regretted being caught, not his actions. He regretted that he'd ended up in a place as close to a literal hell on earth as possible.

Penny still hadn't come to terms with her own lapse in morality. She'd never fully understood it. She'd desperately searched herself for an explanation, a reason for what she'd done. It almost felt like somebody else had taken over her body for that time and only relinquished control once she was in the holding cell. At that moment, she'd suddenly became aware of herself once more, but it was too late.

Being aware of herself was definitely not an issue in the Maze. The only issue was being too aware. There was so much time to get lost in her own head, batting questions back in forth in her mind like an incessant child playing tennis against a wall, never going to win. In recent days Penny had resorted to saying everything out loud. Well, nearly everything. If she actually said everything she thought, Aaron probably wouldn't stick around for long. At one point she found herself falling into an endless circle of thinking about thinking, which then led her to think about thinking about thinking. Fortunately, this was when her head started hurting enough to break the circle.

Penny was still trying to come up with a decent movie quote. Aaron had a pretty extensive knowledge in the subject so every single one she'd said so far he had guessed within seconds. She even tried to catch him out with a quote from *Love Actually*, figuring he probably wasn't a rom-com kind of guy, but he answered without hesitation. Penny had teased him light-heartedly for some time, especially as he went a bright shade of vermillion the moment the answer slipped from his lips, muttering something about how his girlfriend had made him watch it.

This had been a good segue into a new conversation. Penny was interested to learn about Aaron's relationship. It turned out he and his girlfriend had broken up some time before he'd entered the Maze. Penny felt he'd actually got out pretty lightly — at least he hadn't had to suffer the awful blow of losing a relationship right before coming into the Maze, one way or another. Penny reckoned she had the market cornered on bad break-ups forever after what Toby did to her.

'I like that boulder. That is a nice boulder!' Penny said confidently at last. For a moment Aaron looked around, trying to spot the boulder that Penny might have been referring to. She felt very proud of herself that her acting had clearly been that believable. Aaron looked at her in confusion then realised what had happened, his face cracking into an embarrassed smile. He thought for a moment.

'You know what. I think you might have actually stumped me this time,' he said, looking down at the ground trying to rack his brains. Penny nearly punched the air in her success.

Chapter 44

It had now been six months since McKenzie had entered the Maze. He knew this thanks to the now weekly updates from the woman he'd learnt was named Yazmin. The daily news updates had lasted just two weeks and, in the end, McKenzie had been quite glad when they'd ended. The first few came with an immense sense of excitement and novelty, but after three or four it became very apparent that there was little to say. A comprehensive review of the weather was only so useful to him down in the Maze.

Inevitably, he had run into Natasha on the odd occasion. On a couple of those occasions he'd been able to change direction before she'd even noticed, but when he wasn't able to do so he was forced to awkwardly put his head down and pass by as hastily as possible. The most awkward of these meetings had been when McKenzie had been mid-laugh in conversation with Aaron. They had just turned a corner and McKenzie had lost concentration as he laughed heartily, almost causing him to stumble straight into Natasha. He wouldn't forget the look of betrayal on her face as she looked him up and down.

He'd met Aaron after around three months, and they'd stuck together for a short while. It was tough to last more than a couple of weeks with one person. The thing was, the Maze wasn't like anywhere else. He couldn't disappear into another room for a bit of alone time. If one the other person, he couldn't nip out for a walk. That was all they would wake up and start walking, not stopping, until they got bored enough to go to sleep again. McKenzie wasn't sure why he even bothered any more. There was never anything new to see.

There *had* been some new developments. Around the

time that McKenzie had been walking with Aaron, the Maze had left them some fresh clothes to change into in a food room. These were the most welcome supplies the Maze had provided so far. McKenzie had been painfully aware of the stench that emanated from his vicinity. They had even provided a bandana for each of them to tie back their overgrown bird's nest of hair. McKenzie had always wanted to grow his hair out, but maybe not in these circumstances. It would have been much better if he could have actually washed it, too.

Every month now new clothes would appear when McKenzie visited one of the food rooms. He spent more than a little time considering how they actually got there. He'd always assumed that there was some access into the Maze to keep it supplied, but he'd never seen anyone who wasn't a fellow prisoner wandering the halls.

Along with the fresh, beige clothes they were now regularly provided with, further luxuries were being presented, too. In the bathrooms it became regular to find a fresh soap bar, or even on one occasion a roll-on deodorant. Clearly, Diego Flint had begun to realise the error of his ways, or maybe he just felt bad for them. McKenzie even wondered if he'd been replaced. It would explain the sudden change in procedure.

Of all the people McKenzie had met in the Maze, he and Aaron had the best affinity, except maybe Natasha. Unfortunately, there was only a limited number of topics that could be covered and spending every minute of every day with someone was enough to grate on anyone.

Instead, McKenzie had become content to live with himself, something he'd never thought possible before the Maze. These days, he enjoyed the solitude and silence of his own company. He had noticed certain worries developing, however. The two-sided conversations he held in his own head and even out loud were reminiscent of Gollum from *The Lord of the Rings.* It was never particularly encouraging to see parts of Gollum in your own psyche.

Even six months into his life in the Maze, McKenzie felt no closer to leaving it. There were no hints to help him on his way, no clear path ahead. The worst thing was that the hope had gone. McKenzie felt old and withered now, accepting of his fate to be trapped here forever. He wasn't even that bothered by the idea of a life in the Maze; it was hard to picture the outside world enough to miss it anymore. It was a peaceful life in many ways, one without complications. Deep down, he knew he had to find a solution, though.

Chapter 45

Diego had just returned from a week away from the hotel compound after being convinced by Alex that it would be safe to do so. He realised now how much he had truly needed the break. It had become so regular for him to be sat dozily watching the big screen that even when he shut his eyes he still pictured red dots floating around in front of him. It was all he ever thought about now: what was next for the Maze and the people in it and how he could improve it. The week's break came as a small relief from this, but he had been unable to completely take his mind away from the Maze.

He'd also noticed a steady decline in his own mood. He was sure it was from watching the gloomy Mazers all day every day that had led him to fall into a depressive state that very much matched the mood of those on the screen. Alex, too, had noticed this. That was why she had suggested he take a break. The lack of success that the Maze had brought did not help, either. He'd been sure that they would have seen a breakthrough by now, but not one of the Mazers had been released yet, other than Yazmin. Diego didn't exactly count her release as a win.

Nevertheless, she had been a very useful partner since joining the team in the control room. It had been her who had campaigned for the Mazers to have access to fresh clothing and sanitary essentials. The Maze was no longer what Diego had first envisioned, but this was probably a good thing. His intent had been to make life within the Maze a struggle in order to force more social interaction between Mazers and develop faster responses to their situation. Even he could see this was not working.

The Mazers all seemed quite content to live solitary lives, or on occasion hold brief friendships that never lasted more than a few weeks. Diego had pictured groups forming, with four or five people joining together, leading to intricate and complex social circles. Only twice had more than two people spent any time together and on both occasions it had been for no more than a few hours.

Diego had walked into the control room on his first day back to find Alex and Yazmin at the helm, standing shoulder to shoulder in the aisle between the rows of computers. He snuck quietly over to his spot without saying a word, trying to get an opportunity to watch on without them being aware. The two women were too intently focused on the screen to notice him anyway. Diego took his seat silently and diverted his gaze towards what was distracting them, but he couldn't work out what was going on.

'Okay, can we see anything from McKenzie Symms now then, please?' Alex called over her shoulder. Soon the giant screen showed McKenzie sat slumped on the floor, looking thoroughly miserable. Just by looking at the man's hair Diego could tell this was from some time ago.

'What's going on, Alex?' he called, standing up and leaning on the desk in front of him. Both of the women in the aisle jumped and turned in sync. Alex whispered something to Yazmin and the shot of McKenzie quickly disappeared from view.

'Oh, Diego, sorry, we didn't hear you come in. We were actually just working on something for you. Kind of a welcome back gift,' Alex said, smiling slightly nervously. This didn't encourage Diego particularly. Meanwhile, Yazmin had gone scurrying away and was conversing rapidly with several of the operators. Diego raised his eyebrow.

'Am I allowed to ask what you were working on?' Diego asked hesitantly.

'No,' Alex said cheekily. 'It's a surprise.'

'Fine. Catch me up, then,' Diego stated, letting the matter slide. Alex sighed, her shoulders slouching a little as she ambled over and took a seat beside him.

'Honestly, there's not much to catch you up on. Certainly nothing of any interest, anyway. Nobody's points moved at all and there are only two pairs currently interacting.'

'Who are they?' Diego asked, a little excited.

'*Not* McKenzie and Natasha,' Alex replied, rolling her eyes at Diego. He'd really been rooting for the unlikely duo. He figured if anything could prove his Maze a success it would be a pair of star-crossed lovers. Alas, it was not to be.

Alex caught Diego up on the little activity that had happened on his week away. It didn't take long. However, Yazmin was soon scampering back over with something in hand. Diego rarely saw Yazmin without a smile on her face these days, but today it seemed even broader than usual, accompanied with a glint of excitement in her lucid, blue eyes. She held her hand out and Diego took the small rectangular parcel which had been neatly wrapped in vivid pink paper.

Diego tore into the paper, feeling a rare jolt of excitement in the pit of his stomach. It was a cassette. Diego wasn't sure what to make of it at first, he couldn't even think of anyone who had a cassette player these days. He flipped it from side to side, staring blankly in mild confusion until Alex finally realised there might be some explanation needed. Yazmin had been looking at her expectantly.

'Oh, right, sorry!' Alex giggled dopily. 'There's nothing actually on this tape. It's just a symbol, really. We didn't expect you in so early. Anyway, we've made you a-'

'Mixtape?' Diego laughed.

'Well… no. It's a gag reel, actually,' Yazmin stated, looking at Diego warily, as if unsure of his reaction. Again, Diego didn't know what to make of his gift. He decided to go along with it, waving for Alex to start the video. It turned out to be incredibly entertaining, just the mood-lifter he needed on an otherwise gloomy day.

The June summer weather outside was taunting him as he returned to the hotel compound that morning, surrounded by his personal guard. It made the transition back into the reality of the Maze that much more unbearable. The past six months had certainly taken their toll on Diego, causing him to feel withered and permanently exhausted. Having spoken to Diane before he left for the world's shortest sabbatical, she informed him that it was not unusual to begin expressing similar emotions to those you saw on a regular basis. Diego's problem was that the only people he saw were those on the giant screen and the people in the control room it bore down on. The people in the control room weren't exactly a barrel of laughs, either.

Diego took a deep breath as he took in the control room once more. Looking at each face, he suddenly realised he knew nothing of these people's real lives. He didn't know how many of them had families, or what they got up to outside of the control room. The worst thing was, he didn't want to know. It would only remind him of how empty his own life had become.

After a minute of staring vacantly at old Frank shuffling his feet as he hunched uncomfortably over his keyboard, prodding it one finger at a time, Diego returned to the giant screen. A lot had changed in the Maze since its inception. Each Mazer now wore dull beige clothing that was remarkably similar to something Diego would see in any other prison. That angered him. The one thing he had truly wanted was for the Maze to be different from the regular prisons.

Diego had not been keen on many of the changes that had occurred over the last few months, but he had to concede that his initial vision had been some way off the mark. He couldn't expect people to live for months upon months without their basic sanitary needs being met, he saw that now. It was embarrassing to think how cavalier he had previously been about such things as soap and clean clothes.

In the bottom right corner of the screen, the small fact file now marked the Maze at ninety-three point six kilometres in pathways, effectively double the opening size. Unfortunately, the statistic below had not followed a similar trajectory. After failing to show any positive results in the opening three months a decision had been made to officially hold any new Mazers. That meant there had been no new Mazers for four months, leaving the total holding steady at exactly seventy. The only way this was going to change was if anyone was to exit the Maze and, right now, Diego wasn't exactly holding his breath on that happening any time soon.

His gaze was drawn to two dots near the bottom of the Maze, which he knew to be the closest point in the Maze to where he sat at that very moment. The two dots were separate, though one was moving much faster than the other, gaining on the dot in front as they both travelled in the same direction. For some reason, Diego was intrigued by this. He asked for the giant screen to be zoomed upon that section. Such was the size of the standard map that it was no longer possible to keep the dots labelled, so Diego could not see who they belonged to.

As soon as the image was enhanced to focus on the

glaring dots, Diego's eyes widened intently. The dot at the front belonged to Natasha, the dot behind was TJ. Now that Diego could see clearly, he noticed an odd pattern in TJ's dot. It appeared to slow right down for a while, then quickly speed up when Natasha rounded a corner. Diego ran a hand through his thick holiday stubble, relishing in its ability to help him think. Something was off about this situation. It reminded Diego of watching a nature documentary showing a lion stalking its oblivious prey. It didn't bode well. Slowly, more heads began to turn to the screen to watch. Alex, sat at a desk at the front of the control room, turned to look at Diego with a worried expression, one which he returned.

But Diego didn't exactly feel *worried*. He felt a surge of guilt as he watched on in mild hope that something, anything, would happen that could upset the decorum of the Maze. It was a selfish instinct. He knew how much the Maze needed a spark of life, a moment of controversy that would change its history, and apparently he no longer cared who got hurt. For a brief moment, he looked away from the screen and down at his own feet, ashamed.

He didn't have long to be self-deprecative of his own morals. The two dots were replaced by a larger than life shot of Natasha, the camera perfectly placed at the end of the corridor she was walking along, unaware she was being stalked. Diego was able to see the corridor stretch before him for hundreds of meters, marked by the occasional light spots where the lanterns projected their golden glow. He saw Natasha in the foreground, around thirty metres away from the camera, dawdling along obliviously. Behind her TJ lurked, the perfect image of a great white shark's shadow looming under the waves before lurching into an attack. He was waiting at the edge of one of the circles of light, though still easy to make out because of the silhouette he cast.

Diego had to admit he was surprised by TJ's bizarre actions. In his previous encounters, Diego had held no reason to believe he would be capable of such behaviour – not in the Maze, anyway. Of course, he hadn't actually done anything yet. Something then struck Diego. He looked across at Yazmin cautiously; she had returned to a sickly shade of green and her hand was clenched tightly around her water bottle, shaking violently, as she too stared intently at the screen. As Diego watched, she gasped audibly and put her free hand to her mouth. Diego swivelled back around to see what had happened. He stood and slammed his hands onto the desk before him, causing many of the nearby operators to jump.

Chapter 46

Natasha let out a high-pitched scream like no sound she had ever made before. It was more the shock than anything that had cause such a reaction. Her wandering mind had been sent crashing back into the Maze as someone came charging up behind her. Natasha hadn't had a moment to react before they were on top of her. The assailant had grabbed her forcefully by the back of the neck and slammed her unceremoniously against the wall.

Her ears rang and her vision blurred as her head crashed into the wall. The breath was knocked out of her lungs, rendering Natasha incapable of making a sound, or of being able to make out her attacker as they breathed heavily on the back of her neck. She knew full well what was about to happen, but there was nothing she could do. The man had a strong hold on her, forcing her chest into the cool wall. She couldn't even call for help. All she could do was shut her eyes.

She prayed. For the first time in her life, Natasha actually began to pray, to anyone that would listen. She didn't like being in such a vulnerable state, unable to get out of the situation, helpless. It was not a feeling she was used to, and she was going to do everything in her power to do something about it. Natasha wriggled as much as her breathless form could manage, squirming from side to side and ducking down until she was balled up on the floor, her attacker casting an ominous shadow over her. She had never felt so small in all her life. She was quickly hauled back to her feet, but Natasha wasn't stubborn for nothing. She refused to be a part of this, so again her knees crumpled, and she fell to the floor.

Slowly, Natasha's breath had begun to come back to her and her vision was clearing, but the burly man stood above her was not giving up. She received a heavy blow to the back of her head as she struggled to escape his grasp. making her whole world spin. The back of her loose-fitting beige top was seized roughly and hoisted into the air effortlessly with Natasha attached. She heard several seams rip worryingly. Her head now pounding, Natasha finally began to accept once and for all that she wasn't getting away from this. A hot tear slid down her numb cheek and she closed her eyes, allowing her body to go limp.

Chapter 47

McKenzie had heard someone screaming. It was a horrible, goosepimple-inducing sound that had coursed down his spine sending a shiver along his entire body. Immediately his whole demeanour had changed. He had been languidly walking along, his body at ease in this now strangely comfortable environment, but now he was rigid, upright, and full of attention.

He listened intently for another noise. His mental state was so poor that he couldn't rule out that he'd made the sound up. Seconds and then minutes passed, and still there was no further sounds, no signs that he need panic. Yet something told him he hadn't imagined the sound. He couldn't imagine *how* his brain would come up with such a blood-curdling noise.

He began to move hastily along the corridor, keeping close to the left-hand wall, leaning in close until he quickly remembered that the wall was three foot thick and made of solid stone; trying to listen for any noises was a little futile. Something remarkable then happened, something he hadn't seen in the entirety of his spell in the Maze: the walls moved. He had known, or at least had a strong hunch, since his first week in the Maze that they did move, yet he had never once seen it happen. If anything, this further ramped up the panic spreading in his mind, despite his awe at this whole new revelation. The fact that it had come to this moment for such details to be revealed to McKenzie emphasised the importance and urgency of the situation.

The movement of the walls at the very end of the corridor had revealed a pathway to the left, which was now his only option. McKenzie sprinted the remaining distance along the corridor and raced around the corner, skidding a little in his shoes that had soles smooth as a baby's skin by now. He went flying into the wall opposite in his rush to find the source of the scream. The worst thing was, McKenzie was pretty sure he knew who had made the sound. He just hoped he was wrong.

The pathway turned to the right, then immediately left once more, finally turning to the left again. McKenzie couldn't see why those controlling the walls made him go to all that trouble. At first this new, elongated corridor appeared as empty as any of the previous ones he had walked down, but then, some hundred yards in the distance, barely visible in a patch of darkness, something was moving.

It was hard to make out what was going on, but it was clear there was more than one person there, unless a wild animal had somehow found its way into the Maze. The odd, muffled noises echoing down the hallway certainly would support that theory. For a short moment, McKenzie stood frozen to the spot, staring down the stretching corridor. He had never considered himself a hero-type, but right at that moment McKenzie knew he needed to find something deep within himself.

A small squeal of anguish along the corridor awoke McKenzie from his brief slumber. He began pacing powerfully along the corridor, quickly breaking into a run. It felt weird to be running, or to be doing anything other than walking and sleeping for that matter. His joints were not quite prepared for this new, exaggerated motion. Gradually he built up more and more speed, helped by a steady decline along the corridor. Soon his feet were pounding the floor rapidly, truly showing how thin his shoes were. His feet tingled as if a thousand needles were being shoved into his soles. It felt great to be properly running, to feel the limited fresh air whistling through his hair, and for a moment McKenzie forgot about the predicament at hand.

The strange ball of limbs and shadow was now much clearer. McKenzie could definitely make out two bodies, despite the water now filling his eyes. Neither of the two people seemed to have heard his heavy, stomping feet flapping against the floor. McKenzie slowed for a moment, trying to come up with a plan. He came to a stop and hid against the wall opposite, watching the two mangled silhouettes struggling. It was impossible to tell in the poor light what exactly was going on.

McKenzie took a minute to catch his breath. It wasn't easy in the Maze's thin air, especially as his lung capacity seemed remarkably diminished. Eventually, the picture became much clearer to McKenzie. He could now make out a man and a woman from the two shadows. That answered many questions. He knew this wasn't a fight, for one. It also brought a lot of painful memories back, shame inducing memories. McKenzie felt a surge of rage causing his thinned jaw to clench.

He felt his legs begin to stride of their accord. His ears began to pulse with the blood surging through his body. Something had clicked and he felt anger like he hadn't felt for a long time. It was nice to feel any emotion other than the abject, hopeless misery. He broke once more into a run, breathing heavily through his flared nostrils. As he got closer and closer to the two grappling people, he felt every tension from the last six months coursing through his body. Within moments he was in reach.

There was no room in his mind for a tactful, gentle approach. Tunnel vision consumed him; he was a raging bull with a red cloth being waved in his face. Just before he came crashing into the scene, the hulking man suddenly realised what was happening, but it was too late. And too late for McKenzie, too. He had only just realised how large this man actually was. He slammed into the man with a crunching blow and immediately felt the wind disappear from his stomach. He wretched violently, trying to recover himself, as the gruff-looking man fell heavily to the floor.

The hefty man recomposed himself much faster and jumped back to his feet, lumbering up as he slowly approached McKenzie. McKenzie's inner rage had disappeared and was quickly replaced by a sense of dread. He knew he was in trouble now. He still couldn't breathe properly, and his lung's rasped rapidly in his panic. Hunched over, his eye's widened as he watched the man's clumpy shoes get closer and closer. In an instant he felt someone roughly rummaging through his pockets and remembered that there was a third person on the scene.

He looked to his left and was shocked to see a flash of faded purple hair covering the girl's face. It was Natasha. He could feel her heavy, frightened breathing on his neck as she struggled in his pockets. Finally, she pulled out his small penknife and McKenzie caught a flash of her face. It didn't seem like the same Natasha that he had known. Her eyes were wild, almost scary, whilst she bared her teeth like a rabid dog.

Natasha flicked her long hair out of her face and stood to confront the burly man. For a moment the two of them just stood and looked at each other as if they were starring in a western, McKenzie glancing from one to the other. Then, out of nowhere, Natasha had flipped the blade and was charging the man twice as large as she was. He didn't seem to expect this, and he wasn't prepared as Natasha dropped her shoulder and rammed into his midriff. McKenzie was full of admiration for someone so bold and so resourceful. She took down the man with ease.

Then the moment seemed to change, as if an ominous, droning noise had suddenly filled the cavernous Maze. A maniacal look had descended upon Natasha's face as she stood over the indisposed bulk of her attacker. Only now did McKenzie notice that her clothes were ripped in several places. She just stared at the man in disgust for what felt like an eternity, looking wild and angry. Then, in one motion, she raised the hand bearing McKenzie's knife and stepped ever closer. McKenzie couldn't believe what he was watching.

McKenzie knew what he had to do, no matter how much he felt the man deserved this retribution. He picked himself up with enormous effort and leapt towards Natasha, pulling her to the floor and away from the now cowering man. Natasha's menacing glare had remained set on her face, as if the wind had changed, making it stick, and McKenzie suddenly felt terrified as she turned on him. After several moments of intense eye contact between the two, Natasha's shoulders finally sagged, her whole demeanour relaxing. McKenzie allowed himself to breath after a what had been a frantic few minutes. Another minute passed in which none of them moved, all taking deep gulps of the thin, cold air, spluttering a little, deliberately avoiding each other's eyes.

Eventually, the unknown man stood, awkwardly using the wall to drag himself upright. Without looking, he turned and walked away, his tail between his legs. McKenzie and Natasha both watched him go suspiciously. McKenzie didn't know what to say; there were a thousand thoughts and emotions bouncing around his brain.

'Why did you stop me?' Natasha growled with a rigid jaw, still lying on the floor, propped up on one elbow.

'What, you think they would let you out if you killed someone?' McKenzie replied, dryly.

Natasha didn't say anything, just shrugged and looked away. McKenzie thought he could see a tear in her eye. He wanted to ask about what he had just witnessed, but it didn't seem like the moment. He sat up and crawled over to the wall and slouched lazily against it, watching Natasha. She was no longer present in the moment.

Chapter 48

Diego stood frozen, just like everyone else in the control room, his mouth hanging open like he was a cartoon character. There, at the bottom of the map, stood one solitary green dot. The dot that marked McKenzie Symms. After an incredibly eventful few minutes, the dot had flashed from red to green, causing the entire control room to break into a celebratory frenzy. Now the dust had settled, a remarkable hush had fallen over the room. Everyone was just staring in silence at the singular green dot in shock.

Minutes passed by with no-one moving a muscle. The two dots they were all staring at weren't moving, either. On the right-hand side of the screen, Natasha and McKenzie sat slumped against opposite walls. Natasha was still staring along the corridor in the direction that TJ had disappeared, whilst McKenzie kept giving her furtive looks, his face etched with concern. In a way, Diego hoped they didn't leave together. It would make the whole process of getting McKenzie out of the Maze that much easier if they went their separate ways. Finally, the silence was broken.

'You're right,' Natasha muttered, her voice echoing through multiple different speakers around the control room. McKenzie looked at her once more, this time with a look of shock. He had clearly not expected these words any more than Diego had. He nodded glumly but said nothing more. It was weird to see how distant these two had become, especially considering the intimate, life-changing moment they had just shared.

As if these words had somehow woken the entire control room, it quickly became abuzz with activity. Alex came rushing up to Diego, who was still stood motionless, his hands clenched in fists of triumph on the desk before him. He turned to her and suddenly broke into a ludicrous smile.

'We've got work to do,' he said, struggling to contain his ecstasy.

Chapter 49

A day had passed since the most eventful hour of McKenzie's six months in the Maze. He knew this because they had visited the watch together — it was the first time McKenzie had visited for a while, owing to his desire to avoid meeting Natasha there. Neither of them had spoken much. In fact, McKenzie wasn't sure how they had ended up staying together. Eventually they had just stood up and wandered off silently.

In fact, it took some time for anything more to be said. It was Natasha who finally broke the building tension when they reached the watch. She asked McKenzie if he had seen anybody new in the Maze recently. It was an odd question, one that McKenzie hadn't even considered, yet when he did it became even more confusing. He hadn't. When he voiced this to Natasha she nodded knowingly, then began to explain her theory. She explained how she had waited at the watch for three months, expecting to see McKenzie. He felt awful at that moment, but Natasha continued to talk. In all the time she had spent at the watch, she had never seen a new face. McKenzie wondered if it was possible that no new prisoners that had entered over the past three months.

Within the next twenty-four hours, their relationship quickly returned to a state of euphoria similar to that when they had just met. It was tearing at McKenzie from the inside. He liked Natasha, though he only began to realise how much in the silent minutes they had sat apart after her attack. The level of anger and aggression he had felt towards the man was so intense, a fury previously unmatched. That told McKenzie everything he needed to know. Yet, the ideology of a loving relationship seemed beyond his capabilities, particularly down here. That look on Natasha's face when she had stood over a defenceless man kept haunting his thoughts, too. It made McKenzie realise how little he actually knew her, and how much he didn't want to know.

It turned out they had a surprisingly large amount to catch up on. They'd barely spoken since the news updates had randomly begun one day, so they could at least discuss to some extent the world outside. This led to a topic McKenzie had felt scared to talk about before: Natasha's life before the Maze. All he knew really was that she was from Russia and that she was here because she'd been an activist for women's rights. Natasha had always been quite vague about that.

It turned out it hadn't been quite as "peaceful" as Natasha had first made out. Her activist group had been confronted by police during their protest and things had soon escalated. Natasha looked a little bashful for the first time as she told McKenzie of how she was caught grappling with a member of Russian riot police, half in the nude. McKenzie couldn't help but laugh at that added detail.

The days rolled by as the two of them hung out happily. McKenzie had swapped clothes with Natasha, trying to do the right thing. He didn't feel right allowing her to walk around with ripped clothing. In the back of his mind there was a constant debate taking place, but for the time being he didn't need to make an immediate decision, so he let it roll. Eventually McKenzie had to ask about the attack, knowing how unhealthy it was to repress painful memories. Natasha was clearly reluctant, but after a long pause she finally began to talk through gritted teeth.

Chapter 50

It had been a long, cold, tedious three months for Penny. Even the initially refreshing news from the outside had become mundane and dreary, much in keeping with the rest of the Maze. She had met some intriguing people during this time, though these encounters were often coupled with a sense of immediate danger and infinite mistrust, such was the nature of the place. She thought, or rather hoped, that she would get used to the gloomy surroundings she was presented with day after day, but that was far from the case. Every day she seemed to slip slightly further into a pit of her own making, wrestling with her own conscience.

Since she and Aaron had gone their separate ways, much more amicably than the first time, she had struggled to find any long-term friendships. She hadn't come across many other women in the Maze. In fact, as far as she could tell, there were only two women other than Penny in the entire place. She'd met them both briefly, but they didn't seem her type of people, not like Yazmin had been.

After six months and a week, Penny woke slowly to another magnificently dull day. She just sat for a while, slumped against the wall, her head leaning painfully against the cold stone. Fortunately, she had a large thicket of bushy hair obstructing any major pain. She had a strong tendency to wriggle in her sleep which had very often resulted in some painful bruises on her head when she woke. That was happening less and less frequently thanks to her increasingly wild and uncontrollable hair.

For several more minutes, Penny continued to stare at the slate-grey wall opposite her. She wore an inquisitive look as she pondered something. Eventually, she pushed a stray strand of hair that was covering the left portion of her face away, stood up, and, still wearing a puzzled expression, approached the wall, gently running her palm over it, feeling the cold sting of the slate-like stone. Her eyes moved to the top of the wall. She looked along the line that separated the dark-grey wall with the even darker skyline. She jumped up as far as she could and tried to touch the tip of the wall. She got nowhere near; she must have been two feet short at least. To an onlooker this would be incredibly odd behaviour.

As it happened, there *was* somebody watching, though Penny hadn't noticed him yet. He stood a little out of the way, watching silently around a wall at the end of the corridor. He didn't seem to be lurking with any menace or threat, though, just watching with interest. Finally, Penny seemed to gather a sixth sense and turned sharply on her heel to face the stranger. He wasn't exactly a stranger; Penny recognised him as the man she and Aaron had met some time ago when they had naively tried to "defend" the watch.

His name was Marcus. From the little experience of him Penny had, she knew him to be reasonable and friendly. He'd been the only person who had offered to help them in their supposed conquest against Antonio. He looked different now, though. He'd been heavy-set the last time they'd met, but the Maze now gave his skin a loose effect that didn't give Penny the impression of a healthy person.

'Hi,' Penny said nervously, unsure of the meaning of this meeting. It was hard to trust anyone, especially given the dark thoughts that often possessed her own mind.

'Hey,' Marcus replied. His voice was gruff and husky. 'Erm… what were you just looking at?' he asked curiously. Penny's mind wasn't all there yet, having just woken up. She didn't really understand the question at first and it took her a minute to get up to speed.

'Oh. Um, to tell you the truth, I was just thinking about

what could be on top of the walls,' she replied at last, soon realising how daft that sounded. 'I mean, the walls are like… a metre wide or something. They could easily be wide enough to walk on.'

For a couple of minutes, this idea hung between the two of them. Marcus was clearly thinking hard about this.

'Y'know, I can't believe I've never thought about that,' Marcus laughed, embarrassed. 'This whole time in the Maze, I've only ever thought about one level.'

'Yeah, I'll be honest, I have literally only just thought about it now. I can't claim to be a genius, unfortunately.'

'The only problem, of course,' Marcus said, stepping closer to the wall, 'is that there's no way you can get up there.' He bent his knees and leapt as high as he could muster, letting out an aching groan. Even though he was considerably taller than Penny, his hand still fell well short of the wall-top ridge. Marcus landed heavily with an even louder grunt of pain. It was clear he wasn't in good health.

Penny looked down at the ground, her brief moment of hope dashed as quickly as it had come. She thought so quickly she could feel her brain working. Her right hand had automatically shot into the pocket she stored her clunky chisel and hammer in when she had felt the disturbance that had turned out to be Marcus, and they'd remained there since. Now, she twiddled the tools nervously with her fingers as she considered her options. She took out the chisel and anxiously rolled it over and over between her hands. A wild idea came to her, but even as it did, she almost laughed out loud. It was farfetched to say the least. For all she knew, the world above the Maze would provide very little answers.

Marcus was watching her avidly. He'd noticed the chisel, and he was apparently taking a while putting two and two together. At last, a spark appeared in his face and his mouth warped into a slight smile — the smile clearly took a lot of effort to form on his face. There was very little reason to smile in the Maze, so it hurt sometimes when you were caught off guard.

'So, you're the artist, huh?' Marcus grinned.

'Yeah, I am,' Penny replied bashfully.

'That's pretty cool,' Marcus stated, a look of wonder on his face as he stared longingly at the wall to his right. There was a long pause as they both looked around the corridor listlessly. Eventually Marcus shrugged his shoulders strongly, saying, 'Wellll…' as people often did in the normal world when there was an awkward lull. Penny moved to the side still holding her chisel in one hand, and Marcus slowly began to edge forward. Once he had passed Penny, his gait widened, and he strode purposefully away. Penny watched him go, appearing and disappearing in the differing lights.

Chapter 51

It felt like déjà vu. Over the following two weeks Natasha and McKenzie had grown closer and closer. She seemed to have forgiven him for all that had transpired so long ago. McKenzie felt wary, though, knowing where this was destined to end up. He occasionally caught an odd look on Natasha's face as she looked at him and it wasn't hard to read what she was thinking. But, after two weeks, McKenzie finally worked up a steel to speak his mind.

'Hey, look. I've been meaning to speak to you,' McKenzie said slowly.

'Okay...' Natasha said, looking McKenzie in the eyes with a dreamy look which made this so much harder.

'It's just...' McKenzie sighed heavily, his shoulders drooping as if he were exhausted. Natasha's smile faltered a little. 'I know how you feel, you've made that perfectly clear, and I would be lying if I said I didn't feel the same way, at least a little. But the thing is, this place is messed up. I'm messed up. We've been forced together in here, and I'm glad we met, but it's not conducive for a positive relationship.'

McKenzie noticed how hurt Natasha looked. She went to speak, but he jumped in before she could.

'The other thing is, I did something truly terrible. To someone I thought I would never hurt. There is no way I can ever trust myself again. I don't want to hurt anybody else.'

confession, in which

directly at McKenzie. He had a feeling she had tears in her eyes. Without warning, she flung her arms around McKenzie and her whole body sagged, releasing emotions she had bottled up for some time. After several minutes she pulled away.

'I know you're right. I guess I'd been so focused on my campaign stuff for so long, it was kind of exciting to be here, away from those troubles, so that I could focus on me. It wasn't fair to force that on you, too.'

McKenzie nodded soberly. He knew this truly was the end, but he stood still. He didn't want to be the one to turn his back again. That wasn't fair. Natasha looked back up at his face, her own a little blotchy. She gave him an incredibly false smile, trying to convince him she would be okay, and then turned around and ambled away, hands in her pockets.

Chapter 52

The time had finally come. The twenty-four hours after the crazy events involving Natasha, Marcus and McKenzie had been a blur of preparations, random paperwork, and general excitement. Unfortunately, this had then been followed by two dragging weeks of nothingness as they waited for McKenzie to separate himself from Natasha. Diego could do nothing until such a time.

Finally, he had just watched McKenzie and Natasha part ways, surely for the last time, the control room immediately sprung to life. One person after another approached Diego with some issue that needed resolving. He dismissed most of them swiftly as he got to his feet and pulled his navy jacket on. He had somewhere to be. A place he had dreamed of for months. For some reason, he'd always seen McKenzie as the Mazer he would greet at the exit, except for that one dream where he had greeted himself. He tried not to get hung up on the meaning of dreams but that one seemed a little too obvious.

Last week's meeting with his superiors had been the easiest yet; they were almost excitable — *almost* — at the prospect of a first genuine release from the Maze and even began making wild promises of new Mazers upon his release. Diego felt himself getting caught up in the commotion which had gripped the control room, too. Even Diane, who was known as a recluse who usually kept to her office, appeared the day after the green light to offer her two pence. It was remarkable to see how quickly the atmosphere of the entire place had changed, though Diego himself had tried to stay reserved; he knew there was still a lot of work to do.

Pulling his arms into the jacket's sleeves, he edged his way along the narrow gap between rows of desks and began to make his way to the door, calling for Alex to join him. Benji was also in for the historic moment and would be more than capable of running the office whilst they were away. Diego's security team ushered Alex and he to the front doors of the hotel through multiple levels of security and swiftly into a sleek black saloon car with heavily tinted windows. The novelty of riding in such a car had still not worn out for Diego, though this may be because he didn't get the opportunity to get out of the hotel much.

Alex sat in silence beside him as they set off on the relatively short journey to the exit point. As usual, she had her tablet by her side, always ready for any eventuality, though for once she wasn't glued to its glaring screen. Diego often wondered how she avoided throbbing headaches given the amount of time she spent staring at it.

'Do you think he's actually ready?' Alex asked abruptly.

'Who?'

'McKenzie, obviously.'

'Oh.' Diego thought about this. There was of course no way of knowing for sure, but he knew what he'd seen. McKenzie had shown a change in himself. Diego barely believed McKenzie capable of his crime, anyway. He made a mistake, that was for sure, but Diego had never seen anything of that mistake in the Maze and there had certainly been opportunities.

'I believe so, yes,' Diego said calmly.

'You realise that if we're wrong it will be the end of the Maze?'

'Yes, I'm aware of that. But it would also be the end of the Maze if we did not allow McKenzie to leave. That's the whole point of the Maze.'

Alex smiled, as if reassured.

'The other problem we've got-' Alex began.

Diego sighed a little. He liked Alex a lot, but she was

definitely a worrier.

'-Is that we might have a bit of a wait, yet.' Alex laughed. They were already approaching their destination, and as she opened her tablet, Diego saw that McKenzie's green dot was still some way from the exit point.

'Oh, yeah. Maybe we should have thought about that.'

'We?' Alex exclaimed. Diego chuckled, relieving a little of his tension.

*

Five hours later, Diego was sat with his feet dangling out the open car door on the back seat. His face was being battered by a fierce coastal wind as, eighty feet below, waves crashed against the weathered rocks, creating swirls of white, foamy water. Alex sat behind him, her door shut firmly as she studied the Maze's map intently, giving Diego a running commentary of McKenzie's progress. He was getting closer, but they might still have several hours to wait. He wasn't close enough to allow Diego to place a roadblock into action, as many other Mazers were nearby, too. Fortunately, a mid-afternoon's sun was casting its summer rays down upon the car providing them with the comfortable warmth of a lazy Sunday morning, an odd but welcome contrast to the sharp ocean mist they were occasionally hit with.

It was quite tedious, though, waiting for an indeterminably long time. He lost himself for a while by watching the waves crash and swirl in ever-changing patterns against the craggy formations below. It was a beautiful place, fitting for such a momentous moment. It made Diego a little melancholy as he thought about the limitations of his own life. He had only recently returned from a much-needed break, but he already felt withered and aged. Diego was hanging a lot on this moment being a turning point for him and the Maze.

'He turned the wrong way,' Alex muttered behind Diego. She had her jacket wrapped tightly around her body, trying to keep warm against the breeze. Diego kept telling her she would be warmer if she opened her door, but she was more than a little stubborn.

'Great. How much longer?' Diego mumbled, uninterested. He felt like a little kid asking his parents if they were nearly there yet.

'That's probably added another thirty minutes,' Alex stated bluntly. She wasn't much good at sugar coating a situation.

'I'm going for a walk, then,' Diego said, frustrated. He slapped his knees and stood up. He'd expected Alex to make a comment, but she merely glanced his way to acknowledge she'd heard and then returned to her screen.

Diego closed the door behind him. Their car was parked in a stony layby right on a cliff top. It was one of only two cars there; the other, a bulky four-by-four that somehow looked as intimidating as the men stood around it, belonged to Diego's security team. There was no sign of human life anywhere near them. Not an old house lost in time or a vintage lighthouse with a grumpy, bearded keeper. Diego's normally neat and wavy hair was whipping him in the face in an untamed tangle — he hadn't thought to bring something to tie it back with. After a quick look around, he set off along the cliff edge, careful to walk a few yards from the sudden drop, keen as he was to avoid plummeting to his death.

He looked intently at the bricked tunnel that jagged out of the cliffside a few feet below. Soon enough McKenzie would be emerging to his first sight of the outside world. Diego thought it wasn't half bad, as sights go.

Chapter 53

The Maze seemed like a different place for McKenzie ever since the attack on Natasha. Before, he'd viewed the place with a child-like innocence. It was an easy mistake, when nothing sinister had happened to him or anyone else he knew in here. In fact, back then, the Maze had seemed a relatively pleasant community, apart from the surroundings. Maybe it was the added element of desperation surging through each prisoner's body as they slowly came to terms with the idea that there was no outside for them any longer.

Now that McKenzie was alone again, the Maze gave off an eerie, menacing glow that he couldn't explain. It hadn't existed before. His separation from Natasha didn't exactly help. It played on his mind constantly, though he knew he'd done the right thing. He snorted with derision as he imagined bumping into her a week from now. One separation had been awkward enough, let alone a second on top.

He turned a corner, recognising the long, straight corridor that stretched before him. That was a rarity in itself. What was even rarer was being able to recognise his position by the smell more than anything else. Ninety-nine percent of the Maze had the same earthy yet chalky smell, but this was the one place that was different. A now familiar scent of the sea floated into his nostrils, filling his lungs with a rare spark of life.

McKenzie stepped forward eagerly, keen to fill up his body with a rare escape from the Maze. This one spot was the closest McKenzie ever felt to the outside world. He was amazed that nobody had monopolized it. That, if anything, said a lot for the limit of their luxuries. It wasn't like anybody had anything to trade, anyway. Maybe McKenzie was the only one who knew about this spot, he thought. It was plausible — after all, he knew for sure that the walls moved to Flint's liking. Maybe this had been reserved for only he, McKenzie.

He hadn't given a moment's thought to that moving wall. It had been lost in the chaos that followed. He hadn't even discussed it with Natasha. Now he thought about it, that very action of moving the wall to allow McKenzie easy access to Natasha's situation was a sign that Flint did want the best for them. Either that, or it was a selfish act to protect his own reputation.

It added an extra element of paranoia to the Maze to think that those above were constantly watching. McKenzie had long since given up caring for his appearance; nobody could possibly look good in these circumstances. Knowing that there was probably a whole group of people watching him, full of pretentious judgement, was not a pleasant thought. McKenzie didn't know what to think about Diego Flint. He'd pictured punching that smug look from his face for some time. It was hard not to, knowing he was the reason for so many of McKenzie's trials, but there were clearly good intentions behind his warped Maze world.

An odd rustling noise seemed to be coming from somewhere nearby. It brought back slightly traumatic memories as he listened for any further noises from over the walls. That odd noise continued. It sounded like a bird's wings, coming from just ahead. That couldn't be right. McKenzie chuckled to himself. Any bird would have to be incredibly lost to have ended up in the Maze.

He took a steady step forward and was greeted by a flurry of action that happened so quickly it was hard to take in. To his left, another seemingly plain, solid wall had opened to a new pathway. McKenzie knew what this meant and began to fear the worst, judging by his previous experience with moving walls. He took another cautious step forward and peered along the corridor. It was like looking straight into heaven. A blinding light from the other end struck him at the same moment a gale of wind whipped against his face. In the next moment, he was bombarded with a cacophony of bird calls — a small flock of sea birds had clearly made this well-meaning tunnel their new home. McKenzie laughed out loud. Just seeing an *actual* bird flooded his heart with joy. His eyes watered a little, though this could have been from the resounding gust still flowing down the corridor, blasting him directly in the face.

McKenzie edged his way forward into the dark, cavernous tunnel. Unlike any other part of the maze, this pathway had a visible ceiling. Being used to the large, open expanse above him, this made McKenzie feel quite claustrophobic. The ground below his weathered shoes was caked in moss and bird faeces. McKenzie could only think that this had not been intended. He wondered if Flint even knew these birds were here. He took a few steps into the tunnel and had to cover his face as a mass of birds began to panic in the face of their new company. In an instant, the whole tunnel was filled with a melee of wings and razor-sharp beaks. Fortunately for McKenzie, the birds seemed to know their way to the exit.

In the commotion, McKenzie noticed that the wall had closed behind him. There was now only one way out; the square of daylight up ahead that gradually grew larger with each step he took. It became much easier to move forwards now that the tunnel's occupants had fled, and soon McKenzie was shielding his eyes once more, this time from the glaring light that was straining his untrained eyes. As he made it into the light just before the threshold, McKenzie slowed to a halt. He could make out more of what lay beyond, now. He could see the sea, reflecting the golden rays of a crisp sunlight. He could see the sky, a perfect baby blue with barely a cloud in sight.

But from what he could tell, there seemed to be quite a drop right after the short platform beyond the threshold, without any obvious route of avoiding it. The last few steps seemed to take an age. The sunlight scorched his pale skin. It was only now that he began to realise how pale he was — before, he'd tried to convince himself that the greyish tinge his skin was giving off was just a reflection of the Maze's walls. Almost immediately he began to break out in a sweat. It probably wasn't even that hot, but when your body had grown used to a constant chill, it didn't take much.

Despite these minor side-effects of the outside world, McKenzie couldn't help but smile. He wiped his eyes, joyful tears forming. McKenzie just hoped this wasn't some elaborate trick that would see him chucked back into the Maze ten minutes later. He would happily live right here in this tunnel for the rest of his life if that was his only other option. He could learn to love the company of a thousand birds.

Finally, McKenzie stepped past the threshold, passing the final line of moss-covered bricks. He stood there, a bitter wind crushing him with relief. It was the first time in months that he had felt air flowing through his long, straggly hair. It was joyous. He was stood on a small two by two metre brick platform on the edge of a jagged cliff. Down below was a wild sea, slamming violently into the cliff-side. It was a precarious position that McKenzie was keen to get away from. He turned to get a full understanding of his options.

'Hello, McKenzie,' a man said as he turned. It took McKenzie a while to adjust to the light. The man's face was obscured by the sun directly behind him. Slowly, he came into McKenzie's focus. It was Diego Flint. He was sat on top of the tunnel McKenzie had just emerged from, smiling slightly smugly. His legs were crossed, and he gave off the impression of someone had been waiting for some time. Behind him, McKenzie could make out a shiny black saloon car, its fancy image slightly tarnished by a splattering of bird poo. Now that McKenzie looked closer, Flint also seemed worse for wear, as if he'd also suffered the large attack of birds — his swanky suit was littered with feathers.

'Err… hi,' McKenzie replied, unsure. 'Where am I?'

'An interesting question, I guess. Mentally, I would say you are in a much better place than before you entered the Maze. Physically, you are in the state of Oregon, on the coast, as I'm sure you have gathered, but more broadly, you are free.'

It was clear to McKenzie that Flint had been rehearsing these words for some time. It was still impressive, nonetheless.

'Free?' he questioned.

'As a bird,' Flint nodded firmly. 'And you might say I have become quite the expert on birds, in the recent past.' He cracked a cheeky grin. McKenzie couldn't help but chuckle, no matter how much he wanted to hate the man before him.

'I'm guessing you didn't plan for the birds, then?'

'Erm… no, not exactly,' Flint said ashamedly.

There was a pause for a minute or so. McKenzie just wanted to throw his arms out in elation. Then, he realised he could, so he turned to the sea and opened his entire body to the world beyond. Suddenly his whole future was filled with endless possibilities.

'Are you ready to move on?' Flint asked kindly. McKenzie took one last, longing look back down the tunnel he had come down. He kind of missed his home of the last six months in a weird way, but he knew he had bigger and better things ahead.

Chapter 54

Diego was back in the town car, sat opposite McKenzie. After Yazmin, Diego had the sunglasses ready in the doorhandle. They hadn't spoken much since they'd gotten into the car; McKenzie had been too distracted by the simplest things. The funny thing was, they hadn't even passed a single house yet. Diego could only imagine how wide his eyes would get when they reached a town centre. After a while it appeared McKenzie got a little bored of what he saw out of the window, and he turned back to face Diego and Alex.

'So... I'm not complaining or anything,' McKenzie began, throwing his hands out apologetically, 'but I have to ask, why, or how, did I get out?'

Diego grinned from ear to ear. This was the most exciting part of his job; it was a shame it had taken nearly seven months to get to. He leaned forwards to add an extra element of intensity, still grinning.

'I'm so glad you asked,' he said excitedly. Both McKenzie and Alex looked like they wished McKenzie hadn't asked. Diego ploughed on. 'You see, when I designed the Maze, I wanted it to be different from any other prison, but the biggest point to that was to allow the prisoners to prove their own redemption. We've been watching you for months, I presume you've figured that much out by now?' McKenzie nodded silently. 'We have a huge team of operators watching every moment for signs of an improved person beneath the skin. Each prisoner, or Mazer as we call you all, has a certain score that they have to achieve.'

Diego paused, allowing McKenzie to take the information in.

'We in the control room delegate points based on your

behaviours. For example, you gained points the first time you left Natasha, as you showed sorrow for your past mistakes. To answer your question more directly, you achieved your required score in the act of saving TJ Bogle's life, not in saving Natasha's.'

'How does that work? He was hurting her!'

'Yes, I realise that, but in saving Natasha do you not think you were doing something for yourself, too?'

McKenzie thought for a moment, and Diego saw a sudden realisation hit him.

'You see, you couldn't gain points for that,' Diego smiled, 'because it didn't prove you as any different from when you entered. However, when you stopped Natasha, you not only saved a man's life, showing humanity in the process, but you also stopped another person from making a mistake that would have scarred them for the rest of their life.'

McKenzie nodded with a solemn expression. His previously ecstatic face had quickly dropped. Diego felt like he should say something, but he had no idea how McKenzie was feeling. He'd been watching this man for six months, but there was no way he could empathise with his situation. For the rest of the journey McKenzie stayed silent, returning to staring out of the window. However, now he seemed more pensive than in awe as he watched houses and shop fronts pass them by. Soon enough they'd returned to the hotel complex that hid the Maze. As McKenzie got out of the car, he looked the building up and down in slight confusion. Alex was watching him very warily, which angered Diego more than anything. He didn't want McKenzie to be seen differently by the outside world — in his mind, McKenzie had proven he was now a different person.

Chapter 55

This weird, slightly dystopian hotel front for a prison complex wasn't helping McKenzie re-adjust to the outside world. He couldn't help but snap his neck rapidly from side to side as he took everything in. He, Flint, and his assistant Alex trooped straight through the hotel lobby, flanked by a small army of security guards. At first McKenzie thought they were guarding against him, but it soon became clear that wasn't the case. For one thing, they hadn't taken away his knife, so they clearly didn't think he was that much of a threat. He walked mere feet away from Diego Flint and could easily attack before any guard could stop him.

None of the hotel staff gave them a second look as they passed. Clearly this was a regular occurrence for them. Eventually they came to some heavy steel doors, locked by a security code. McKenzie continued to follow Flint through the doors, taking in his surroundings in silence as Flint led him into a private room. Noise came from an open door further down the corridor that he figured was the main hub of activity. For some reason, he really wanted to see what was in the room.

Now that he was back in a public place with regular people passing him in the corridors — their hair neat and tamed, their clothes stylish and clean — McKenzie couldn't help but feel self-conscious. He was still wearing Natasha's ripped, beige clothes that were much too small for him whilst his hair and beard were oily and uncontrolled. He wished Diego would just allow him to clean himself up before anything else, but that didn't seem about to happen.

Alex left them to return to the noisy room ahead and, perhaps even more staggering, none of Flint's security outfit followed them into the room either. Flint ushered McKenzie into a seat on one side of a plain black table and closed the door behind them. This room looked remarkably like a police interrogation room, only there was no two-way mirror. McKenzie was pretty sure there must be a camera somewhere, though; Flint couldn't be *that* confident in his judgement of McKenzie, or of his own abilities to fend off a desperate prisoner. McKenzie had to remind himself: *No, you're not a prisoner anymore.*

Flint sat opposite him, releasing a deep exhale of breath. Now they were in a more comfortable light, McKenzie could see he looked older and more tired than McKenzie had remembered seeing him on the news. It gave McKenzie the impression that all was not well with Flint. Maybe his conscience was catching up with him. *Good, he deserves it*, McKenzie thought. Then another part of his brain felt sorry for Flint; McKenzie wasn't sure he did truly deserve whatever was troubling him.

'So,' Flint began calmly, 'I guess the easiest place to start is: what's next for you?'

McKenzie let out a harsh bark of a laugh. Considering he'd had months to himself, he'd spent very little of that time contemplating the future. Given his dire situation it was hard to imagine a positive future. Ever since he had stood on that platform overlooking the cliff, his mind had been abuzz with a million ideas. It had been indiscernible to him.

'You know, you'd think I would've thought about that, but the truth is I kind of gave up on ever getting out. The outside world began to feel like a distant dream.'

'Okay. What would you like to do?' Flint prompted.

'I guess I would like to travel. Being trapped away in one corner really made me realise how little of the world I've seen.'

Flint nodded exuberantly. Clearly this was a good answer.

'And... what about relationships?' Flint asked tentatively. McKenzie paused, staring at Flint's face in disbelief that he'd just asked that. He looked away at the blank white wall to his left. He didn't really know how to answer that. His rationale made no sense when he actually thought about it, but for some reason he was sure it was the only way.

'Okay. You don't have to answer. The truth is, I already know what you're thinking, I just wanted to tell you that it didn't have to be that way,' Flint said reassuringly, as if McKenzie was a confused teenager. It bugged McKenzie how nice Flint seemed. It would make everything much easier if he was a bit of a jerk.

'Can I ask *you* something?' McKenzie asked, a provoking thought striking him.

'Of course,' Flint replied, seemingly delighted that McKenzie was engaging. It was like the weirdest therapy session ever.

'How many others have got out of the Maze so far?' he asked. Clearly, he'd struck a nerve. Flint laughed contemptuously and ran his hands through his thick, dark hair, leaning back in his chair. They were classic ticks. After a few moments silence, Flint braced himself to speak.

'Well, I guess there's no hiding it from you, you'll find out soon enough. You're the first, technically.'

McKenzie's mouth widened. He had so many questions.

'What do you mean "technically"?' he asked hurriedly.

'Well, one other was released, but that was because she was found to be innocent, not because she proved herself worthy.'

'You mean you put an innocent person through that hell?'

'Well, it wasn't exactly my fault. How was I to know if the judge didn't?' Flint replied defensively. McKenzie shrugged.

'It just seems a lot more risky when you realise someone might not deserve that.'

'Yeah, well.' Flint shrugged, too.

For an annoyingly long time Flint continued to pepper McKenzie with questions and advice regarding his future prospects and mental state. McKenzie sort of wished there was a clock in the room, but he figured that would only give the illusion of time moving more slowly. During Flint's rambling anecdotes, McKenzie began to drift off and daydream about all the luxuries that lay ahead: a hot shower, a good old fashioned American cheeseburger, the smell of freshly cut grass. It was a little cliché, but now he truly understood the meaning of appreciating the little things.

Eventually Flint finished his final spiel, McKenzie barely noticing when silence fell upon his ears. After a moment or so of Flint staring at McKenzie expectantly, McKenzie finally realised he was awaiting some form of response. He started, pretending he had been deep in thought, trying to cover his own lapse in concentration. Flint stood, seemingly realising he had been chewing McKenzie's ear off, and directed him to the door. Accompanied by his security team, he led McKenzie to an elevator and then into a thirteenth-floor room that had everything McKenzie had been dreaming of.

Chapter 56

Penny hadn't moved for over a week now — she'd been too intent on her work. It was the hardest her chisel had ever had to work, though she wasn't creating a piece of artwork. She hadn't been able to shake the idea in her head about what lay above, on top of the Maze walls.

For an entire week she had been fixated on one piece of wall, chiselling away contently. The only thing Penny wished she had at the moment was some music. She was able to hold a tune in her head for a while, but it became incredibly frustrating given her limited knowledge of lyrics. She usually spent about thirty seconds at a time listening to a song in her head, followed by another three hours of trying to remember the lyrics.

After an unending day of contemplation, Penny had finally come up with a solid plan and sat down to put it into action. Like a child in pre-school, she crossed her legs and sat down adjacent to the wall. At the bottom of the wall she scored a mark, around a foot from the ground, then set into a rhythm that had continued for days on end.

She was building a ladder, carved into the wall, so that she could climb her way to the top of the Maze. After a whole week, she was still only four rungs down, with another six to go. The stone Maze walls seemed to get denser and more difficult to chisel the deeper Penny got. It didn't help that her chisel was wearing thin and dull. Every time she sharpened it, it seemed to last less and less time. It was already considerably shorter than when she'd first entered the Maze, and Penny was sure it would be useless by the time she finally finished the last rung.

Penny was exhausted, which made a surprisingly nice change of pace. Her arms ached with a devastating numbness after working non-stop for days. The worst was that she'd barely made a dent yet, almost literally.

Penny had just started the fifth rung when she heard footsteps approaching from around the corner. It wasn't the first time somebody had crossed her path. Most had just wandered passed without a word, as was the norm these days in the Maze. Only one person had actually stopped to find out what she was up to and even they had seemed disinterested after a minute or so. She felt like the only person who thought this might serve a genuine purpose.

The footsteps reached a mild crescendo and Penny saw the same man that she'd met just before starting on the ladder: Marcus. He looked at her with immoderate bewilderment, clearly shocked to see she hadn't moved in the week that'd passed since they'd last met. He smiled knowingly.

'You decided to do it, then,' he chuckled approvingly.

'Well, I couldn't just keep doing the same thing over and over again for the rest of my life,' Penny replied, trying to play it down.

'You know, you could save yourself a lot of time by making half as many rungs,' Marcus stated, pointing at the wall. It was obvious he'd worked out *exactly* what she was doing. Penny looked suddenly at her work and realised he was right, blushing a little. The only problem was the perfectionist within her couldn't now change her process. It would look stupid, half-finished. That's when she realised this ladder was more than just a way to the top of the Maze. It was another piece of art. Probably her most abstract piece ever.

'Yeah, I could have done with that kind of thinking a week ago,' Penny laughed. She glanced at Marcus again, suddenly having a thought. 'You wouldn't happen to know where the nearest food room is, would you?'

'Well yeah, I've just come from there actually. It's just back there.' Marcus pointed over his shoulder with his thumb.

'Oh, that's good,' Penny mumbled, thoughtfully. She stared at her work a little desperately. She really didn't want to leave it now.

'I can go get you some things, if you want,' Marcus stated, taking her not-so-subtle hint. Penny smiled gratefully, trying to make it seem like that hadn't been what she'd intended. Marcus wasn't buying it for one second.

A day later Penny was still grafting her way through the endless chore. It had certainly become more bearable in the last twenty-four hours, though, now that she had a new pair of hands. Marcus was currently taking a break, leaning against the wall, his forehead sweaty. Penny had somehow forced herself to give up her chisel for a short time whilst she ravaged her way through the assortment of foods Marcus had provided. She winced at times as Marcus roughly slashed and thumped at the wall, pushing herself to shovel food into her mouth as fast as possible so she could take back control. She couldn't bear to watch Marcus for long.

So, after a rushed food break, followed by a slightly longer break of holding her indigestion-riddled stomach, Penny got back to work. She could only imagine how daft she looked to Marcus, sweating profusely as she toiled away, pulling demented faces. Penny had long since given up caring about being judged — or judging anyone else, for that matter. The Maze really was a great leveller in that sense.

It was nice to have some company for a change. Marcus had taken a real interest in her project, more than likely because he felt bad for Penny and thought she was having some kind of mental breakdown. Penny liked to believe it was because he too was interest to see the Maze from above.

After another three days with only limited breaks in which she reluctantly allowed Marcus to take over, Penny finally began work on the final rung. Marcus had pleaded with her to just go up the ladder early; they both knew the final rung was pointless. They could easily climb onto the wall without it. But Penny was determined to complete her task. Marcus was surprisingly respectful of that, given how irrational she was being. Maybe her mild screaming fit had caused him to back down; Penny hadn't realised until afterwards that she had been waggling the chisel a little threateningly in his direction. He'd disappeared for a while after that, mumbling something about collecting some rations for the trip.

He was gone for longer than usual and Penny began to fear she'd scared him away indefinitely. Marcus was always the one to go and collect supplies, Penny was so protective of her greatest work that she refused to leave its side unless she had to use the bathroom. After a few hours, or what Penny guessed passed for a few hours these days, Marcus did return. Penny hadn't been to see the watch since she'd started working on the ladder, so her awareness of time reminded her of the horrible weeks before the watch.

The first few weeks of the Maze had been the worst time of Penny's life. She was still trying to get over the life-changing turn of events right before she entered the Maze, let alone being able to deal with the crippling loneliness and malnourishment that she was faced with. They had nothing back then, no clothes, no soap bars, not even a toothbrush. The Maze had become much more tolerable since then, and it had all started with the watch. Yet, as Penny thought, she realised that it might just be that she had become acclimatised. She had gotten used to expecting very little from life. That was a thought that she didn't want to linger on, especially given her current productive streak.

Finally, a full two weeks after she had begun working on the ladder, full of youthful naivety, Penny etched her final mark into the stone. She quickly pocketed the completely blunt and useless chisel, hoping that it had served a valuable purpose — the idea that such a minor item, one that she'd given little thought to before entering the Maze, could make such a huge impact on her life and potentially others too gave Penny a shiver of goosebumps. She stood back and folded her arms, covering herself from a sudden chill as she took in the finished product. For the merest of silent moments, Penny and Marcus just admired what was essentially an incredibly boring creation. Chuckling at this thought, Penny stepped forward and placed a hand on a rung halfway up the ladder, beginning to climb.

Chapter 57

It was certainly an eye-opener, if nothing else. Marcus stood atop one of a thousand criss-crossing walls that stretched on for as far as he could see. It was a bizarre, other-worldly experience, viewing the Maze from above. Marcus could make out several fellow prisoners marching along corridors at various junctures, passing in and out of his sight as they walked under the golden lanterns that created this somewhat magical spectacle.

The lanterns glowed below him like a million fireflies on a warm summer's night in Arizona. Marcus felt his shoulders sag as he breathed in a sigh a warm relief, allowing himself to picture a barbecue smoking in a summer haze, laughter all around in the glorious euphoric mood that swept over his hometown during the warmest months. There wasn't a single worry around.

Eventually, the scene faded and he returned to the hush of the Maze, yet a jolt of that same euphoria had lodged its way into the pit of his stomach. He looked to his left and saw Penny looking as wide-eyed as he imagined himself to be at that very moment. It was certainly more beautiful than he could have ever imagined from down below, but it gave few answers to their struggles.

Having taken in the Maze for a long while, Penny nudged Marcus and began to walk steadily along the wall. This new world created a whole new set of problems. For one thing, they only had one entrance and exit, and everything looked remarkably similar, perhaps even more so than before — it would be very easy to lose it. There was also the minor issue of falling off the edge of the wall. It was easily three feet wide, yet a momentary lapse in concentration could lead to a very painful and heavy fall, not to mention the hassle of finding the ladder again.

Marcus had never suffered from vertigo, but up here, above the Maze, he felt extraordinarily shaky. He was thankful Penny was ahead of him, all he had to do was watch her feet.

Marcus still had a plentiful supply of food stuffed into the incredibly deep pockets of his inmate clothing, but he couldn't help but consider what happened when they finally ran out of food. He had no intention of building another ladder. Penny didn't seem to share these concerns; she didn't show any concern whatsoever as she continued on at a frenetic pace ahead of Marcus. She kept pausing to allow him to catch up at junctions before setting off once more, a resolute expression stuck on her face. Marcus was considerably larger than Penny, who was sure to have a low centre of gravity along with the dainty balance of a ballet dancer. As such, he found it much harder to move with confidence along the walls, the alarming drop on either side daunting.

They reached a long passage of extended wall and Penny began to stretch further and further away from Marcus until she faded into the darkness beyond visibility. For several minutes Marcus was left alone in the spooky land above the Maze. The darkness seemed to press more heavily up here, the black space above him seemed heavier. Even the loneliness seemed worse. He was beginning to regret his decision to leave the comfort of the corridors down below. The idea that the Maze was the most comfortable place for him at this stage in his life began to unravel his insecurities.

Just in time, Penny came into view. Marcus was shaking violently as the weight of his anxieties began to heighten to a brand-new level. He finally caught up and felt a giant sense of relief, being able to stand on firm ground. He took a deep breath and made to kneel down for a moment. Penny, meanwhile, was full of a restless energy, feverishly turning her head from side to side in search of something that was nowhere to be seen. As far as Marcus could tell, the walls were a barren wasteland that provided nothing of any use. In fact, all they were doing at the moment was getting further and further away from any food or bathrooms.

'Do you think maybe we should head back?' Marcus asked tentatively. 'We don't want to get turned around, do we?'

Penny wasn't listening. She murmured some form of acknowledgement but offered nothing in reply. Instead, she knelt down and started inspecting the floor in front of her. Marcus raised an eyebrow behind her back.

'Erm… what are you looking at?' Marcus questioned, his voice high-pitched as if he were talking to a crazy person, or a dog.

'Come and look,' Penny whispered. 'There's footprints in the dust.'

Marcus felt as if his worst suspicions had been realised. To humour Penny, he knelt by her side, steadying himself on one lean arm. To his surprise, she was actually right; there *was* footprints on the wall, and they definitely weren't hers. They had to belong to a man.

Penny smoothly ran one finger through a dense layer of dust until she reached one of the footprints. They seemed fresh, as if somebody else had passed this spot in the last twenty-four hours. Marcus was struggling to believe that could be true. Penny's gaze had become distant and vague as she looked out into the dark horizon. Marcus followed her line of sight but couldn't understand what she was thinking.

'Aaron was right,' she mumbled indistinctly.

'What?' Marcus asked, bemused. He'd met Aaron on the same day as Penny, but he had no idea what Penny was talking about.

'He told me months ago, when we first met, that he saw a light. He was right.'

'How'd you figure?'

'Well, clearly someone else has been up here, and I can't imagine anyone else from down below has managed to climb up. I certainly haven't seen any other ladders anywhere, have you?'

'Well, no. But-'

'This must be how they get around, the people who replace the food and supplies and...' Penny stopped, mid-thought. 'That's how they took Yazmin, too.'

Now Marcus was really confused. Penny seemed to be having a fairly detailed conversation with herself about people he barely knew.

'What are you talking about?' he snapped. She looked straight at him.

'There are *obviously* people who come in to maintain the Maze. You must know that by now? Unless you thought it was fairies or something?' Penny sniggered. Marcus nodded, taken aback. 'I was travelling with a girl, Yazmin. She went into one of the bathrooms one day and next thing I knew she had disappeared. The door opened and no-one was there. They must have pulled her out through the ceiling! And if they're using the walls to travel, that must mean there's a door up here somewhere!' Penny squealed excitedly.

Marcus felt his jaw drop a little. He was glad Penny was switched on, because he wasn't too certain that they could around in the Maze. There might not be any edges, but they must be real and solid. Penny is right, one of them must hold a way out of here.

Chapter 58

It had been over a month since Natasha had last seen McKenzie. The childish part of Natasha that believed in happy ever afters had been sure they would meet again, but he seemed to have just vanished into thin air. Natasha had stormed her way around the Maze over and over again, day after day, without success. She had begun to concede that McKenzie was actually gone, hoping that he had somehow found a safe way out of the Maze.

A terrible thought flickered through her mind — she imagined the man who'd attacked her stood looming over a whimpering McKenzie. For some reason, she felt more afraid for McKenzie than for herself. She ambled along now, devoid of hope, little to encourage her day-to-day existence. She was abruptly startled out of her stupor by a familiar female voice booming over her head. Natasha had quite forgotten that today was announcement day. It had become as meaningless and futile as anything else by now. Nevertheless, it was at least a brief change from the same old routine. She sat down to listen attentively to the world above.

'…Some more exciting news for you,' the voice echoed along her corridor from both directions. 'Happy Independence Day to you all, as today is July fourth!' The jolly youthfulness of the woman made it hard for Natasha to listen. It was very hard to relate to that content feeling down in the Maze. The woman continued to deliver what she considered to be pick-me-ups for the prisoners for several more minutes until it was time to wrap up. Natasha was barely listening by that point.

'Finally, perhaps some news from closer to home will cheer you up. We are delighted to announce that a few days ago one of your fellow Mazers was released and will now begin his integration with society. Congratulations to McKenzie!' the woman finished, her voice continuing to echo eerily along nearby corridors for several seconds.

A flood of mixed emotions filled Natasha up. She was overjoyed to hear McKenzie was safe and free, but it was certainly a kick in the teeth for her and everyone else still stuck in the Maze. Natasha just wished McKenzie could have told her how he'd done it, at least.

Natasha allowed herself to drift away, filled with thoughts of McKenzie and jealousy of the outside world. She wandered along absent-mindedly, her head in the clouds, or at least in the void of darkness above her. It was probably the lowest she had felt since entering the Maze. It was certainly the loneliest. McKenzie had been the only friend she had known in here and knowing he was actually gone felt dreadful. She hated herself for feeling like that, wishing she could just be happy for him. If anything, his release proved it was possible; that should be a positive. She tried to resolve herself to only think of the positive. She felt like a completely different person to the Natasha who had first entered the Maze, full of purpose. She had been so strong and full of willpower that nothing would have ever set her off course. That wasn't true, of course. That Natasha *had* been derailed by the Maze.

Footsteps from somewhere nearby broke Natasha's trail of thought. Two sets of footsteps, for that matter. They sounded loud, as if they were running or stomping angrily. There were distant voices accompanying the footsteps too, echoing strangely along the Maze walls. Yet Natasha couldn't see anyone down the corridor. Her eyes narrowed in expectation, certain somebody was about to leap out at her. Ever since she'd been attacked, Natasha had felt jittery and overly paranoid about every little noise she heard.

A movement in the darkness caught Natasha's alert eyes,

but to her amazement it was above the Maze walls. Looking up anxiously, she spotted two bodies in the same beige, loose-fitting uniform that she wore. For a moment she froze, both in shock and amazement. She craned her neck to watch the two people, breathing in against the wall they were stood on so they wouldn't spot her. After a minute or so of tailing slowly behind them it became clear that they were not hostile. Natasha moved away from the wall to make herself known. The two fellow prisoners had stopped and were inspecting the top of the wall on their knees. Natasha cleared her throat and two faces glared down at her: a man, and a woman.

'Hi,' Natasha waved, awkwardly.

'Hello,' the two people replied graciously, as if nothing was abnormal about this situation. It was hurting Natasha's neck to keep looking up at them like this, she wasn't used to looking up much these days.

'How the hell did you get up there?'

'Built a ladder,' the woman said plainly, as if it were the most obvious thing in the world.

'Out of what?' Natasha asked, bemused.

'The wall,' the woman stated simply once again. This confused Natasha even further. When she continued to frown the woman finally decided she needed to elaborate. 'I have a chisel,' she said, digging a hand into her pocket and waving a grubby metal instrument. This answered a lot of questions. Now she was simply impressed, that must have been some undertaking. For the first time, Natasha focused on the man hidden slightly behind his friend. He looked queasy and nervous, unbecoming to his naturally large frame.

'What's it like up there?' Natasha asked.

'Why don't you come and see for yourself?' The woman responded. 'The ladder is only about five hundred yards that way,' she added, gesturing with a nod of her head.

Natasha didn't even take a second to think. Almost immediately she turned in the direction the woman had pointed her in and made to set off. She took a few steps before stopping in her tracks.

'What were you guys looking at?' Natasha asked, full of sudden intrigue.

'There's footsteps up here, we're trying to follow them,' the woman said. Natasha was astounded by the woman's frankness. It was like someone had given her a truth serum, such was the monotonic nature of her responses. Natasha knew as much as anyone that there was no point lying down here, there wasn't much to be gained and they were all in the same boat.

Chapter 59

TJ had never felt worse in his entire life. He was full of a deep sorrow that was amplified by the miserable atmosphere of the Maze. He almost wished someone could punish him, but he supposed being stuck down here was punishment enough. He was torn by a desire to find the young woman and make a much belated apology, and a desperate aspiration to hide for the rest of his life, afraid to face his failings.

It was harder than ever to keep plodding along every day. Hearing the last announcement had woken TJ to a lot of hard truths. He was almost certain that the man who had been released was the man who had intervened, saving the girl. If that were true, it seemed somebody was watching them and, worst of all, now they had seen TJ at his lowest. That couldn't possibly have had a positive response. It was going to take a long time to prove he was worthy of release now.

It was horrible to know that Yazmin would have seen his actions. It wasn't exactly unusual for people to look down on TJ based on some of his questionable life choices, though he didn't care about most people. He did care about what Yazmin thought. It had been nice to know someone who actually looked up to him and respected him for his actions, only now he had tarnished all of that.

TJ had decided he needed to visit the watch. He hadn't been for some time, afraid he might run into someone he didn't want to run into. But now, he decided that a reminder of the world outside might help cheer his mood up.

The area around the watch seemed strangely silent. TJ didn't pass a single person on his way and the corridor, which was usually occupied by at least one or two people, was empty. He figured that, like him, many had become tired of the watch; it had undoubtedly lost a lot of its initial magic.

TJ stared longingly at the relatively simple watch. It seemed so ornate and luxurious compared to the rest of the Maze. He touched its cold silver rim, trying to grasp at the closest thing to his old life. The air around the watch somehow felt different, as if a bubble of other-worldly air was preserving it. TJ felt the strangest desire to kneel before it. He had never been a religious person but right now he felt willing to try anything.

He didn't kneel, his mind full of doubts, but instead he lingered for as long as he dared and quickly disappeared before anyone could run in on him.

Chapter 60

Like Yazmin, McKenzie had slept for hours and hours, making the most of a soft, warm mattress. When he emerged from the room, shadowed by two of Diego's security guards, he looked a completely different man. His long hair was now tied stylishly in a bun, gleaming a golden brown. Diego wondered how he had learnt to tie it so well. His straggly beard had gone too, replaced by a razor-thin stubble which shone in patches of blond and ginger. Despite being in the Maze much longer than Yazmin, McKenzie looked in much better health. He'd looked after himself well, for the most part, and particularly so since he had met Natasha.

McKenzie sat with Diego for lunch in the deserted hotel restaurant, wolfing food down in great gulps. He didn't seem to care what food it was, either. At one point Diego caught him stuffing a croissant into some marmite. For a few minutes, Diego even worried for his own fingers. Eventually, McKenzie had gorged himself enough and leaned back on his chair, his bloated stomach bulging under his fresh t-shirt. He watched Diego lazily for a minute as Diego read the newspaper lying on the table, though he became bored and started scanning the room for things of interest. Diego was glad to see an excited spark within McKenzie's eyes.

'Right,' Diego said, swallowing the last mouthful of his bagel and tapping the table meaningfully. 'Are you ready?'

McKenzie nodded stiffly, his jaw contracting a little. They stood together and made their way to the hotel lobby, where an unusually large crowd was gathered. One of the operators whispered to his friends and pointed not-so-subtly in their direction. McKenzie looked a little taken aback, worried they were all here to show their malcontent.

Diego knew it was quite the opposite, however. All these people were Maze workers, and they had assembled to cheer him off.

The two of them stopped just short of the hotel's front doors. Diego turned to look directly at McKenzie, his eyes then flickering to McKenzie's breast pocket where his sunglasses were snuggly resting. McKenzie smiled and let out a short snort, pulling out the glasses and putting them on. There was an expectant silence filling the room from the onlookers. Diego held his hand out and McKenzie took it without hesitation.

'If you ever need any support, please get in touch,' Diego said simply, patting McKenzie gently on the back. McKenzie nodded and, without another word, walked straight out the door. Everybody watched him leave; and when the door swung shut there was an outburst of cheers and fist pumping. Nobody had come to collect McKenzie, so he was to be driven home by one of Diego's own personal team. Diego slowly turned and realised this was a perfect time to address the flocks of operators that were watching on so intently. It meant a lot to him to know they were as invested as he was.

'Thank you all for coming to see Mr. Symms off. It is great to see how invested you are in our collective project, but we have much work to do. This is one small step in a marathon we must endure. I'm hoping over the coming weeks that we'll begin to see some real progress. Now, for heaven's sake, can we get back to work? This isn't exactly subtle!' he finished, laughing.

*

Diego's meeting with the board the previous week had given him some much-needed good news. Mr. Jenkins had informed Diego that five new people would be allowed to enter the Maze. This seemed to buoy the entire crew in the control room, after such a long period of inactivity.

A week after McKenzie left the hotel, hopefully for the last time, the Maze was preparing to welcome the five new Mazers. This was going to be their most challenging, complicated entry, especially given the recent developments involving Penny and Marcus. The whole control room had been on red alert for days since the two of them had made their way onto the wall tops. It made simple tasks like replacing food much harder for fears of being spotted and, in the very worst case, Penny and Marcus could find their way to an unauthorised exit. That would surely mean the end of the Maze for Diego.

As much as his whole project hinged on the two people wandering above the Maze, Diego was still excited to see how it would play out. A development like this was exactly what made the Maze stand out; it offered the Mazers opportunity to think for themselves. Penny and Marcus had now been joined by Natasha, and Diego was sure more would follow when they found the ladder. Curiosity was enough to get the most of anyone; it offered a tiny glimmer of hope and salvation.

After the incident with TJ, the board had been incredibly adamant that there would be no-one high-profile entering the Maze any time soon, at least until one of the current number proved themselves worthy of release. Diego, situated in his usual corner, watched on as the Maze disappeared completely on the giant screen — a rare occurrence — to be replaced by five different rooms, all identical in every way. At the moment they were all empty, but soon enough each one would be full of activity. The new Mazers were saying their final goodbyes at that very moment.

The room in the middle was the first to see any activity. Two people moved steadily over the threshold, one clad in the stone-grey uniform of the Maze officers, the other in a dull beige outfit that Diego had fought to the hilt against, unsuccessfully. The uniformity between the Mazers' outfits was far too similar to a prison jumpsuit for his liking. The woman in beige looked around the room in bewilderment, just as many before her had. She had a hardened, resolute expression which showed no sign of fear — impressive given the great sense of the unknown facing her behind the daunting black door.

Within minutes the other rooms were occupied by other pairings of guards and Mazers. Once again, Diego had a sick feeling, wishing something would go wrong. He caught himself, mentally chastising the part of his mind that lived off everyday drama. As he watched the screen, he glanced down at the tablet he was holding, keen to learn more about the newest Mazers. It was the first time he'd had a chance, given his suddenly hectic schedule. The board hadn't been joking when they said these people weren't high-profile. In fact, as Diego skimmed the files, he wondered if any of them even deserved to enter the Maze. The selfish side of him knew that wasn't an option. If he started turning criminals away, he would be left with nothing more than ruins.

In fact, the new Mazers' entry day was completely uneventful. All five moved through the dark veil of a doorway with little more than a question. Alex looked at Diego with a distinct glance that made Diego sure she knew what he was thinking. He couldn't help but smirk.

'Where did the good old days full of drama go?' he joked.

Chapter 61

Tara stepped out of the claustrophobia-inducing darkness, into the relative light of a new world. It was some sight. A cavernous expanse of absolutely nothing stretched for miles above her. The cool grey walls before her looked worn and battered, covered in scratches and markings that had been left by previous prisoners. The whole place gave off a pungent, rotten smell that made Tara's nose wrinkle in disgust. She figured there weren't going to be many showers happening during her time here.

Despite the gloomy outlook that her first impression of the Maze gave off, Tara was full of surprising resolve. She had forced herself to see this unfortunate chapter in her life as an exciting adventure more than anything else. She had been given the opportunity to explore a place that very few others would ever see and, more importantly, a chance to rediscover herself.

She stood in the opening for several minutes, taking in everything around her with wide eyes full of wonder. Pathways veered off to her left and right, and one continued to stretch before her. She took in the lanterns that glowed a perfect golden yellow, the only light source in the entire Maze. She also took in the unerring silence, perhaps the hardest thing to become accustomed to. The modern world was so loud all the time that it was hard to get a moment to herself. That wouldn't be the case down here. She was suddenly incredibly aware of her own breathing and her heart beating firmly in her chest.

There was an eerie silence about the place, yet Tara was somehow aware of the steeped history the weathered pathways carried. She could almost see the haunted faces of those who had been in the Maze for months and months as they had walked past this very spot. She felt sorry for them.

At least she had some idea of what to expect. She'd seen the news updates coming from the Maze over the past months and steeled herself for the worst when she was given her verdict.

Tara was not a fool. She knew full well there wasn't going to be a physical exit she could just stumble across. Those in control couldn't risk dangerous criminals finding freedom before their time was due. Tara was prepared for the long haul, knowing the Maze had only just released its first prisoner after more than six months.

Satisfied that she had taken in the Maze to its fullest, Tara took a long stride forward and began her venture into the corridors, full of a realistic optimism. The pathway ahead of her seemed to stretch on endlessly into the distance, without a curve or bend in sight. Tara held her head high, endlessly scanning her surroundings. Every little scratch in the wall fascinated her. It was like discovering an ancient civilisation, steeped in its own culture. She saw names, arrows, and random indiscernible scribblings as she made her way along the corridor, finally making her way to a new junction.

She checked the pathway to her left, which continued onwards surrounded by the great stone walls, then made to look right but jumped back in shock. A man was slumped on the floor right next to the turning. At first Tara wasn't sure if he was even alive, such was his ill-fated appearance, then she noticed his shallow, gentle breathing. He didn't even seem to notice Tara, though his eyes remained open. Tara stared at him for a minute and began to truly realise the degree of her task in the Maze. She couldn't even begin to guess how old the man was. His features suggested he was probably in his late twenties, yet his uncontrolled, dishevelled beard flecked with grey and accompanied with sprouting ear and nose hairs made it much harder to tell.

He was impossibly pale, too, like an old man who didn't get enough sun. Looking around at the unfathomable ceiling above, Tara supposed the latter part of that was probably true. There wasn't much chance for sun-bathing down here. Worst of all was the aroma of the defeated man that floated all around; a stifling, warm stench that Tara had always associated with nursing homes. Tara cleared her throat to announce her presence. The man didn't even flinch, not even an eyelid. She squatted down beside him, beginning to really panic that she was going to witness a man die by her side. It really wasn't a good endorsement for the state of the Maze. Finally, the man slowly turned his head to face Tara as if he was afraid it would fall off if he moved too quickly.

'Hi,' Tara stammered. She suddenly felt self-conscious that she looked too normal to be in this man's company. It was like she was mocking his struggles, which she had no intent of doing, especially as she knew she could well be in the same situation in six months time. The man opened his mouth to speak, but barely a croak come out. His throat sounded like it was made of sandpaper. He started coughing violently, spit flying over his clothes and the floor in front of him. He made no attempt to cover his mouth and Tara supposed that normal sanitary habits were obsolete for the man at this point.

He tried and failed again to speak, again bursting into a coughing fit. Tara flung herself away from the phlegm raining down around her. Allowing the coughing fit to pass, Tara turned back to the man, rubbing his arm soothingly.

'Why don't I ask some questions and you just nod or shake your head?' Tara asked softly. The man nodded slowly, his neck stiff. Tara thought quickly, not knowing what to ask first.

'Have you been here the whole time?' she asked in the

same, unfamiliarly gentle tone.

Again, the man nodded. His face was set in an emotionless expression, his jaw rigid and taught. Tara felt a fleeting feeling of sorrow for the man, before realising she was in exactly the same position. She stared along the corridor they sat in, looking out into the fading light. She couldn't believe the Maze had done this to someone, and that no-one was helping him. She had allowed herself to believe a false pretence that no harm would come to her here. That clearly wasn't true.

'Were you attacked?' she asked, almost hoping he had been. Unfortunately, he shook his head. Again, she looked away, it was hard to look at the man, especially knowing he could be a reflection of her own future.

'Is there anything I can do for you?' she whispered, a little desperately. The man didn't answer at first, apparently thinking. Then, very slowly, he shook his head. Tara couldn't comprehend this. How could he just sit there, waiting to die? Was this place really that bad?

The man leaned forward with immense effort, straining every sinew in his neck. He opened his mouth to speak and uttered two words: 'Good luck.' He collapsed back against the wall, his head cracking against it. Tara continued to squat beside him, her mouth slightly open as the man remained motionless, no longer breathing. She'd only been in here half an hour at most and this was how she was welcomed. For a moment she wondered if this was a test, an actor placed to make her doubt herself. If it was, he deserved an Oscar.

She stood, still looking at the man's face, hoping he would suddenly let out a deep breath. He didn't. It took her a long time to move away from his body. She searched his pockets for some sign of the man's name or anything. There was nothing but a few mouldy crumbs. Finally, she turned and walked in the opposite direction, constantly looking over her shoulder, expecting to see the man dash away. He didn't. For the next few days Tara barely thought of anything else. How could she? She had never seen another human die before her very eyes, and it had taken the Maze less than an hour.

Chapter 62

Diego didn't notice it for some time. He had settled back into his chair after the hushed excitement of the morning, stuffing his face with a fresh bagel complete with cream cheese. That had become his regular lunch pattern over the past few weeks. Engrossed in his food, he barely looked up at the screen. The new Mazers appeared to be settling in just as the seventy before them had. He glanced up at one point and quickly had to double-take. The statistics for the Maze were always updating in the bottom right corner and Diego could have sworn that the number of Mazers had been adjusted to eighty-three that morning, yet now it stood at eighty-two. Unsure of himself, he stood up slowly and approached Benji who was leaning on the note stand at the front of the room looking thoroughly bored.

'You may think I'm crazy,' Diego whispered, keen not to be overheard. If he was right, he didn't want to cause a panic and if he was wrong, he didn't want the embarrassment. He was supposed to know everything about the Maze. 'I think the number of Mazers has changed.'

Benji's elbow nearly slid from the table. His brow furrowed in a puzzled expression. He too began to stare at the bottom right corner, squinting a little behind his square-rimmed glasses. He looked back at Diego, clearly doubting himself as much as Diego himself was. If it wasn't so unlikely it would be much easier to believe. Diego's mind began to wonder, questioning if somehow Penny had found her way out through the wall-top paths. But then, surely Marcus would have gone, too.

'Scottie, come over here, would you?' Diego called, waving to the young, dark-haired operator. Scott was so excited he practically skipped over to them.

'Have you noticed that the number of Mazers has gone down?' Diego asked seriously when Scott had reached them, his voice unusually business-like.

'Well, yeah. That'll be because of Aaron,' Scott replied in a matter-of-fact way, as if this was some stupid test. Diego looked at Benji and could see he was just as nonplussed.

'What do you mean? Where has Aaron gone?' Diego asked. This was becoming embarrassing. How did Scott know more than he did? Scott laughed, still believing this to be a joke that he didn't fully understand. Then he noticed their unmoved faces and realised they really weren't joking.

'W- well,' he stammered, suddenly unsure of himself, 'he hasn't *gone* anywhere yet. He- he died.'

Diego let out a dramatic gasp. This couldn't be true. Scott looked like he didn't know what to say. There was obviously something he wasn't telling Diego. He looked around the room for some support from his fellow operators. Several of them gave worried glances in their direction, no longer focused on their own screens. Diego stared venomously at Scott, silently challenging him to explain.

'Last week we had a visit from Mrs. Tompkins, a member of the board,' Scott blurted out, stumbling over his words in his hurry. 'She came to see us when you weren't here and told us we needed to intervene less. She even told us that if anyone was sick, we should do nothing, just let the situation play out... so we did.'

'And why didn't you tell me, or Benji, or Alex?' Diego demanded.

'W- we were specifically told not to,' Scott muttered, bowing his head so he didn't have to look Diego in the eye.

A fury had taken hold of Diego. How dare the board come down here and undermine his leadership of the Maze. *It was his idea!* He stood, frozen to the spot with fifty eyes all watching his seething silence, like waiting for a bomb to explode. Benji looked just as surprised and confused as Diego felt himself, and Diego would bet on Alex not knowing about this, either. She didn't have it in her to betray him. His fists clenched in anger. He didn't even bother trying to hide his feelings from the onlooking crowd.

Diego quickly strode to the door and marched his way out of the complex, heading straight for the boardroom in the middle of the hotel. He didn't even know what he'd find when he got there, but he was ready to fight anyone he came across. He was shocked to look behind him and see Benji's stormy face, his arms swinging aggressively by his side. Together they entered the elevator in silence and waited, the enraged emotions filling the enclosed metal box palpably. The elevator pinged as the doors opened and Diego all but broke into a run along the deserted corridor. He crashed through the boardroom door without knocking to be greeted by a library like hush. Only two people sat in the room, both quietly poring through reems of notes: Mr. Jenkins and Mrs. Tompkins. Diego's mouth curled into a nasty smile. Just the people he had wanted to see. They looked up as the door slammed shut behind Benji.

'Ah, I'm guessing you've heard, then,' Amelia Tompkins stated, a sinister sneer breaking across her face.

'How dare you?' Diego roared. 'A man has died! How can that possibly be a good thing?' He wanted answers immediately. Seeing her smug smile had only further fuelled his fury.

'Why don't you take a seat?' Mr. Jenkins suggested calmly, his low voice remarkably soothing. Diego slumped into the nearest chair and sat watching the pair of board members sat opposite him, waiting expectantly.

'I appreciate you must be feeling... frustrated,' Jenkins

began, 'but we must explain. We never anticipated or wanted anyone to die, not necessarily.'

Diego tutted and threw his hands in the air.

'Oh, that's such a relief,' he uttered sarcastically, his voice full of contempt.

'You will surely concede, though,' Jenkins ploughed on, 'that the Maze had not seen nearly enough progression over the last seven months?'

'Perhaps. But that is no reason for anyone to die.'

'I will repeat, we didn't want anyone to die, though I understand it is hard for you to accept. We decided that we needed to be a little more radical with our processes and we decided that we had to undermine you because otherwise the results would be on your shoulders.'

Diego stuttered, unsure what to think. He looked at Benji to his left, who had remained silent. He shrugged his shoulders.

'So, you're saying you were actually trying to protect me.'

'Yes, Mr. Flint. You seem to forget, but we are on the same side,' Mrs. Tompkins stated derisively.

Diego began to calm, his breathing less agitated. He sat up more attentively in his chair.

'Okay, what do we do next?' he asked, his tone completely different.

'It is our belief that we need to allow things to take a more natural course to create an organic environment. We can affect the environment, yes, but we need to interfere less with the Mazers.'

Diego nodded. Annoyingly, this made a lot of sense, yet his conscience was unable to settle.

'And what happens when someone else dies?' he asked tentatively. The two board members looked at each other meaningfully.

'If we are correct, that should not be an issue. We hope

that this will create a better Maze in every way,' Tompkins replied.

'And the media? They are going to have a field day when they find out.'

'They won't find out,' Jenkins added firmly, almost threateningly.

Diego left shortly after, his mind full of a thousand questions. The board *might* be right, but what if they weren't? Diego couldn't sit back and watch more people suffer, people who he was supposed to protect. He made his way back down to the control room, his eyes not leaving the floor in front of his feet. The control room was serene, with every eye on the giant screen. Diego glanced up and saw three officers carrying the limp body of Aaron over the wall tops. Diego really hoped Penny wouldn't see this. He looked around the control room, full of suspicion. Did the board truly expect all these operators to keep their silence?

Alex was stood at the front of the room, her arms folded angrily. Diego approached her cautiously. She was as incensed as Diego had been, confirming his earlier suspicions. Diego repeated his conversation with the two board members, but to his surprise that didn't seem to ease her mood as it had his own.

'How can they think allowing these people to die is making the Maze better?' she retorted. Diego tried to explain the reckoning that nobody else would die, but this didn't help, either. Alex stormed out of the room leaving Diego as confused as ever. He was so used to Alex being right about everything that he had an involuntary reaction to take her side, but even he had to admit the Maze needed something to change, otherwise the Mazers would all die eventually, anyway.

Chapter 63

Penny and Marcus had just spotted some of the Maze workers for the first time. Penny dropped to the floor and lay down as flat as she could possibly make herself, whispering harshly for Marcus to copy. She was sure the workers wouldn't want them on the top of the walls, otherwise they would have made it easier to get up. It was hard to make out in the darkness, but she could have sworn they were carrying something. It was probably just food.

The three of them passed as silently as ninjas, not giving Penny and Marcus a second glance, and soon disappeared from view. Penny knew they must be heading for an exit, so she was quickly on her feet, keen to follow. Before she could set off in pursuit Marcus grabbed her ankle. She tried to shake him off, but he refused to budge.

'What are you doing?' she hissed in a hushed tone. She knew the workers must still be within earshot.

'You can't,' Marcus muttered, still clinging on to her leg.

'What? Why not?'

'Where do you think they're going? They're going back to a building that'll be filled with security. You'd get caught straight away!' Marcus half-shouted, half whispered.

'I have to try,' Penny stated stubbornly. With an almighty effort she twisted her leg free of Marcus' grasp and made a run for it. She glanced back after a few seconds and saw that Marcus was still lying on the ground, watching her go pleadingly. This was no time for sentiment; if she was very careful, she could actually get out of this hell today.

For the next hour she snuck along the walls, just about keeping the three men within sight. She couldn't risk being caught, at least not before she saw the outside world at the very least. It had taken her ten panicked minutes to catch up to them after Marcus' interruption, having headed in the wrong direction at first. Fortunately, they were moving very slowly, being weighed down by a large sack of something Penny couldn't make out.

Marcus' words kept biting at Penny as she edged her way in slow motion along the walls, matching the pace of those she was pursuing. Maybe he was right, maybe Penny would be greeted by a hundred guns. Even that would be better than sitting around waiting to die, though. At least it was an adventure, a story to tell. If she could take one breath on the other side, it could sustain her for another day. She wondered what Marcus was doing right now. Probably trying to find the ladder to get back down. He had wanted to leave almost as soon as they'd got up here. Penny could tell that much, even though he didn't dare say it.

She thought of Aaron, too, and Yazmin. It was strange how these people she would never have known otherwise had come to mean so much to her. But she had always known she was different, more ambitious. She was fuelled by something more than just a desire to survive.

Finally, Penny thought the end must be in sight. It had been painful, trudging along at such a slow pace. She wanted to stop for a while, her legs aching, but she couldn't risk losing the three workers. Up ahead Penny swore she could make out something other than utter darkness. There seemed to be a glint, like a mild star up ahead, and Penny was sure it must be a wall. She put on a turn of speed to close the gap slightly, crouching down as low as possible to the point that her calves were screaming.

Jagged edges of stone jutted out at her from the darkness ahead. The workers were only a few metres away from the edge of the Maze and Penny was still too far back. Her mind was racing with the enormity of her decision. She had to go through with her plan, and it was now or never.

A crack of glorious light had started to appear in the plain black wall and she could make out movements of several people on the other side. Her stomach dropped a little. It would take a miracle not to be caught but she was going to try anyway. How much worse could her life get?

The light widened and widened until it was a full doorway, the thick door swinging backwards into the light. Penny could see that it had been moulded to blend into the surroundings. The workers moved into the light and were soon at the threshold. Penny, unseen in the background, had slowly been creeping closer and closer. As the workers disappeared around the door and into the bright light of the outside world, Penny put on a burst. The door began to close exceptionally slowly. Penny had to hope it was operated by a machine. If somebody was pushing it on the other side, she wouldn't stand a chance.

Only a foot of doorway remained open when Penny reached the threshold. She paused and took a deep breath, before heading into the unknown. At first, she couldn't make out anything; the light burned her eyes. She squinted, throwing one arm up to shield herself, too. Taking in the room, she could see it was warmly decorated with natural wood and calming, simple colours — such a refreshing view after so many months seeing the same cool grey of the Maze's walls.

The room was deserted, the previous occupants clearly distracted by the arrival of their colleagues. Penny's heart leapt; she couldn't believe she was so lucky. On the other side of the room a large, wood-panelled door stood slightly ajar. Cautiously, Penny approached. She couldn't hear a thing from the other side and as she peered through the gap, the adjoining corridor appeared just as deserted as the room she was currently occupying. It troubled her how silent it was. She was sure there would be guards or at least cameras somewhere, but her adjusting eyes couldn't see any.

The door swung backwards noiselessly when Penny pulled it and she slowly crept into the empty corridor. She looked both ways, concerns growing inside her head. Now that she was actually out of the Maze, the magnitude of her foolishness suddenly hit her. Even if she could survive five or even ten minutes, Penny knew she would be caught at some point. And what was it for? A breath of air that didn't taste bitter and metallic, and burnt corneas.

Penny wandered along the left corridor, no longer holding the pretence of sneaking around. It wasn't worth it. She walked straight down the middle of the pathway, her eyes darting in all directions, expecting to be intruded upon at any moment. There wasn't a sound, though. No sign of the workers she had followed for so long or any of their colleagues. She reached a plain white door on her left, sealed closed. It looked like an entrance to some kind of hospital lab, which seemed very out of place. She leant against it and listened intently, revelling in the warmth of the material. It was so nice to see something other than stone. Penny would quite happily never see another grey wall; she'd had her fill by now.

Again, there wasn't a whisper from what she could tell. She pulled on the handle, but the door didn't budge. She tried again, but still nothing. Shrugging to herself, she turned away and carried along the corridor. More doors lay ahead, some looked like mere janitorial stores whilst others had glass windows so that Penny could see what lay on the other side. None of them were of any interest to Penny until she reached another of the white laboratory doors. This one was slightly ajar.

No longer concerning herself with remaining unnoticed, Penny reached for the door and hastily pulled it open. She half expected to find a crowd of people suddenly staring back at her like she'd entered the wrong tavern in an old film. There were no heads turning her way, though. There wasn't a single sign that another person had passed by recently. Penny began to wonder if this was all some weird dream that she was stuck in, that her mind had somehow concocted an empty Maze of hallways to mirror her actual life. If that were true, Penny really hated her subconscious self.

She it knew it couldn't actually be true, mostly because she always woke up when she realised she was dreaming. She stood in the centre of the empty room, baffled, her hands on her hips. She didn't understand, the people she had followed through the door had disappeared mere seconds before Penny had entered, and yet they were nowhere to be seen. She turned in a huff and pushed the door back open, continuing along the corridor. The whole place seemed far too much like a hospital for Penny's liking, with more doors than she could count leading to new corridors and rooms unknown. The floor was even the same ocean-blue rubbery material that she remembered from her last visit to hospital.

Up ahead, Penny could make out a patch of light and her stomach lurched forward in eagerness. She picked up her pace until she reached a section of corridor walled on one side by eight-foot-tall glass panes. On the other side sat a courtyard with grass, trees and even a colourful little bird going merrily about its business. Penny couldn't remember its name for the life of her. She pressed a hand against the glass, longingly. The whole scene was lit by late afternoon sun beaming golden rays that made Penny's whole body tingle with goosebumps. For the first time in months, she was completely distracted from her own self-involved troubles as she took in the wonder of the moment. It didn't last long.

Something moved in the corner of her eye and her eyes darted in its direction, at first thinking it was probably just a fly. It wasn't a fly, but a camera. It had just moved so that its lens was now focused on Penny. Her heart sank, knowing that her brief escape from the Maze was surely over. She backed away slowly from the camera, refusing to blink as if she were holding it in a staring match. At any moment Penny envisaged doors all around her crashing open and being surrounded by armed guards.

Chapter 64

Yet again, Diego had been left stunned by the actions of the Mazers. This week was getting weirder and weirder, and not for the better. In keeping with the board's wishes, Diego had swiftly come up with a plan to entertain Penny's attempt to gain freedom. A mass exodus of officers had taken place in a matter of minutes and Penny was to be greeted by a new maze of empty corridors and random rooms.

Diego watched along with the rest of the control room as Penny made her way through a whole new corridor full of a much more natural light. The cameras were much more limited in this new environment and at times they lost track of Penny's movements, but it was fascinating to watch her explore this new realm. Diego was torn in his decisions. This new world of corridors offered an expansion to the Maze, one that might just provide life to it. Yet, he didn't feel comfortable rewarding Penny for her efforts to escape. For the time being Diego was content to watch Penny and see how things unfolded. After all, that was what the board would have wanted from him.

The control room was more active than Diego had ever seen it before. Operators and officers alike were dashing here and there, filling in paperwork and desperately trying to find a corner of desk space to work from. The act of clearing the officers from their own maze-adjacent halls had been swift and efficient — the only problem now was that they were working in the same space as the operators. With all the extra action the Maze was seeing right now, this was far from ideal.

Diego had vacated his usual spot in the back corner. He was used to being left in peace and quiet by the operating team, but with little breathing space for anyone he couldn't exactly expect that luxury. Soon enough he had been crowded out, and with a feeling of suffocation closing in around him he quickly leapt out of his seat and forced his way to the front. Neither Alex nor Benji were anywhere to be seen. They were probably busy dealing with the aftermath of Penny's "escape", or with Aaron's death.

The latter still troubled Diego. It made him feel sick to think of someone dying under his care. That was certainly not why he had designed the Maze. He wanted to talk to somebody about it, to announce it to the world, but he knew he couldn't. It would destroy his Maze and his own reputation. His eyes stared at the desk in front of him morosely, though his mind was elsewhere. All around him people fluttered by in pandemonium, not even acknowledging him. It felt incredibly easy to get lost in himself given how many people were around.

Instead, he tried to focus on Penny. He tried to picture what was going through her head. Before today she had seemed a very level-headed person — for the most part, at least. It unsettled Diego to think that a well-mannered, creative person like Penny had been driven to do something so crazy. The last twenty-four hours had heightened Diego's self-doubts to a new level. Suddenly, Alex came bustling through the crowded room, working her way up to the front. looking irritated by the noise and heat emanating from the crowd. For some reason her anger cheered Diego up. Seeing her flared nostrils and pouted lips always put a smile on his face.

'Is this really necessary?' she huffed impatiently, looking around the room and clutching her trusty tablet tightly to her chest. 'Can't we just send her back now?'

'You know what the board will say,' Diego stated.

Alex rolled her eyes.

'I never thought you'd be so willing to go along with the

board, especially on this.'

'Well, maybe they actually have a point. The Maze hasn't exactly gone to plan, has it?'

'Well, no…' Alex faltered. 'But this is crazy. You've literally let somebody escape.'

'She hasn't exactly *escaped*,' Diego replied, defensively. 'We know exactly where she is.'

Alex sighed heavily and turned away, watching the screen. Penny was currently out of view, having disappeared into an adjoining room.

'I know you think you know Penny from having watched her in the Maze, but have you ever thought there might be more to her? She might actually be dangerous.'

Diego pondered this for a minute. Despite the nature of the Maze, he had tried to block out everything he knew from their previous lives. He didn't want to judge them on their past mistakes, which now he thought about didn't make a lot of sense. Penny strolled back into view, clearly comfortable that she wasn't about to be arrested. She looked like a toddler who had just started walking, so keen to explore the world around her. She certainly didn't *look* dangerous.

Chapter 65

Penny had just finished another long day in the coffee shop. She had spent several hours with their accountant that afternoon, running through numbers and trying to find a positive spin. There was no avoiding it; their little shop seemed destined to close. She sat in the driver's seat of her car, her head leaning on the steering wheel. She'd locked up and flopped into her car some time ago, but she couldn't bring herself to leave the car park. She was the only person around and it was a little eerie, hidden behind their little dream, illuminated by the glow of a singular, flickering streetlight.

She hadn't told Toby yet, though even he must have worked out that something was wrong. Business just hadn't picked up the way they had hoped. Everyone was too invested in the chain stores that were putting businesses like hers and Toby's out of commission. She slammed her head against the wheel, immediately thinking herself lucky that she hadn't set off the airbag. That would have really topped it all off. Leaning back in her chair, she spotted a stray fox that had been scavenging in a nearby bin giving her a glare, its fur fluffed up in defence. It soon realised she wasn't a threat and went back about its business, scampering away down the narrow side street.

She must have sat there pondering the future for an hour at least. She kept picturing herself starting the car, driving home, and telling Toby the news in a variety of ways but none of them ended very well. Each time she actually went to turn the ignition key, something stopped her. A light drizzle broke out, spattering droplets onto the windshield. Penny gave a little shudder and finally decided she could put it off no longer.

Just as she reached for the ignition she glanced into the

seat to her right. Her satchel lay open, files spilling out in a heap of papers. She had never been the most organised person. Maybe that was why *The Little Spoon* had failed. Penny's eye caught the document on top of the pile. It was a confirmation statement of their building insurance policy. In an instant, a flood of thoughts and feelings hit her. Her hand pulled away from the ignition key. A horrible thought had struck her, she hated herself a little for even thinking it. Yet, she was having a hard time dislodging it from her mind.

Her brain was working at triple speed now. It would be so easy, yet surely there was a simpler way. One that wouldn't risk everything they had worked for, let alone her own life. She desperately tried to think of an alternative, but the more she tried, the more the idea seemed to burn brighter in her mind. Out of instinct she pulled her phone out. She quickly scrolled through her social media, more out of habit than anything else. When she closed the tab, a picture of herself and Toby arm-in-arm stared back at her from her home screen. It was the first day they had opened *The Little Spoon*. It had been such an exciting day. She felt a lonesome tear trickle down her cheek.

Wiping her face quickly before setting it resolutely, Penny switched her phone off. She had learnt that much from TV, at least. She got out of her car, frantically scanning her surroundings for any sign of onlookers. There was no-one to be seen. There hadn't been for the whole hour she had sat in her car. At least, she hoped not. Jangling her keys as she pulled them from her pocket, she reached the door and opened it quietly, checking one last time that nobody was watching her. There didn't even seem to be any CCTV. That unsettled her a little.

Inside, the entire shop was filled with an expectant hush, as if it knew what she was about it do. She didn't switch the lights on. The glare of the streetlights gave Penny enough light for her to see what she was doing. She moved stealthily to the kitchen. For some reason the darkness seemed to encourage silence. She wasn't used to seeing this place in the dark, but she knew where she was going well enough to navigate the obstacles.

In the kitchen, she set about her work quickly and silently, still alert for any sign of passers-by in the evening calm. Luckily there were no windows in the kitchen. As quickly as she had thought up her not-so-cunning plan, it was set in motion. She rushed out of the kitchen, hoping beyond hope that it would work. She locked the door behind her, her eyes darting suspiciously to overlooking windows and shadowy corners, half-expecting someone to leap out accusingly. She tried to reassure herself: even if someone was there, they wouldn't necessarily know what she'd just done. She leapt into her car and hurriedly started the engine, her hands shaking at the wheel. It was done. Only time would tell if she would get away with it as she pulled away from the scene of the crime. Penny never noticed the other car, parked in next door's bay and hidden by a low, brick wall.

Chapter 66

Natasha had been on the wall tops for about a day before she found Marcus again. She could tell straight away that he was down about something. He told Natasha about his companion, Penny, the woman Natasha had seen him with. Marcus told Natasha that Penny had followed some people dressed all in black, assuming they would lead her to an exit. Immediately, Natasha began speculating about whether she'd succeeded. Even if she had found an exit, surely she would be captured instantly? Oddly, Marcus didn't look too upset about this. It was something else that was bothering him.

'Were you and this Penny... close?' Natasha asked, trying to be delicate.

'Oh, no,' Marcus blustered. 'We'd only met a couple of days ago, actually. I just happened to bump into her when she was making that ladder. I helped a bit.'

'So, what's troubling you?' Natasha questioned him again.

Marcus sighed deeply, his eyes dropping and his shoulders sagging cartoonishly.

'I don't know... it's just... I kind of got my hopes up about this. I thought there might be some answers. If anything, I feel further away from the exit than before.'

Natasha nodded; she understood that only too well. It was tough to keep yourself going day after day without a clear end in sight.

After that, Natasha didn't really want to stay above the Maze any longer. Marcus said he was starving as he obviously hadn't been able to eat since they'd climbed up; the only food was on the level below. Together, they walked for several hours, debating on multiple occasions which way they needed to go to reach the ladder. Natasha wondered if it would be easier to just jump down. Not knowing the answer, it wasn't worth the risk. It wasn't like there were ambulances or hospitals around in case she broke an ankle. This temptation became much harder to resist when they came across one of the food rooms. Natasha felt her mouth salivating at the smell of the baked goods that floated up to them.

The only thing Natasha had discovered from her time above the Maze was that the walls *did* move. She had suspected this for a long time, and now she was almost certain. The only thing that made her doubt herself was her mental state after seven months inside; it was enough to make her think some outlandish thoughts. She was almost relieved when she looked out upon the Maze and saw a wall in the distance turn and create a new corner. It meant she wasn't completely insane.

Finally, after several more hours of enduring hunger and drowsiness, they spotted the ladder a few pathways away. Once they had climbed down, Natasha noticed how jaded and thin Marcus looked. Fortunately, he knew where the nearest food room was, having visited on multiple occasions when he was helping Penny. They set off at a much more meaningful pace. Marcus looked much steadier on his feet now he was back on firm ground. He was a tall man, so Natasha imagined it looked a lot higher to him up above the Maze.

Fifteen minutes later, they had arrived at the food room. Natasha was shocked to find that it was already occupied. Two women were in the room, helping themselves to the food. One was stood on the far side, her back turned to the door as she selected items from the various platters. The other was sat at the canteen-style table with her feet up as she chewed on a slice of watermelon. She looked remarkably comfortable given her surroundings. Judging by their appearances, neither of them had been in the Maze very long; their hair was still in good condition, not overgrown, whilst their complexion still had a slight rosy glow that suggested recent exposure to sunlight.

Natasha cleared her throat to announce their arrival. The two women looked up like rabbits caught in headlights; another clear sign they weren't completely used to their surroundings. Natasha and Marcus stood shoulder to shoulder in the doorway, bedraggled and pallid in appearance. The women stood on the far side approached, a friendly smile on her face. It was strangely refreshing to see someone genuinely warm and welcoming. Everyone Natasha had met in the last few months had developed a cold outer shell, having been trapped here for so long.

'Hiya, please come in. Don't let us stop you,' the standing woman said, waving them in. She had a high-pitched, bubbly voice that Natasha had come to know as out of place down here. It was unsettling to meet someone so friendly. Natasha's instincts were screaming at her that it was some kind of sinister trap. Nevertheless, they were both starving so they entered, awkwardly watching the two newcomers out of the corner of their eyes', avoiding their gaze. For the next few minutes, they all ate and drank in silence, the two new women taking in the room as they munched away with a mixture of wonder and grim realisation.

'So, I'm guessing you guys have been here for a while?' the woman who had welcomed them in asked, now sitting at the table. She looked them both up and down as she said it, and Natasha felt she should be a little offended but she couldn't blame the woman. She couldn't imagine how dishevelled they looked at that moment.

'Yeah. Seven months, roughly,' Natasha said through a mouthful of tasteless white bread. The two women's eyes widened, and they looked at each other.

'So, it is true,' the second woman stated. 'There has really only been one person to get out?'

'Er... yeah, I guess so. We've only heard about one.' Natasha shrugged her shoulders. Marcus seemed too busy cramming things into his mouth to exchange pleasantries.

'What do you mean you heard? How did you hear?'

Natasha smiled. It was like introducing somebody to a colony.

'Well, they do these announcements every week so we can learn about the outside world. They told us in one of them.'

'Oh, cool,' the second woman replied. Natasha thought that was more than a little bit of an overstatement. She didn't correct her, though. She just nodded. The newcomers would soon learn.

They returned to an understood tranquillity after that, each party hoping the other would leave soon enough. The two women certainly didn't look like they were in a hurry to move on. Natasha had no idea how long they had been there before she and Marcus had arrived. The first woman to speak was deep in thought, her blank eyes unstaring, directed at the plastic canteen table. She looked to be the older of the two, though they both looked fresh and cleansed thanks to their recent arrival. She abruptly stood up and approached Natasha and Marcus, who had been sat leaning against the wall. Natasha always looked forward to actually sitting on a chair, but even that luxury had been temporarily taken away from her.

'You know, it would be great if me and Tara could stay with you guys for a while. We don't know the Maze too well yet, is all.'

Tara turned her head at the sound of her name. She clearly didn't necessarily feel the same way. Natasha and

Marcus looked at each other doubtfully. The spiteful part of Natasha felt these newbies should learn the Maze for themselves, like she had. Of course, she had had McKenzie to help a bit. She thought about McKenzie for a moment. He probably would have helped, despite his fears of becoming too close to another person. The nameless woman wrung her hands nervously as she waited for an answer.

'Are you two, erm… together?' she asked nervously.

'Oh, no,' Natasha replied instinctively, though maybe a little too quickly. 'In fact, we only just met, really.'

'Oh, really? Even after seven months you're still meeting new people? How big is this place?'

Natasha chuckled.

'No. It's not that. It's just… nobody really talks to each other down here. They just go about their business.'

The puzzled expression on the nameless woman's face concerned Natasha. These two women really didn't have a clue about the Maze, and it was going to be harder for them. There were so many unspoken, unwritten rules between the prisoners that they wouldn't know or understand. Maybe they did need some help. Natasha exhaled deeply and rolled her eyes.

'You know what, we will help you. You're going to need it,' she stated. Marcus turned his head sharply to face her. He obviously didn't want to be spoken for. 'Well, I'll help you, at least. You might want to tell me your name, though.'

'It's Georgia.'

'Natasha.'

'No, Georgia.'

'No, I mean-'

'I know what you mean. It's just a stupid joke.' Georgia smiled. Natasha didn't think she'd heard a dad joke like that for at least seven months. She actually laughed, a high-pitched, girly giggle. Soon, she another

Penny had been out of the Maze for over half a day now. She knew that because there were *clocks* on the walls here. Though, she was beginning to think that she wasn't out of the Maze at all. Flint was plainly a very intelligent man. Penny figured he knew somebody would find this exit and had simply created an extension to the Maze, only one that looked completely different. If that were true, he was more than intelligent; he was a genius.

There were two things troubling Penny about this new section. Firstly, she knew she'd followed three people through the door, yet there was no sign of them — or the others that she had seen through the door, for that matter. There wasn't a single clue as to where they had disappeared to. Penny could only presume they had gone through one of the now locked doors. The other concern was much more real and much more immediate. Penny had searched a large portion of the new set of hallways and nowhere had she come across any food, or even a bathroom. She hadn't eaten too long before entering this new Maze, it had only been around a day ago, but she needed to find somewhere soon, and she didn't want to be going all the way back to the other Maze.

The new Maze seemed to be made up of a square building, full of long, criss-crossing corridors. Four corridors edged a courtyard in the centre of the building, visible through long stretches of glass panelling. Despite being so close, Penny had been unable to find a doorway into the courtyard. It was just teasing her, desperate as she was to feel fresh air flow through her hair, and to touch the leaves of the trees dancing in the swirling wind.

The majority of doors she passed were locked, even ones Penny could only imagine were tiny janitorial cupboards. It was eerily silent and empty, most of all because it felt like this place should be filled with people doing busywork. Knowing she was the only person here made Penny feel lonelier than she ever had in the main Maze. It wasn't all bad, though. Although she couldn't actually get outside, being able to see a hint of green life and bask in the golden sunlight filtering through the windows was glorious. She was glad she had come, just for the change of scenery as much as anything.

She wondered what Marcus was doing and if he had come to his senses and tried to follow her. Without anyone to follow, he wouldn't have a chance of finding this place. She also speculated how Aaron was doing. It had been so long since Penny had seen him now. Aaron was in no way her favourite person, but they had developed a closeness during their time together in the Maze when Penny had really needed someone to lean on.

Penny had turned so many corners at such a frantic pace in her enthusiasm to discover everything about this place that she had lost her bearings. She had no idea how to find the door back to the Maze anymore. She resolved herself to start searching once more, thinking that the workers would surely have to show up at some point when food needed to be restocked in the Maze. She began attempting to retrace her steps, muttering to herself as she passed different doors that she remembered. At least this place had some landmarks and variations in its design that made it slightly easier. If she had been turned around in the main Maze, she wouldn't have had a chance of finding her way back.

For the next couple of hours Penny strolled the halls, alone. Every now and then she spotted a memorable door that helped her track down her whereabouts. Time seemed to be passing slower now that she had a constant reminder of it. Penny realised she actually quite enjoyed the separation from that particular aspect of societal structure. In fact, other than the basic necessities, there wasn't a lot Penny missed. She quite enjoyed the solitude. Especially knowing that nobody was going to sneak up and attack her. For the last seven months, she had lived in constant fear of those around her.

Penny turned yet another corner and felt her heart leap from her chest. At the far end of the corridor, she was sure she spotted somebody's foot. It had only been for a brief moment, but Penny was positive she had seen it. She sprinted the entire length of the corridor at speed, her worn shoes struggling to grip the shiny floor surface. As she reached the corner the foot had disappeared down, she tried to slow but skidded ten feet past. Recovering her balance as quickly as possible, Penny turned the corner and was infuriated to find the hallway to be completely empty. She had been so sure that she had seen something, yet she was doubting herself now. After all, she was pretty hungry, and it was a definite possibility that she was hallucinating.

Nevertheless, she began storming down the corridor, forcefully hauling doors open and half-expecting to come face to face with an ashen-faced worker who had somehow been trapped with Penny in this abandoned set of corridors. She had no such luck. Penny was about to give up when she heard the slightest hint of a noise coming from just down the corridor. She moved a little closer and realised it was somebody coughing. They coughed once more and then fell silent. Penny moved on her tiptoes in an attempt to catch the worker off guard. She reached for the door and gently tried to pull it. As she anticipated, it was locked. The worker hadn't been that foolish, but Penny was prepared to wait, for days if that was what it took. She took a heavy breath and sat across the hall, leaning against the wall opposite.

Chapter 68

TJ had almost given up on himself, right up until he had spotted those people racing along the top of the walls. His general self-loathing had led him to slump against the wall and just wait for the end. There hadn't been an end in sight, no way that he could get over what he had done or even do something to put it right. The Maze was ready to swallow him whole, wrapped up in his own emotions.

He sat at the very end of a corridor, looking down the entire length of it. He could see far into the distance, staring into the impenetrable darkness that stretched on forever above the Maze. But then that darkness had been broken. Two people went half running, half walking by, dressed all in beige just like he was. They must have been a kilometre away, but TJ could make them out as clear as anything, lit from below and drastically contrasting the darkness that threatened to smother them.

They were gone before TJ could blink, but he was on his feet just as quickly. It felt like a sign, telling him to follow them, like he was meant to be watching that particular section of the sky at that exact moment. He began scrabbling his way along the corridor in his haste to catch up with the two figures in the distance. By the time he had reached the end of the corridor, they were long gone from sight. TJ felt weak from malnourishment, having not eaten for days now. He had come to the conclusion that he didn't deserve to eat. Or breath, for that matter.

Despite his famine TJ felt more alert, his brain sharper than it had been in months. He thought rapidly, replaying his fellow prisoners' movements in his head. He knew they had run to his right and he could easily follow, but how would he get on to the wall anyway? They must have created something to help them climb; TJ knew he had to find that.

Half an hour later, TJ stumbled upon a food room in his search for this magical object that would get him onto the walls. He wanted to carry on, but he couldn't ignore the earthquake of rumbling his stomach was sending out. Soon enough he had gulped down enough food to last him another week at least and he briefly sat down on one of the rickety plastic chairs to catch his breath, his stomach now bloated yet content. TJ felt the relief of a little nourishment coursing through his veins, and he was quickly back on his feet, keen to get back to searching.

He was just heading for the door when somebody else went rushing past. What was unusual was that they didn't give the food room or TJ a second glance. They went rushing past so quickly that all TJ saw was the merest flash of purple. It was enough to fill TJ with dread. He would have recognised that messy tangle of outgrown purple hair anywhere and it immediately made him shiver with self-hatred. He cowered away in the corner of the room, hoping beyond hope that the woman wouldn't come back. TJ huddled up in the corner with his arms wrapped tightly around his knees. The shame spiral he had briefly been torn away from by the two mysterious figures had come crashing back over him.

He desperately wanted to get back searching for whatever it was that had helped the people to get up onto the walls, but for the time being he was unable to move. He only wished he had a safety blanket to cuddle up in. TJ suddenly snapped himself back to reality, realising how stupid he was being. This wasn't him. He was a strong and stubborn man. Before the Maze, he had never once had a moment of self-doubt. Now it controlled his every action.

It took TJ quite some time to recover himself, but eventually he got back to his feet. Again he approached the door, much more cautiously on the second attempt. At the threshold he glanced warily from side to side as if expecting a heavy load lorry to come rushing past. But there wasn't a single person in sight, so TJ slowly set off to the left, following in the footsteps of the purple-haired woman.

It didn't take long after he set off to discover how exactly those two people had got onto the walls. After just three more turns TJ abruptly came across the answer. The wall had been cut to pieces, leaving a ladder of rungs carved deeply into the stone. The floor was littered with a dusting of stone shavings that had once stood firm as part of the wall. TJ couldn't help but be impressed by the sheer innovation. He had never once considered climbing onto the walls before, let alone how he would go about doing it.

TJ didn't waste a second, he climbed straight up the ladder and onto the top of the walls. It was quite a sight from his new vantage point, widening TJ's eyes to this whole world. As there was no sign of anybody else in the gloom above the Maze, TJ guessed and headed off to the left, taking in his new surroundings with boyish eyes.

He walked for hour upon hour without a single sign of the others he had seen. TJ had no idea just how many people were up here by now. He was sure others would have seen the first explorers of the Maze walls — they weren't exactly subtle up above the Maze, standing out against the dark ceiling. TJ spotted several people down below, mere specks to him from so far away. He came to a halt, considering his next move. There was nothing around him but a gloomy void of emptiness. Down below, TJ spotted a man walking by. He couldn't believe what he was about to do.

'Hey!' he called, waving. The man looked at TJ with a look of mild shock.

'W- w- how…?' he stammered, confused. TJ shrugged it

off and continued.

'Have you passed anyone else up here? I- I lost my friends,' TJ lied. He had already guessed the answer based on the man's reaction.

'Er… no, sorry.'

'Okay, never mind.' TJ turned and walked away before the man had a chance to question him. TJ couldn't believe he'd just asked for directions in the middle of the Maze. How ironic.

A little further along, TJ knelt down, stopping to think. So far, the wall tops had been a severe disappointment. He thought it would be a new opportunity for him to rediscover himself, but that wasn't turning out to be the case. On closer inspection he noticed that the floor he was standing on was caked in a layer of thick dust. This told him that nobody had passed by recently; his were the only footprints coming and going from his current position. Sighing heavily, he turned and headed back the way he'd come, accepting that this couldn't be the right way.

For another day he walked around the walls aimlessly. It was a much faster way of moving around the Maze, especially as there were no dead ends to worry about. At one point he had to take on an ambitious leap across one of the hallways when the wall he was walking along ran out. Finally, he ran into something other than open air, something solid. It was a wall! He had reached the edge of the Maze. He stretched out one hand and rubbed it along the rough, rocky wall. It seemed incomplete in its finish with several sharp edges jutting out from the wall. It was incredibly out of place with the smoothed, polished finish of the rest of the Maze.

*

For the rest of the day TJ made his way around the Maze, sticking as close to the wall as possible. Occasionally he had to make his way back over to the wall in a panic, thinking he had somehow strayed away. Even stood ten yards away, the wall was so dark it was almost impossible to tell it was still there. There was no doubt in his mind that the Maze's end would provide some form of answer for TJ. Somehow, TJ knew it was why he was up here. Sure enough, up ahead he spotted something out of the ordinary: a light. It grew in size and intensity as TJ watched from afar and he saw somebody moving about, silhouetted dimly by the glow. Just as quickly, the light began to disappear, and TJ knew he was too far away to get close enough. He didn't even bother racing after it. He knew, like a train pulling away from the platform, the moment had come and gone.

Chapter 69

It was a bit of a rag-tag group, coming together out of circumstance, yet Natasha couldn't help but think that it worked. Marcus had reluctantly been dragged along with the three women, or at least he'd made a good go of showing his discontent. Natasha got a feeling that he wasn't as displeased as he made out. As they walked, Marcus was easily the most vocal and excitable. Natasha had to admit that it was refreshing to have the innocent energy that the two new prisoners brought. She was working hard to allow them to keep that purity as long as possible and not drag them down.

It turned out the two women had only been in the Maze for a day, or so they estimated. Natasha had smiled knowingly when they commented on the lack of clocks in the Maze and began to lead them towards her watch. At that moment, she was prouder than ever of her accomplishments within the Maze. It only took them a short walk to reach the watch. It didn't have such an awe-inspiring reaction from the two new prisoners. After all, just a day before they had been able to see as many clocks as they wanted. They had never understood the suffering that someone like McKenzie had. Somehow, seeing the watch seemed to lower the atmosphere within their new travelling group. Tara and Georgia seemed to have grasped a whole new understanding of the hardships of the Maze. If this was a luxury, this tiny watch, then they were in for a tough ride.

Natasha quickly guided them away before the last drops of positive energy dissipated. For a while the group fell into an unspoken understanding, each just happy for the company. The two women were still new enough that little mementos and landmarks left their eyes wide. Every little scratching of direction or random scribbling triggered an excited squeak from Georgia. Natasha imagined it was like travelling with a toddler. She concerned herself with Georgia's future, doubting whether she was strong enough to survive the mental challenges the Maze brought. She committed to save judgement on Georgia's character until she knew her better.

'So, where have you guys been sleeping?' Tara questioned. 'We haven't passed any beds yet.'

Natasha laughed heartily, sure that Tara must be joking. She promptly realised that wasn't the case. When she thought about it, it was perfectly reasonable for there to be beds in the Maze. Why not? There were bathrooms, after all.

'There are no beds,' Marcus mumbled glumly. 'We sleep here, on the floor.'

Tara looked down in disgust, suddenly walking on tiptoes. She could only imagine what else people did on the floor if they slept there, too. After another minute of silence, Tara found her voice again.

'Have any of you seen someone die yet?' she asked despondently. Natasha halted to an abrupt stop at the front of their party, a distracted Georgia walking into her from behind.

'What do you mean? Did *you* see someone die?' Natasha asked, shocked.

'Yeah, like ten minutes after entering,' Tara stated, gazing off along the corridor. Natasha looked at Georgia and realised this was news to her, too. 'I figured it was a normal thing here, what, with the lack of food.'

Natasha's mind was suddenly racing. She couldn't believe someone had actually died in here. Natasha had always thought, or rather hoped, that someone was looking out for them to stop any harm coming to them. A stubbornness deep within Natasha was refusing to believe Tara. Their little group fell into a mournful silence as Tara described her experience with the man. Natasha wondered if she had ever met him, in a way hoping that she hadn't. If she had, she would forever carry a burden of responsibility knowing that she could have done something about it. Natasha wanted more than anything for somebody to change the subject and distract her mind.

'What if we built our own shelters?' Georgia suddenly blurted out when Tara had finished her heart-breaking monologue. She had obviously been away in her own thoughts, disregarding her companion's speech. Natasha was still unsure of her feelings towards Georgia. She seemed a little faraway, perhaps as a coping mechanism to hide her true feelings in this strange world. Despite that, Natasha couldn't help but admire her plucky, happy-go-lucky attitude. It reminded her of the youthful and optimistic Natasha who had entered the Maze.

'What do you intend to build these shelters from?' Marcus asked bluntly. 'Sorry to be the one to tell you, but there aren't many materials to work with,' he chuckled derisively. Natasha gave him a warning glare and he stopped abruptly. She didn't appreciate him making sarcastic comments like that. They had enough to worry about without bringing each other down, too.

'I'm not saying we should build big wooden huts or anything, just basic living spaces. Maybe we could use our old clothes to separate areas out, and use some food trays for structure?' Georgia's voice was distant and dreamy, as if she was always afraid she might wake a sleeping baby. Her idea gave Natasha a surge of inspiration, though she had no idea how they would actually make it work. Marcus didn't say anything, and Natasha presumed he was sceptical at best but had decided to keep that to himself, afraid of another penetrating glare. Tara, meanwhile, seemed lost in her own issues. Natasha felt awful that she had endured such an experience so early in her Maze life but there was very little she could say or do to help. It was down to Natasha to entertain Georgia's overactive mind.

Natasha had decided that after the watch she would show Georgia and Tara the other carvings in the Maze. She felt like the least enthusiastic tour guide in history, and it wasn't like the attractions sold themselves. Again, the two newcomers showed little to no interest in what the Maze had to offer. The novelty just wasn't there for them. When Natasha thought about it, a rough carving, though impressive, was hardly much to get excited about, and it was a reflection of the Maze that she and all the other prisoners had. The final frontier was the newest addition: the ladder.

'Is there actually anything up there?' Tara asked as they all looked it up and down pensively.

'Er… no, not really,' Natasha mumbled, and that was the end of the world's worst tour.

Chapter 70

Alex and Benji loitered on either side of Diego, chirping their opinions and, in the process, perfectly reflecting the two sides of his conscience. Alex was desperately pleading with Diego to intervene with Penny, a hint of a tear forming in the corner of her eye. Diego couldn't think of a time he had seen her so worked up before. Benji, who had been sat next to Diego in the board room a week ago, was much more mellow in his arguments, and his opinions were much more in line with Diego's.

Before them, a potential disaster was unfolding on the giant screen. TJ had somehow managed to follow Penny into the officers' quarters and was huddled in a corner with only a solitary, unlocked doorway between them. Diego still had no idea how he had got there. He was under the impression that the door to the Maze had locked behind Penny, but apparently that wasn't the case. Not knowing everything that was happening in the Maze was by far the biggest drawback to this new laissez-faire approach. He felt riddled with worry every time he saw one of the operators approaching him.

As a result, Diego had barely slept in the last two days. He had spent every waking hour studying the movements of the Mazers so that he would face no more surprises — or so he had hoped. Despite his best efforts, TJ had slipped under Diego's radar and forced his way out of the Maze. This left Penny in a potentially perilous situation, especially given TJ's recent history around vulnerable women.

The only thing protecting Penny at that moment was TJ's concerns that he'd been spotted by a guard, rather than a fellow prisoner. If he had known it was another Mazer he'd spotted at the far end of the hallway, Diego was sure TJ would have acted differently. Instead, he had tried his best to lock and hide himself away from view, but he had given himself away just as Penny was moving out of earshot. Now the two Mazers were locked in a stalemate, both sat waiting for the other, under the impression that they were the only Mazer in this peculiar section.

Everyone knew the importance and danger this scenario presented. TJ had already proven he was capable of terrible atrocities and Diego had to presume that he would seize on this opportunity he had been presented with. That was definitely the opinion Alex took on the matter and it was why she was imploring Diego to do something about it. Unfortunately, his knew pledge to be less involved with the Mazers had left Diego's hands tied.

'You realise, of course, that this pledge you supposedly made was only made to yourself. You don't actually have to follow it!' Alex argued, exasperated.

'Maybe Penny needs to suffer to learn,' Benji replied in a low tone not intended for Alex to hear. Unfortunately for him Alex's senses were primed as she fought her case.

'Trust me on this, nobody needs that kind of suffering,' she retorted harshly. Diego frowned as he listened to the pair bickering. He wondered what Alex meant by that.

For what seemed like hours the three of them squabbled and argued between themselves, constantly going around in circles of debate that slowly drove Diego to the brink of insanity. Every time one of his colleagues made a point he swung to their side like a pendulum, all the while knowing he had to make a decision soon enough. The giant screen pictured the two Mazers sat on either side of the door, waiting for the other to make a ‌ Diego watched Penny thoughtfully. Perhaps ‌ ‌ ‌ both ‌ and Alex at the same ‌

Another hour later, the singular volunteer officer was

prepped and ready to enter the Maze once more, adorned with a tray of assorted foods. Diego found it oddly satisfying that the officer who had volunteered was Ben, a man who had previous experience with TJ. Ben was the officer who TJ took as a hostage in a bid for freedom in what felt like a lifetime ago. Now that he thought about it, it made perfect sense for Ben to be the only volunteer. He was the only one with a good reason to help.

Diego had promised Ben that, should everything go to plan, he would come nowhere near to TJ. He also reminded the officer that Penny's only form of weapon, her chisel, was so blunt by now it was almost completely useless.

The door to the stairwell swung open with a gentle woosh and Ben stepped forward, the food tray rattling as his hands shook slightly. As soon as he stepped over the threshold of the doorway, the door was rapidly shut behind him, almost pushing him forward. It was as if there was a rabid monster on the other side rather than two scared and confused Mazers. Ben was an instant celebrity from that moment. Once again, every eye fell upon the giant screen as he took on the stairs one by one, rattling with every movement.

Once in the officers' quarters, Ben's task was simple. Unfortunately, the two Mazers were just about as far away from the stairwell as possible, so he had a fair trek on his hands. Every minute that went by felt like an hour for Diego as he nervously chewed his nails, hoping he had made the right decision. Alex and Benji's silence comforted him a little, as they would be arguing again if they disagreed. Diego wanted to scream at Ben to hurry up as he watched him plod sluggishly along the corridors. All the while, Penny and TJ sat either side of a one-inch door on the verge of a potential catastrophe.

Finally, Ben approached the corridor that Penny

occupied, his padded shoes allowing him to approach silently. Diego didn't think Penny would have noticed his footsteps anyway, she seemed lost in thought as she stared at the wall opposite. Diego had to applaud her patience and resolve to sit there and wait, not even knowing what waited for her on the other side. From the camera focused on Penny, Diego spotted Ben peer around the corner anxiously. To his left, Diego heard the chief officer Gavin muttering instructions frantically over the hush of the control room. For a moment, all stood still, Ben frozen to the spot with fear. Then, in an instant, everything kicked into action.

Ben swiftly made his way across the corridor, playing his role perfectly he dropped a portion of the food as loudly as possible. A spoon fell with an echoing clang that reverberated around the control room. It did exactly what he had intended. Penny's neck twisted like that of a hawk who'd just spotted its prey. She was on her feet in a flash and Diego suddenly worried that Ben didn't have enough of a lead. His heart stopped beating as he waited for the camera to flick to a shot of Ben, and he breathed a sigh of relief when he saw him scampering along the corridor as fast as his feet could carry him. Penny was only just in view, way in the background. She had completely forgotten about TJ, sensing a new opportunity.

TJ, brought to life by the commotion on the other side of the door, had also got to his feet. Diego risked a look away from Ben for a moment and saw the Mazer leaning against the door, listening intently for signs of life on the other side. TJ's feet twitched nervously as he knelt awkwardly against the door but, soon enough, he too was on his feet, and he swung the door open to reveal an empty hallway.

Three corridors away Ben and Penny were involved in a

foot race. Ben had the advantage of a full stomach, though, ironically, he was weighed down with a tray of food. Despite his load, Ben had to slow his progress to keep Penny in sight. If this was to work, he couldn't get too far ahead. Penny struggled along behind, her chest heaving with rasping breaths.

Back some way across the white corridors, TJ was still staring up and down the deserted hallway. Looking in the direction Penny had disappeared minutes before, he noticed something new. Something was lying on the floor where the corridor split into an intersection. Diego watched him race over to the splattered fruit that was spread across the gleaming floor. He glossed over the food and immediately his eyes focused on the silver spoon lying close to the wall. He snatched it up and stood, wildly scanning his surroundings for a sign of life. Penny and Ben were long gone.

Chapter 71

Penny had followed the worker for ages now, barely able to keep up. Something told her that the man wanted her to keep up, though, which was strange. Part of her mind wandered back to the other person she'd abandoned on the other side of the locked door, and Penny questioned if she had made the right decision. She'd been lured away far too easily, and now it was dawning on her that this was almost certainly deliberate, a way to divert her attention.

It was too late now. Even if she wanted to turn back and retrace her steps Penny doubted she could find that door again. She focused her efforts on the figure she was pursuing, doubling the strain she was putting on her empty stomach. A stitch clutched at her midriff with blinding pain and Penny cursed the old wives' tale, that, evidently, was not true.

As she turned yet another corridor in a blurry haze of unwilling sweat, she spotted the man open a door at the far end, promptly disappearing from view. She panted heavily as she held her stomach, bent double. She longed for this to be the final corridor. With another burst of speed, she set off, keeping her eyes firmly locked on the door as it closed. The man hadn't looked back at her, and Penny wasn't sure if he actually knew she was following him. She hadn't exactly made much of an effort to be quiet, though.

The door slammed shut and Penny's hopes fell to a pit in her gut. Penny was sure the door would be locked, but she wasn't about to give up now. She slowed to a walk as she approached the closed door — half the battle was won now that she knew where the man had gone. The door was wide and heavy-set, made from a dark timber. Penny recognised it almost immediately and, all of a sudden, it dawned on her where the man was going. She should have put it together much sooner.

Her hand was already halfway to the handle but she recoiled, hesitating. Her mind was whirring intensely as she considered her options. Penny had loved her time in this weird and wonderful part of the Maze, but she had to admit that without food or water it couldn't last much longer. Not to mention the solitude. Penny had marvelled in the independence of arriving in the hospital-like corridors but, having not seen another face for several days, it had become tiresome.

It took her a minute of deliberation, but, once again, she reached forward and this time she grabbed the smooth silver handle and pulled. The room was empty now. The man she was following had wasted no time and Penny didn't either. In three large strides, she crossed the small intersecting room and went to open the next door. The only problem was, she couldn't open it. There was no handle, no button, or even a keycode to enter. She contemplated this and began feeling the seal around the door for some kind of hidden lever or button. Nothing.

Penny took a step back. She had been certain that the man was meant to be leading her back to the real Maze, but now there was an obstruction stopping her from getting back. Just as she questioned this, the door made a sudden creak and began rolling open mechanically. With several rattling clicks and clunks, the Maze presented itself in its fullest. It was more staggering and mind-blowing than Penny had remembered; her elevated view made it all the more spectacular. It was almost welcoming to see it, which unsettled Penny a little.

She stepped forward, taking in the familiar glow of the golden lanterns. There was no sign of the man she was following, but that didn't matter now. All she wanted to do was find a food room. She didn't even care about finding the ladder, she would jump down if she had to. At the very thought of food, her stomach gave an angry growl. Setting off on the narrow wall top, Penny soon discovered that walking along the elevated pathway wasn't as easy as she remembered. She staggered a little, her legs wobbling from sheer exhaustion. *Not much longer*, she told them. Her eyes were adjusting to the gloom once more, and Penny was sure that the Maze was somehow darker than before.

It didn't take her long to find the shining doorway of a food room. It gleamed like a beacon in the dark, guiding Penny towards it. She knelt down on the wall, her whole body shaking as she slowly began to lower herself. For a split second, she dangled on the edge, trying to control her fall as gradually as possible, but her arms couldn't take the strain and she fell heavily, landing awkwardly on one foot. A horrible crunch of bone made her wince, but she was mere meters away now.

Steadying herself, Penny rose to her fullest and hobbled into the food room, quickly grabbing handfuls of food and slumping into one of the plastic chairs. Her whole body groaned with gratitude as she sunk in her chair. It was crying out for sleep, but Penny knew she needed to eat first. She began cramming food into her mouth as quickly as possible, relishing in the flavours. Quickly though, she fell into a deep sleep, her mouth still half full with a cheese sandwich.

Chapter 72

One down, one to go, Diego thought. Ben had successfully lured Penny away from the officers' quarters and back into the Maze. There had been a brief moment that panicked Diego, before Penny crossed the threshold into the Maze, but in the end, she seemed only too willing to return. Now only TJ remained, and a debate had sparked between Alex and Benji, echoed across the entire control room in murmurs and whispers.

Diego couldn't take it any longer. He bowed his head low and quietly made his way from the room, careful not to draw attention. To seek refuge, he sought out the psychologists' office and Diane. As he closed the door, the faint humming of babble still audible from the control room went silent. He pinched the bridge of his nose and scrunched his face up. When he turned, Diane smiled warmly. In that simple action Diego felt a wave of relief flow over him.

'Trouble?' she asked, knowingly.

'Isn't there always?' Diego replied. Without thinking, he flopped onto the chaise-lounge with a distressed sigh. For several minutes neither of them spoke, and Diane continued with her own work.

'You know,' Diego began, speaking softly to the ceiling, 'I'm beginning to think this was a bad idea.'

Diane leant forward in her chair, watching Diego closely. He had his eyes closed, though, as if trying to remove a severe migraine.

'The funny thing is, when I took this job, I was almost certain that was true. Now, I'm not so sure,' Diane said.

Diego sat up with a puzzled expression.

'Oh, don't get me wrong, there's a lot wrong with the Maze. But it can be fixed,' she continued.

'You think?'

'I do. Anything can be fixed. I wouldn't be a very good psychologist if I didn't believe that.'

'Okay. Any chance you know how?' Diego asked furtively, rubbing his face vigorously.

'I'm afraid that's your job.'

Diego gave another deep sigh as he slouched back down. He wasn't ready to go back out there just yet. Diane seemed more than happy to allow him to hide out in her office. Maybe she felt sorry for him. If the positions were switched, he wouldn't have, after all this project was his stupid idea. He closed his eyes and allowed his thoughts to drift away carelessly; they were filled with images of TJ and masked officers. It didn't take long for him to jump back to his feet — he couldn't procrastinate and suppress his problems forever. Besides, if he got too comfortable, he may well doze off.

Diane looked away from the papers she was scribbling on to say, 'I'm sure I'll see you again soon,' as Diego made for the door. As soon as he opened it, Diego heard a cacophony of rumbling debates chasing him up the corridor. It was enough to make him shrivel up into half a man, yet he stepped confidently out of the office and walked back towards the control room with his head high.

Chapter 73

It was a sign of the times that TJ had eaten the floor food, like a stray dog. He had waited as long as possible, staring the scraps out as they lay there goading him, barely straying more than a few yards down the hallway in any one direction. For hour upon hour, he waited for another sign of life, for another person to show themselves, but they never did. Even with nothing else to do, watching the clock on the wall was mind-numbingly excruciating. He approached the food with caution, a paranoid nerve twitching in his head, telling TJ that this was surely a trap. He sniffed and prodded at the remnants of a few broken sandwiches and, in the end, decided there was nothing for it. He wolfed the lot down in a matter of seconds and sat back, smacking his lips. Now he desperately needed to quench his thirst.

That set off a growing feeling of panic in his mind. He had barely explored this oddly uninhabited territory, but from what he could make out there didn't seem to be much in the way of sustenance around. He told himself that those in charge of the Maze would have to make sure he was fed. Then again, what if this wasn't part of the Maze? It certainly felt different. TJ got the feeling that he wasn't supposed to be here. Even if Flint and his pals did know TJ was here, why should they look after him? After all, he was the one who escaped.

It didn't take long for TJ's confidence to waver to the point of non-existence. He needed to get out of this place. He felt oddly drawn back to the Maze, as if he were homesick. Fortunately, TJ was confident enough that he knew the way back, despite the chaos that had led him to be locked in a cupboard for the best part of two days. He stood up shakily and began walking slowly, trying to retrace his steps. After a while he started walking backwards, realising it was easier if he saw things from the same perspective as the day he first arrived. Surprisingly, it worked well. As TJ marked off memorable doors he had passed on his way he marvelled in his own genius for a moment and let out a triumphant cackle.

It was slow work, walking backwards, but within a few hours TJ had successfully steered his way back to the memorable door. Stepping inside the familiar, box-shaped room, TJ came face to face with another large door with no handle or button to open it. Instant panic rose again, that panic that constantly bubbled gently beneath the surface, now rising in a tidal wave. He was trapped. He couldn't get back to the Maze. TJ didn't understand — he had been sure Flint would have wanted him to return. Then a gentle beep made TJ stiffen and he watched the heavy door slowly come ajar.

*

'There you go. It all worked out in the end,' Diego stated smugly, rubbing his hands as if he'd planned the whole thing.

'Maybe the board were right. If we just leave them to it things might just work out,' Alex added. Diego grinned broadly. 'What?' she snapped.

'I never thought I'd hear you say those words,' he chuckled.

'I said maybe.'

Chapter 74

It had been over a year since Natasha first entered the Maze. She barely thought about McKenzie and the early months, except for every day. She'd made a whole group of friends now, but not one of them could make the place less lonely. It was amazing to see how much the Maze had changed in the last few months, and Natasha had to credit most of that to Georgia. She had an insatiable energy that had helped drive a whole new community.

Every night, or their version of night in the Maze, Natasha liked to climb up the new ladder and onto the wall tops to look out on their basic shanty-like town. Somehow, Natasha had become an unofficial leader of their community, looked up to by others for answers she could never have. There were no answers to be found in here — Natasha had accepted that some time ago. For the first few months of her new gloomy life, Natasha had seen this as a great opportunity to spend more time with herself and become a better person. It was almost impossible to be a better person in the Maze, though. There were very few books and no internet to learn from, no new skills to learn. The only two things Natasha had improved were her patience and her long-distance walking.

They had built their rickety shelters along the same passage that housed the watch, giving a more permanent idea of time structure. It had helped Natasha develop a more regular routine that she'd previously been missing, even before she was thrown in here. The passage had the feel of a small-town high street with people coming and going regularly. Some refused to stay, preferring to carry on in their misguided belief that they would be the one to discover the secret exit to the Maze. Natasha and her fellow founders; Georgia, Tara, and Marcus; had accepted there

From up above, Natasha could see every shelter, there were no more than ten at any one time. Some people had taken this as an opportunity to have a home in the corridors, some just stayed for one night to get some slightly more comfortable sleep, whilst others stayed for a week or two and then moved on. One of the first to appear, a man named Paxton, had been with them for several weeks as they set up the shelters and gradually grew the community, then one day he'd disappeared without a trace. Natasha hadn't heard from him for two months now and he hadn't been mentioned over the loud-speaker. In fact, nothing had been said over the speakers from the outside world for the past two months, now Natasha thought about it.

The little individual shelters were incredibly delicate. It hadn't been easy collecting enough materials to create them and even now they were strung together by the bare minimum. Natasha was thankful there was no wind down here, otherwise they'd have to put them back together every five minutes. Each frame had been built using fragments of snapped food trays, stacks of plastic cups, and whatever other scraps they could find, which was very little. They were then covered with used clothing to provide privacy, an unheard of luxury in the Maze. The shelters weren't much to look at, but it had given them a sense of purpose and togetherness as Natasha and her new friends had built them, and they were still better than anything else on offer.

After a short while of pensive peace, Natasha climbed her way back down the ladder. It had been built by an eccentric woman named Penny who claimed she had already found an exit of sorts to the Maze. Despite this most wild of claims, Penny seemed reluctant to explain herself when Natasha had questioned her. Natasha didn't understand the vagueness either, surely it was either an exit or it wasn't? And if she *had* found it, why hadn't she taken it?

Penny had disappeared as quickly as she had arrived. After spending a week putting together a haphazard version of her ladder with far less rungs, she had hastily set off on a march through the corridors. Natasha had watched her go, all the more certain that the Maze had affected Penny's mental state. She could barely hold a conversation at times, lost in her own thoughts and ludicrous ideas. Natasha couldn't help but think that someone running a social experiment would be fascinated. The general social skills of those that came and went were shot to pieces, with each person wary and edgy around their neighbours.

The Maze had once again changed; it no longer felt innocent. Natasha had never experienced a sensation quite like it, but somehow she knew that something was wrong within her environment. The lack of news from above didn't help either; it felt like Flint and his team were trying to cover something up. It was noticeable in their little village, too, with the atmosphere as cold as the plummeting Maze temperatures. Natasha had grown used to the relative warmth that was provided by the summer above, but now the Maze was as cold as it had ever been. Every time she woke, Natasha found a thin coating of frost covering the wall where her breath had formed moisture.

The worst of everything was the lack of comprehension Natasha faced on a day-to-day basis. In stereotypical old movies, she'd seen prisoners counting down the days until their release. That wasn't possible for Natasha, or anyone in here, which only added to the feeling of helplessness. She had no idea when, or even how, she would get out. At least she had a group of friends that were all in the same situation. Natasha couldn't remember feeling so close to anyone in her whole life. These were people who would all be completely lost without each other.

Just as Natasha was clambering slowly and carefully into her vaguely private quarters, a commotion broke out at the far end of the stretching corridor in which their camp was built. Somebody was screaming a berserk tirade, their shouts echoing in a multitude of confused voices against the stone walls. Alerted by the sudden interruption, Natasha bounced back upright, and the back of her head crashed against the top of her den, making the whole thing come toppling down. Cursing loudly, she swung a foot aggressively at the rubble and stormed off angrily in the direction of the disturbance.

Chapter 75

Tara felt the full wrath of an angry Natasha as she came dashing through their camp. Natasha looked livid, like Tara had never seen before. Somehow her hair was flailing around her despite the lack of even the merest of winds. However, this was soon forgotten with the news that Tara brought. After weeks of searching and studying the Maze's many nooks and crannies, finally they had been rewarded.

Tara had been stationed to watch over the mysterious sea-salt smell that filtered along one specific corridor in the hope that its source would present itself. For weeks and weeks she had been returning every day for the slightest suggestion of change, all based on a "hunch" that Natasha had, one that she refused to share with Tara.

The corridor was a complete throwaway from the dull and gloomy grey of the rest of the Maze. According to Natasha it had once been just the same as any other corridor, at least as far as she could remember. Now, however, the walls and floor were covered in a thick, spongy layer of green moss. This had led to a pool of dew forming on the floor, making the pathway treacherous at best.

It had taken a full month, but a strategically thought-out position above the Maze had allowed Tara to watch on, jaw agape, as the wall split apart to reveal a new passageway diverting away from the main Maze. This new passage looked somehow different, even from Tara's poor viewpoint, and instantaneously she was hit with an immense stench of sea air mixed with something that almost made her retch. If she hadn't been so focused on what was going on below, she probably would have. Whatever was on the other side of that false wall must have been dead for some time.

Tara didn't get any longer to consider this as somebody quickly appeared around the far corner; an older-looking man Tara couldn't remember meeting before, which was saying something. She was under the impression that everybody who currently resided in the Maze had passed through their camp at some point or another. Of course, there was no way of knowing that for sure — they had no idea how many people were even here, and apparently they had been wrong.

The man had hobbled towards the newly formed gap in the grey concrete and peered along the corridor. Even from a distance Tara could tell that the Maze had taken its toll on the man, as it had for the younger people, too. Despite this, whatever he saw at the other end caused an unmistakable glint of excitement in his eye. He paused for the merest of seconds and hobbled on, out of sight.

Tara waited for as little time as she dared and quickly scrabbled to her feet, heart pounding. She knew she didn't have long, but the drop to the Maze floor seemed more daunting than it ever had before to Tara, though she knew she had to take the risk. Bending her knees delicately, she gripped the edge of the wall firmly with one hand and dangled one foot over the edge. The floor still seemed an impossibly long way away. She did the same on the other side and twisted awkwardly in the process, hanging limply for a moment, eyes scrunched tightly. She forced herself to open one eye and look down slowly. Her feet were still some way short of the floor, but she was surely running out of time.

Without another moment to stop and think, Tara let go of the wall and fell, landing like a superhero on one knee. As she did, Tara heard a horrible screeching noise and turned back to the passage a little along the corridor, heart now in her mouth. Sure enough, the concrete walls were closing shut once more, the bases dragging against the floor causing an awful noise that sounded much like nails on a chalkboard, making Tara's arm hairs stand on end.

With all her might, Tara pushed off from the ground and dashed along the corridor, trying to ignore the blinding pain shooting up her left leg, emanating from the knee she'd landed on. As it turned out, that wasn't a practical way to land at all. Worst of all, she was too late, the walls were all but sealed shut and, despite Tara's best efforts, they wouldn't budge an inch. It looked like it wouldn't be her day to escape. At least she could tell Natasha her hunch had been right — if that had indeed been Natasha's hunch. *Natasha.* Tara quickly sprung back into action at the very thought. She had to get back as quickly as possible to tell her and the others. This was huge, maybe the biggest thing to ever happen to them down here.

On her way back, Tara's mind was racing with a million ideas of how they could force the walls open and what she would do on the other side. She ran on for some time, oblivious to the stitch in her gut and her heaving breaths, until a thought quickly dropped like a lead balloon to spoil her plans. As if the whole world had just come crashing down around her. Tara came to a halt and bent over, hands on her knees. She quickly slumped to the floor when the pain in her knee reached a whole new level of excruciating agony.

If we got out now, we would always be on the run. None of us would have proved anything to the rest of society. We wouldn't have proven our worth. These thoughts flowed through Tara's mind and suddenly the Maze seemed to make a whole lot of sense. It was like Diego Flint was stood there, explaining it all to her like a simpleton. It had always been there to see, yet they had all been too focused on escaping and fighting the system that they had never considered anything else.

Tara was back on her feet in a flash and running with a renewed vigour and energy. In less than an hour she came careening into the camp, yelling herself hoarse in an attempt to gain as much attention as possible. She wasn't sure why, but it felt more dramatic that way. The first face she saw was Natasha's riled and bristly one, clearly frustrated that she had been denied her makeshift bed. As Tara began to explain what she'd seen, Natasha's face had softened and she'd quickly forgotten her grudge.

The rest of the camp was gathering around them attentively, and Tara had to start her story again for their benefit. By the end there were several wide, glistening eyes staring intently at her. She hadn't experienced anything like this attention level for so long that it became quite overwhelming. She was sure many of the crowd that had listened to her story were thinking wildly of their freedom, much as she had been a little over an hour ago. She couldn't blame them, any suggestion of an escape from the Maze was enough to torment anyone. Tara turned meaningfully to Natasha.

'I think we should talk in private,' she muttered in an undertone, inaudible to the others slightly behind. Natasha nodded and ushered Tara away from the thronging crowd. A few minutes of palpable silence later, Tara and Natasha were well clear of any prying ears. Tara wasn't really sure why they needed to be so private, but she couldn't help picturing the state of pandemonium caused if this news broke out. As they'd walked, there seemed to be an unspoken understanding between the pair, and as Natasha turned to face Tara she had a knowing smile on her face. It was an ugly look matched with a slightly desperate hunger for the outside world. Tara had never seen such a side to Natasha; she'd always seemed so at home in the Maze.

'It's an exit, isn't it?' Natasha half asked, half stated.

'Yep. But how did you know?' Tara questioned.

'I didn't really, it was just a hunch.' Natasha shrugged.

'And that's why you asked me to watch that exact spot every day for a month?'

'Yep,' Natasha stated assuredly. 'So, who was it?' she asked in a matter-of-fact way. Noticing Tara looking back at her blankly, she elaborated: 'The person who went through. Did you recognise them?'

'Oh,' Tara made to explain, then paused, baffled by Natasha's understanding of the situation. She didn't even bother asking. 'Erm, no. I couldn't really make him out.'

'Him? Are you sure it was a him?'

'Yeah, it was definitely a man, but like I said I couldn't see who it was. He looked older, if that helps.'

'Everyone looks older in here,' Natasha stated sardonically, shaking her head disappointedly. For a moment, both of them stood in silence, Natasha vacantly staring off into the distance.

'I think I know what this means,' Tara stammered timidly. Natasha nodded, her eyes still glazed over.

'We have to prove ourselves, don't we? Otherwise, the exit would always stay open?'

Natasha nodded again, this time more slowly and much less pronounced. She didn't say another word as she turned slowly on the spot and began trudging her way back to their little community.

Chapter 76

The last three months had been incredibly frustrating for Diego to watch. Since her first day, he had been routing for Natasha to find her way out of the Maze. Three months ago to the day Natasha, reached the level required for her freedom and Diego, like he had with all the other Mazers who had been released, had prepared himself to set off to meet her on the other side of the exit chamber. Natasha, however, was far more stubborn and invested in the Maze than even Diego had realised.

Over the following weeks she barely left her little town, and when she did it was only to go on short foraging trips to the nearest food room or to go to the bathroom. It was infuriating to watch, not just for Diego but for everyone in the control room, knowing the person on their screens could have been free some time ago and, worst of all, not being able to go and shout it in her face.

Ironically, the town Natasha had helped create, which Diego had crudely named Watchville, was the reason she had been granted a release, or should have been, at least. She had been placed into the Maze after involving herself in anti-establishment organisations. She had, for the most part, acted peacefully and righteously, yet her very idealisms that countered a democratic society were troubling. The fact she was willing to accept democracy and even be part of creating her own society showed a change Diego was ecstatic with. This was exactly what the Maze was for and how it differed to those normal prisons full of dingy cells. Those prisons would only have amplified Natasha's anti-governmental feelings to a new extreme. Diego had seen that very phenomenon happen before.

Finally, after endless days of waiting for some solution to appear before his eyes, it presented itself to Diego. On the far side of the ever-growing Maze one of the original batch of Mazers, Dougie Richards, had also finally reached the points he needed to be released, his light on the giant screen joining Natasha's as green. He happened to walk around a corner at the right moment as the increasingly erratic Penny sat sharpening her chisel blade maniacally. Dougie had, rather bravely in Diego's opinion, having spotted the wild look on Penny's face, talked her down like she was stood on a ledge. It was a goosepimple-inducing moment of sheer honesty and brave unity between two people that were facing an enduring struggle, and as they had all watched on in the control room, briefly distracted from the Natasha dilemma, Diego had spotted very few dry eyes.

*

Almost a week later, Diego was finally sat under a whimsically flimsy umbrella at the end of the moss-cocooned tunnel that led out of the Maze. He was being buffered by a heavy wind that was bringing with it sheets of rain that were hitting Diego with a vicious sting, leaving his open-skinned arms blue yet prickled with nasty red spots. He couldn't help chuckle at his own stupidity, he was bound to catch a cold now, yet tradition was tradition and he wanted to welcome the released Mazer as he had with all the others before Dougie. Well, all three of them.

Now reasonably practiced in the process, Diego welcomed Dougie as quickly as possible without rushing through the details, hoping to get out of the rain and into the warmth and dry of the car waiting nearby. To his great relief, Dougie accepted the story quickly and with few words, merely shrugging his shoulders in recognition. Within minutes they were into the car, the rain pounding against the darkened windows and the metal roof like a thousand pinpricks. As the door closed, Diego felt a wave of warm relief fall over him, reminding him of his childhood when he'd get back in the car after wet and windy soccer practices.

No sooner had the door closed, though, than he felt a violent vibration in his right trouser pocket. Without reaching for it he knew it would be Alex, mostly because she was the only person who ever phoned him these days. He also somehow knew that it was going to be serious. After all, Alex knew where he was. His eyes darted quickly to his left and looked questioningly at Dougie before answering it. Dougie was already gazing unblinkingly out of his passenger window, and his eyes appeared droopy; Diego doubted he would be paying much attention.

'Diego, you need to get back quickly,' came Alex's rushed voice from the other end as soon as Diego picked up her call.

'Why, what's wrong?' Diego asked, lowering his tone and glancing once more at the unperturbed Dougie.

'We- we've got a code green,' Alex stated, leaving Diego perplexed.

'What's a code green?' he asked dumbly.

'Well, we don't actually have one, I was hoping you might infer, but never mind. Just hurry up.'

A long, high-pitched tone told Diego the call was over. He quickly leant forward to the driver and muttered to step on it. Meanwhile, Dougie had barely raised an eyebrow, and when Diego looked more closely his eyelids had sagged completely closed and his chest was rising in slow and shallow breaths. Within a remarkably short time, the car pulled up back outside the hotel complex, Diego immediately opening his door and slammed it behind him, startling Dougie into life. The now released Mazer hadn't stirred at all during their journey, other than his head lolling from shoulder to shoulder every now and again. He was blinking rapidly as he came to his senses in the parking lot. Diego opened his door swiftly in his haste to get back into the control room. He had forgotten the effect the light would have on his fellow passenger, and Dougie was quickly throwing his arms in front of his face.

The lashing rain had now eased, and the gloomy clouds that had lingered above so ominously had passed, too, replaced by a much friendlier white sky. Placing a hand rather more forcibly than he had intended on Dougie's shoulder, he led the former Mazer to the double doors. All the while, Dougie kept his arm over his face, blinking uncontrollably in his efforts to regain his sight. Through the lobby they went, Diego keeping a hand on Dougie's shoulder to steer him in the right direction.

The aged Mazer staggered in his blindness and Diego had to hold more firmly as they strode purposefully through the corridors towards the control room, surrounded by a team of Diego's security. These days, the security measures hardly felt necessary. Diego couldn't believe he'd once felt so afraid of what the general public might think of him. As it turned out, people didn't seem to care much about what wasn't directly in front of their eyes.

'I'm going to take you to our psychology expert, Doctor Diane Cooper,' Diego explained hurriedly as they walked through yet another empty corridor. 'She'll help your transition back out of the Maze and answer any further questions you have. I know it's been an odd day for you, and it must be overwhelming, but remember I- we- are here to help you.'

'Okay,' Dougie grunted with little emotion. He still seemed half asleep, and Diego felt more pity for him than any of the other Mazers who had exited so far.

Around a final corner they went, and Diego knocked sharply on Diane's door, not waiting for a response. Diane was, as usual, neck-deep in paperwork and personal files. On the right-hand side of her desk, a tablet was lying flat, showing somebody walking through the Maze. Diego recognised the person quickly as the man he was supporting and came to the quick conclusion that Diane had been expecting them. For some reason, that humoured and annoyed him at the same time. It was aggravating how ahead of him Diane always was.

She waved her hand nonchalantly towards the sofa that was laid along one side of the room. Dougie freed himself and quickly made his way over, collapsing heavily onto the shiny tan leather covering. His eyes were still flickering rapidly as he attempted to adjust to the light, lying back to face the harsh office lights. Diane had put her head back down to her work immediately and remained silent for several moments as Diego stood there awkwardly.

'We'll be okay now, thank you, Diego,' she stated, not looking up.

'Oh, right, okay. Well… I'll pop back later, then,' Diego replied, slowly turning to leave.

'Do you mind dimming the lights on your way out, please?' Diane requested. As he left, Diego reached for the switch on the wall without another word.

A minute later, he was back in the control room and was greeted by an awed silence. Many eyes were looking up at the giant screen and Diego quickly turned his attention to it, too. The left-hand side of the screen was focused on Natasha, sat cradling her knees, apparently deep in thought on top of one of the many Maze walls. Diego couldn't quite make out where exactly she was. Even to him, much of the Maze looked the same. He moved his eyes to the right of Natasha and scanned the map hastily for her green dot. It wasn't too hard to find as she was the only Mazer with a green dot beside her name.

She was sat right by the Maze's exit, facing the exact spot that the wall opened up to face the fresh sea breeze. She was deep in thought, her eyes glazed over. There was no other Mazer near her, which was odd in itself these days, what with Natasha being the hub of her community. What was even stranger was that she was so far away from their little village. She had not ventured past the two facility rooms in weeks, with little need to. She had accepted the truth that there was no such thing as an exit some time ago and that she therefore had no reason to go off exploring the further reaches of the Maze.

'What's going on?' Diego asked hurriedly, pushing his way to the front to stand beside Alex.

'They know,' Alex muttered, busily fiddling away on her tablet.

'Right... know what exactly?' Diego asked, once again finding himself frustrated that he wasn't in the know. He was supposed to be in charge here.

'About the exit. Tara, she saw Dougie leave and went to tell Natasha straight away.'

'Oh... oh, right. What's happened since?'

'Well, not a lot, really. She's just been sat there, staring.'

Both of them turned and watched Natasha. She looked completely lost in her thoughts. Diego knew how intelligent and intuitive she was, and he was sure she would have worked out everything that was going on around her. She probably even knew they would be watching her, though she showed little acknowledgement of this. He held a remarkable amount of respect for her; after everything she'd been through, she was still such a strong character. Watching her now, he couldn't help but realise how well he'd come to know somebody he'd never met in person. He couldn't wait for that moment. Something suddenly occurred to him, and he checked the map on the right portion of the giant screen once again.

'Erm… this might be a stupid question, but what exactly are we waiting for?' he asked Alex.

'What do you mean?' she responded.

'Can't we just open the doors?'

'Do you think she'd actually go through? Without even talking to Tara and the others?'

'There's only one way to find out, I think,' Diego declared, a smile spreading across his face. His clothes were still soaked through, and his hair slicked back from the miserable weather that had drenched him whilst waiting for Dougie, yet he couldn't wait to get back out there again. He'd been waiting too long for this moment as it was.

He strode purposefully from the room, almost breaking into a run in his clamour to be back outside the exit. 'Wait for my word,' had been his last words to Alex, an unusual level of authority in his voice. He had snatched one of the many tablets that was lying unaccounted for on his way out so he could watch Natasha's reaction as the doors opened. For a brief moment, he wondered if he was assuming too much. He'd learnt so much about Natasha over the last year, but if that told him anything it was that she was incredibly unpredictable. *Maybe*, he thought, *she won't leave her friends. Maybe she'll stay in the Maze forever.*

Chapter 77

Natasha's mind was racing. She'd expected the wall to open up when she approached, just as Tara had said it had done for the old guy — she was that certain of her right to freedom. When it didn't, the entirety of the past year had flashed through her thoughts, full of doubts about herself and her place within the Maze, and within the greater world. It was so easy to get lost in her own perspective, and suddenly one solitary shut door had made her question everything she thought about herself.

Now she looked back, Natasha realised she had only ever fought from her own perspective. She was in the Maze because of that perspective. All along she had believed her cause to be the correct one, that she was fighting for a noble right. Now, she doubted that. She managed to find her way onto the wall, unaware of her surroundings, sitting down on the freezing stone and rocking slightly back and forth. Her whole world felt rocked.

There was nobody around, not that she felt like talking to anyone. She questioned whether anybody would understand her troubled mind at this moment. Then again, maybe everyone in this Maze was facing the same struggle of self-doubt. She felt ashamed of how little she knew of her so-called friends with whom she had shared a hallway for the past two months. She didn't know why they were in the Maze, or anything of their pasts, really. For some reason, that topic always seemed kind of taboo.

She abruptly felt a tear trickling down her cheek but made no effort to wipe it away. What was the point? She wasn't trying to impress anyone. However, it did trigger a new flow of thoughts. There was a sudden awareness of how much the Maze had changed her. Before the Maze, she had never shown much of her emotions. The little sadness or anger she'd revealed on the outside had usually been in the form of aggressive yelling. The Maze had forced her to open up to others. Nobody could survive in the Maze without people around them, that much Natasha was sure of. The feeling of a shared struggle for all that lived in the Maze's separate ecosystem had brought out a new side to Natasha. It was this new, more mentally healthy side that had given her the strength to build a community with Tara and Georgia, but it was the same side that now made her desperate to leave. She, at least, believed that she was ready to join society once more. There was also someone she wanted, needed, to see desperately.

The more she thought about it, the more Natasha realised how different she had become. She used to be so independent, void of sentiment or any desire to let her life be controlled by a need for others. Now, sitting there staring blankly at the plain stretch of wall before her, she suddenly missed the friendly faces of Tara, Georgia, and all the other passers-by in their smallest of towns. For the first time ever in the Maze, Natasha felt truly alone, and she quickly understood the overwhelming terror that others had succumbed to long ago.

She slowly began to stir out of her trance and was just untangling her crossed legs when she heard an echoing, scraping noise race towards her along the corridor. Her eyes widened and she stood rapidly, dizzying herself — such were the heights up here on the wall tops. She glared longingly at the same blank wall she had been staring at all day, but it was no longer completely blank; she could make out a strip of dull, natural light filtering through a gap in the wall. Her mind whirred into action, and she was quickly on the move, hoisting her legs over the side and tentatively lowering herself down the high wall. She reached an impasse but didn't halt in her mission, instead dropping quickly from the wall and landing with finesse. No sooner was she on the floor than she was back up and racing along the passageway leading straight to open air. The gloriously fresh smell of sea salt was filling her lungs more and more with every stride, and Natasha breathed it in with glee.

Seconds later, she'd reached the hole in the wall, which was now wide enough for her to slide her gaunt body through. Doing so, a powerful wind buffered her back a little, but she persevered on, the light growing ever brighter. It took her a few moments of slow progress to look down and notice, to her horror, that she was walking on what appeared to be a thick layer of bird faeces and feathers. She'd assumed that it was hay or something similar. With her shoes wearing remarkably thin, Natasha opted to walk on her tiptoes, her face set in a permanent grimace. Slowly but surely, she made her way across the threshold into a golden, sunlit evening, judging by the low sun that was casting a glorious road of enticing amber across the still sea below.

Despite the tranquil appearance of the evening, Natasha could tell that it hadn't been so for the whole day. The grass-covered cliffs before her were soaked through, the grass a forest green that only came after a heavy downpour. This must be the calm *after* the storm.

'I can't tell you how good it is to see you,' a male voice stated matter-of-factly. Natasha's heart skipped a beat as she turned, wide eyed. However, her shoulders sagged a little when she saw the long, dark-haired man sat on top of the passage she had just left. He was smiling at her adoringly as if they were long lost lovers, but Natasha had never met the man before. The man seemed to become aware of this fact, too, and his demeanour changed. 'Sorry,' he started, standing. 'I'm Diego, Diego Flint. I'm sure you know who I am, just like I'm sure you know a lot of things.

We've all been watching you very closely, and I have to say, I am so glad this moment has finally come.'

So many thoughts crossed Natasha's mind, and so many questions, too. She, of course, knew Flint was the man behind the Maze, everyone did, but she was certainly taken aback to see him there greeting her so welcomingly. In her mind, she had painted Flint as an evil, mad scientist who had created the Maze to torture those he thought had in some way wronged society. On first sight, this seemed unfair to say the least. Diego Flint seemed much the opposite. The very fact that he spoke about her in such a personal way suggested that he actually cared about those living in his creation. For a moment, she stood there a little dumbstruck, taking it all in.

'What do you mean "this moment has finally come"?' she asked. There were so many questions stumbling over each other, trying to get out, that it was a struggle to pick one. In the end, it seemed a little daft to ask something so meaningless.

'Ah.' Flint sighed dramatically. They were still stood twenty metres away from each other, with Flint stood some five metres above her, yet she noticed a flicker of nervous fear spread over his face. 'Erm… well I suppose there's no point beating about the bush,' he uttered, clearly doing exactly that. 'The thing is, you've actually been able to leave the Maze for three months, it's just this is the first time you've gone anywhere near the exit.'

Flint broke off with a look of concern on his face, as if worried Natasha was going to break into a sudden outburst. She didn't. She had been almost certain this was the case once Tara had confirmed her theory. Only for a brief spell whilst she waited atop the Maze wall did she doubt this. She merely shrugged, and with that shrug came a release of all her troubles and questions she had ready to fire. She turned to look at the lowering sun over her shoulder, then turned back to face Flint.

'Do you mind if I sit here for a bit?' she asked, clearly taking Flint aback.

'Oh, of course not,' he replied kindly. 'Why don't you come and join me up here?' he added, sitting once more with his feet dangling over the edge of the tunnel's roof. She awkwardly clambered her way up, her legs unused to the uneven terrain after so long in the Maze.

'Don't your eyes hurt?' Flint asked after a minute or so as they sat side by side, looking out at the amber sun.

'No, why? Should they?'

'Well, no, not exactly. It's just, all the others have been covering their eyes because it's so much brighter out here.'

Natasha thought about this pensively, then realised Flint had been talking about McKenzie. She wondered silently how she could bring the topic up without sounding too desperate and pathetic. She still wasn't ready to show that side of herself to the rest of the world. Flint just sat there silently, and Natasha knew he was waiting for the barrage of questions that would inevitably come.

'Can I ask you something?' she said after several minutes in which she lazily watched a seagull soaring around at eye-level.

'Of course,' Flint nodded curtly.

'Why did you create the Maze? Really?'

'It's just like I said in those interviews. I created the Maze as a new option for the correctional system, to save people sitting around in blank cells for years and years, and coming out with nothing but bitterness to show for it.' He said this as if bored, which Natasha realised he probably was. He must have been asked that question every day for the last two years. 'It's true. I didn't lie in those interviews,' he stated in reply to Natasha's slight look of disbelief. His look of indignation made Natasha feel quite sorry for him.

'I'm sorry, it's just... you haven't been in the Maze. It's horrible, and that's coming from me,' she explained, not looking at Flint.

'Well, don't you think it kind of *had* to be horrible. I couldn't exactly make it a luxury palace. How are you supposed to learn anything about yourself then?'

He chuckled a little, reiterating his belief that this idea was ludicrous. Natasha simply nodded vaguely. He *was* right, of course.

'That's all very well, but sometimes I didn't go to the bathroom for, like, three days!' she exclaimed, to which they both laughed this time. Flint became abruptly serious once more, though.

'I'm no fool, you know. I know the Maze is not without its problems. In fact, there are probably more problems than there are solutions at the moment, but it's still a start. It'll get there.'

'Why are you telling me this?' Natasha asked, a little staggered by Flint's openness. He sighed heavily.

'I guess for you this must be hard to comprehend. You don't know me from the next guy, but I can't help but feel I know you. I feel I can trust you.'

Natasha breathed a sigh of relief. For a brief moment, she had a terrible feeling that Flint was going to confess his love for her. That would make the whole watching-her-every-minute-of-the-day thing a whole new level of creepy. The very thought made her cringe deeply. Realising Flint was now looking at her expecting a response, she stiffened her face once more.

'So, the Maze hasn't exactly gone to plan, then?' she asked, suddenly sounding motherly in her attempts not to sound smug.

'No, I guess that's fair to say.' Flint's whole body sagged, looking remarkably downbeat. Natasha wanted to get away from the topic as quickly as possible, sensing a rant coming her way, but she had one last question she had to ask.

'Er… *Diego*,' she began tentatively, 'how long was I supposed to be in the Maze for? It's something that was bugging me for ages, because I never got given any time sentence before I entered.'

To Natasha's surprise, Flint showed a flicker of a smile.

'Well,' he began importantly, 'in theory, you had no exact time limit. The idea was that each Mazer – that's what we called you guys – had a set point score they had to reach to be allowed to leave. This changed depending on the severity of the crime, and you could gain or lose points based on your actions. You gained your pass by helping to create your little town,' he finished with a gleaming smile, like he was a proud dad.

'You can lose points? Natasha responded. It seemed every answer produced five more questions. 'So, what about…' she tailed off. She hadn't thought about that particularly low day in the Maze for a long time.

'Of course you can lose points. Otherwise, those who hadn't necessarily proven themselves would get out far too soon.' Flint paused for a few moments, thinking. 'His name is TJ,' he said at last, rather stumbling the words out. 'I know this is no consolation, but that was one of my lowest days watching the Maze, too. I seriously considered ending the whole project after that. It didn't seem fair on you or anyone else to be in the situation I had created.'

Natasha didn't accept this attempt at an apology. Fortunately, Flint didn't seem to want her to.

'I guess I should say thank you, though. You may have put me in that situation, but you also helped save me,' she muttered. For a moment she debated whether to say anything more, but it seemed her mouth had decided for her. 'There is someone else I would like to thank, too. Do you....'

'I don't know where he is. He told me he would be travelling for a while, and the last I heard he'd taken a plane to France.'

'Oh, okay. I think I'm ready to head back now,' she said, failing to hide her disappointment. The sun had disappeared below the shimmering sea and, in the failing light, Natasha was beginning to shiver.

Chapter 78

Penny was no longer the person she thought she had been when she entered the Maze. It had turned her into an outcast, lost from any form of society. Even the tiny little community that had been created next to her tree seemed farfetched for the person she was now. She spent each and every day wildly racing through the corridors, her feral eyes ravenous for an escape route to the real world.

Despite its ever-present lure, Penny had decided not to return to the wall-top. It had clearly been a dead end, and all it had done was make her hungrier for daylight. Her brief spell there had been the only time she'd seen the light of the sun in the past year. The Maze appeared to offer more dead ends than anything these days. Penny had forced herself to remain optimistic, refusing to believe that there was no exit. Her perhaps naïve optimism was the only thing that had kept her alive this long. Only occasionally did the Maze get the better of her, but when it did she felt like giving up. On those occasions, she felt like nothing more than a shell of a person, her spirit broken, numb to the world and everything going on within it.

Penny couldn't remember the last time she'd actually held a respectable conversation with another person. When she did bump into a fellow prisoner, her mind was always too preoccupied on her singular mission to find the exit that she barely listened to anything they had to say. She only paid attention long enough to listen whilst they answered her rapid-fire questions about their recent explorations. Nothing useful had ever come from that, either. Every other prisoner seemed to look at her like she was crazy. Penny didn't see what was crazy about wanting to get out of the Maze and she felt almost sorry for them, knowing they must have given up a long time ago. It also made her angry at Flint. These people didn't deserve such a miserable fate, destined to wander aimlessly around the same corridors for eternity until their bodies finally caved in to the inevitable. It was a morbid thought that drove Penny on day after day, determined not to settle for such a fate.

The Maze itself had stumped Penny. She was well aware that the walls moved around, creating new routes on an almost daily basis, yet she couldn't comprehend how she hadn't found the exit yet. She had no idea exactly how big the Maze was, but she was sure she must have scoured every inch of it at least twice, without any success. She questioned whether those controlling the walls had deliberately stopped her finding her way out. This thought was the one to derail her on her days of despair, for if that was the case then what hope did she have?

Much of the time, she found herself gravitating towards the salty smell of one particular corridor under a hunch that this held some secret to her desired escape. More regularly than any other spot in the Maze, she returned to search the walls for any clue of a secret passage she was yet to uncover, without any luck. Twice when she had returned to the spot the stench of sea air had seemed much stronger than usual, but she'd convinced herself that was just her hopeful mind playing tricks. It was one of very few spots of any interest through the entirety of the dull, characterless Maze walls, and Penny had created three of the others. The rest of the Maze was nothing but unmarked grey stone passageways that told very little of those who had passed through them.

Penny still had her chisel with her, now neatly strapped to her waist. She was sure to keep it until the day she died, as a tiny reminder of the loved ones she had on the outside. At least she hoped she still did. She had no idea how her mom was, or her brother, or anyone else for that matter.

She couldn't picture them in her head anymore, such was her feeling of estrangement. She still carried her reel of pictures, too, though she didn't look at them anymore. The last time she had, Penny had come over inconsolably sad, unable to get a hold of her emotions.

These days, her chisel served just one purpose: to draw out maps of her search. She would often spend hours, even days sometimes, etching out maps of the nearby corridors for her future self. She was sure this would help one day when she found a new pathway open. It had already happened once or twice and her heart had leapt with excitement as she surged forward, only to reach a dead end or get sent on a long loop to where she had started. On the second occasion, she had once again been sent into a spiral of doubt, spitefully convinced that someone above was holding her captive and away from the magical corridor she needed. Somehow, it was worse that her slim hopes had briefly been lifted.

Even though she was almost constantly on the move, she had not seen Aaron for many months now, and she went through phases of hating his guts for the sheer audacity of escaping before her, — as she had wildly concluded — or being full of concern for his safety. It more leaned towards the latter these days, after realising that the speakers attached to the walls would usually announce if somebody had found the exit. She hoped it was sheer misfortune that had led to her and Aaron not meeting for nearly six months by her calculations, yet something nagged at the back of her brain telling her that was incredibly unlikely. Especially given her last sighting of him. He had looked sickly at best, and worryingly thin.

Thinking about her old travelling buddy, she was briefly cast away from her endless pursuit of the gateway to the real world, quickly coming to her senses as she stumbled another prisoner as it was highly unlikely to be anything else. It wasn't exactly a person, but rather their makeshift shelter that Penny had stumbled over. Unfortunately, makeshift was a very apt word and the shelter wobbled ominously for a moment before collapsing emphatically in on itself. Penny heard a wild spree of cursing from within the shelter as she stood there watching the person within struggle to get out. Looking around, she realised in her distracted state she had strayed into the small community of tiny shanties that lay in place along the same corridor as her tree.

The whole corridor seemed oddly serene and still, unlike any time Penny had visited before — that was, other than the extremely aggravated woman who had finally emerged from the cocoon of clothing and assorted materials she had used to build her shelter.

'Why would you do that?' she hissed aggressively, apparently aware of the silence around her.

'I didn't mean to,' Penny stated defensively, but the woman continued to glare at her as though she had just killed a beloved pet. 'I wasn't really paying attention to where I was and next thing I knew, I had hit something.'

'Yeah, me!' The woman turned away and looked at the crumpled remains of the closest thing to a home she had had in the Maze, waving her hands furiously and muttering under her breath. Penny only heard snippets such as, 'Gonna take me weeks to rebuild,' and, 'Wasn't even looking.'

Eventually she appeared to come out of her strop and turned to face Penny once more, this time with a much kinder expression.

'I'm sorry, it's just that it took me quite a long time to

build.'

'No, I'm sorry, you're right I should have been paying more attention,' Penny replied hurriedly. 'But how do you get in and out if it's so delicate it'll fall at the slightest touch?'

'Carefully,' the woman chuckled, clearly reminiscing about some inside joke that Penny didn't quite understand. 'What's your name?' she asked suddenly, apparently coming to terms with her ruined home.

'Oh, I'm Penny.'

'*The* Penny?' the woman blurted out. 'The one who went out of the Maze? The one who made that?' she asked, pointing at the tree a little way along the corridor in a frenzy.

'Er… yeah,' Penny replied, a little taken aback by this sudden revery.

'No way!' the woman yelled. Penny became aware that there was movement from several of the other makeshift shanties, but the woman didn't seem to care now. 'I'm Georgia,' she added, goggling up and down at Penny, making her feel quite uncomfortable.

'Um, nice to meet you. Is Natasha about, do you know?' Penny asked, trying to get the subject away from herself. However, this prompted another rapid change in mood from Georgia. She quickly looked glum and concerned, glancing down at the floor.

'No, well, Natasha hasn't come back.'

'Come back from where?' Penny prompted hastily.

'The exit,' Georgia stated plainly.

'*What?*'

'Yeah, she went a few days ago and nobody has seen her since. We reckon she actually got out.'

Georgia said all this as if it were matter of fact. Penny

was still staggered by the statement about an exit.

'What do you mean "the exit", though? You mean the one on the wall tops? 'Cos I told Natasha that it was useless going that way.'

Penny noticed a flicker of pity flash across Georgia's face.

'No, I mean the actual exit, by the sea.'

Piece by piece, Penny was beginning to put this information together.

'You mean, that's actually an exit? How do you know?' she asked, full of intrigue now. Her mind felt clearer and more focused than it had for months.

'We saw it. Well, Tara saw it. A man left, too, just before Natasha.'

Now, Penny didn't know what to say, or think for that matter. She had had a suspicion about that corridor for some time, but something didn't make sense. Why did Natasha get out and not her? She'd never been given a sentence that she could remember. What was she supposed to do, just wait until the door opened for her one day? That wasn't Penny's style. She wasn't exactly prepared to wait.

Others had started to gather around the pair of them, Penny and Georgia, all emerging from their relative slumbers in a dozy state. There must have been ten to fifteen people gathering, making Penny feel a jolt of claustrophobia. She wasn't used to groups of people at all anymore. Penny figured it must have been the middle of the night, or, for all they, knew the middle of the day.

'Everyone, this is Penny,' Georgia called out to the masses, greeted by a wave of excited murmuring and awed chatter. Penny gave a little nod in her awkward state. She had no idea how to interact with one person anymore, let alone fifteen.

'Hi, everyone. I hope you don't mind me asking but

who's in charge now Natasha's gone?' Penny asked cautiously. She knew this would be a sore subject and sure enough she was greeted with an awkward silence as the group looked to one another. Eventually, another woman stepped forward.

'We haven't really decided that,' she said softly. 'I guess making that decision would be like admitting she's actually gone,' the woman added, shrugging her shoulders.

'Okay, well, why don't I speak to you and Georgia then, as you two seem to know what's going on,' Penny suggested decisively. The woman made a quick glance to Georgia and then nodded once to show her approval of this idea.

Chapter 79

No sooner had they left the crowded hallway than it became apparent that this wouldn't just be a friendly chat. Tara had to march swiftly to keep up with Penny who had set off purposefully, staring vacantly at the empty corridors ahead of her and turning corners without even breaking stride. After a few minutes of silence and quizzical looks from one another, Tara and Georgia nearly walked straight into Penny as she halted suddenly and turned on them.

'I want to know everything,' Penny demanded, her eyes scarily feral as she looked down at the pair of them. Neither Tara nor Georgia came close to Penny in height, and she suddenly seemed quite intimidating, far from the picture Tara had held of her previously from what she'd been told of the creator of the tree. Georgia had turned expectantly towards Tara, so she had to concede that she would be telling her story once more.

Ten minutes later, if it were possible, Penny's eyes were even wider. She was twitching frenetically and unable to stay focused on their conversation as her brain went into overdrive.

'So that's the answer? The exit?' she questioned hurriedly.

'Well, yeah, only it doesn't open to everyone, does it?' Tara pointed out. If it did, they all would have left the Maze by now.

'Yeah…' Penny said slowly, distracted by whatever she was thinking so quickly about. 'But what are you waiting for, if you know where the exit is, that is? Why don't you just move the camp to the exit?'

Tara paused for a moment. Before this statement, she had at least thought Penny was quite intelligent, even if she had been driven slightly off the rails by the Maze.

'If we did that, nobody would ever get out,' Georgia stated. 'They're clearly watching us, and they'd know we were there, so they wouldn't open the doors for anyone.'

'I don't care. If I can't get out, then no-one should,' Penny declared, much to Tara's shock. She had not expected those words to come out of Penny's mouth. 'I've done as much in this Maze as anyone else. If it wasn't for me, you lot wouldn't be squatting by the tree.' She waved her hand wildly in the direction of their camp.

For a minute, a tarnished silence fell over the three of them, stood in an otherwise silent corridor. Tara didn't quite know what to say to Penny. She seemed so desperate to get out that it had made her distraught with anguish and recklessness.

'Look,' she began after a prolonged silence, none of them making eye contact. 'I know it sucks, it more than sucks, to be told that someone is somehow better than you and more worthy of release, but we have to keep going about our lives, trying to survive. We're here for a reason, after all. Maybe we should try and focus on that reason, rather than forcing an escape.'

For a moment, Tara's words seemed to be sinking in, then Penny's whole demeanour changed erratically. She crumpled in on herself and fell to the floor, cradling her knees as she wept.

'I can't,' she said between deep, gasping breaths as she tried to fight back her tears. 'If I stop fighting, I'll just give up and I don't want to give up. I won't let this place get the better of me,' Penny added stubbornly. Tara felt a surge of empathy towards her as she watched in shock, but, for the first time, she also felt a rage growing towards those behind the Maze. Penny had become an unstable wreck of a person because of what they had put her through, and it wasn't fair. Whatever she had done on the outside, surely it wasn't worth all this hurt.

Chapter 80

'You see, that's the problem,' Natasha indicated, waving at the giant screen. They were watching Penny, Tara, and Georgia talking. Against all protocol, Diego had allowed her to accompany him into the control room, perhaps because he felt such a strong affinity and level of trust towards her, having watched her progress for so long. But, if he was honest, it was because he thought she could offer a different perspective to the Maze's struggles. 'This woman has so much fight within her, who's to say she couldn't do great things given the right help?'

'Well, her criminal record, for one,' Diego retorted.

'Perhaps,' Natasha snapped back. 'What I'm saying is, she could be nurtured to learn how to use her fight and courage for better purpose, rather than being locked away until she becomes a dejected shell of a human.'

Diego considered this for a minute. Something of Natasha's thoughts made sense, but surely those who had committed crimes deserved some form of punishment?

'So, what are you saying? I ditch the Maze and set up an apprenticeship scheme?' he chuckled as if this were a ridiculous idea. Natasha remained dead-pan and stony.

'No, of course not,' she bit back. Alex was stood by Diego's side and seemed shocked he was allowing Natasha to speak to him like this. 'If you actually want my help, the best I can suggest is to actually be honest with the people in there. The worst thing was not knowing *anything* about your own future. Maybe explain that a physical exit doesn't exist and clarify what they can do to help their release. But, most of all, you need to stop acting like the almighty. You do not decide these people's fate, that is not your job. As I was saying, Penny has so much fight that, if directed in the right way, she could do great things for great causes. *You* don't know what she could do. Maybe her finding her fight should be just cause for her release. Not everyone is the same, remember.'

The whole control room had frozen as they listened to Natasha's impassioned speech. Diego didn't know how to react. The stubborn, spiteful creature inside his brain was nagging at him to ignore her and brush it off, but a much larger part of his conscience was telling him Natasha was right. He had known much of that himself, though before now he had never dared confront it. He was very aware of the many eyes which had turned to face him and waited with bated breath for his reaction. If anything, this spurred him to be the bigger person.

'You're right,' he stated simply, taking a deep breath and pulling himself to his fullest. To his left Alex was looking at him in disbelieving shock. He would talk to her later; he needed her help more than anyone elses if he were to make these changes. Still stood at his fullest, he turned towards the watching audience of operators. 'Natasha is indeed right. Until this point, I have allowed my own ego to get in the way of the success of our shared venture and I apologise now for wasting much of your time. Now we must do better. Over the next couple of days, I will be working with you all on new plans for the Maze. This *will* mean a whole lot of changes, but it will only make the Maze better.'

He finished confidently and didn't wait to see the response. He didn't care. He knew Natasha was right and that he was right to take her advice. He turned away and ushered Natasha from the room, heading towards the exit where he knew a car awaited to take her onward from her experience in the Maze. This thought brought up a new question for Diego. As of yet, the car didn't have a planned destination.

'So, what's next for you? Will you go back to Russia?' he asked curiously. Natasha looked back at him with a knowing look. Diego nodded his head slowly. 'You're gonna go find him, aren't you?'

For a moment, Natasha looked deep in thought, as if struggling for the words to explain this.

'It's not like I'm crazy in love with him,' she said at last, a little defensively. 'It's just, I've never felt that connection with someone before, probably because I've never allowed myself to be that vulnerable before the Maze. I guess I'm just curious to see if it was just the Maze.'

Natasha finished with a little embarrassment, as if she were a fourteen-year-old girl ashamed to admit she fancied someone. Diego smiled. Maybe, just maybe, the Maze might have produced some good after all.

About the Author

A student of sport, I have in recent years found an unlikely calling in the field of creative writing. It has always been an ambition of mine to sit down and write with meaning and purpose but like so many I struggled to find the time. When lockdown hit, I found myself with much more time and the opportunity to explore a new world of my own creation, one that was full of the difficult themes I faced, living alone during the first lockdown.

'The Maze' is my first full story, though it has since woken a real drive within me and I have been constantly niggling away at several other ideas.

My background and passion in terms of reading is one of fantasy and sci-fi, dating back to the classics of 'Dune' and 'Foundation' that set the tone for the genre and moving on to the ever adapting world of fantasy. I find great pleasure in finding a book no one else is talking about, diving into the fascinating world that the author has created and finding the great undertones that lie within.

www.blossomspringpublishing.com

Printed in Great Britain
by Amazon